HYDRAULIC LEVEL FIVE

Sarah Latchaw

OMNIFIC PUBLISHING
LOS ANGELES

Omnific Publishing
1901 Avenue of the Stars, 2nd floor
Los Angeles, CA 90067
www.omnificpublishing.com

First Omnific eBook edition, August 2013
First Omnific trade paperback edition, August 2013

The characters and events in this book are fictitious.
Any similarity to real persons, living or dead,
is coincidental and not intended by the author.

Library of Congress Cataloguing-in-Publication Data

Latchaw, Sarah.
Hydraulic Level Five / Sarah Latchaw – 1st ed.
ISBN: 978-1-623420-22-2
1. Contemporary Romance — Fiction. 2. Divorce — Fiction.
3. Mexican-American — Fiction. 4. First Love — Fiction. I. Title

10 9 8 7 6 5 4 3 2 1

Cover Design by Micha Stone and Amy Brokaw
Interior Book Design by Coreen Montagna

Printed in the United States of America

For my sister, who fell in love with Colorado.

HYDRAULIC LEVEL FIVE

When water pours over an object hidden in the heart of the river, water reverses upstream and creates a whitewater hydraulic. River travelers are often trapped in its dangerous churn indefinitely...

Prologue

Untitled Draft 1.1
© Samuel Caulfield Cabral
The Real Water Sirens

"If you're going to be a nixie," says the boy, "you need an 'N' name. Water nacken and nixies only have names that start with 'N.'"

Two children, pale and dark, slight and tall, stand in silent battle over the fairy tales woven through the waters of Bear Creek, swollen cold with melted Rockies snow. The nacken king watches his nixie queen. Today, she lugs her pink banjo to their shaded kingdom. That fancy banjo will be ruined in ten minutes.

"Neelie Nixie?" she suggests.

"Neelie's a nice name."

Pale girl sweeps jelly-grimed fingers through his hair so wind-wild, it could snap brush bristles. He jerks away. She knows he will, but still, she tries.

Blue eyes send a thousand warnings. In another world, his mother called them "sky eyes." She walked him to his alphabet classroom, smoothed his cowlick and said *love you eyes of blue, so blue I could fly. Sky Eyes!* He moved to hug her, but she held him back. She rose from silk-clad knees, wistfully touched his cheek in a silent "be good," and left. He was good, dutifully organizing his crayon box and cubby hole, far away from other baby-faced boys and girls. Kids were as odd to him as scratch-n-sniff stickers, until Bear Creek.

The nacken king watches his nixie queen, whose smile is now a furrow too sad for any seven-year-old. The thing is, her frown mirrors his own.

A countdown to one, and snarls and splashes echo over firs as they tug-of-war with limbs. The nixie queen has a small tear in the hem of her shirt, a scraped knee, and a soaked bum. But she holds her revenge until he bends to rub life into his chilly toes.

She doesn't think. She lunges.

The boy yelps as she pummels square into his side, tumbling them both into the creek. Their heads dip under and they sputter when icy ribbons wrap bodies and freeze clothes. The boy pushes her off of him and scrambles to his feet...only to fall again.

She laughs, but her laughter quiets as tears well in her king's blue eyes. He furiously slaps her helping hand away and swipes at his cheek.

"Caulfield..." she says.

"Leave me alone." He springs out of the creek, yanks on his shoes. *Squish squash squish* over to his bike.

When he is gone, she falls onto the blanket and pulls her pink banjo to her side, a meager comfort. Corn-husk hair splayed, she stares through the web of quivering branches and plots how best to guard her tender heart from Caulfield.

Caro, it's a deviation from my normal work. When Kaye finds out, it's World War III.
~SC

SC, from what I hear, she turns into a hellcat every time her name and "Neelie Nixie" are uttered in the same breath. There's no pleasing her, Sam. Don't even try.
~Caro

Chapter 1
READING WATER

Reading the anatomy of a river—its eddy and flow—helps a paddler harness its power and thwart danger.

"Arrrgh! Angel!" I paddled against the current in a vain struggle to turn the open-topped kayak before we hit the massive whitewater hydraulic churning twenty feet ahead.

"*¡Ajúaaa, vámonos!* Come on, Aspen Kaye, paddle! That damned play park is getting *surfed*." Angel's muscled arms furiously kicked up frigid river water.

"Don't call me Aspen—crap!"

We'd tried to surf that "damned play park" every single rafting trip for the past six years, since we first tackled the Shoshone stretch of the Colorado River. Each April, we immersed ourselves in the beautiful, white-capped Rockies to hit the rapids in their prime—when snow slid down the mountains into the river, making for wild whitewater. I had this obsessive idea that we'd be able to ride the top like a surfboard.

Our friends hollered from the cataraft. I vaguely heard Santiago command Molly and Danita to tighten the straps around the gear as he pulled the six-foot oars from the river, bracing for the hit. Wetsuits were a necessity—the difference between hypothermia in two minutes or twenty. Adjusting my helmet, I glanced over my shoulder at the hydraulic, just beyond Angel's grinning, goggled face. Sun hit the wave and fractured into a million sparkling drops, spitting ice into the air, ready to swallow us whole.

"'Kay, Kaye, remember, tuck in if we capsize!"

"Yeah, Angel, I know, we've done this six—crap! Crapcrap*crap!*"

"Here...we...GO!"

I shrieked as the kayak began to jerk. I leaned back and clutched my paddle, squeezed my eyes shut. For a moment, when I felt the duckie dip and lift, I thought we'd done it—we'd surfed the wave. Then the kayak flipped up, followed by my feet. Pulling my knees from their harnesses, I kicked out of the kayak and let the hydraulic attack me. Water hit me like an igloo wall, and I screamed obscenities before I was sucked under. Bright sky swam by, followed by fluid gray, then sky...gray...sky...gray. I forced my arms around my knees and balled up, tumbling over and over and over. I wondered if I'd ever see the surface again, and then I saw sky, and only sky. I gulped precious air and whooped.

"Spank-me-son-of-a-shrew, that's *cold!*" Raucous laughter erupted around me as I grabbed my paddle and let the current carry me to the overturned duckie.

"Watch your mouth, Kaye! You're cussing like a kindergartner." Santiago—Angel's youngest brother—steered the cataraft our way.

I wasn't one for outright cussing (Lyons was small and word from the playground got to our folks fast), so ages ago, Sam and I had come up with alternatives. With his brilliant mind and my big mouth, it was flipping magical, the way we'd strung innocent words together into phrases that sounded downright dirty. "Steaming, unholy waste, plague and atrocity" was solid Shakespeare.

Samuel and me. My gut twisted sharply. Plume-plucked puttocks.

I grabbed the duckie's side cord just as Angel swam up, and together we flipped it over. "You okay, *manita?*"

I nodded, teeth chattering too hard for words. We drifted until we found the rest of our caravan taking-out along a steep, rocky slope.

Angel pulled off his helmet and shook his military-cut hair. "Oh, Kaye, we almost surfed that mother this time."

"Yeah," I panted, still winded. We secured the duckie, and then Angel stalked off to the bushes for a piss.

My entire body trembled. Molly unfolded her long frame, sturdy as a ponderosa pine, and pulled a bottle of Jack Daniels from a wet bag. "Have a swig of this."

I took the bottle and swiftly threw it back, amber flames licking my throat. I coughed and waited for seeping warmth.

"You are going to drown yourselves one of these days if you're not careful..." I simply nodded and dug through the wet bag for my fishing hat. "Why don't you head over to the hot springs? They'll heat you right up." Reaching under my chin, she unlatched my helmet like I was a five-year-old and gave me a shove.

Danita and Santiago stretched out on flat rocks like seals, black and sleek, heads lolling in the sun. Danita Maria Cabral...a tumble of gleaming black curls, curvy Latina hips. The Cabral gene pool certainly kicked out some lovelies. She waved me over. I saw the no-nonsense eyebrow lift behind her designer sunglasses and tried a pre-emptive strike.

"You're wearing Dior shades on a rafting trip?"

"They're old." She ripped the sunglasses from her eyes. "If you keep trying that hydraulic, one day either you or Angel won't break the surface."

"Yeah, Molly said the same thing."

"Well, maybe you should listen to me, Kaye." Molly planted herself next to me on the rock. "You take too many risks. Ice rappelling, paragliding...and I heard about how you skipped out on Vail's last ski day to chase avalanches in the backcountry with Hector...in cow costumes, no less!"

"Hector and I didn't go leaping and twisting off cliffs. Just two friends taking a leisurely ski down a scenic mountain. We were *udderly* safe. Get it?"

Santiago's ears perked up at the word *ski*. "Dang, Kaye, you cliff-huckers." Cliff-hucker? Hmmm...it had potential for my cuss-word stockpile.

"We live in Colorado, playing on mountains is in our blood," I reminded them.

Danita huffed. She couldn't stand Hector Valdez and thought his penchant for risky sports was a bad influence.

I eased my muscles into the water. Before long, Angel's heavy footsteps plodded our way, then his deep voice cut through the quiet.

Despite the cool spring air, he'd rolled his wetsuit down to his waist, showing off his beautifully muscled chest. Once upon a time, he'd been pimply and pudgy, never acknowledged save by our small group of friends. But he left for the Air Force Academy and came back confident and...well...hot. One hand clutched his water shoes, the other, the Goon Bag—our consolation prize of cheap, nasty wine.

"Tra-di-TION...Tra-di-tion! Tra-di-tion!" He shimmied in his best Tevye impersonation and tossed me the Goon Bag. "Drink up, Kaye! Shlapp that hard, *hermanita*, you earned it today."

"Yessir, First Lieutenant Valdez." Lifting the plastic bag over my head, I gave it a couple of good smacks and trickled crappy wine into my mouth.

"How's the water?" He beamed at Dani and stooped for a kiss. She twisted her head away, taking his grin with her.

Danita sucked furious air through plump, pink lips. "Angel Esteban Valdez, you *pendejo*, I am so sick of watching you and Kaye try that same old stupid surfing stunt on a *class five* hydraulic! What if you'd drowned? *Ave María Purísima*, you are no better than Hector!"

"Dani—"

"I'm not exactly keen to lose my fiancé right before the wedding, especially since you just got back..." She lapsed into Spanish, winding down.

Angel gave her the minute of venting she needed. "I'm sorry you were worried." His dark eyes shone with regret, though I noticed he hadn't actually apologized for trying to surf the rapid. "But I know what I'm doing. There's that stretch of calm water right after the rapid. If we didn't have that, there's no way we'd try to surf. Trust me, *mi amor*." Danita sniffed, but she didn't say any more. While patient to the point of being lackadaisical, even Angel had his breaking point. "Anyway, I found this burned-out Ford up the hill, behind those aspens. It must be fifty years old. The upholstery's gone and the windows are broken out, but it's a good place to set up camp."

The car it was.

It was a tranquil night. Just the rushing water, the cadence of evening birds, rustling aspen leaves. Angel grilled burgers over a small campfire. Danita and Molly chatted on their sleeping bags. Santiago leaned against the old car, mini flashlight in his mouth, hunched over a book.

The sun faded. Amazing didn't do it justice—I was never one for clever descriptions. It had always been *him*, so lyrical and perfect.

"Kaye, listen to this." Santiago held up his book. "It could totally be us right now: 'As the sun set, the entire mountainside went up in flames like parched timber. It crept behind the Matterhorn, painting them in bottomless blues and purples and stars…' Creepy, huh?"

I anxiously crossed my arms over my chest. "What are you reading?" I already knew the answer.

"*Water Sirens.*" The other three's heads shot our way and Santiago mistook their concern. "Yeah, yeah, I know it's been out for like, six years. I'm probably the very last person in Lyons to read it. But damn, Kaye, your ex can write an awesome story!"

"Don't I know it."

"I can't wait to read the other five books!"

"Yup."

"I'm still not sure what a nixie is."

"Nixies, nacken, sirens…They're all seductive water spirits known for drowning their victims."

"So, why are water spirits battling…what are those monsters called?"

"The Others."

"I mean, did Cabral have some sort of obsession with mythology when you guys were together?"

I couldn't believe I was having this conversation *again.* Not ten months after our marriage crumbled, Samuel had struck gold with his debut novel, and ever since, I'd been subjected to readers, critics, and entertainment journalists prying into my personal life.

"Knowing him, they're most likely metaphorical nixies. Something along the line of being lured in and drowned by his ex-wife?"

Danita winced. Santiago was unfazed. "Why the Alps, though? What's wrong with Colorado?"

I couldn't tell him how the Swiss Alps were like Camelot to my ex. His birth mother had taken him on a ski trip to Zermatt when he was five. He stayed in the lodge while she hit the slopes and the nightlife. It was the one and only "family vacation" she'd ever spent with him.

"Probably changed it so I wouldn't sue his sorry tail."

He tilted his head like a cockatiel. "Why would you sue him?"

Danita groaned. Molly muffled a laugh. Did this man live under a North Face-embossed rock?

"Santiago, how far into Samuel's book have you gotten?"

"Um, about one-third."

"Do any of those naughty lil' nixies seem familiar to you?" I knew my bitterness was loud and clear and I'd become *that* person. But Neelie Nixie was a sore spot for me.

Santiago shrugged. "I'm not paying too much attention to the characters. The action scenes are much better."

I practically had this bilge memorized, I'd stewed over it so long. "'She had the soft mouth of an angel,'" I hinted, "'but what came out of it was so awkward, it made the comparison farcical.'"

A blank look. Santiago probably didn't know what farcical meant.

Molly jumped in. "How about 'eyes as deep as ancient forests'? I always liked that one."

"'Fashion sense of a hobo'?" *Thanks, Danita.*

"'She could drink a ladybug under the table...and that was about it.'" Molly laughed. "Smart boy, your ex."

"'Chaos stalked her so frequently, she should have slapped it with a restraining order,'" Angel piped up from the campfire, flipping another pineapple skewer.

"Oh har har har. You all can quote that brilliant Byron's little snipes like scholars. How about some burgers there, Valdez? It's almost eight o'clock."

But Danita, mouth quirking, added one more to my pile of published shame. "'In the sack, Neelie didn't care if she won...she was just happy to be nominated.'"

"Dani, you tramp, that isn't even in there!" Oh, that was it. I leaped from my sleeping bag and dove, evoking a screech from my traitor friend. But then, a figurative light bulb flickered over Santiago's stubbly head.

"You—you're Neelie Nixie? Seriously?"

I hated that cartoon nickname. Hated it almost as much as I hated my first name—Aspen—courtesy of my hippie parents. Seriously, what had Samuel been *thinking*, sharing all of that personal stuff with millions of strangers?

"Wow…Kaye." Santiago's eyes went wide as they flicked across the page. "Is it true you have a heart-shaped freckle on your—"

Samuel Cabral was going to die when I saw him again, I thought for the thousandth time. *If* I ever saw him again…

Steaming, unholy waste, plague and atrocity—Angel and Danita's wedding.

Chapter 2
BANK SCOUT

Before navigating a treacherous stretch of river, a paddler must get out of the craft and scout the rapids from the bank.

I stared at the blank whiteboard, tapping a dry-erase marker on my knee. I never had problems coming up with ideas in my beloved brainstorming room. Warm purple walls. Cushy art-deco chairs. A marvelous cascade chandelier I'd found at a local art festival, made entirely from recycled eyeglasses. And the centerpiece: my big whiteboard.

Tap tap tap tap tap...I tossed the marker on the table and ran a hand through my loose curls.

He was coming home for Danita's wedding. Two months to mid-June. Two months until I had to stand across from him at the same altar and witness another couple pledge to love each other for the rest of their lives.

I stared at the whiteboard, willing ideas to just auto-populate. Nope, still blank. I needed Molly. I found her at her desk, ginger hair twisted up with a pencil.

"Is that the new website for the Rocky Mountain National Park?" I asked, impressed.

She looked up from her screen. "Whaddya think?"

"Perfect. I love the photography. Hey, I can't wrap my mind around the Fine Arts Center pitch. Brainstorming?"

"Yup, I could use a break." She saved her work and grabbed a marker.

Molly and I had been in business together for nearly a decade, since we founded TrilbyJones in our humble freshman dorm room. Following graduation, we secured a small-business investor and a loan. Once word spread and business rolled in, we took on a staff of six. Now I handled client accounts and Molly was art director.

Boulder proved to be a killer location. From Pearl Street to the Flatirons lording over the town, it had everything a granola kid could want. Buying and renovating the dilapidated Victorian to house TrilbyJones was the only occasion I'd ever spent a dime of Samuel's alimony. Our offices were downstairs. Upstairs was my apartment, lovingly decorated by Sofia Cabral—Samuel's tender mother. She insisted I needed a beautiful home of my own, something brand new for my fresh start. I'd cried in Sofia's plump arms for an entire afternoon.

Sofia. Even now, almost seven years after my divorce, Sofia was still *mi madre*. Like Samuel and me, Alonso and Sofia played together as children, but in the shabby streets and fairy-tale gardens of Ciudad Victoria, Mexico. When Alonso left with his brother for Harvard, an opportunity he couldn't turn down, it nearly broke Sofia's heart. But he came back, married her, and they made their home in Lyons, Colorado. Lyons was a teeny tiny town in the shadowy imprint of hulking mountains. It had hippies and Hispanics and farmers, microbreweries and music. It had my father, my mother, and my Cabral *familia*. Boulder was a great place to work. Lyons? It was home.

"We should move the press release here, after the radio spot," Molly said, putting the final touches to our now-full whiteboard.

A rap at the door interrupted us, and Danita stuck her head in.

"Hey!" I swooped in for a hug. "What are you doing in town?"

"It's not like I haven't just spent an entire week in the wide world of nature with you." Danita laughed. "I want you to look at something for the wedding. Do you have a minute to pop across the street for lunch?"

"Sure. Molly, thanks, I owe you one."

"Bring me back a brownie." Fisher's Deli was famous for their huge, cake-like brownies packed with walnuts. Those things would kill my hips one day, but it would be worth it.

A drizzle brushed my face like the lightest of feathers. We didn't have many days like this outside of the mountains, as Colorado was embroiled in the longest stinking drought on record. Danita and I claimed a table under the canopy and absorbed the balm and breeze. Our waiter winked at her. The wink didn't faze either of us. I'd trailed my buxom Chicana friend long before she had cleavage that pervert boys ogled, and was used to being eclipsed by her bountiful blessings. If I didn't know better, I would assume she torched metal in heels and a push-up bra. But I'd seen her many times in her welder's jumpsuit, sparks flying, face sweat-streaked and dirt-speckled beneath her visor as she gently wielded molten iron into something exquisite. The dresses and heels were a vestige of womanliness in a testosterone-dominated world.

"So, dear Danita, why dost thou need my sage opinion?" I asked around a mouthful of turkey and Swiss.

She smiled sadly, and I realized I'd stolen a quip from Samuel. "It's the ceremony program." She pulled out a sheet of lavender cardstock and tapped her nails over it, not passing it to me, thinking.

"Um, do you want me to look at that?"

"I spoke with my brother today." A fly ball from left field clobbered me in the noggin. "Kaye, you tend to get defensive, so can you hear me out?"

I nodded, wary.

"Samuel's coming back to Lyons for my wedding."

"Yes, he's one of the groomsmen."

"You'll probably be around him more than you're used to."

I chuckled mirthlessly. "Dani, I've only seen him four times since he left. That's an understatement."

"Can you two get along in public?"

"If not, Sofia will take us out back and swat our rears." She didn't laugh. "Seriously, Danita, no weirdness. Water under the bridge. I think we can be civil to each other."

"I just want to make sure. I heard what happened at Thanksgiving two years ago. And you're my maid of honor…"

I opened my palms. "I wasn't prepared to see him, then. Look, can I just preview the program?"

She slid it across the table. Music selections, scriptures...the editor in me checked all of the names for correct spelling. Wait.

"Why is my last name just a question mark?"

Danita fiddled with her napkin. "I didn't know what to print."

"Just ask, Dani."

"Okay. I wasn't sure...your name."

Comprehension dawned. *Oh, Danita*. I'd never changed my name back to Trilby after...well, after. It'd been such a pain to switch in the first place that I didn't want the additional heartache on top of the other crap. As years passed and my business took off, I'd never bothered with it. I gave Danita a weak smile, guilty that she had to deal with my baggage.

"It's still Kaye Cabral. You know that."

Her eyes were pinned to her half-eaten salad, and it occurred to me that maybe my retention of the Cabral name might be upsetting at the wedding. Great aunts, old-school relatives from Mexico. Bitter ex-husband?

"Do you really think it bothers Samuel?" My heart sank.

"I really don't know how Sam feels about it. I'm more worried about you, frankly."

"Me?" Ah. "So you're thinking I'm not over him, when he's over me."

"Yes." Leave it to Dani to cut straight to the heart of a matter. "Things have changed somewhat. You see, he's bringing Caroline."

"His agent? I figured she'd come along because of the book tour."

"No, Kaye. I mean they're seeing each other. Romantically. He's bringing her to the wedding as his date."

I felt as if the wind was knocked straight from my chest. Sure, Samuel had his casual girlfriends—actresses, singers, other writers—splashed across gossip mags and entertainment shows. He was a shining novelist, Broadway's wonder-boy playwright, not to mention hair-raisingly handsome. If he kept a woman around long enough, they'd discover he played a mean Spanish guitar.

But Caroline Ortega...That one really stung. I knew Samuel would never risk that precious writer/agent-editor-publicist-whatever-she-was relationship unless he was serious about her. At least, the Samuel *I'd* known never would.

I fought to regain my composure. "I thought he was seeing Indigo Kingsley—the chick cast as Neelie in *Water Sirens*? She took him to the Oscars just a couple of months ago."

"I don't think it was as official as the mags made it out to be." Danita's brown eyes dug through my nonchalance.

"Well, thank goodness I have a couple of months to prep. Gotta look hot to show up the new girlfriend." My laugh was weirdly high.

"Actually, you don't have two months. He'll be in town early for his book tour."

"How early?"

"He flies in two weeks from tomorrow." I dropped my sandwich. "He said he'd be at bookstores in Boulder, Colorado Springs, then Denver before taking a break to spend time with the family."

Why hadn't I heard anything yet? Caroline always used Trilby-Jones to plan local signings for Samuel's *Water Sirens* series, given his hometown hero status. I delegated the projects to Molly, preferring to stay out of his life completely. We'd never get them arranged…unless…

Oh no. Freaking *hell* no. Caroline wasn't using our firm, and I could only guess why.

"Bastard!"

Dani reached across the table and awkwardly patted my hand. I jerked it away and busied myself with paying my bill.

"Print whatever name you like in the program, Danita. I don't care. See you this weekend." When we parted, I wearily slipped from the café and headed upstairs to my apartment, calling it an early day.

Caroline. Brilliant, refined Caroline Ortega. A lovely woman he could bring home to *sus padres*…someone who shared his heritage and not just a love for bluegrass. Why didn't I see her coming? Years later, stuff like this still surfaced and, like hidden tree roots, knocked me flat.

Maybe I needed to unearth those roots and deal with them, starting with my last name.

Since he'd left me almost seven years ago to "find himself" at New York University, I'd only seen Samuel four times.

The first was a brief, devastating visit to New York City, just weeks after he'd moved. I was still in denial that he'd actually left me forever. I saw him for a total of two minutes. I came home, filed for divorce, and no one knew about that trip except for his parents.

The second was to negotiate our divorce settlement. We'd stared at each other across the gulf of a conference table in Jaime Guzman's law firm. Samuel was haggard—unshaven, clammy skin, glazed, blood-shot eyes. I didn't look much better. Shell-shocked. There wasn't much to negotiate; we'd only been married for nineteen months. Aside from a trust from Samuel's birth parents, we didn't have any assets. Little did I know, he already had a book deal in the works that would eventually make an obscene amount of money. Every four-zero alimony check he insisted on mailing went directly into a savings account and remained untouched.

The third time I saw Samuel was several years later, again at Jaime Guzman's law firm, to renegotiate that cursed alimony. He wanted to fly all the way to Lyons to "talk it out," though a conference call would have been logical. I argued I wouldn't touch a cent of his fortune, and he countered that I could do whatever I wanted—it didn't concern him anymore. I folded, my heart too heavy to fight.

The fourth and final time I saw Samuel was the day before Thanksgiving, two years ago. Sofia had called, asking me to swing by the house for her famous mango pie. She assured me that Samuel wouldn't arrive until later. Silly me, I should have known she was up to something by her hopeful, agitated tone. But I was completely and utterly caught off-guard when the door swung open to reveal none other than my ex, as striking as ever.

He had filled out a bit, no longer a skinny kid but a full-fledged man. Over his shoulder, I saw the old Gibson guitars out and tuned. A part of me ached for that close camaraderie we'd shared, before hormones and kissing and sex messed everything up. I felt the warmth of his olive skin beneath his soft sweater and jeans when he hugged me, breathed my name. For a moment, I was home—that perfect place everyone hunts for in music, and comfort food, and scents.

Then, that perfect place slapped me with a goodbye letter and I remembered how he'd thrown this—me—away, with the callousness of a con artist. Disgusted, my arms fell to my side.

I despised him. I despised how his blue eyes were full of innocence and childlike hope but not a fleck of contrition. How he made me feel like a mud-slopped doormat because I yearned to pick up that guitar anyway. My fingernails itched to tear through the tender skin of his neck.

My parting words were something along the lines of, "You abandoned me like a spoiled little boy!" I viciously told him, "I never wanted the whole damned marriage in the first place."

He accused me of marrying him for his family and bitterly asked, "Are you glad you have them now that I'm gone?" Suffice it to say, Sofia's staged intervention was a bust.

After that surreal, disastrous Thanksgiving, he emailed me three times. Once to apologize for the fight, which I accepted and returned likewise. Next, asking if I wanted to see The Twiggies with him in Denver. I didn't reply. He tried again. And again. And again. Again, I didn't answer.

Then he stopped trying.

Chapter 3
HUNG UP

When a craft is snagged, but not wrapped or flipped by a river obstacle.

Untitled Draft 2.3
© Samuel Caulfield Cabral
Festivarians and Firecracker

Storming the stage is the Tripping Marys, a local band playing the Rocky Mountain Folks Festival at Planet Bluegrass. Greasy hair, ripped jeans and flannel, they work the crowd until everyone is a die-hard four-leaf-clover.

A loud "fuck" flies from the mouth of a groupie and Caulfield's adoptive parents cover his and Maria's ears. Next to them, nine-year-old Aspen and her dad, in matching Bob Marley T-shirts, twirl each other with sticky hands, blissfully unaware of his parents' disapproval.

"Maybe we should see the dance troupe again," Caulfield's father suggests.

He shrugs. "They were okay." He says the same thing about the fiddler, the man playing spoons, the music petting zoo, the face painting. He wouldn't mind seeing the jugglers again, only because Aspen is enthralled with their pin-tumbling hands. He likes to watch her laugh more than he likes to see snow-capped peaks pierce the sky. When she laughs, her entire body laughs.

His aunt tenderly sweeps a hand through his hair, but his body twists from her touch. She is not his "Mamá." That title is for one person alone – a queenly redhead who wears pink and speeds along the shoreline of Boston in a convertible.

Aspen tugs his shirt sleeve, peering up with eager eyes. "Let's get closer. I wanna see the guitars." They push their way past hundreds of long skirts and wooden beads, rumpled cotton and hemp. He still smells the cotton candy she ate, above Festivarian sweat and pot and pine-sap air. His father follows close behind. They duck under arms and jostle their way to the very edge of the stage.

The band switches their electric guitars for acoustics, easing into a ballad. The shoving calms and the crowd settles onto the ground.

"Wow," Aspen breathes, eyes glued to the guitarist's fingers as they skim over strings. Her good ear turns to the stage. "Caulfield, I want to learn how to do that." She clutches the boy's hand. He doesn't twist away.

"I do too, Firecracker."

She wrinkles her nose. "Why'd you call me that?"

"I dunno. You're kind of exciting and explosive, and you surprise me a lot."

"Oh...I guess that's okay."

The ballad is a sad, fervent melody. Simple chords snake through their ears and bind the children together as they sway, sucked in, bewitched. It drowns out the mad cacophony of tribal drums. Gone are the sculpted red devils, cloggers busting moves, rainbow bumper-stickers, the mountains themselves. When the music plays, all else churns in a muted gray.

It's in this one-song sub-universe that Caulfield and Aspen become Festivarians. Every August, like pilgrims, they return to Planet Bluegrass to wade through crowds and let the music swallow them.

Over and over, until life drives them thousands of miles, thousands of days, apart.

Caro, is this what you want in the guitar back-story?
~SC

SC, absolutely. Now I want to hang around podunk Lyons until August, just to catch the music festival (and bag one of those jugglers). A shame we'll have movie promos by then. A side note—'Aspen' seems fascinating, can't wait to know her better. I have a feeling about this book. It's different from Water Sirens.
~Caro

Caro, that's just it—this is not Water Sirens. It's too personal. I don't think I'll even publish this.

SC, darling man, such an artistic temperament.
~Caro

Tears dripped from my eyelashes as I dialed Hector's number. Samuel had a date for the wedding. Not one of his casual girlfriends, but the type of woman men took seriously. Successful. Ethereal. From what Danita said, Samuel met her at NYU when she worked as a lowly editorial assistant at one of the big publishing houses. But she had connections, passed along his book, and made both of their careers. And, as much as I hated to admit it, she was nice. I loathed her. I loathed him. I loathed the perfect marriage they'd have, the beautiful Hispanic babies they'd make.

Yet, a bigger, better part of me just wanted my childhood sweetheart to be happy.

"*Hola*. Please leave your name and number, and after I've doctored the tape, your message will connect you to a terrorist plot and be brought to the attention of Homeland Security. *Buenos dias*."

"Hector?" I tried to catch my breath between laughs and sobs. "I need you to be my date for Danita and Angel's wedding stuff. I know you're already a groomsman but if you'd just pretend to be interested...I'll do the winter climb on Longs Peak. There, I've committed. Love the new message."

Just as I hung up, the phone rang.

"Hector?"

Silence. "No, this is Molly. You okay? You didn't come back to the office."

Sobs won out. "Fricking Caroline. He's in love with her! He's bringing her home to meet the family."

"Whoa. Calm down there, Kaye-bear."

"Molly, I'm alone with my glory days photo album, a lousy bottle of merlot, and…and I have split ends." I frowned at a lock of scraggly blond hair, rolling it between my fingers. I bet Caroline didn't have split ends.

A pause. "Are you drunk?"

"Not enough."

Another pause. Rustling in the background, followed by a quiet curse. "Okay, on my way up in fifteen. No one should drink alone."

"Bless you, Molly." I dropped my cell phone and hunkered down in my broken-in leather chair, photo album still opened to the picture Sofia took after Samuel's baseball team won State. *"Let's do the fairy tale—all of it," he'd proclaimed as he wrapped me in his arms, jersey damp with sweat. He placed his dirty baseball cap on my head. "Only you, Kaye…"*

My fingertips smoothed over his boyish face from long ago. We had so much time, then.

I'd always known my last name would one day be Cabral. Alonso and Sofia Cabral were warm, and disciplined, and solid. Church every Sunday. Family dinner every evening. "*Te quiero*" spoken all the time. Not so in my home. My parents didn't believe in "antiquated traditions" and had something of a common law marriage that ended before I began kindergarten. The final shake-up happened when my hippie father refused to take me to the doctor for a ruptured eardrum, insisting holistic medicine was the better approach. By the time my mom brought me in for treatment, the unchecked, perforated eardrum had rendered me permanently, partially deaf in my left ear. Surgery eventually improved my hearing, but it would never be one hundred percent. There was a huge fight, and my dad moved off the farm.

To be fair, Mom was not the easiest person to live with. She was a reserved organic farmer who cares more about cross-pollination hazards in planting heirloom tomatoes than heartfelt conversation. Dad worked at his girlfriend Audrey's organic grocery store, and that's where I spent my weekends. So when I visited the Cabral home, I'd follow Alonso and Sofia with longing eyes and pretend I was their younger daughter.

Then *he* came. Samuel Cabral. He was Danita's six-year-old cousin from Boston, a quiet, serious little person whose face was grayer than any Latino boy I'd seen and eyes, too blue. Alonso's brother had died years ago, and now the wife was dead, too. At first I was jealous of the new boy. The Cabrals adopted him, just like that, when I'd put in countless months winning them over. But something about Samuel resonated within me. He was haunted. So sad—like a scolded puppy—and I wanted to fix that.

I knew the circumstances surrounding his mother's death were horrible because everyone whispered and when I asked, they'd only say, "she died." Even as adults he never spoke about it, *ever*, and I never pushed. Perhaps I should have pushed.

I tried to be his friend. He shot me down. Then, slowly, he was friendly back. Little things, like standing up to Danita when she teased me or offering to halve his sandwich with me. From then on, he usurped Dani as *mi mejor amigo*.

Playing by St. Vrain Creek. Guitar lessons. Baseball games. Camping trips. Summer Jobs. Prom.

Our first kiss.

First date.

First time.

First marriage.

First love.

First everything, to our detriment.

It was eerily silent in my apartment. I dialed Dani and took a deep breath.

"Danita, print 'Kaye Trilby' in your programs."

I heard Dani sigh. "Oh, Kaye, it's not that big of a deal. You're still *familia*. I'm sorry I'm being a bridezilla."

"No, you're right—a real friend tells the truth. It's time to let go, let Sam have his family back. I'm going to the Social Security office tomorrow to fill out the paperwork, then it's done. I'll be Kaye Trilby again by the time your wedding rolls around."

"If you're sure..."

"Yes."

Animals...Home and Garden...ooh, another cop show marathon.

"Heck no, Kaye! How drunk are you?" Molly hurried past the marathon and settled on some ghost hunting series.

"I don't get it." She took a handful of popcorn. "When they ask ghosts questions and they don't answer, why do they listen to a million hours of audio footage? Wouldn't they already know if the ghost talked back?"

I foolishly topped off her glass, then mine. "The voices only show up on tape. See, listen closely." She turned the television volume up as they looped the audio portion in question. *It's here. It's here. It's here* flashed in the caption.

She squinted. "Sounds like a weak radio signal."

"Maybe it's saying 'Casssssady.'"

That got a rise out of Molly. Cassady Bakke pulled into Lyons in a powder blue VW Campervan a year ago and secured a job at Paddler's Outdoor Adventures. With his long brown hair, hemp bands, and broken-in jeans, Cassady called himself an itinerant philosopher. I placed my bet on a disenchanted kid from northern Minnesota. But Molly was enamored, and she was a persistent princess.

She pushed back the quilt and stood, only to stumble because it was wrapped around her feet. She staggered to the bathroom for the third time.

If Molly so desired, she'd never have to work a day in her life, but she'd snap like a taut wire if she sat still. Her father was a real estate developer. Her stepmother could sport a cocktail dress like a cougar. She was a waif compared to big-boned Molly, and the witch enjoyed drawing the contrast. The one good thing Molly gained from that woman was her stepsister Holly (of all names) who truly loved my friend.

The ghost hunting grew hokey, so I flipped to an entertainment channel just as a familiar face flashed across the screen.

Oh, you have got to be kidding.

"After a tumultuous schedule in Europe, Indigo Kingsley heads to LA with heart-throb author Samuel Caulfield Cabral. She has just wrapped filming on Water Sirens, *the movie version of his best-selling book."*

Footage rolled of Samuel and Indigo at the Oscars, Samuel in a dashing tux and Indigo in a flowing buttercup-yellow gown. His hand rested on the small of her back. She was magnificent...platinum blond hair piled high, long silky legs. Was she as broken over Samuel's new relationship as I was?

"Sources say the duo is still going strong, though the in-demand author has been seen out-and-about with close friend, Caroline Ortega. Is this a spritely brawl in the making? Maybe we'll find out in two weeks, when he'll launch his latest book, The Last Other, *in Denver, Colorado..."*

Growling, I hurled a pillow at the TV just as Molly returned. She looked at me soberly—as soberly as possible—and smoothed the creases from my forehead.

"Oh, Kaye-bear, don't be sad. You know most of the stuff on those shows is a lie." I tossed back the rest of the wine in my glass. "He's thirty now," she continued gently. "You can't expect him to be alone forever. What if he wants to be a dad someday?"

I went green and stumbled for the bathroom Molly had just vacated. She ran behind me, tripping over the quilt again.

"Oh geez, wrong thing to say. I'm sorry!" My friend patted my back as I clung to the toilet. "Umm, how to fix this? He's a jerk! An elitist snob. Their children will be brats. His head is so far up his own—"

"Thanks, Molly, that's fine."

"Are you going to...you know?" She made a gagging motion from her mouth to the toilet.

"I don't think so." Pulling myself up from the cold tile, I splashed water on my face and steered clear of the mirror. I hadn't been seriously drunk since college.

Molly scoured the Internet while I lay down next to her, my head spinning. "Frickin' famous cliff-hucking author." Molly's fingers stopped clicking.

"What's a cliff-hucker?"

"No, no, no, cliff-huck*ing*. Extreme skiing?"

"I like 'cliff-hucker' better."

She hit play on a video, actual footage of skiers hucking off overhangs in Zermatt. I wondered if it was the same ski resort Samuel had stayed at with his mother. I pulled a pillow over my head. "Argh!"

"What's wrong, pillow-face?"

"Look at me—I'm a basket case. Who in their right mind cries over being jilted so long ago? I wish Samuel could feel this…this cliff-hucking horrible."

"Cliff-hucking floozy, Caroline." She pulled the pillow off of my face. "You know what you need? *Revenge.*"

I stared at her dubiously. "I don't know…"

She shook her head, ponytail swishing back and forth. "No, no, hear me out. Picture this: hot dress. Shiny blond curls. Beautiful legs. Heels."

"No heels."

"Heels. You walk—no, sway—into the book signing, all sexy. He's slack-jawed. *Salivating* for you. Make him forget about Indigo, Caroline, Candy Cane, whoever."

She had my full attention. "Go on."

Molly took another swig of merlot and flung her arm dramatically. "You *slam* your book down, lean over the table, get right in his face and say…"

"Sign it, mother cliff-hucker!"

"No!" She doubled over in laughter, rolling off the couch. Then she grabbed my ankle and pulled me with her. "I love you, Kaye. You should stay with me during this book release, until the media frenzy blows over." She patted my cheek, but missed and hit my nose.

"I love you, too. And I think I might."

"If you don't do the whole book-signing scenario, the least you can do is find a date for the wedding."

I anxiously picked at my thumbnail. "I've asked Hector and I think he'll agree to it."

Her face softened. "You know, Hector is a pretty handsome guy. And he's been by your side through a lot."

"Hector's a good friend."

"Have you ever considered he could be more than a friend?"

I had. After the split, Samuel had Sofia and Alonso—they'd moved to New York for a year to be with him. I had the Valdez boys, pulling me out of very dark times with everything from skydiving (I sprained my ankle) to mountain climbing (sprained my other ankle). I had new passions in which Samuel played no part. Now that he'd moved on to someone else, maybe…

I'd met and dated men since Samuel. I'd even slept with a few and felt sick afterward—partly because I wanted them to be Samuel, and partly because I *hated* that I wanted them to be Samuel. Did he ever really love me *that way*, or had he confused friendship love with romantic love? If I was ever to escape from the churning vortex that was Samuel Caulfield Cabral, I needed answers.

It was here, sprawled on the area rug of my living room floor, my body absorbing merlot like a warm wine cork, I decided I'd do whatever it took to get unstuck.

Molly dropped an elbow over her eyes and groaned. "I'm supposed to see this Dylan-wannabe tomorrow with Cassady, one of his 'friend dates.' I'll be lucky if the little people with jackhammers in my head keep it to a dull roar."

"Samuel asked me on one of those a while back," I murmured.

Molly shot up from the ground. "A friend date? No! When?"

"Two years ago, after Thanksgiving. Want to see?" I sat up and held the coffee table to steady my tilt-a-whirl brain, then opened my account and pulled up four emails. Molly skimmed them over my shoulder, gasping:

> Kaye, come with me to Denver next Saturday? The Twiggies are playing at Three Kings Tavern—think you'd like them.

"How did you reply?"

"I didn't."

"Kaye!"

"I replied to the first one. I just…didn't know what to do with the other three."

"So instead of facing him, you tucked tail and ran?"

I grimaced. "Something like that."

She pushed me out of the way and leaned over the keyboard. "You are going to reply to him now, missy."

Dread filtered into my veins, followed by an odd recklessness. Why not reply? After that Thanksgiving, he couldn't possibly dislike me more. And maybe, if he replied, I might get the answers I needed.

"This is kind of like drunk dialing. Drunk emailing." I tossed a piece of popcorn at her. It soared over her head and bounced under my dining room table. "What should I say?"

"You could start by apologizing for missing the concert."

"Fine. You type, I'll dictate. 'Dear Cabral…You white-hot unholy cliff-hucker.'" Molly glanced back at me, unsure. I waved for her to continue. "Trust me. 'Sorry I missed The Twiggies concert. I do like them, you're right.' That's it."

She shrugged and typed the rest. I read it over her shoulder, swaying a bit:

> Deer cabral, you white-jot unjoly cliffhuckr. sorry I missed the twigging concert. I do lick them, your right That's it.

I clucked at all of the mistakes. "No no, delete 'That's it.'" Molly back-spaced, clicked send, and clapped her hands gleefully.

"Kaye, you did it! That man is not going to know what hit him."

I stared at the screen, my face blanching. "*No.*" Diving for the keyboard, I clicked into the Sent folder and saw the brainless, double entendre-riddled message sitting there, dated just seconds ago. "Molly, you actually sent it?" There had to be a way to retract it, take it back, *something*. I considered pulling my laptop apart and destroying whatever tiny port of sail waved that doomed virtual message to sea.

"Hey, s'okay. You know Samuel, he'll get a kick out of it."

"You're right about one thing." I peered through my fingers at the embarrassing, irretrievable message. "He definitely won't know what hit him."

I hoped Samuel still had a sense of humor.

Chapter 4
PEEL OUT

Paddling into the core current. A downstream lean is needed to remain balanced.

I tried not to check my email account every hour. When my phone buzzed, I forced myself to wait a full minute before I read the message. Each time, I held my breath...then exhaled when I saw the sender was Molly, or a client, or my mother, or one of the many monthly newsletters I subscribed to for my job. What did I care if the Denver Zoo had a new exhibit coming, called "The Scoop on Poop"? Who paid money to see a heap of animal crap, anyway?

After a week, I gave up hope of his responding. Either he was paying me back for not replying two years ago, or he didn't want to out of respect for Caroline. Knowing Samuel, it was probably the latter. He wasn't one for playing games with other people's heads—just his own.

So, if he didn't want to talk to me, why in the name of pogo-sticking Peter was I on my way to his book signing?

Molly.

"Remember, smug and professional," Molly commanded as she whipped around curves on the rock-lined road to Boulder. "There's no revenge sweeter than rubbing your hotness in his face." Cassady choked in the front passenger seat as he swallowed green tea from his thermos. I patted his shoulders and felt them quake with laughter.

"Yes, Molly, I remember. How about I rub my *happiness* in his face, instead?"

She ignored me.

"Besides, this isn't revenge per se," I continued. "This is getting answers. Untangled."

"Whatever you want to call it, Kaye." I saw her roll her eyes in the rearview mirror. "Walk confidently up to that table— "

"—look him in the eyes— " I echoed for the hundredth time.

"And say in a sultry voice— "

"Welcome back, Cabral," I replied in my best sultry voice.

Cassady now laughed aloud. "Wasn't that a seventies sit-com?"

I slapped my forehead. "You're right, it's too cheesy. How about I just say 'Samuel'? That's sultry, right?"

"Why don't you just be polite and normal?" Cassady reasoned. "That will make a bigger impression."

"Why do you think she wouldn't be polite? She's not going in there to rip off his face. She just needs to project confidence." Molly glanced at me over her shoulder, the Subaru veering to the right as she did. "Confident, not killer—right, Kaye?"

I desperately clung to the handle above the door. "Molly, road!"

"Oh!" She swerved back into her lane just as the right tires of her Subaru rumbled along the shoulder, kicking up wet gravel.

Cassady reached over Molly's massive car organizer to fiddle with the radio, settling on a classic rock station. To Molly's not-so-secret glee, he'd asked to tag along and have Samuel sign a book for his sister. "How's the studying going back there?"

"Still skimming." Samuel's latest, *The Last Other*, launched two days ago. Despite the high demand for copies, I managed to obtain one from the bookstore after work. But with our entire TrilbyJones team putting in long hours to prep for the new Rocky Mountain National Park campaign—"Colorado's Craziest Adventure"—I had no time to read. Now I rushed through the book.

While there was a romantic subplot in the series, it didn't belong to Neelie, for which I was eternally grateful. *The New York Times* hailed the series as "brimstone beauty in a post-apocalyptic landscape." *The*

Guardian described Samuel Cabral's work as "bound together in a masterfully allegorical black ribbon." Whatever. The books were action-packed, epic mysteries set in various mountain ranges, which Samuel's mythology inhabited. Each book culminated in some sort of bizarre good-versus-evil showdown. Caught up in the struggle was Neelie Nixie, a naïve but well-meaning water sprite on a quest through ashen wastelands to discover the fate of her friends: Nora, Noel, and Nicodemus.

Many of the storylines were taken straight from our imaginative playtimes in St. Vrain Creek, which ran the length of Lyons. When we were little, Samuel had come up with dramatic rescues from tree forts, leaps over the river into enemy territory. Like the scene I read right now: Neelie rappelled down a mountainside in the Alps with her crew, uncovering another clue in a long string of tense arrows that pointed to the conclusion.

The Last Other was the final book, thank goodness. Now that the *Siren* series was finished, I felt more magnanimous. When I took myself and Samuel out of the equation and read the story for what it was—simply a story—it was good. But then I'd stumble across another little characteristic, such as Neelie biting her fingernails, and feel resentment once more. For the record, I didn't bite my fingernails…not since last week.

"Kaye, do you know how it ends yet?" Molly called, yanking me from the book.

"No, I'm only about half-way through."

"Did he write about me?"

"Ummm…sorry." I was beyond certain the "Molly" character was a rosy twelve-year-old who'd shipped off to boarding school in the fourth book, but she disagreed. She still waited for a hip, New Age nixie to strut onto the stage of Samuel's series in vintage cowboy boots. I caught a glimpse of Molly's disappointed face in the mirror. The only sound was the pleasant, steady beat of the windshield wipers and Cassady's fingers drumming the dashboard.

"So, Kaye, had any trouble with the media this time around?" he asked.

"Not so much. But I've stayed with Molly the past several days." By now, I was an old pro at laying low following a *Water Sirens* book release. "My apartment phone's probably ringing off the hook, and so are Mom's and Dad's. They aren't too happy with Samuel right now."

"How'd they figure Neelie was based on you?" When the first book was released, Cassady was somewhere in northern California, working at a vineyard and boycotting razors.

"After *Water Siren*'s success, one of the local reporters rooted into Samuel's past and played a matching game with his real-life acquaintances and the book characters." I explained how the reporter concluded that one Kaye Cabral, née Trilby, was the inspiration behind the author's quirky heroine, "Neelie Nixie." The news feature was picked up regionally, then nationally, making my life an insane obstacle course of the media. I'd gotten a new cell phone number and email address for friends and family only, had our receptionist screen all guests, and installed a peephole and deadbolt on my front door.

Alonso told me Samuel was concerned about the press reaction to the reporter's findings. I asked him to tell Samuel, "It's a little late for that, don't you think? Be glad I'm not suing for invasion of privacy." Alonso, kind man that he was, insisted his son hadn't meant to be malicious. In the following books, Neelie wasn't as recognizable, but the damage had been done. It didn't matter whether Neelie's traits were mine or not; readers just assumed they were.

"Five minutes, Kaye," said Molly. "Better skip to the end."

Hazy-eyed, I saw that we were already in the outskirts of Boulder. Crap! I flipped to the last few pages, searching for Neelie's name. I didn't see it. I turned back a few more, but still no Neelie. Odd, wouldn't his main character be in the last scene? There was Nora... Noel...ooh, Molly's character was back from boarding school...but no Nicodemus. And no Neelie.

"Molly, slow down—look out for that news van backing up," Cassady said calmly.

I glanced up and gasped, letting the book fall shut. We were smack dab in the middle of a three-ring circus—local media trucks, cameramen covered in plastic ponchos, cars fighting for parking spaces, honking horns, hundreds of fans with brightly-colored umbrellas standing in lines out the door, just to get their book signed. Nerves shot through my body and settled in my stomach. I had no idea the signing would be *this* big. When TrilbyJones planned similar events, we'd kept them low key per Caroline's request.

"Maybe I should just wait to see him at the rehearsal dinner."

"We're here, we're going in." Molly hit the horn as a beat-up Festiva pulled out in front of her.

"But Monday's my name-change hearing. I don't think I should be sick for it, and with the rain…"

"Do you even need to be present for that?" Cassady pointed out.

"Kaye! How is it possible that you can dive head-first into white-water rapids and not bat an eye, but when it comes to having a friendly exchange with your ex-husband—who, may I remind you, was your best friend for years—your feet freeze?"

I took a deep breath and repeated my mantra. *Answers. Answers. Answers.*

"There's no way you'll find a parking spot anywhere near the bookstore," Cassady said. "Why don't you and Kaye go in, and I'll find something down the street, eh?"

Molly gazed passionately at Cassady, as if he'd just suggested they elope to Vegas. Opening their doors, they flipped up their hoods and dodged around the car, ignoring the honking drivers behind them. Molly swung my door open and pulled me into the rain.

"Come on, Kaye, let's make a run for it."

Tucking Samuel's book under my raincoat, we dashed for the bookstore, hopping over puddles. I was glad beyond belief I'd talked Molly out of putting me in heels, though she had managed a more feminine pair of boots and a dress. We'd also taken care of my split ends, not that my hair stood any chance in this wet weather. Dragging me behind her, Molly tried to push her way through the bookstore door only to be rebuffed by a dozen women and one lonely man.

"Line starts back there," one of them said snippily, rivulets of rainwater streaming from her umbrella and bouncing off our hoods.

Molly put her hands on her hips and glared. "Look, we're not here for the nixies. There's this fantastic cookbook, *Heroin for Breakfast*, I want to pick up. Heard of it?"

"Ahhh…" The girl stared at pink-faced Molly in a new light, her umbrella drooping.

"Come on, Molly. We need to hurry up and get that book before three." I smiled at the umbrella girl. "My boyfriend's getting paroled today. I'm so excited to see him again—it's been years!"

The girl nodded mutely, stepping aside to let us through the door.

The inside of the bookstore was even more chaotic than outside. Hundreds of people swarmed through book aisles, chatted, compared costumes. I recognized quite a few of them. We could have had an impromptu high school reunion, with all the old classmates who drove over from Lyons to see Samuel Cabral again. My eyes searched the store for the front of the line, where he'd be. There was a massive display with panoramic mountains and *The Last Other* sweeping across the top in gothic font.

I spotted Caroline talking with the bookstore owner, tall and regal in an obviously expensive, tailored suit. Her black silk hair was business-bobbed and swished whenever she shook her head. I'd met her briefly when she initially visited TrilbyJones and she'd been nice, but all work—just like now.

I stood on tip-toes to peer above the sea of fans, then hopped onto a shelf ladder.

There he was. Or rather, the top of his head. I could barely make out a muddy-haired man bent over a book, scrawling in the cover while he spoke with the young lady in front of him. The cuffs of his dress shirt were rolled, exposing tan, graceful wrists. I'd always loved the way his hands moved, whether they were playing a guitar, smoothing over my skin, or simply signing a book. The strong lines of his face were softened only by a slightly rounded nose, just like Alonso's, and dense lashes that canopied his gaze. He looked up, returned the girl's copy, and gave her that lovely, lazy smile of his. His eyes, blue as mountain lakes, cut across the crowded bookstore floor.

My heart hammered hard. So hard, I was sure Molly could hear it next to me. She offered me an encouraging smile then tugged my hand.

"Kaye, restroom. You have raccoon eyes from the rain."

I let her pull me through the crowds, between bookshelves and into the ladies' room. A few people did double-takes as we passed, and I wasn't sure if it was because they recognized me from town, or because I looked half-stoned. My hands trembled so badly, Molly had to fix my makeup for me.

"Take off the raincoat. Now turn around." She fluffed my hair, pulled stray strands off of my knit dress and gave me the green light to strut my stuff.

"Okay, Molly. What's the plan?" We edged along the side of the wall, skirting the book line.

"First, calm down. Next, try to put yourself in his line of vision. When he sees you, he'll wave you up to the front. After that it's up to you, hon."

I twisted my fingers together. There was no way he'd see me through this crowd—the whole thing was ridiculous.

Answers, Kaye. You came here to be friendly, butter him up.

Molly nudged me again. But when I turned around to tell her to give me a minute, I saw it wasn't Molly, but an old classmate of mine...what was his name? Alan something.

"Kaye Trilby! Or Cabral. Or...Trilby."

Murphy, that was it. "Hey, Alan, good to see you."

"Good to see you too! So, you here to see Cabral? Heh, obviously. Who isn't?"

Embarrassment prickled my cheeks. "Yeah, something like that. Old friends, you know." Molly had disappeared. I scanned the crowd for her frantically, only to see her make her way to the security guard near Samuel.

"Don't I know it! There are people here I haven't seen in years. Half the old baseball team...oh! I saw Jennifer Ballister on her way out, looking pretty pleased with herself."

I had to chuckle. That sounded like Jennifer.

"Now that your boy is famous, everyone wants a piece of him, I guess."

"He's not my—"

"Speaking of which." Alan flung an arm over my shoulder, hitting me with a waft of body odor. I shrank back. "Tell me what it's like to be a famous character in a book series, and now a movie!"

"Samuel didn't intend for Neelie—"

"Neelie's a pretty hot ticket. All of my buddies are half-in-lust with her."

Ew. Now I was really uncomfortable. I glanced over at Molly again and saw that the security guard was currently standing next to Samuel, waiting to speak to him. Molly gave me a thumbs up. Crap crap crap.

"Reading *The Last Other* must have been especially weird for you," Alan prattled on in my bad ear, and I realized I'd missed a good chunk of what he'd said.

Wait. "Why would reading the book be *especially* weird for me?"

"Ah...I don't know, I just think it would be strange to read about Neelie dying. I mean, it was pretty sad. I was even choked up."

Everything else faded away as I absorbed what Murphy had just told me. Neelie died?

Samuel *killed off* Neelie?

My hands trembled, but this time it wasn't from nerves. It was fury. He killed off Neelie! *My* Neelie! Oh man, I was going to be sick.

The security guard made his way over. I stared past him, seeing Samuel. His eyes were on mine...questioning, intense as ever.

He killed off Neelie.

"Ma'am, if you'll follow me. Mr. Cabral would like to speak to you."

I nodded, sliding from Alan's arm. He gave me a good-natured pat on the shoulder.

"It was nice to see you again, Kaye. Say hi to Cabral for me."

"Yeah, you too." I kept my eyes fixed on Samuel, vaguely catching curious chatter from the book line about my free pass to the front. Molly sidled up next to me, bouncing with excitement. And then I stood in front of him, arms clutching his book.

He smiled tightly. "Hello, Kaye."

My voice failed as his pale eyes swept over me, taking in my dress, my hair, my face. *He killed Neelie.*

"Was that Alan Murphy with you?" When I didn't answer him, he grew concerned and waved a hand in front of my face, snapping me out of my shock.

I dropped my book on the table and glared at him expectantly.

"Nice to see you again, too," he said, chuckling.

"How could you do it, Samuel?"

The smile fell from his face. "Do what?"

"You know."

"I'm afraid I don't."

I leaned in, my voice not one ounce sultry. "You *killed off* Neelie."

He looked baffled.

I thought my hiss was too low for anyone else to hear. I thought I'd been discreet. But a stunned silence hung around the table for several uneasy seconds. And then behind me, a desperate "No!" followed by grumblings rapidly intensifying to a dull fury.

"You...you bitch!" one woman screeched.

"Are you insane? You just gave away the ending!" cried another.

Oh holy hell.

My traitorous weak stomach did a floor routine. Ever so slowly, I looked over my shoulder and found a dozen fuming young ladies, no more than twenty in age, clutching multiple copies of the entire *Water Sirens* series. In addition to black nail polish, fishnets, and boots that could do serious damage, each sported a "Deep in the Heart of Nixie" T-shirt and murderous eyes. Word spread down the line. I knew I was about to be taken out swiftly and viciously, as only a group of rabid readers with pointy books can take out a fink.

I looked to Samuel in sheer panic. He stared back, stunned. Not the "stunned" I'd been going for. He blinked once, twice, then sprang into action and grabbed our elbows, steering Molly and me into a room behind the massive *Water Sirens* display before we were pummeled by hundreds of hardback novels.

Caroline followed. He muttered something to her about damage control. She told him, "ten minutes," and slipped out of the room.

"What was that asinine stunt, Kaye?" He rounded on me, his face severe in its irritation. "Did you even read the book?"

"Not…closely. I h-haven't finished."

"Of all things, I can't believe you'd do something like that!"

Wait, did he believe I did that on purpose? Only a garbled word or two left my mouth. Thankfully, Molly pinch-hit. "Now hold on a second, Sam. That was an accident."

But Samuel ignored her, his ice eyes boring into mine. "Do you seriously still have it in for me?"

"Why would you think that?"

"Danita told me."

Danita! A double agent! I flopped down in a chair next to a small table. Of course she'd spill to her brother—blood before best friend. Well, she could find someone else to complain to about Angel's lack of interest in wedding planning.

"It was a mistake, Samuel, I swear. You think I want to get my tail kicked by your groupies?"

Samuel turned away, exasperated, pushing hands through his executive hair. "You are entirely too rash, Aspen Kaye. Always have been and probably always will be."

"Hey!" I finally stepped up to the plate. "First, don't call me Aspen. Second, what I did was an accident. You, however, very *deliberately* killed Neelie. It was premeditated."

"For the last time, she's *fictional.* Besides, I thought you hated Neelie. You can't have it both ways."

Ugh, he caught me there. "That's true, but she's still *me.* And the media thinks she's me. Can you imagine the heyday they'll have with this? The kind of questions I'll get? 'So, care to comment on why your ex-husband wants you—'"

"I've made public statements in the past about how there is no relation between you and Neelie, I've evolved her character, and I've even personally requested they leave you alone." His voice could have frozen fire. "All I can say is, just read the damned book."

"Kaye," Molly warned. I fought to rein myself in.

"Look. I may be rash, but at least I don't angst over every little thing. When we were children, I'd stand at the gas station register for a full fifteen minutes waiting for you to pick out a candy bar."

Samuel shifted his feet and I could tell I'd gotten to him. "Your point is?"

"That you wouldn't have killed Neelie without thoroughly thinking it over. And that, my friend, is what upsets me." I met his blue eyes, so much colder than I recalled. Up close he looked worn—bags under his eyes, thinner since I'd seen him last. I felt a tug in my chest and some of my resentment dissolved.

"I don't have time for this," he said and sighed, collapsing into a chair. *And here comes avoidance.* "Both of you might have to stay in here, lay low until the crowds thin. Can I have someone get you drinks from the coffee shop? Latte? Iced chai?" He looked pointedly at me.

Another tug. It was difficult to fume at someone who remembered your favorite beverage. I started to refuse, but earned a jab from Molly's elbow. I'd almost forgotten she was there, a wide-eyed spectator to our volley. "Sounds great, Samuel. Thanks!" she replied too brightly.

He nodded, but made no move to leave his chair. A gauche silence settled into the room, finally becoming too much. I cleared my throat.

"Your readers are very...devoted."

"Publicity events have only been this crazy for the past couple of years, since people started paying more attention to what I did than what I wrote. But I have a dedicated fan base, yes." His celebrity status still made him self-conscious. Neither one of us liked to draw attention to ourselves. "I'm surprised to see you here," he continued.

"Usually when I'm back in the area, Molly's the one bustling around this sort of event." He nodded to my friend.

Molly and I looked at each other. He didn't even know Trilby-Jones had been ditched. "Don't they loop you in on the business side of things?" she frowned.

Samuel shook his head. "With the last book, the movie script, and that commission for a play, I don't have time to mess with the little details."

Little details. Ouch. "You—or rather, your publicist—didn't use TrilbyJones this time around."

"Oh." He had the decency to look apologetic. "I'm sorry about that. I can talk to Caroline, I'm sure it's just a misunderstanding."

"It's okay."

"Caroline's agency is actually teaming with a Hollywood publicist, coordinating efforts for the movie. It might have been their call."

Play it cool. "Samuel, I said it's okay. TrilbyJones focuses more on regional accounts, anyway."

"So we were an exception?"

"We don't turn down clients just because they have to fly in to meet us," I said a little too primly. Molly quietly snickered and the corners of Samuel's mouth quirked.

"Well, I don't think losing our business will hurt TrilbyJones. Besides, I've been told you have a hefty savings account, just in case."

Oh, we were *not* going down the alimony war path. I opened my mouth to say as much, but was interrupted when Caroline returned.

"Hello again." Her posh hips swayed in a way I could never hope to emulate, and I saw Samuel noticed it, too. She leaned down next to his ear and whispered. He murmured something back. A single, manicured finger slowly, deliberated traced down his arm in a manner too intimate for friendship. My heart twisted painfully as I watched this sleek-coated Afghan hound mark her territory.

Samuel stood up. "Excuse me," he mumbled, jamming his hands into his pockets and making for the door.

"Wait!" I cried. Gah! Where did that come from? Samuel turned around, his eyebrows raised. *Think fast, Kaye.* "Can you sign my book, please?"

"Oh, right." He flipped open the front flap, whipped a Sharpie from his pocket, and began to scrawl.

"Make it good. I want it to fetch a high bid on eBay."

A smile flitted across his face, at last. Snapping the book closed, he handed it back to me, fingers barely brushing mine. Then he escaped from the room, Caroline fast on his heels.

I glanced at Molly. Her eyes were wide, mouth pinched like a lizard's, and I knew she'd also caught the flirty exchange between Samuel and his agent. "Holy hell!" she silently mouthed. Well, maybe now she'd believe me about Samuel having moved on.

Caroline returned, alone, this time with two iced chai teas.

"Wow, this is great," Molly said.

"Thanks, Caro—" I began.

"Please don't." She determinedly set the plastic cups in front of us. Then she turned to me with a hard glint in her dark eyes. What was with these flinty New Yorkers? "I have an idea of why you're here and what you want," she said calmly, "but I suggest you abandon your plan."

I stared at her in utter confusion. She leaned in closer—so close, I could see the tiny pores of her nose. Her palms were flat on the table, face level with mine.

"I'll be frank. The last thing Samuel needs is an ex-wife nipping at his heels, stirring up trouble. You had your time, now it's over. So if you have a decent bone in your body, you'll let him live his life, enjoy his success."

My mouth popped open. "What...what on earth makes you think I'm after Samuel? I'm not exactly a 'crook my finger and they come running' kind of woman."

She gave me a sardonic "oh please" look.

"Listen, *Caroline*," Molly cut in, "she just wants to have a chat with her old friend, not that it's your business."

"Everything about Sam is my business. Don't take it personally." Caroline flashed a cool, patronizing smile. "I think you're a genuinely nice person, Kaye. But Samuel Caulfield Cabral is a little out of your league."

Ouch. I didn't know whether to spill my tea on her suit or cry in the bathroom.

"Out of her league? Oh, let me tell you something, princess." Molly sat up in her chair and waggled a finger at Caroline, but her baby face didn't lend her the intimidating effect she was going for.

"My friend is one of the most loyal, generous, wonderful people I know. If anyone's out of her league, it's your asshat client."

"*Molly*," I hissed, begging her to step down.

Caroline simply glanced at her expensive-looking watch. She straightened her back and smoothed a graceful hand over her suit. "Time to run, thanks for the chat. I'm staying with the Cabrals, so I'm sure I'll be seeing you both." She hustled out the door, leaving us stunned in her whirlwind wake.

She nearly took Cassady down as he entered.

"There you two are." I'd never in my life been so glad to see one person leave and another arrive. Molly gazed at Cassady, who was soaked-through and frazzled, as if he were Superman. "Circled that bookstore three times, getting eyed up and down by half your ex's fan club. Who was that haughty little ice queen?"

"Cassady!" Molly gushed, "You just missed what is probably the world's biggest harpy, hands down. How'd you find us?"

"Finally met Samuel Cabral, just cut in line and before security threw me out, managed to get my sister's book signed and ask if he'd seen either of you. Ya know, Kaye, I was kinda expecting your Beelzebub to have horns and a pitchfork. I'm disappointed." Water droplets dripped from the ends of his curling hair, down his forearms. Molly shifted uncomfortably in her chair. "Didja get what ya wanted?"

"Not really. But I got a chai and a signed book." I held up the bookstore booty for which I'd sold my dignity.

Molly shot up from her chair, tossing her nearly full chai in the garbage. "That's it. I need to get out of here."

Cassady grimaced at his wet clothing. I almost suggested we stay another ten minutes to give him a chance to dry, but I wanted out as badly as Molly. I gave him a rueful smile.

"Sorry, Cassady. Let's go."

"Are you happy?" I read the note in the front cover of my book again. Really, Samuel, no need for sarcasm.

He'd signed it "*The Unjoly Cliffhuckr.*" I laughed. Okay, I had that one coming.

"That didn't go exactly like I'd planned." Molly's shoulders slumped dreadfully. Cassady rested an arm on her seat, offering something like comfort without actually touching her. Men.

What the heck happened? I'd been entirely prepared for "Sexy Kaye" to knock him out of his celebrated author chair with one breathy word. Instead, I left feeling even more sapless than before, my backbone nothing but a wiggling pile of Jello. His chilly tone, remoteness…he made it clear he wanted me gone. Of course, it didn't help that I'd nearly incited a fan riot.

My ego took a hard hit today.

I still wanted answers from Samuel, but extracting the reason why he stopped loving me wouldn't be as simple as just asking. For Tom's sake, he'd killed off Fiction-Me. If that wasn't a clear (and creepy) declaration that he wanted me stricken from the archives of his life, I didn't know what was. Our meeting wasn't easy and familiar like Thanksgiving, two years ago. His defense walls were fortified, complete with a moat, spikes, and fiery arrows.

And that was the next order of business: slipping past that pure-bred guard dog, Caroline. I definitely needed reinforcements to handle her. Molly couldn't take Caroline on her own, and Danita would have been perfect for the job, but I couldn't ask for her help. One, Caroline was a guest in her parents' home. Two, I'd told her I could be an adult when I was around Samuel, and I'd already blown that promise. And three, she had too much on her mind, with the wedding just five weeks away.

Then, like a ray of sunshine (or a hard tackle), it hit me. I knew who I'd ask for help. She was frightfully open about her dislike for me—our personalities didn't exactly mesh. But, as a matter of principle, she might be game. She was a woman who'd also been cast off by the love of her life. A woman who could meet *two* Carolines head on and emerge without a scratch. A woman who knew every dirty trick in the book and had the legal chops to cover her tracks.

My former divorce attorney and fellow scorned woman, Jaime Guzman.

Chapter 5
BOULDER GARDEN

Maneuvering around boulders tightly scattered across a rapid requires precision and skill.

"Rain gear?"

"Yes."

"First aid kit?"

"Mm-hmm."

"Angel's trail mix?"

"Yes, Danita."

"How about tissue paper?"

"Dani!" I smacked the custom metal picnic table she was beneath. Her feet jerked, the only part of her that was visible. I heard her hiss at me.

"*Santo Dios*, Kaye, never do that while I'm working!"

"We've day-hiked since we wore high-top sneakers."

"Sometimes you forget things."

"One time. *One time*, and you'll never let me live it down."

"Yeah, and that's one time too many that I've had to wipe my butt with fern leaves."

One of the welders hovering over what looked to be an agricultural weed sprayer chortled, and I realized he could hear us over the sparks and clanks echoing through the metal service center.

"Don't worry, you're covered this time." But Danita had a tendency to make me second-guess myself. I unzipped my hiking bag to make sure the packet of tissues was there, just in case.

I'd also brought *The Last Other*. After causing a fan-girl revolt last week at Samuel's book signing, I felt guilty enough to give it a fair, closer reading this time—even if it meant reading Fiction-Me bite it nixie-style. But between multiple work projects (summer was tourist season), my maid-of-honor duties, and plotting my great endeavor in moving on, I'd had little time to read.

Molly and I planned to hike the six-mile trail to Bridal Veil Falls in the northeastern part of the Rocky Mountain National Park. She wanted scenic waterfall photos for the brochure she was assembling, so we decided to make an excursion of it. Danita and Angel were joining us. The wedding was four weeks out, and they needed a break.

Hector Valdez was also hiking the trail with us. He'd just finished a three-day mountain biking adventure for Paddlers, leading a group along the punishing terrain of the park. But Hector was an animal—more extreme than any of us, and could handle it. "Love to come, *por supuesto*. Nothing like a nice, quiet off-day."

Danita shoved away from the table, shed her visor, and attacked her face with a rag. Only eight in the morning and she'd already spent three hours bending iron. I held out a hand to her, and she took it, pulling herself up.

"Jeff, this one's good to go," she called across the shop.

"Yup. See ya Monday, Cabral."

The staff of Jeff's Welding and Machine were men of few words, but they had a healthy respect for Danita and she'd earned it busting their balls on more than one occasion. She had a working knowledge in everything from custom fabrication to industrial machinery, and she was sex on legs. Jeff had a long waiting list of welders wanting in on his shop, just so they could work with the hottest ironhead in Colorado.

"Give me a moment to finish some paperwork, then we'll head out."

I followed her to an office cluttered with Post-its and empty coffee cups. Just as she grabbed a clip board, my cell phone bombastically wailed from my purse. Digging through my bag, I checked the display. Jaime Guzman. I'd left her a half-insane message, explaining how I needed someone out of the way and asking if she had the power to do that. After I'd hung up, I realized how it sounded. So, I definitely couldn't answer with Danita standing right here and not expect a Spanish Inquisition. I dropped my cell back in my bag and put on my best innocent face.

"Who was that?" Dani was bent over her clipboard, jotting.

"My mom."

"Isn't she working the farmer's market today?"

Oh, Dani was good. "Um, yeah. I suppose I should give her a call once I get in my car, see what she needs." Argh! Lying was as easy for me as quantum physics.

Danita's pen paused, and she pointedly stared at me. I hated lying to my friend, but if I'd said *no one*, she'd definitely know it was *someone*. And that someone was my divorce lawyer—definite red flag. Getting unstuck had better be worth this.

"I want to take a quick shower at Mom and Dad's before we leave. You can make sure Mamá's all geared up for the hike." Normally, Sofia would wave us off the front porch with a "*cuídate mucho, diviértete*." But Alonso was neck-deep in press deadlines for *Latin Colorado*—his regional magazine—and she hadn't hiked the National Park in a long time.

"You realize, Dani, you will just get filthy again."

"Look, I don't want to stink like molten metal all day. Pure feminine sweat is much more alluring." Then, as an afterthought, she added, "Samuel and Caroline won't be there, if that's worrying you. They're in Denver for another book signing."

Oh crap, did she know what went down at the Boulder book store? I studied her face—no, she didn't. I'd made Cassady and Molly promise not to breathe a word to Dani. A naughty part of me—Victim Kaye—wanted to enlighten her about the "Caroline Incident" and watch smugly as she busted Caroline's posh rear. But she'd ask why I ambushed her brother in the first place, then declare I got what I deserved. Honestly, she'd probably be right.

"Done."

She capped her pen, grabbed her purse, and we ran out the door. We hopped in our separate cars—her beautifully restored Coronet muscle car and my Jeep Wrangler. I was on my third Jeep now (the second met a sad, sad end in a winter weather incident involving three elk and a guard rail). It had a deep blue paint job and was my baby.

We plowed down the tar-patched Main Street fenced by tall evergreens and a smattering of small businesses, including The Garden Market (where Dad worked) and Paddler's, past Planet Bluegrass, which dwelled in the shadow of Steamboat Mountain.

The Cabrals' home was in the foothills above town, on the edge of the Hispanic neighborhood. Their beautifully crafted cabin was in stark contrast to the number of small homes and trailers the trip took me by, many occupied by migrant workers. There was a gas station with faded Corona signs, an authentic restaurant with peeling cornflower-blue paint, and a taco truck which sold the best breakfast burritos this side of the Rockies. I drove past the tiny grocery store, where I'd spent many hours shopping with Sofia and sneaking strawberry *Jarritos* into her cart. There was the Spanish-speaking community church I'd attended with the Cabrals. Sometimes Samuel whispered translations into my ear or sang the English versions of hymns until his father gave us a "you *niños* stop talking in church" look. Despite the worn-out feel of the neighborhood, the road was a scenic stretch of Virgin Mary garden statues and mountainside.

Five minutes to the Cabral home, just enough time. I picked up my cell phone and dialed.

"Jaime Guzman," answered a gruff voice.

"Jaime. Kaye Cabral."

"That's not what I hear." Of course. Jaime followed court business religiously.

"Force of habit. Listen...about my message. I know what it sounded like—"

Jaime cut me off. "It's okay, I know some people. How much money do you have left in that hefty Cabral Alimony Fund?"

Was she actually considering a hit? "I...I don't want you to kill anybody."

"Relax, Trilby, I'm messing with you. So what, do you want me to bash Cabral's knees while he's in town? It's about time. Hold on a minute."

I heard dogs yipping, followed by the clatter of what I assumed was a food dish. Jaime bred and trained black Labradors, the closest relationships she had save for her twin brother. She was obsessively proud of them. I made the mistake once of asking her, in a very crowded restaurant, if she'd considered breeding Labradoodles. She declared loudly, "No powder-puff poodle is going to fuck my dogs!" No one was shocked. It was Jaime Guzman.

"Back. It's breakfast, you've called at a bad time."

"Jaime, I don't want you to hurt anybody. Just mess with them a bit."

"Psychological torture. Even better."

This was such a bad idea. "Listen, I need some real answers from Sam, but there's a problem. Several, actually." I explained how I wanted someone to monumentally sidetrack Caroline while I worked to pull information from a leery Samuel.

A pause. "Have you ever considered getting a pet? It's a lot more rewarding."

"No offense, Jaime, but pets aren't my thing."

"Fine, it's your self-esteem. Now back to my original question: How much of that alimony money do you have left?"

I squirmed, not liking to bandy about my sizeable bank account. "All of it, except for the twenty thousand I used as a down payment on the TrilbyJones mansion."

She whistled. "More than enough for a large charitable contribution. This gives us resources—sky's the limit. I've got some ideas that will kill two birds with one stone."

"Two birds?" Jaime embraced this more enthusiastically than I thought she would, and it made me nervous.

She sighed. "Hopeless. Two birds. Bird Number One: get Caroline out of your hair. Bird Number Two: get in a jab or two at ol' Sam. Someone has to, since you won't. I still think you're an idiot for trying to refuse his divorce settlement. The both of you are utter pantywaists."

I ignored that. "So, when and where do you want to meet? Your office?"

"No, I need to keep this separate from law firm business, legal ramifications and all." Oh crud, what was she planning? "How about the Lyons Café, Tuesday evening, seven o'clock?"

Public was good, safer. "I can make it by seven. Please don't do anything until we talk it over first."

"Just research. Tuesday at seven, Trilby. Bring your checkbook." The line went dead before I could say goodbye.

We were lucky the rain held off. It had poured yesterday, a typical afternoon mountain shower that reduced the path through the thick forest to mud holes. The Bridal Veil Falls loop was lush with wildlife—one of my favorite trails. It followed a stream through a couple of valleys, aspen groves, steadily-climbing slopes, and eventually broke into astounding views of hazy mountains. The trail also passed an old homesteader ranch, preserved by the park.

We'd been on the path for a couple of hours, the high altitude and sun stealing our breath and crisping our backs. I could barely make out Hector's loping stride far ahead as he lugged Molly's camera equipment for her. Angel and Danita walked in front of Sofia and me, pushing through branches and hopping over dead tree trunks.

"*Señora* Cabral, whaddya think of Samuel's new girl?" Angel asked, never one to beat around the bush. "I've never seen so many suitcases."

"Don't be ridiculous, Angel. You've seen hundreds of suitcases," Danita snarked, side-stepping a puddle. "Airports, hotels, department stores..."

"Your closet." He wrapped his thick arms around her waist and planted a passionate, sloppy kiss on her neck.

I don't believe Danita and Angel had ever suffered a misunderstanding between each other. They were the bluntest people I knew. While he laced his straightforward nature with humor, she was no-nonsense, plain and simple. The only misstep occurred on the very first day of Kindercare, when Angel told Danita she was pretty. Then Dani, bawling, kicked Angel in the knee because she thought he was teasing her. That was the first of three times I'd known Dani to cry. The second was the day Angel left for Afghanistan, and the third, when he came home.

"So, *Mamá?*" Angel wasn't going to let it go.

Sofia picked several big leaves and slipped them into a Ziploc bag. She collected leaves—alder, poplar, cottonwood—and pressed them into decorative tiles.

"I'm not sure what to make of Caroline yet. They haven't dated for very long."

"But they've been friends for several years now," Danita countered. "It seems to be a natural course."

Sofia gave her a stern look. I'd been on the receiving end of it many times, and I knew to shut up when it was directed at me. Dani did, too.

"Samuel hasn't been forthcoming one way or the other, Danita. You shouldn't read too much into it."

My thoughts were torn. This morning had been...odd. It wasn't difficult to see the wheels cranking in Sofia's brain when Danita and I picked her up for the hike. Earlier, while Dani showered, I followed Sofia through their elegant, airy home, helping her finish breakfast dishes and fold towels.

"Kaye, can you take a few towels up to my daughter? I haven't replaced them in any of the bathrooms yet." I would have thought nothing at all of her request, but she didn't look me in the eye. Samuel used to be the same way—he'd avoid eye contact when something was up.

"Sure." She handed me a stack of six fluffy towels.

"While you're up there, *mi corazón*, would you please put these in the guest bathroom and Samuel's bathroom?"

I trudged up the stairs, past the multitude of framed family portraits and Mexican artwork, and tossed a few towels in Danita's bathroom where she yelled at me for letting in cold air. Then I entered the guest bedroom and chuckled mirthlessly, understanding Sofia's plotting. Luxury luggage was scattered around the room, clothing spilling out as if Caroline had frantically gone through them this morning. An army of hair and facial products lined all available countertop space in the attached bathroom, signaling that this woman had settled in for a long stretch.

Sofia wanted me to see that Caroline was sleeping alone in the guest bedroom, rather than in Samuel's room.

Good lord, Sofia. She'd never given up, even after I begged her to let it go because her hope was too painful. I hated to burst her bubble. Samuel and I had snuck out after curfew all through our teenage years, even though our visits were innocent (somewhat). And while he certainly respected his parents enough not to flaunt his sex life, that didn't mean he and Caroline weren't doing a little boot-knockin' mattress-dancing in secret. I nearly gagged when I saw the floozy's barely-there black lingerie peeking out from one of her suitcases. If she and Samuel weren't already sleeping together, she certainly planned to before long.

When Samuel and I dated, we tried to wait until we were married. But lust and hormones wore us down, and we caved the night he put a diamond engagement ring on my finger. All we'd wanted was for the other to be happy. Sadly, that single flower didn't make me happy, now that I held the whole, decayed bouquet. How different a man he'd grown into, from the deep-feeling boy I'd once known.

I dropped the towels on the counter of Samuel's bathroom and made my way back through his room. I'd been in here a few times since we split. Instead of hurting, it was strangely comforting—a warm, familiar embrace. His encased fossil collections, countless Moleskine notebooks, a shelf full of smudged baseball trophies. His high school letter jacket was still in his closet, hanging in a plastic dry-cleaning bag next to a row of grown-up suits, slacks, and dress shirts. He'd only worn it once or twice. While he'd been a star left-fielder and one of the best base runners on Lyons High's varsity baseball team, he wasn't a letter jacket kind of guy, and favored a black ski coat because I told him it made his shoulders look sexy.

I shouldn't have snooped, but a piece of me was caulked in the walls of this room. There was a five-by-seven picture frame lying face down on his desk: his high school graduation. Samuel was in a cap and gown, grinning for the camera. I was piggy-backing behind him, arms wrapped around his neck, my cheek pressed next to his. The picture had once been in our apartment after we married. I thought he'd taken it with him to New York, but he must have abandoned it to his parents, probably along with a pile of other mementos.

I'd heard Danita turn off the shower down the hall a while ago and probably should have cleared out right then. But something caught my eye on Samuel's desk—a pile of papers, typed and marked up in his handwriting. A single phrase jumped out, and so did my heart: *Planet Bluegrass*. What the heck? A brief scan told me it was a draft chapter of his writing, with the heading "Hydraulic Level Five"...a whitewater story?

A throat cleared behind me. I dropped the page, spinning around to see Danita in the doorway, arms crossed. Her damp hair curled around her shoulders, but she was dressed and ready to hit the trails.

"Looking for something?" The corners of her mouth twitched.

So busted. "Nope! Just dropping off towels." She swatted my tush as I swept by, and I yelped.

"You're bad, Kaye. Come on, there's nothing in here you haven't seen before."

Nothing, except for Samuel's draft chapter that had something to do with Planet Bluegrass and whitewater hydraulics. It was enough of a mystery to stir my nosiness. Already, my brain plotted ways to get another peek at that manuscript...

"You're awfully quiet."

Sofia's voice pulled me out of my reflection. I took in our surroundings and was surprised to see we were already at the old McGraw Ranch, a hundred-year-old home surrounded by meadow and gnarled pine trees. She'd huffed alongside me for a good hour, face flushed and glistening, and I hadn't been stimulating company.

"Sorry. Just enjoying nature."

We walked around to the front of the old wood cabin and found a porch. Dropping our packs, we settled against the wall while the other three wandered through the tall grass, exploring the site. I was alone with Sofia, and sudden inspiration struck. Maybe she would be more forthcoming than Samuel. I settled for directness.

"Sofia, why do you believe Samuel left our marriage?"

She frowned, torn. "That's for you and Samuel to discuss, *mi corazón*."

"But I want to know what *you* believe."

"Why are you asking this now, after all these years?"

I avoided Sofia's warm eyes, fiddling with my very fascinating shoelaces. "I've thought a lot about his motives, lately, because of the new book, and the wedding, and...and Caroline. She's Mexican-American, like your family. I know how passionate Alonso is about preserving your heritage, and it would be a lot easier for her to understand and to fit in..."

"Oh, Kaye, asking me this puts me in an extremely difficult position, do you see?" She stooped over and plucked a blade of grass, wrapping it around her fingertips. "Alonso can be...difficult. He loves you, though. I won't pretend he wouldn't have been thrilled if Samuel had chosen a Hispanic woman to marry, for reasons that have nothing to do with you. Samuel didn't care one lick about it. *Mija*, I do know this about my son: he has struggled for so long to find his place in this world, a label and a compartment. But you and Samuel together, you created your *own* compartment, your *own* culture."

"So why did he leave it—us—for New York?"

Sofia sighed. "I'm not sure I truly understand his reasons, either. But whatever you may think, he is not a selfish man."

I knew that about Samuel, and it was one of a number of reasons his leaving me hurt so badly. He wasn't selfish—too generous, even. He had his private purposes other than the "my life is over" line of bull he fed me.

"He is also a poster child for order and logic. Chaos distresses him." Sofia tucked a strand of hair behind my ear. "But you, sweet child, are a messy whirlwind. You'll jump in before you think and then try to sort it out once you're already in the thick of it."

"Samuel has always accused me of being rash."

"Yes, but he loved that about you, too."

"Not enough." I couldn't help but notice she'd used "love" in the past tense. Sofia's grief-stricken eyes sought mine. Even now, the destruction of our marriage still hurt our family. There it was, that familiar ache in my chest.

Sometimes I wondered how Sofia could possibly be Danita's mother. Danita was a realist. Sofia, however, lived in a state of perpetual optimism, whether she wished for sunshine, world peace, or for Samuel and me to shrink down to ten-year-olds so we could swap toys, hug, and make it all better. But she hadn't been there to hear Samuel's words before he left…

The afternoon it happened was burned on my brain, ugly and raw. I only pulled out his cliché-riddled words and turned them over in my hands like broken crystal when I felt particularly masochistic. His voice had been so collected, calm.

"It's no use, Kaye. I've already made up my mind. I'm sorry, so sorry…I can't be married to you anymore."

He was there on top of the bed, threadbare gray T-shirt and athletic shorts clinging to his body, face down in his pillow. I remembered how his shoulder blades tensed beneath my hand, damp with sweat from his brutal morning jog. His running shoes were kicked off at the foot of the bed, like he'd just shucked them and collapsed.

Samuel was in perfect shape from years of baseball and jogging, so he must have run for miles that morning to work up such exhaustion.

Even after he said the words again, explained how he hated feeling as though his life was already over at twenty-three, I didn't believe them.

I blamed them on his stressful job. All summer, he'd worked horrendous hours which left him fatigued and miserable. Like most local papers, they pushed their underlings to death, allowing them the chance to "prove their mettle."

I blamed his words on never seeing each other. Between my PR agency internship and his job, we were two ships passing in the night. I was usually asleep when he slipped into our bed. In the morning I crept quietly, showering and dressing, fighting the urge to wake my half-naked husband while I got ready for work.

I could still feel his lean, beautiful body moving over me, slick with sweat. It was as familiar as my own. I shuddered…

"Kaye, whatever you think, please don't doubt that he loved you," said Sofia.

Loved in past tense. A cynical little snort escaped—I couldn't keep it in.

We hit the trail again, traveling further up the incline and eventually catching Molly and Hector. After a couple more miles, she set up her camera equipment on the rock steps at the base of Bridal Veil Falls. We sat and swung legs over slick steps. A sheath of cool mist sent a chill slithering up my spine.

"*Oye mamacita*, you cold?" A tattooed arm came around me—a different arm than the one I'd been recalling. Not the same, but still a comfort.

I smiled. "A bit." Early May in the mountains was brisk, especially under the fall's spray.

Hector zipped open my backpack and pulled out my fleece, tossing it over my shoulders. "What's eating you, Cabral? Your face is all scrunched like someone cracked your favorite skis over their knee." I hadn't told Hector about my name change, and I didn't feel like correcting him just now.

"I'm simply enjoying the ambiance of the place. Bridal Veil Falls is a favorite of mine."

Hector's eyes crinkled. "You did not just use the word 'ambiance' all snooty-like, did you? *Ahm*-bi-ance."

I gave him a playful shove. "How else am I supposed to pronounce it?"

"You don't. Normal people use words like atmosphere, surroundings, mood, or leave it out altogether."

"Ambiance *is* a normal word."

"Nah, it's a snooty word. Hey! I got a joke for you."

My smile was big now. Hector had a thing for "Hippie Tom" humor. "Shoot."

"What do you call Hippie Tom with a haircut?"

"This sounds familiar."

"Just go with me. You call him 'the defendant.' How do you know if Hippie Tom's been to your house?"

"I dunno, how?"

"He's still there."

I laughed. I shouldn't have expected any less. This was the guy who, when we exited the theater after seeing *Titanic*, shouted, "Hurry up, Kaye! There's only enough cars in the parking lot for half of us!"

"It's...pretty bad, Hector. You should hit the stand-up circuit—start at the next CU faculty meeting. Where do you find this stuff? The Internet?"

"I try, *mamacita*, I try. It's worth trolling for hippie humor to see you smile." He grabbed my hand, gave it a squeeze, and let it drop in my lap. Tiny hairs on the back of my neck stood up. "So, are you serious about doing the Longs Peak winter climb with us? You usually turn me down."

"Are you serious about being my date for Danita and Angel's wedding?"

"Yup. I assume it's because dickhead has a date." He grinned at me, his eyes glinting mischievously. "Hey, Kaye?"

"Hey, Hector?"

"How many hippies does it take to screw in a light bulb?"

I groaned. He'd told me this one a million times. "None, they screw in sleeping bags."

His eyes widened in mock shock. "Gosh, no! I was gonna say 'one to change it and three to relate to the experience.' You and your filthy mind."

I jumped up, stuffed my fleece in my backpack, and stretched my legs. It was time to hit the trail again. Smiling down at my friend, I brushed a hand over Hector's sandpaper head. "Thanks, seriously. You are too good to me."

"Well, I take what I can get."

His words held more than simple playfulness. I was now more determined than ever to move on. Hector deserved better than "taking what he could get." It should be given to him, whole-heartedly. I wasn't in a position to do that now, but someday, once I got to the bottom of my past with Samuel, maybe I could be.

Chapter 6
STANDING WAVES

Large waves are often a sign of deep water.

Untitled Draft 1.6
© Samuel Caulfield Cabral
The Tree House Sign

No one prepares them for the rain.

Bear Creek bakes and crackles under a punishing sun. All summer long, Maria, Esteban, and Caulfield spend dusty hours in the backyard, constructing a tree house from scrap timber while Aspen sits between tree roots, playing with her Barbie doll. She's cut its hair short, so now its bald plastic head has tufts of blond sticking out like river reeds.

Caulfield's *padre* helps build when he can, and the frame and floorboards are sound enough to hold their weight. They hammer two-by-fours onto the frame to create walls while a clunky transistor radio cranks out pop tunes. The tree house is nearly complete, save for the north wall and a good coat of paint. Maria insists upon red. Esteban wants blue. Caulfield has no preference, as long as they don't splatter paint all over the sign he has meticulously created:

Club Caulfield. Must be ten or older to enter.

Caulfield remembers seeing similar signs on night clubs in Boston while he watched laughing, brightly-dressed women and men stumble in and out of neon doors, along fractured pavement. He waited in the car, in his pajamas, for his mother to finish running errands, ducking low in the seat whenever one of the glittery people came too close. Long minutes passed. Then an hour. He feared his mother forgot him. *Hey there, Sky-Eyes*, she slurred when she returned, *see anything fun?* How could he tell her about the man throwing up in the gutter? The greasy-haired woman tumbling into a taxi cab, a single white breast hanging out of her shirt? His cheeks burned red. His mother climbed into the car and they peeled into the street, city lights blurring by his window. He pressed his forehead to the glass, feeling its coolness...

Caulfield likes the idea of using a sign on their tree house. It means he doesn't have to hurt Aspen's feelings to her face, and she'll simply know she isn't old enough to climb up the rope ladder.

Aspen annoys Maria and Esteban. Even Caulfield admits she's grown whiny. The more they try to escape her, the tighter she clings. Thus, the sign outside of the tree house in looping red letters.

The others are certain it will do the trick. Caulfield, though, is not. Aspen is as stubborn as super glue.

And that is what leads to the three of them – Maria, Esteban, and Caulfield – doing a grueling set of sit-ups beneath the Coach's stony gaze. Rain pelts the porch overhang, filling the silence with simple *plip-plops*. Aspen sits at her father's Birkenstock feet, soaked to the skin, sobbing and sneezing into her hands. Snot streams down her face and she wipes it on her T-shirt.

Caulfield hasn't felt this horrible since his mother died.

"Forty-eight...forty-nine...fifty. Well, who's going to tell me what happened?"

Each child mutely wheezes and puffs while Coach stares them down, one by one.

Esteban panics, trying to remember if it was, in fact, his idea to leave Aspen in the tree house without the rope ladder.

Maria stares defiantly back. Aspen got what she deserved. How were they supposed to know it would start thundering and lightning within the short span of two hours? It *never* rains in the summer, in Colorado, unless you're up in the mountains. As far as she's concerned, Aspen is being a baby.

Caulfield fumbles with his ball cap, guilt-ridden. The sun was shining when they went inside to watch a movie in their basement. They were only going to leave her up there for half an hour, but the movie was hilarious and he forgot.

How could he *forget* her out there?

They are all grounded, for sure. His aunt nearly burst a gasket when Coach showed up at their home, the man frantic because Aspen was supposed to have been home an hour ago. "How could you children be so irresponsible?" she chides in Spanish as she wraps a shaking Aspen in a towel. She allows Aspen's father to drive them to exhaustion with sit-ups until someone confesses.

The Coach's hazel eyes bore into Caulfield's, strokes his bearded chin. Esteban drums his fingers on his knees. Maria traces circles on the muddy porch slats. Caulfield can't take it anymore.

"It was my idea. I took the rope."

Maria and Esteban exchange incredulous looks, relieved to be off the hook.

"No cop-out, you two. You went along with it." He exhales and rubs his daughter's cold-numbed cheek. She still hiccups from crying. "Go on inside, flower. Maria, Esteban, you too. I'll deal with you in a minute."

The three scramble out of the cool, mud-drenched air, and the screen door slams behind them. An anxious Caulfield is alone with the Coach. Aspen's father pats the porch swing.

"Why don't you hop up here and we'll have a talk. Man to man."

Caulfield scurries to obey. "I'm so sorry, sir. I didn't mean to hurt Aspen."

The Coach drags a hand over his face. "Now, I know my little girl can be kinda overbearing sometimes."

"Overbearing?"

"A downer. When you're a ten-year-old boy, you just want to hang out with other ten-year-old boys. And girls, if you count Maria. And that's fine. But you and Aspen have something special. She pretty much worships the ground you walk on, you know that?"

"Yes. sir."

"And I think you like her a lot, too. Sort of like your little sister."

"Yes, sir."

"Well, that's cool. But she's younger than you are, and sometimes two years is a big difference. Do you hang out with other third graders?"

"No, sir."

"Just remember what it was like when you were in third grade. How you wanted to do things the older kids did, but weren't big or strong enough. So keep an eye on her. Look out for her when you can. None of this leaving her stuck in tree houses business. Can I count on you to do that, Caulfield?"

Caulfield solemnly nods. "I promise, sir."

The Coach holds out his big, calloused hand to the boy and they shake on it. "Far out."

The two step into the bright foyer from the bluster outside, shaking out their raincoats and hanging them on his aunt's coat rack. Aspen flies to Caulfield, wet clothes snapping. Her eyes and cheeks are pink, nose raw from sneezes. Her blond hair is snarled and stringy, like clumps of dirty flower roots. She stops short of hugging him.

"I'm sorry. *Lo s-siento,*" Caulfield stutters over his wobbly Spanish. "I was really mean to you."

Aspen sniffles. "If you don't like me, tell me. You don't have to make a stupid sign."

"I like you. But sometimes we want to be by ourselves, without kids hanging around."

"But you guys are kids, too."

"Yeah, but we're older. We're supposed to take care of you." He tugs her ear.

Aspen's breath trembles from her crying jag. "Next time you get bored playing with me, tell me to go away and I'll do it. Just don't make a sign again."

Caulfield feels his heart crack a bit. He pulls his young friend into a hug and kisses the top of her wet head. "I'll never get bored of you, Firecracker."

Caro, I'm used to writing more darkly for the Water Sirens series. This seems too simple. Is the childlike sentimentality coming across as contrived or genuine?
~SC

SC, I don't even know what to say. The things I learn about you. Structurally, I'd say genuine, but a strong sense of place is missing. I suppose it's good we're in Lyons, you can get some inspiration. Speaking of inspiration, I think I'd like to pay a visit to that tree house...and I'm definitely over ten.
~Caro

Caro, the tree house is gone. We weren't exactly master carpenters. I'll work on the sense of place. Thanks, Caro. You're amazing.
~SC

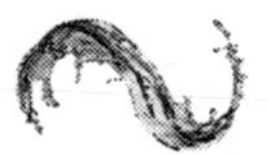

The Lyons High athletic department laundry room was my hideaway.

My father coached the Lyons varsity baseball team, one of the few commitments he'd made and held to with any long-term consistency. Since he spent so much time in the coach's office during baseball season, I'd tag along and launder the team's smelly towels. No, this wasn't a deep metaphor for some secret desire to be dominated by men, sexual repression, anything like that. The simple fact was, the place was cozy. It was secluded and rumbly, and smelled like Downy. I had come here since I was old enough to know not to eat laundry soap. I'd prop my back against the warm dryer to do homework, read a book, or just think.

This morning, I cooled my heels in the laundry room before Danita's bridal shower. I hadn't had a moment alone since my horrible hangover the morning after Molly and I drank our weight in merlot. *The Last Other* was open on my lap. Amazing, how four hundred pages of nothing but words could cause such a frenzy in readers and media alike.

I was a fourth of the way in and Neelie's death loomed heavy. Every page I turned, I cringed, expecting something to fly out of the sky and pummel Fiction-Me. The way Samuel built suspense…I didn't know a lot about writing, but I could tell the difference between being wrapped up in a story and just passing time. His story was so vivid and bizarre, it almost made me forget I was peeved he killed off my character. But sometimes Samuel was abstract with his ideas, and it rankled my questing mind.

> **Her eyes were keyholes, swollen, obliterating her peripheral sight. But she could still see. Before, there'd been nothing but flashes of pain and weakness and the Others hovering above her, sharp jabs hitting her body over again. Now the Others were gone and only Nora, Noel, and Nicodemus remained, carrying her over mountain slopes roiling with stripped ancient pines and white snowflakes. They swirled through the keyholes like flecks of cold ash. Neelie thought maybe she'd always seen through swollen eyes, with no peripheral, nor had she missed it. There was nothing but tundra, ripples of ice...and the back of Nicodemus's body as he pressed forward through the pass, forever trekking ten feet ahead to break the shell of snow, grinding it down...**

The door swung open, startling me out of the frozen mountain scene. Through glazed eyes, I saw my dad leaning against the washer, an agave smoothie in each hand. His sandy hair was snarled, cotton T-shirt threadbare under his baseball jacket.

"Breakfast?" He held up a smoothie.

"Sure, thanks. Hey, Dad, I've got another one for you."

He groaned. "Did you see Hector yesterday?"

"Yes, just listen. Hippie Tom's daughter comes home from a Dead concert…" I snickered through the joke as I followed him out of the laundry room.

My dad didn't think Hector's jokes were funny, but he did like Hector Valdez. He had also cared for Sam, though they often went toe-to-toe over my father's recreational drug use. When Dad kicked the pot to keep his coaching job, things got better at home and they eventually developed a respect for each other beyond Sam's star status on Dad's state championship team. His flight to New York hurt my father deeply, but I thought Dad would welcome him back with open arms if the prospect arose.

I plopped down in his desk chair and opened my book again.

"So…what are you doin'?"

"Reading."

"Yeah, I can see. What are you reading?"

I buried my face in the pages. "*The Last Other*."

"Wait, isn't that Samuel's book? Why're you reading it?"

"Because he asked me to." Well, more like dared me to, but close enough.

"I see."

Dad didn't move, smoothie still in hand. Finally, I bookmarked my spot and hopped up from his desk chair. "Look, Dad, I'd love to stick around, but Danita's bridal shower is this afternoon and I have some errands to run."

"Will Sam be there?" My father never wasted words.

"Ah, I really don't know. I doubt it."

"Cool. If he bothers you, let me know."

I smiled, knowing the worst he'd do was pass along some new age book, and kissed his hairy face. "He won't bother me, Dad."

Danita didn't want a traditional Mexican wedding, though Sofia had angled for one. This included the bridal shower. I suggested having it at my mom's farm, but she shot that down before I'd even completed my sentence. Angel's plane hangar was also a no-go, but it inspired me. I found the perfect venue on the edge of Lyons—a little bed & breakfast whose owners were flight enthusiasts. I talked them into exhibiting their radio controlled hobby planes after the shower. Molly had even bought up all of the Matchbox planes and helicopters in Boulder toy stores to give away as party favors.

Sofia, Molly, and I were in the B&B kitchen, putting the final touches on trays of prosciutto-wrapped asparagus, stuffed mushrooms, and toasted brie cheese and pears on baguettes. I may not have been a fashionista, but when it came to menu planning I was in familiar water. Molly lifted the box lid from the sheet cake and halted, knife poised over the corner piece.

"Ah, Kaye?" she said.

"Yes?" I arranged pansies around stacks of pineapple slices.

"So...is there something Danita hasn't told us?"

Sofia's head shot up from where she was mixing punch. "Why, what's wrong?"

Molly gestured to the cake with her knife. I dropped the flowers and peered over her shoulder at the cake, seeing what she saw.

Oh sweet Mother Mary. Dani was going to kill us and bury our bodies in the foothills.

Instead of each slice of cake having a frosting flower in the center, two dozen little baby booties stared up at us like pairs of pink eyes. Sofia laughed softly behind me.

"Oh...my. This is unexpected."

I groaned. "Of all things! Who confuses *bridal* shower with *baby* shower? I mean, how do these people stay in business?"

"Flo's the only lady in Lyons who makes cakes," Molly explained. "She's eighty-five, give her a break."

"What do we do?"

"I say leave it. Then when Danita sees the cake, we snap photos like crazy and enjoy the moment of payback."

Any other time and I would have thought it was funny. But guests would arrive in ten minutes and all we had was a sheet cake that screamed *Surprise, Dani is knocked up!* I wrung my hands, thinking quickly. Got it. Rushing to the refrigerator, I pulled out a package of strawberries, shoved them under cold water, then dumped them on a cutting board.

"Okay, women, here's the game plan. Sofia, pry those booties off the cake. Throw them away, put them in a freezer bag for several years down the road, I don't care. Molly, help me slice. We'll make strawberry hearts for each piece."

We worked swiftly, patting berries dry and placing them over the spots where the baby booties had been. I was so focused on the task that I didn't notice my former father-in-law hovering over my shoulder until I was finished. I very nearly took him out with my paring knife. It clattered onto the counter as my hand flew to my chest.

"Alonso!" I squealed in a pitch nearly too high for human ears, and threw my arms around his neck. Alonso was editor-in-chief of an understaffed magazine, and I felt I hadn't seen him in years. He hugged me back with that signature Cabral embrace.

"*Hola, mijita.*" He smiled at my enthusiasm. I was a twenty-seven-year-old small business owner, but still "*mijita*" to Alonso—one of the hazards of remaining in your hometown.

When I was little, I was convinced I would marry Alonso. I'd said it before, I really was very determined to become a Cabral. Tall, curly black hair, clean-cut and kind, he was a prince who'd stepped right out of a Disney movie. Danita may have gotten her exotic facial structure from Sofia, but her regal stature and glorious hair were all Alonso. However, when I saw Alonso take time to play Candy Land with Danita rather than settle in with a joint, the idea of marrying him was swiftly abandoned for my desire to have him as my father. I never told my dad that.

"Kaye, you've done an incredible job."

"It's the least I could do, Alonso." Danita had done the same for me.

He patted my shoulder one more time then turned to Sofia. As he did, I saw that Samuel and Caroline had come in with him. Dread churned in the pit of my stomach. They wandered around the B&B foyer, speaking too quietly for me to hear. He rested a hand on top of her head, rather sweetly, and she pulled it down to her lips and kissed his palm. Then he looked toward the kitchen. Before I could duck under the counter, he was making his way over. I hunted for a tray, arranged plates and cups, anything to appear too busy to interrupt.

"Hello, Kaye."

"Samuel." No Cabral hug this time. I didn't expect it. An awkward silence hung between us as I nervously shuffled veggies on the relish tray. Thankfully, Alonso saved me.

"Son, I'm going to scout out those Warbirds in the yard. Care to join me?"

"No thanks. I should probably stay here for a bit." He nodded toward Caroline, who picked at a flower arrangement.

Come on, Alonso, don't leave me hanging here, I pleaded with my eyes.

"Suit yourself. Come find me when you've had too much of the ladies."

"Will do." Samuel turned to me expectantly.

I scrambled for something to say. Sarcasm usually fit the bill when nothing else came to mind. "And so the big bad author returns. Should I have made security arrangements when planning the bridal shower, keep the fan-girls away?"

He wasn't sure how to take my cynicism, and settled on a painful chuckle. "No, that's not necessary. The nice thing about coming home is everyone's seen you in braces and high-water pants."

"You mean your relatives aren't clamoring for your autograph?"

"You're the only one who's asked me to sign their book." He had the decency to look away when my cheeks colored. "What's playing? I like it."

I listened to the folk music mix I'd thrown together for the shower. "Ah...New Greeley Bluegrass Group, just released an album."

He smirked. "Do you lick them too?"

Cue tongue-tied syllable babble...yep, there it goes. "Listen, Sam, about that email. It...well, I didn't..."

"You didn't mean to send it?"

"No."

"I figured that one out on my own."

"Of course you did. Molly and I, we...um...and you know."

He laughed, fingers rubbing the back of his neck. "One of those. I'm just impressed you still have emails lying around from two years ago." I took the opportunity to briefly sweep my eyes down his body. Untucked button-up shirt, faded jeans. He looked refreshingly normal, not like the debonair "Samuel Caulfield Cabral" of entertainment news and gossip rags.

"Well, you know me, hold on to everything. You should see my work accounts. Did you go, by the way?"

"Go where?"

"To see The Twiggies."

He cleared his throat. "Nah. I ended up having to fly back to New York early, so it wouldn't have worked out, anyway. Don't feel bad about it."

"I don't."

"Yes." Another awkward pause. "Do you still get out to Planet Bluegrass for Rocky Mountain Folks?"

"Every August. This band playing now, New Greeley? They'll be there."

"I should try to go this year. It's been a long time."

I folded my arms around my ribs. "You should take Caroline. I bet she'd like it...Maybe you could even write a book about Planet Bluegrass," I hinted.

A strange expression flitted over his face. "Maybe."

And then Ms. Ortega herself spotted us across the room. Resplendent in pearls and tailored-to-a-tee slacks, she sidled up to Samuel with the grace of a Manhattan socialite, looping her arm in his. I was suddenly self-conscious of my off-the-rack brown dress. Next to Caroline, I might as well have worn a shapeless paper sack.

"There you are," she breathed to Samuel. He smiled back. Mother cliff-hucker, I wanted to throttle them both.

"Kaye, have you actually met Caroline? The book signing was rather chaotic."

"We haven't been properly introduced." Heavy emphasis on *properly.* "She's worked with my TrilbyJones team, but not me."

"Of course. This is my close friend and agent, Caroline Ortega." *Just friend? Well, Kaye, he's not exactly going to introduce her as his lover, is he?* "Caroline, this is Kaye Cabral."

Cabral...I froze, stunned. He didn't know.

What to do? Correct him, not correct him? And Danita. I'd think twice before I listened to her over my own instincts. Obviously he didn't have a problem with my bearing the Cabral name in front of his girlfriend.

I tried to match Caroline's lethal grip as she murmured, "A pleasure to meet you, Ms. Cabral," her face tighter than a fat man's Speedo.

"Ahm, actually, my name is— "

"Angel's here," Samuel interrupted, glancing at the door. I saw Angel barrel into the room, scooping up his little sister in a bear hug. "We're dragging him out to the golf course while you do your thing."

"I hardly think you have to *drag* him out to the golf course. Most men would go willingly." Caroline flashed flirty eyes. What did *she* know about Angel?

"Oh no, they really have to drag him," I countered. "Angel doesn't like to golf. He prefers man versus nature kind of things—rafting, rock climbing, spelunking."

"Beating his chest," she teased.

Oh, cliff-hucking floozy was going down. She could scorn me, make fun of me. But *no one* made fun of First Lieutenant Angel Valdez unless they'd earned the right. I opened my mouth to lay into her, but Samuel interrupted, his eyes caution lights.

"Angel will like this. The groomsmen are going mini-golfing." He had the gall to look apologetic. And was that smugness I saw in Caroline's face? How could he possibly be friends with this woman, let alone date her?

But then I realized he said they were going *mini-golfing*. Hector was in the wedding party.

I forgot about Caroline as haunting images of the last mini-golfing excursion invaded my mind, making me tremble. Hector hitting his bright orange ball into the creek, then forgoing the net to wade into the water himself and pluck it out. Hector putting the ball so hard, it skipped over the green and pelted some poor child in the head. The kid was fine, but he'd cried and his dad had yelled at us. Hector dropping his shorts after a wager with Cassady that he couldn't break par for the course. We'd been escorted out. I'd be surprised if the mini-golf staff didn't bar him at the gate.

"Ah, Samuel, not such a good idea."

"We're mini-golfing, Kaye, not whitewater rafting. We'll bring everyone back in one piece." That soft smile crept over his mouth, and dang it, it still got to me.

"If you get kicked out early, you can't come back here."

Just then, the guest of honor walked through the door and a dozen shrieking women rushed her. Danita was as lovely as ever, but a deep glower was etched in her features as she scanned the room. Samuel looked in her direction, distressed.

"I suppose we better hit the road before it gets too wild." He gave Caroline's shoulder a quick squeeze. "You going to be okay?" he asked her.

Panic flashed across her face, then retreated. Begrudgingly, I knew I had to play the good hostess.

"Caroline, follow me and I'll get you one of those 'Hello, My Name Is' stickers. You don't mind wearing one, do you?"

She grimaced and smoothed a hand over her soft Angora sweater. "That's fine."

I started to walk away, but Samuel caught my eye. The cold blue from the book signing was entirely gone, replaced by nothing but warmth. "Thank you," he mouthed.

I narrowed my eyes, and he got the message. I wasn't doing this for him, or for Caroline. I was here for Danita, and I was going to give her a perfect bridal shower if it killed me.

Whatever made Danita so sour when she first arrived dissipated, and soon she laughed with the rest of her guests. The bridal shower went well, despite the near-disaster with the sheet cake, the glares Molly sent toward Caroline, and my spilling a glass of punch down the junior bridesmaid's back. Angel's little sister was nice about it, but she was not pleased with the red stain streaking the zipper line of her lavender blouse.

Caroline was quiet, aside from the occasional name-dropping or comment about how she saw the same gift in Fifth Avenue's such and such culinary boutique, and how divinely it whisked eggs, brewed coffee, cooked a seven-course meal. I tried not to notice how impressed the other ladies were with her high-class exterior, how they emulated the refined way she crossed her ankles. It didn't bother me in the least when Molly's stepmother—who was so tan she'd nearly turned to leather—asked Caroline what it was like to date a famous author and have her name appear in gossip mags. Then my own mother, for Pete's sake, asked about the hype surrounding the movie. Thanks, Mom. After Caroline finished expounding upon the dreariness of having one's life become tabloid fodder, no one asked her anything more.

We played your typical shower games, ate cake (everyone commented on the precious strawberry hearts), and fawned over Danita with all the attention due a bride-to-be. She loved it, and I was in high spirits. When I drove back to Boulder that evening, I felt rather proud of myself. I'd given my friend her dream bridal shower and managed not to gouge out the eyes of my ex-husband's new girlfriend, all in the same day. This was progress.

Of course, that progress might collapse like Jericho after I met with Jaime Guzman Tuesday night. I wondered, for the thousandth time, if involving Jaime was a mistake.

Chapter 7
PUNCHING

Heavier, larger rafts cannot avert hydraulics like canoes or kayaks are able to, and the paddling crew must speed up and punch directly through the hydraulic to avoid ensnarement.

I should have known when I left the TrilbyJones mansion to find that my Jeep's battery was dead, it wasn't a good idea to meet with Jaime Guzman.

My nerves were already a mess. For the past three days, ever since I read the part in *The Last Other* where Samuel wrote about Neelie's lack of peripheral vision, I tried to pay attention to all of the little details going on around me, rather than focusing straight ahead. But enough was enough. I'd stumbled over a fire hydrant. Missed my mug when pouring tea. Shook a loosely-capped ketchup bottle and splattered it all over Molly. I decided to take whatever cryptic passages Samuel wrote with a grain of salt.

I arrived at five after seven. The smell of burnt grease stung my nose and eyes when I entered the nearly empty Lyons Café. Jaime waited for me, already pissed. Tucked into a cracked faux-leather booth, she had shoved a cup of coffee to the side, half finished. Her lips were pursed tightly, fingers drumming the table to Roy Orbison and rattling the chrome napkin holder and table tents.

"You're late."

"Sorry, car trouble."

Jaime snarked. "Right."

With her sharp Latina features and round eyes, Jaime was naturally beautiful. If she ever decided to don lipstick, skirt, and heels, she could probably bring a courtroom to its knees. But like me, Jaime was a little rough around the edges. Okay, a lot. Her sleek black hair was tucked under a pageboy cap. In fact, her entire body was hidden in the baggy cargos and snarky T-shirts she favored. Another winner tonight: a mustard yellow one with "*Illiterate? Write for Help*" scrawled across the front.

"For the record," she said, "I'm not doing this out of the goodness of my heart. I'm on the clock." I froze, menu half open. "Relax. I'm not charging you exorbitant legal fees. Just a little pocket change to save face."

I exhaled. "Please don't *ever* volunteer for a children's charity." I nodded to her T-shirt.

"Unless it has to do with Labradors, *this*—" she motioned between us "—is as charitable as I get."

I scowled at her implication.

"*Qué tan burro eres*, Trilby, don't get your little feelings hurt."

"I'm hardly a charity case." I sniffed indignantly.

Jaime gave me a dubious look. The waitress came—neither of us was hungry, so we just ordered more coffee. We talked about a pot bust over by Platteville, then a Lab she had begun to train (she nearly had me convinced to get a furry, slobbery friend), until a respectable amount of time had passed.

As I blew on my steaming cup, Jaime dug into her messenger bag and slapped a black leather binder on the table.

"What's this?" I reached for it, but she kept a firm grip.

"Research. I've done homework on your gal Caroline, and she's a piece of work. Did you know she's a beauty queen?"

I shook my head. I didn't know much about Caroline Ortega, save for her involvement with Samuel.

"Runner-up Miss North Carolina, 1998," she said, opening another sugar packet into her mug. "Hispanic Daddy's a fast-tracked VP at a diversity-conscious 401(k) company in Raleigh, even though his

Ortega line was in the US a hundred years before the CEO's granddaddy munched rotten potatoes in Ireland. The company got hit really hard three years ago. Mama's become a Stepford wife, but she used to be a painter in Mexico City. Daughter was a champion equestrian and member of the varsity cheer squad. Total suburbia 'keeping-up-with-the-Joneses' types. But Caroline's smart and hardnosed. She was guest editorialist for the local weekend paper…in middle school. She earned her way into NYU. And Samuel obviously sees something in her that's attractive, so don't underestimate her prowess."

"I already know she's on a different playing field. Why do you think I called *you* in to deal with her?"

Jaime clanked her spoon in her coffee. "Whatever. From what I can tell, Caroline's whole life is about appearances. What certain people think of her. She's a publicist *lamehuevos.*" Evidently, she forgot I was something of a publicist, too. "So if there's one thing Caroline's afraid of, it's…"

I stared dumbly at Jaime. "Looking bad?"

Jaime rolled her eyes. "Not just looking bad. Hell, if she worried what everyone thought of her, she wouldn't have gone ape shit on your iced chai latte. That's low class. So's Starbucks, but to each her own." I hoped Jaime never visited Seattle, for her sake.

"So…" I motioned for her to continue.

"So, Caroline's afraid of looking bad in front of the right people."

"Samuel."

"Samuel, the Cabrals, Hollywood, New York somebodies, the media. Now we come to killing two birds with one stone." She slid the folder over to me. I pushed my empty mug aside and flipped it open. It was filled with print-outs of articles, paparazzi pictures, financial contributions, public records, even both Samuel's and Caroline's NYU grade transcripts. Son-of-a-shrew, how had she compiled all of this? Divorce lawyer, of course. Woman was in the right profession.

"Not everything is in there. I'm still digging up stuff. But it seems as though your boy had quite a wild time after your separation."

I shifted in the booth, uncomfortable with where this was going. "I know. Alonso and Sofia had to go out to New York for a year."

"After that his record is squeaky clean, except for his asinine romantic blurbs on Page Six."

"Yeah, I know about those, too."

Jaime continued. "As a publicist, Caroline's worth her weight in gold if she's managed to keep these post-divorce hijinks buried. I suppose he's still fairly new on the tabloid scene, so it could only be a matter of time before an enthusiastic reporter finds out. It's a PR nightmare waiting to happen..." She looked at me pointedly.

Anger and fear churned up my throat. This is what she meant by two birds? I slammed the dossier shut and slid it back to Jaime. "And you won't help the media. You are not to use his arrest record in whatever little Machiavellian scheme you have cooking, do you hear me? Stick to the trifling stuff."

"Trilby—"

"Absolutely not! I'm not going there. Besides, do you think he'd give me the answers I need once he found out I leaked this to the media?"

"Geez, just a week ago you were after both of their *cajones!* You really suck at revenge, you know that?"

I held firm. "Then I suck at it."

"I could take care of everything in one swoop. But you don't want to play dirty, I guess." She shrugged.

"Nope. Thanks for your time." I tossed a few dollars on the table and began to slide out of the booth, but she grabbed my forearm.

"Fine, fine. I have a Plan B."

Oh crud. Had she dug up his library fines and parking tickets, too? I set my purse down and tentatively settled back into the bench. "I'm listening."

"Okay. Your main goal here is to get Caroline out of the way, right? Keep her busy while you get a chance to, ah, *work* Samuel over for answers. *Press* him for information." She smirked at me.

"Don't be crude, Jaime."

"Not my concern. It's just my job to clear out Caroline and get in a little jab at Samuel."

I nodded. "Nothing cruel."

"I can work with that." Apparently she *had* been working with that. She slid a paper from the back of the binder—a large flow chart, complete with color coding and footnotes. "Tell me, close personal childhood friend and former spouse of a famous author, did Samuel Cabral have any pets?"

I frowned. "Yes, a guinea pig named Mickey."

"Seriously? He named a guinea pig 'Mickey'? This guy is screwed up."

The corners of my mouth quirked at the memory. "Actually, he let me name it. And it was 'Mickey' for Mick Jagger, not for Mickey Mouse."

"That's not...in Ireland it means..." She shook her head. "Never mind. And what happened to poor, poor Mickey?"

"He developed enteritis. Samuel gave him radish leaves that had bacteria. Guinea pigs are really sensitive to bacteria, I guess, and... he found the little fellow all curled up, dead. He was only twelve..." *Wait a second.* "Why does this even matter?"

Jaime pointed to number one on her flow chart: The Los Angeles Guinea Pig Charitable Fund. I snorted. It seemed she'd already learned about Mickey, probably from Hector—he had a big mouth.

"You make a donation in Samuel's name, hefty enough to get big-time notice." My eyes followed her finger down to the dollar figure, then bugged out. *Sweet Mary, for guinea pigs!* "We'll tip off the LA press, they love bizarre human-interest stories like this. And believe me, the LAGPCF—*está cabrón*, that's a mouthful—will eat up the attention. They'll want Samuel to tell Mickey's sad story at his upcoming events." She tapped her finger on a calendar—Samuel's public appearance schedule. "If he doesn't, it will make him look like a stuck-up asshat who's unwilling to go to bat for this poor little animal charity."

I laughed. A few café patrons turned around, and I covered my mouth. "Caroline will hate this. It's great, but this won't keep her busy for long—maybe a day or two."

An evil spark glinted in Jaime's eyes. "Not when you hit Caroline and Sam with everything else on the chart, one after the other—you'll have to help me fill in some of these blanks. Remember, Caroline's all about keeping up appearances. Embarrassing press for Samuel is embarrassing press for her. And if Samuel has any pride, he'll just want the publicity punches to end. You'll get your answers, one way or the other."

"Jaime, I like Plan B a lot better. But some of this...It won't take Samuel long to figure out where it's coming from."

She gave me a strange look. "Don't you want him to know it's you who's screwing with his life?"

"Well, yes and no. I like the idea of spilling trivial skeletons-in-the-closet since he already crossed that line with Neelie Nixie. But..."

"You're chicken shit," she scoffed. "I don't believe this. You know what I think?"

"What?"

"I think you like blaming Cabral for your inability to move on, because it's easier than blaming yourself. You actually prefer being stuck. Total avoidance technique, see it all of the time in divorced couples."

"Says the woman who hates all men." My hackles bristled.

Jaime's mouth twisted into a warped smile. "It's not just men, it's everybody. I'm your classic misanthrope. But I know it and I embrace it. You, Trilby, are in denial."

"You don't know what happened."

"So tell me. You certainly didn't during divorce proceedings, left me blind in the batter's box. It's a good thing Samuel didn't want to clean house because you definitely didn't stand up for yourself. After looking over those public records, I'm willing to bet you knew a lot more than you told me."

I banged my fist on the table, rattling the saucers and silverware. "I was barely twenty-one! Most people haven't even *met* their spouses at that age, you know that? I'd already married the love of my life, lost him, and I was only just old enough to cry over a drink at happy hour. What do you want me to say? I failed at love. Even if he's the one who left, I *failed*, and I wasn't about to start airing our dirty laundry for the world to see. Especially to you."

Jaime let me rant, simply pursing her lips until I finished. "Does this mean you aren't going to tell me what happened in New York?"

"You're a ruthless bitch, you know that?"

"Yes. Feel better?"

I took a shaky breath. "Yeah."

"Good. That means I don't have to play your shrink and remind you how you started your own business, managed to keep your friends, learned new hobbies—none of which you failed at, blah blah blah. So, Plan B. Are you in or not?"

I closed my eyes and nodded. "Yeah. Sorry for calling you a bitch."

"Shut up, Kaye. Welcome to the club." She raised her cold cup of coffee to me and threw the last drops down her throat.

I wondered to which club I'd just gained membership.

I wrote a check to the LA Guinea Pig Charitable Fund. My hand quaked the entire time—I could buy a beach-front property for the same amount I'd just scrawled across the line. Jaime had the check couriered, along with a letter explaining the anonymous donation given in Samuel Cabral's name. The letter also told the sad, sad story of Mickey Cabral—the ill-fated family pet who'd been poisoned by tainted radish leaves.

It actually felt relieving to get rid of some of that insane alimony stockpile, knowing it was going to a (sort of) good cause and I wondered if Jaime had stumbled onto something here.

We made plans to meet at the café again Friday night, when I was back in Lyons, to hammer out post Operation Mickey-gate. She wanted to do lunch, but I had a lunch tradition that I wasn't about to forgo.

Every Friday at noon, my group of friends gathered at Paddler's Outdoor Adventures to kick off the weekend. Our Friday lunches were a convenient way to make plans and let off steam. We originally started eating lunch together years ago on Saturdays, the summer after Samuel, Danita, and Angel graduated from high school. I was sixteen and worked next door at the Garden Market, saving up for college. When college was over and Saturdays often booked, we switched to Friday lunch.

So much of our lives were encapsulated in that hour spent hunched over kayaks spread with carryout and sodas.

Cassady introduced us to the joys of eco-sneakers at a Friday lunch a year ago, when Paddler's shelved a trial stock. I fell in love with a pair of green and white Veja slides, made from reclaimed rubber and plastic bottles of all things, and never looked back. Molly never looked back, either—that was the first time she met Cassady.

It was during Friday lunch that Danita first confessed her love to Angel, who was home on two weeks' leave for our Glenwood Canyon trip.

Then there were the weekends Samuel came home from college. When he rolled into town, he'd go straight to Paddler's, pull me away from my lunch, and kiss me soundly. Sometimes that kiss continued in the Garden Market back room with tangled tongues and frantic groping. That is, until Audrey Wexler's elderly mother caught us behind crates of whole grain bread, rounding second base and heading for third. After the word "underage" passed her lips, we tried to be more discreet.

Though life shifted and changed, the tradition continued.

When I pulled up to Paddler's around noon, I was already beyond frustrated. The morning had been spent calmly arguing over the phone with a ski rental client about why "*Going down with you since 1973*" was not a family-oriented business slogan. Then our webmaster called the minute I hung up, telling me that one of the TrilbyJones servers crashed and we were on back-up.

Everyone was already there, crowded around an overturned kayak, when I entered. Warm pine paneling covered the walls, lined with wet suits and helmets, colorful kayaks and canoes, oars, and mountain bikes. Framed eight-by-ten photos were scattered between outdoor rentals, our faces bright behind ski goggles, whitewater helmets, or rappelling gear. There were six Shoshone rapids pictures—one for each year Angel and I tried to surf the unconquerable hydraulic.

Today was tamales from Sofia. Santiago, Hector, and Cassady were all in town instead of leading an adventure group. Danita was in her spattered jumpsuit, legs crossed, and Molly sat next to her in a pencil skirt. The boys tore into another pile of stuffed corn husks, save for Cassady. Not that Cassady didn't eat meat. But because of his diet, grease tended to make him woozy. I thought it was funny. Molly thought it was adorable.

I scouted the plate of tamales.

"Looking for something?" Angel asked, grinning from ear to ear. He knew what I wanted.

"Any chance there's a bean and potato lying around?"

"Over here, Kaye." Hector held up a hot corn husk. "Hope you don't mind, but I didn't think you could eat the entire stash yourself."

I dropped next to him and he handed me the tamale on a paper plate. "You'd be surprised. I tend to be an emotional eater when it comes to Sofia's tamales."

"Bad day?"

"Kind of a roller coaster week. I'm realizing I have a lot more leftovers to clean out of the fridge than I originally thought."

Hector gave my shoulders a squeeze. "Have I ever told you what a turn on your food analogies are?"

"Hmm. Men and food. It's spot on, though—that old saying about the quickest way to a man's heart?"

Danita lifted her tamale in a toast. "Hear, hear."

"That's so true," Molly chimed in. "It always ties back to basic needs, doesn't it? Food, sleep, sex. You meet those three, you've got a happy man."

"C'mon, Molly, you make us sound like cavemen," said Cassady. "We have brains, you know. We like to use them, even." Molly's face fell. Cassady nudged her gently.

"And we want someone we can laugh with," Hector added. "When everything else, er, peters out down the road, you'll need that." Hector didn't remove his arm from my shoulders. It made me uneasy, but I didn't scoot away. This was normal for us, and I'd never once felt anxious about it until the past week.

"We like to feel useful, too," said Santiago. "I had a girlfriend who would ask me to gauge the air pressure on her Camry's tires. She knew how to do it herself, but then I got *rewarded* when I helped."

"Good one, *hermano*," Angel said, giving Santiago a fist-bump. "Don't forget our Superman instincts."

"Superman instincts?" I asked.

Danita looked heavenward. "Superman instincts—a man's need to protect his woman. Angel has this bizarre fantasy that I'm Lois Lane, ready and willing to fling myself over the railing at Niagara Falls, just so he can swoop in and rescue me."

"We're saving *that* one for the honeymoon. I've got my red underwear and cape packed and I'm poised for action!"

The women groaned, the men whooped it up like...well...cavemen. This conversation was starting to take a turn for the worse, so I steered it back. "Speaking of food analogies, anyone up for the Band Game?" A chorus of refusals rippled around the room. I scowled. It wasn't that bad of a game. The idea was to use a food analogy for a band. Rolling Stones: beef sirloin marinated in Jack Daniels whiskey. Samuel and I created it when we were kids.

Hector manned up. "I'll play, Kaye."

"In," said Cassady.

Molly was in after that. The rest cleared up the tamales and dug through boxes of new equipment, trying on a shipment of yellow life vests.

"Okay." I started them out easy. "Harry Connick, Jr."

Molly snapped. "Shrimp Etouffee with a side of red beans and wine."

"Niiice," said Hector.

Molly pumped her fist. "All right! The Beach Boys."

"Simple," said Cassady. "Your archetypal cherry-flavored snow cone. Mamas and the Papas." My eyebrows shot up. These guys were getting better.

I snapped, barely beating Hector. "Ambrosia salad, extra mandarin oranges." I grinned, ready to take it to the next level. "Voodoo Loons."

Only blank stares met me. No one had heard of them. I was about to pick another band, when I heard *his* voice behind me.

"Bangers and mash with a jug of bootleg moonshine to wash it down."

Oh for the love of…it was the unholy cliff-hucker. I swiveled around and saw Samuel leaning against the doorframe. His arms were folded across his chest, a fitted T-shirt and jeans casually clinging to his lean frame, and his normally coiffed hair was unruly—it must have been an off-day. His eyes sparked with quirking lips to match. The game was forgotten, and everyone around me, save for Hector, jumped up to hug Samuel or slap him on the back, greeting the prodigal son with open arms and dragging out the fatted calf, calling for a feast.

But Danita embraced her brother with the warmth of an ice sculpture. Yes, there was definitely something going on there.

"How on earth did you manage to shake Tweedle-Dee and Tweedle-Dum?" she asked. Tweedle-Dee and Tweedle-Dum were two photographers who kept tabs on Samuel, popping up whenever he strolled around Lyons.

"Disguise." He shrugged, as if people snapping pictures of your every move was perfectly normal.

"Groucho Marx glasses?"

"Tempting, but no. My old baseball cap and sunglasses." He held up his familiar Lyons High ball cap, now frayed around the bill. "How's the head, Angel?" I noticed that his eyes kept drifting to me instead of Angel. Ha, I'd been right—I'd *warned* him about mini-golfing.

Angel rubbed the knot on his forehead where Hector's golf ball had nearly knocked him out. "Much better. I told that mini-golf chick I didn't need to go to the hospital after Hector beaned me."

"You could have had a concussion, *mi ángel*," said a concerned Danita.

Samuel made his way over while the two continued to bicker and sat next to me.

"Hey, Kaye."

"Um…hey?" *How much more awkward could this get?* "What are you doing here?"

"Isn't this Friday lunch?"

"Yeah, but…"

"Danita asked me to swing by, but I won't stay long if it makes you uncomfortable. I just want to catch up with everyone."

Hector leaned around me to glare at Samuel. "*Hombre*, you just can't show up like this after all this time."

Samuel lowered cool eyes on Hector. "I didn't know I was uninvited."

"You kind of uninvited yourself when you skipped out on—"

"Hector." I laid a calming hand on his inked forearm.

Hector took a deep breath, then tried a different tactic. "So, Sam, *¿dónde está tu hermosa dama?* She didn't want to come along?"

The other conversations died away and everyone focused on Samuel and Hector.

"Caroline couldn't make it. She's caught in a PR mess with several regional TV networks in LA. Actually, an odd thing happened."

Suddenly, my flaking nail polish was extremely interesting.

"What happened?" Danita asked.

"Well." He glanced at me sideways. "Do you remember that guinea pig I had back in sixth grade—Mickey?"

"The one Kaye named after an Irish penis?" said Dani. *Flippin-A.* My face began to burn. I hopped up and walked across the room. "You poisoned it."

"For the last time, I didn't poison it! Not on purpose, anyway—but that's beside the point. Someone made an extremely large donation to a charitable fund that specializes in guinea pig rescues."

"And…?" Dani waved him on.

"And, they did it in my name. Mickey's too." The entire group broke into raucous laughter, save for Samuel and myself. "I ask you, who with that kind of money could possibly know about Mickey?" He looked at me.

"Samuel, you brought that thing to science class every other week," I countered. "Any one of those students could have spilled the story." I tacked on a laugh to avoid suspicion, but what was the point? He obviously knew it was me.

"So, how much money are we talking about, Sammy?" Angel shouted over the laughter.

"Enough to build a brand new center, complete with office space, a small research lab, and a guinea pig 'learning lounge.' The LAG-PCF—I think that's the acronym—wants to name the center after me." More laughter. He waited until it died down before continuing. "Anyway, someone alerted the media to this 'human interest' story. Caroline's been on the phone all morning, putting out statements, press releases, talking to the charity to convince them to name the center after Mickey instead of me. And now someone at PETA has expressed interest in the story…"

Crap, crap, crap—we hadn't considered PETA. Or *I* hadn't, anyway. Something told me Jaime might have.

"You're going to end up in a PETA campaign, Samuel!" said Angel. "Now you'll have to pose for one of their magazine ads—you know, sprawled sexy-naked across a floor while guinea pigs crawl all over you?"

"Be sure to cover your nethers, there," Cassady deadpanned. "I've read that guinea pigs are vicious."

Laughter erupted ten-fold. Hector held his sides. Tears streamed down Molly's face. Even Samuel couldn't help himself and chuckled quietly. A part of me was relieved he didn't seem to be angry about Mickey-gate.

"Anyone up for celebrating the newly-christened Mickey Cabral Center for Rescued Guinea Pigs at my apartment this evening?" Molly asked as the laughter died down.

"Sorry, can't," Danita said. "I have an early morning tomorrow at the shop. I'm putting in extra hours before the wedding."

"Got a group heading over to the national park tomorrow, but could swing by for a coupla hours," said Cassady.

Molly turned to me.

"Um," I straightened a photo on the wall. "I have plans." Seven set of eyes fixed on me with astonishment. I felt a bit offended. "Really, guys, is it that strange to have weekend plans with someone outside of our circle?"

"For you? Yes," Molly shot back.

Come on, Molly, not in front of the ex. "It's not like that, seriously. Just meeting a colleague for dinner."

My friends' simpering faces told me they didn't believe it. But really, I couldn't reveal I was meeting with Jaime Guzman, my former divorce lawyer and self-proclaimed people-hater. They'd know something was up in a heartbeat. Suddenly, the photo in front of me became the most fascinating photo in the world. I studied it intently until they went back to their own conversations.

"This is in Glenwood Canyon?"

I jumped. I hadn't even noticed Samuel come up behind me. But now he was so close, I could smell his aftershave. Too close. I took a small step away.

"Yes."

"Do you like it out there?"

"Yes."

"I'd always wanted to spend time on that stretch of river, more than just passing through. I think it's beautiful."

"Mm-hmm."

He smiled at my one-word answers. I certainly wasn't going to make it easy for him. "Is this a whitewater rafting trip?"

"Yep."

"I never pegged you for an extreme sports enthusiast, Kaye. But in retrospect, maybe I should have. You certainly have always had a fearless temperament."

Okay, now he was baiting me, and dang it, I wanted to bite.

"Come on, Kaye. Talk to me."

I bit. "What, Samuel, you want to have an in-depth conversation, despite—how did you put it in *Water Sirens*? 'What came out of her mouth was so awkward, it made the comparison farcical'?"

"All right, I'll give you that—it *was* a mean thing to write. But the phrase doesn't work without the rest of that sentiment, Kaye," he said gently, his smile growing bigger. Smug male, he *wanted* that reaction from me. "You, however, seem determined to recall only negative." Oh, I remembered the first half of that sentiment—'soft mouth of an angel'—but I wasn't about to toss it around in front of him. "I'm trying not to be patronizing," he continued. "I'm just a little worried, I suppose."

"You don't need to play Superman to my Lois Lane, Samuel," I whispered roughly. "In fact, you shouldn't. You gave up that right a long time ago."

"That's true. But it doesn't mean I can't worry. Or shouldn't. Class five whitewater, chasing the perfect snow…that's nothing to mess around with." His eyes grew serious as he tapped a different photo—one of Hector and me—snapped in Vail backcountry after a day of crazy skiing, our poles held up like winners' trophies.

I huffed, feeling like a fifteen-year-old kid again. Samuel had the power to do that, and he still did it well. Of all things, worrying about extreme sports…in Colorado! And then I remembered the draft story I saw in his bedroom, the one about whitewater hydraulics. Something clicked into place. "Samuel, how do you even know about that class five hydraulic at Glenwood Canyon?"

"Angel told me."

Et tu, Angel? My friends occasionally kept in touch with my east coast ex, though I never thought they'd discuss me with him. I frowned. "*You* probably would have surfed that damned hydraulic the first time out."

He paused, caught off-guard by my comment. "I'm not faultless, Kaye. Far from it."

"I never thought you were."

"Yes, you did."

What to say? I felt his hand rest, ever so carefully, upon my shoulder. "I'm sorry I disappointed you," he whispered.

My fists tightened. This was my chance for answers. Caroline was busy with Mickey-gate, he even freaking apologized. Why the heck wasn't I taking my chance? *Come on, Kaye, just ask him.*

Samuel glanced down at his watch and my window passed. "I've got to run. I'm supposed to do a telephone interview with ABC7 in LA for their news broadcast tonight and they want to know Mickey's story. Maybe a little bit about my latest book, too."

"Oh...sure."

He laughed quietly. "Have fun on your date tonight."

Before I could spill my guts about Mickey or anything else, he brushed my shoulder, waved goodbye to the others, and was gone.

Jaime was right. I was sabotaging myself.

I grabbed my purse, also ready to head out but Danita grabbed my elbow. There was a no-nonsense glower on her face. "Oh, Kaye, we need to chat."

Busted. Mickey-gate would sink me yet.

Chapter 8
RIFFLES

Little waves caused by shallow water and rocky riverbed.

"Mom, I've got a thinking question for you." I crated dozens of spring produce items spread across the counter while my mother, Gail, prepped them for tomorrow morning's farmers market. After Friday lunch, I wandered over to the farm, killing time before I met Jaime. I tried to read more of *The Last Other* while Mom scrubbed asparagus, but something Samuel said bothered me so much, the words blurred past. After re-reading with no luck, I closed my book and sought out my mother.

"Sure, what is it?"

"When Samuel and I were growing up, did I think he was perfect?"

My mother huffed—not surprising. My mother huffed at most anything. Either that, or freaked out. "Oh, Kaye, you thought the sun rose and set in that boy—his entire family, really. It was so odd, the way you two had your little made-up games, your pranks and cuss wars...you certainly spoke a different language than the rest of us. You acted tough around him, fought with him, like you were fooling us. But we saw." Her brown eyes grew distant as she remembered.

"What is it, Mom?" She studied my face. "Just say it, please—whatever you're thinking."

She sighed, struggled, then gave in. "Well, I can't help but wonder if your dad and I handled your engagement to Samuel as best as we could have."

"What do you mean?"

"It's just...you wanted to be married so badly, I think, like you were determined to do the opposite of what Tom and I did. I know our failed relationship did a number on you, more than either of us was willing to admit." She picked up a bunch of asparagus, smoothing a cracked finger over delicate stalks. "Maybe we should have tried harder to talk you out of marrying so young, I don't know. I could tell Samuel was hesitant, but you were so persevering, so enthusiastic. And the two of you seemed to love each other so much."

I fidgeted with the hem of my shirt, stewing over what my mother said. Was she right? Had my desire to marry been driven not by my love for Samuel, but my determination to steer clear of my parents' treacherous footprints? "You thought I was too rash in my marriage. Do you also think I was too rash when I filed for divorce?"

"Well, I'm not sure. It's hard to make a judgment call like that when I don't know all of the details." She misted the crates with a water bottle, glancing at me from the corner of her eyes.

Of course she didn't know everything. I never told her about the day Samuel left or my very brief trip to New York City. I'd never breathed a word of it, except to Alonso and Sofia. Spilling the painful details of the most wretched moments of my existence was too much to ask, and I opted for dignity over honesty.

Mom still eyed me as she moved on to the strawberries, wiping one on her dark green apron. Maybe it was time to unload a few of those heavy secrets. I drummed up the courage, struggling over a million different ways to phrase my words, not wanting to upset her.

"There are a lot of people who think I filed for divorce too quickly. Dani does. Molly might too, even though she's never said it. It's just... there are things..."

My mother paused in her misting. "Like what?"

My teeth craved a thumbnail so I stuffed my hands in my sweater pockets. "What if...something happened that made you think someone wasn't who you thought they were? And it hurt, really bad. So badly, you just wanted to rip out your heart and hurl it back at them."

Mom grabbed my arm, smearing dirt on my shirt. "Oh my God, did Samuel hurt you? What did he do? I'll kill him if he laid a hand on you!"

"No, Mom, geez. Samuel would never do anything like that." I shook off her hand. I knew she would react badly—that's why I hadn't said anything. "I only meant that when I followed him to New York, I saw something…shocking, I guess, and it made me question a lot of things. He'd already been gone for several weeks and I was a head case, half-expecting him to come back, stunned he'd left in the first place. Now I wonder if I was rash in filing for divorce. But when someone says they can't be married to you, how else are you supposed to take it, right? And then he dragged the divorce out for five months, never signing, never talking to my lawyer, like he couldn't even be bothered with me, like he didn't care enough to stop his 'new life.' I was so incredibly angry—"

"Wait, when did you go to New York?"

"A few weeks after he left. We'd talked about moving out there after I finished at CU, remember, so he could attend grad school? But it was never set in stone. I thought maybe I'd only misunderstood him, but…"

My mother stared at me, confusion rife on her face. This was a bad idea.

"Just don't worry about it, Mom. I'm second-guessing myself, that's all. Nothing new."

My mother smiled sadly and awkwardly patted my shoulder. "You and me—we both bottle up everything and never say a word to anyone until the cap comes off. Then, when others try to catch up, half the time it doesn't make any sense."

It struck me then how very similar my mother and I were. My father had always been a well-meaning but fickle man. He and I had a decent relationship, and I had his impulsive genes, but I was my mother's daughter. Private, stubborn, I preferred to internalize my fears and failures, dealing with them in my own way.

My dad had loved Gail, just not enough to ever marry her. He'd always claimed he didn't believe in that archaic tradition (that's supposedly why he hadn't married Audrey, either). My mother...my mother loved him, still did. Even though she'd tried to date here and there, it never amounted to anything. And while she managed to carve out a contented existence between me and her little farm, she was never quite happy. Mom was stuck—just like me.

This couldn't happen. I had to do something, before I, too, met Mom's fate.

But...what if getting unstuck meant letting go of Samuel? Not just physically separating myself from him—I'd tried that already, and it hadn't worked. What if it meant letting go of the love I still harbored for him, buried amidst bitterness, anger, regret? Was that what Jaime meant when she said I wanted to be stuck? If so, I didn't know if I was strong enough to let go.

I glanced at my watch—six thirty. I didn't have enough time to run home and change before dinner with Jaime. Ah well, the tattered sweater would have to do—it's not like she would mind.

"Let me get this straight. Not only does Danita Cabral *not* care we're screwing with her brother's life, you have her blessing?"

"Yes. As long as it does not, and I quote, 'in any way, shape, or form interfere with her wedding, or events thereby pertaining to said wedding.'"

Once again, Jaime Guzman sat across from me in the Lyons Café as we waited for our order. It was a bustling Friday night, despite dust-laden high winds. Gusts beat against the windows and rattled the hole-in-the-wall restaurant. Nevertheless, it was cheery inside. This time, amidst the noise of conversations, clanking dinner plates and jukebox music, I felt more comfortable with her. I'd even committed to our dinner date past coffee by ordering a tuna melt and side salad. She chose a platter of cheesy fries, and that was it. The same pageboy cap still covered her hair, another snarky T-shirt worn proudly—a drawing of a Dutch girl with wooden shoes and tulips. Across the bottom it read: *AmsterDAM, you're good looking.* She said it was her special Friday night date shirt.

"You're kidding. I thought she and her brother got along."

"They do, and that's the odd thing. There was bad blood between them right after he left for the east coast, but they managed to sort through most of it. Heck, she usually takes me down a peg or two when I bash him. But I don't know..." I was still puzzled over Danita's enthusiastic high-five over Mickey-gate. "Lately, I've gotten strange vibes from her. First she convinces me to change my last name, move on, Samuel's with someone else. Now she's all but begging me to drag out this vendetta."

"Hmmm." Jaime twisted a paper napkin, winding it around her finger. "Maybe she has an ax to grind with Cabral and she's letting you do her dirty work. From what I remember about Danita, hasn't she always been kind of vindictive?"

"Dani can be, but if you've got her on your side, she's a strong ally." I snapped my fingers, remembering the icy looks as of late. "You know, lately Dani has been casting evil eyes at Samuel."

"Do you think it might be significant?"

"It's never taken much to set her off. For all I know, it could be entirely separate incidents."

"But huge enough for Danita to want to fuck with her brother." Jaime cringed, catching her words. "Forget I just said that."

"Nice. Maybe you'll clean up your mouth now."

"Not a chance." She took a swig of ice water, wiping her mouth with the back of her hand. "See if you can find out from Danita, or Angel even, what the fight was about. It could be something useful."

Dani had asked who was helping to plot my "Neelie Nixie" revenge, not believing I could be this devious on my own. She informed me Lyons was too small a town for secrets and her boss's brother's wife's best friend had seen me and Jaime Guzman at the café Tuesday night, so engrossed in our conversation that we hadn't bothered to order food. Welders were horrible gossips.

"Just don't buy into everything that Jaime Guzman sells," Danita had warned. "You heard about the way she worked over her ex-husband when he ditched her for that chica who works at the bank. Half of the Hispanic community still isn't speaking to her." Her ex still got gay porn in his mailbox to this day. I promised to keep the pranks harmless and she seemed content, even supplying the picture I now handed over to Jaime: A stunned twenty-year-old Samuel stared up from the glossy four-by-six photo, liquid-lined and magenta-shadowed eyes glowing from the camera flash. He was clad in a red knit miniskirt that belonged to Dani, heels, a blond bombshell wig, a pointed black bra—and nothing else.

Halloween was serious business, each year's costume topping the next. One year, we'd done some creative work with a gothic get-up and pillows, and went as Wednesday and Pugsley Addams. Another Halloween, in junior high, we were a Bee and Beekeeper. But my favorite was when I'd gone as a devil, and Samuel, an angel. The original intention was that I would don the halo and white feathery wings, but we'd switched at the last minute. My photo album had a snapshot of Samuel innocently pressing his palms together in prayer while I jabbed his rear with a pitchfork. I think we were fifteen and seventeen that year.

The drag picture was completely unlike the quiet, virtue-conscious young man I'd loved. And yet, in the picture, it was so obviously Samuel. I was sorely disappointed I'd missed that CU party. At the time, I was in my senior year of high school and up to my neck in a research paper on *The Grapes of Wrath*. But Danita had taken many pictures. So had dozens of other people, which was why Jaime and I used this photo—to throw Samuel off our track.

"Perfect." Jaime chuckled at the photo. "As funny as it is, it's the last thing a serious author wants floating around on the Internet."

I was willing to bet John Updike never wore drag.

"On to the next order of business." She tucked the photo into her dossier and pulled out her articles and flow charts. "The photo gets sent to *HollywoodDays* first, then posted around several blogs if no one bites. Our goal is for an entertainment network to air a blurb about it, at least on their website..."

Our food came out. Soon, I was engrossed in plotting and didn't notice the café goings-on around me. Jaime, however, was a practiced multi-tasker—every time the bell above the door jingled, she glanced behind me to see who had walked in. Her eyes widened.

"Damn! Is that her, Trilby? She's stunning."

I whipped around. Yup, it was. Samuel and Caroline shook dust off their jackets and scanned the restaurant, searching for an empty table. He was dressed in the same casual T-shirt and jeans, though he'd thrown on a fleece—Lyons still grew chilly at night, even in late May. Caroline was as posh as ever, hair sleek as onyx. I glanced down at my own ratty sweater and tennis shoes, and slid down into the booth.

Jaime laughed. "Oh, she'll be fun to mess with. Look how she's crinkling up her nose—I think she's had work done on it." She scrambled to clear away her flow charts, pictures and papers, and stuffed her top-secret dossier in her messenger bag. "Bet she's never been on a Lyons Café date. Look, a couple of girls are asking for his autograph. HA! Caroline signed it, too."

"Oh crud." My face fell into my hands. Jaime popped another cheesy fry in her mouth, chewing gleefully while I peered at her between my fingers.

"What's wrong, Trilby? Still scared of that Manhattan skank?"

I shook my head. "Samuel thinks I have a date tonight. This is embarrassing."

Jaime's eyes gleamed. I knew that gleam—it was her eleventh-hour courtroom revelation gleam.

"There's no reason he has to know you aren't on a date," she whispered swiftly. "Change of plans, just follow my lead."

A flash of panic rippled up my spine. What did that mean? Before I could ask, she rose from the booth and waved over Samuel and Caroline. She transferred her plate, drink, and bag to the empty spot next to me. "Move—I want the window seat. Left-handed." I rolled my eyes and stood to let her in. When she was settled, her arm came up behind me, resting along the top of the booth seat. Since when was Jaime ever affectionate? I squirmed when she didn't move. I tried to sink further into the booth, my tomato face still hidden in my hands, but she yanked me up by my shirt collar.

Two sets of expensive shoes stopped in front of our booth. I slowly peered up. Samuel grinned down at me and then at Jaime with a smug "I've-got-your-number-now" look. Caroline crossed her arms, fingers tapping impatiently.

"Neelie Nixie. Fancy running into you here."

"What a coincidence," Caroline muttered under her breath.

Jaime kicked me beneath the table when I didn't say anything. Finally, she stepped up. "You can count the restaurants in Lyons on one hand, Cabral, so it's really not improbable to see someone you know. Or do you only use those fingers for typing up your stupid fantasies?"

Samuel's smile faltered. "It's always such a pleasure to see you, Jaime. I hear you've taken up the causes of small furry rodents." Crap. I should have known the minute he saw the both of us, he'd put two and two together.

"I'm not sure what you mean."

"Tell me, are you thinking of branching out from breeding Labradors? I hear guinea pigs are popular with children these days."

Jaime's eyes narrowed. "Yeah, so's Candy C."

No! I *told* her not to go there with the records. Samuel's mouth fell open in stunned silence, but he shut it and let the comment slide. The lines around his eyes tightened. And while I didn't look at her, I felt Caroline's heated gaze upon us like a missile lock, sizing up the situation. I jabbed an elbow into Jaime's ribs, warning her to shut up. She dug her fingers into my shoulder, hard. She had a painful grip, but it was enough to wake me up. *Time to grow a pair, Kaye, and defuse this thing.*

"Um, did the two of you want to join us?" I gestured to the other side of the booth. "We're almost done eating, but..."

Caroline cleared her throat. "Thanks, but we'll probably just head over to Smokin' Dave's. It's too crowded here."

"We were just at Smokin' Dave's, and you said it was too crowded," said Samuel.

"You agreed with me," she fired back.

Jaime and I shared a glance—there was tension in Versaceville. Samuel scratched the back of his neck and sighed.

"Caro, can we just grab a table and eat, please?"

"Fine." But surprisingly, instead of finding a different booth, "Caro" glided into the seat across from Jaime, meeting my eyes in silent challenge.

Samuel looked to me for approval. I nodded, and he awkwardly slid in next to her, across from me. Caroline wrapped protective fingers around his. He moved them under the table, out of sight. I gagged a little, my tuna melt now nauseating.

Jaime grinned at me, getting what I meant by the *Hound from Hell.* "The moral support's touching, but you can move your arm, now," I whispered to her. Ignoring me, she held out a hand to Caroline.

"Nice to meet you. I'm Jaime Guzman."

"Caroline Ortega—Samuel's date for the wedding." She gave him an insider smile, implying they were much, *much* more than wedding dates. I looked away. "So, Jaime, how do you know our Kaye?"

Our Kaye?

"Well, Caro, *our* Kaye is the hottest little *tamale blanco* on this side of the Rockies. I wish *I* was her date for the wedding, but you know how that goes."

Caroline and Samuel laughed politely and perused their menus. They thought she was kidding…

But they didn't see Jaime's other hand slide under the table and grasp my thigh. I gasped. Frickin' twisted muffin, was she putting the moves on me? Horrified, I glanced across the table to see if Samuel and Caroline had noticed. They were busy ordering their food. I started to get up, but she pinched my leg, hard.

"Ow!"

Leaning over, she whispered into my bad ear, something like, "Go with me."

Then I knew what she was doing. Woman seriously had no shame when it came to messing with people. I started to tell her I wouldn't play this game, even if it meant the eternal subterfuge of a thousand Carolines. But then, the reckless feeling stirred in me—the stupid one that argued, *Why the hell not? Cross that line, girlfriend!* It was the same voice that urged me to surf class five rapids with Angel, cliff-huck with Hector, and crash book signings with Molly. *Aw, what the heck. Might as well be a lesbian with Jaime.*

I tossed up my hands in futility. "Whatever, sweet cheeks, have it your way. Should you tell them or should I?"

The Manhattan camp's attention was suddenly on us. Samuel halted, water glass halfway to his lips. Caroline's tapping fingernails stilled.

"It's okay, Kaye-baby. I've told you time and again: there's no reason to hide our love." She leaned over and nipped my ear.

Samuel dropped his glass. It clattered to the table, cold water and ice cubes sloshing over the edge and onto our laps.

"Shit, Cabral!" Jaime yelped, jumping up. "What is your problem?"

He blinked at me, eyes wide, as if antennas sprouted from my skull. (I thought, for a moment, maybe they did—this had to be a fantastically weird dream.) He froze, watching while the rest of us grabbed napkins and mopped up the table before it spilled over the edge and onto our shoes. Finally, he sprang into action, muttering apologies while he scooped up soggy napkins and tossed them on an appetizer plate. Our waitress came by with a tray, took away the mess, and wiped it dry. When we settled back into our seats, Jaime's arm came around me again.

"Yeah, Kaye's pretty much the best partner ever. Doesn't nag, doesn't get all insanely jealous when another gal talks to me. Did you see how she played it cool with our waitress just now? Didn't even check out her rack. And she's got the cutest little ass I've ever seen."

Samuel's sharp eyes were riveted to my every move—how I shifted in my seat, pushed the food around on my plate. I knew he was deconstructing the situation, flushing out my bluffs and tells until he was satisfied he had the truth. It had always unnerved me when he watched me like that, so intensely.

Caroline, however, gushed fountains of pure honey. "I just can't tell you how happy I am to meet you, Jaime. I'm glad Kaye has a significant other in her life, also."

Jaime's face was so openly sweet, it was sick. "It's swell, isn't it? I like to think she's a really lucky lady, too."

I unconsciously leaned away from Jaime. He saw it. At last, he leaned back in his booth with a smug, and perhaps relieved, smile.

"When I first met Kaye, I thought maybe she was…you know," Caroline happily continued. "I could just tell."

Argh! Hound. "Yeah, the lack of heels and hair product is a dead giveaway, isn't it?"

She nodded, missing my sarcasm.

Samuel groaned, his face falling into his hands. "Caro, come on. Let's leave them alone so they can finish their dinner. We can find a different table."

"Oh no. I really want to get to know Kaye better, spend some time together. I mean, you've known her forever and I've only known her for a few weeks. You don't mind, do you?" she asked Jaime.

"Not at all."

No, no, no! I shouted silently. I didn't want Caro latching on to me like a soul-sucking starfish.

Samuel, sensing my distress, came to the rescue. "Probably not a good time for that, *cariño*. I'm sure Kaye will be extremely busy helping Danita with the wedding. Right?"

I nodded emphatically. "Really, really busy. Dress fittings, rehearsals, company coming into town, organizing vendors. So much to do. Maybe we can do lunch or something, sometime."

"Of course." Caro turned to Jaime. "Well, that means you'll have free time on your hands, with Kaye so busy."

Jaime choked on a half-cold French fry. *Ha, she didn't see that one coming.*

"Absolutely!" Samuel grinned wickedly at his adversary, sensing a chance to pay her back for a number of grievances dating back to playground days. "Think of all the things you two have in common, all of the stories you could swap."

Jaime's eyes narrowed at him. "Oh, don't I know it! Ever since Kaye and I reconnected, all I've heard from this one is best buddies, guitars, lesbian sex is so much better, yap yap yap."

Samuel didn't miss a beat. "So, how did the two of you start dating, Jaime? Attorney-Client happy hour?"

Jaime dove in enthusiastically, pulling out every stereotype in the book and pausing only when the waitress returned with Samuel's and Caroline's salads. She wove an elaborate tale about how we met at an LGBT mixer at the Lyons Civics Center—we were the only two there, so we just kind of fell together. Since then, we'd bonded over our love for military consignment stores and erotic art. We'd even marched together in the last annual Denver Gay Pride Parade, donning rainbow wigs and carrying signs that read*: Better Gay than Grumpy.* And now we bided our time in the proverbial Lyons closet, living in our own "bubble of beautiful lesbo love." I coughed into my napkin at Jaime's alliteration. Samuel's eyes met mine, shining with amusement.

Not to be left out, Caroline nodded sympathetically, watery eyes meeting mine. "I understand. It must be difficult to live in such a small town, Kaye, especially when your father is the high school baseball coach."

I was unnerved she knew about my father. Then again, I knew about *her* father. It reminded me to keep my cards close—Caroline was not as ditzy as she appeared. "We like to keep our relationship quiet, here. Really quiet. As in, don't tell anyone please."

"Of course." She speared a cucumber slice.

"You'll have to join me some Saturday for Harley club while Kaye's wedding prepping," Jaime said. "Our biker bitches would really dig you." I wondered if Jaime really knew biker bitches and, if she didn't, what she planned to do with Caroline. I probably shouldn't know.

"Oh!" Caroline turned to Samuel. "Speaking of lesbians, you have a talk show scheduled next Tuesday. They had a cancellation and want you to discuss *The Last Other*. Probably ask some questions about that ridiculous guinea pig and the PETA boycott, too. I could just throttle whoever pulled that stunt."

Jaime's body shook with mute laughter.

The conversation safely turned to the book tour (*oh thank you, thank you*). My near-incitement of a fan-girl riot was blessedly overlooked. Caroline mentioned another talk show appearance two weeks from Saturday.

"Samuel, that won't work," I replied. "That's the same day as Angel and Danita's bachelor-bachelorette trip—the weekend before the wedding?" They'd opted out of strip clubs and body shots, instead wanting to honor their upcoming nuptials in an activity befitting our circle of friends. We were going skydiving. Half of us were licensed after a summer's worth of free fall and parachute training.

"I forgot about that. Caro, can we reschedule?"

She whipped out her smartphone and shook her head. "No go. I worked really hard to set this one up, Samuel. Maybe you can throw yourself from a plane some other time."

"Cancel then. This is my sister's wedding and I'm not missing anything she has planned. Although, why she wants to kill off her entire wedding party with one deft plunge, I'm not sure."

"I'm surprised, Cabral," Jaime said. "It seems like you have a lot of experience pushing the limits. Now *Trilby* here, she'll throw herself out of anything that's remotely dangerous. *Trilby's* insane." *No, Jaime. Please, no, not my last name. Not here, not now.* I nudged her with my elbow over and over until she shoved me away, annoyed.

We waited, bated breath, for Samuel to react. When he didn't so much as bat an eye, I relaxed. Jaime, however, wasn't going to let it go.

"Like I said, Kaye *Trilby* is a real dare-devil. Skydiving is a walk in the park for her."

Caroline rolled her eyes. "We get it, understood you the first time. Kaye's amazing at extreme sports, likes to take risks."

"No. I don't think you do get it."

"*Jaime*," I hissed. I scrambled for a subject change while the two verbally dived for each other's throats.

But then, beneath the table, well-known, warm fingers wrapped around my fidgeting ones, holding them still.

My eyes flew to his. They were cool, veiled. Either his poker face had gotten a lot better or I couldn't understand him like I used to—I don't know which upset me more. I wanted anger to be in every fleck of blue, not this unnerving calm. There was the barest hint of urgency there, almost as if he waited for some cue, something from me I couldn't comprehend. Jaime and Caroline still busily sniped at each other, somewhere in my blurred peripheral. But I lost myself in wild rivers and wide blue skies...everything I cherished about Colorado.

He traced the inside of my palm with his thumb...so very subtly, I wasn't sure it was deliberate. I capsized.

But so help me, whenever I was swamped, I always broke the surface. My steel guard snapped up, stemming the torrent of emotions that threatened to overwhelm me. Gritting my teeth, I pulled my eyes back...and my hand. "I think it's time to head out," I said flatly.

Jaime broke from her argument with Caroline in an instant and gathered up her things. "Finally!" she exhaled, shoving me from the booth.

The night air was crisp. The sky was clouded over when we exited the café, but the wind had stopped. I breathed deeply as I pushed through the door, savoring the farm-tinged mountain air. Streetlights bounced off pavement and it glowed orange. I started toward my car, but Samuel put an arm around my shoulders and pulled me tightly to his side, halting while the others walked ahead. His breath was hot on my ear.

"What are you, eight? You think I don't know what you're up to?"

"Tell me, what am I up to?"

"You and Jaime, and all of these ridiculous games you're planning. Now you want to duke it out, after all these years?"

Oh, that got me. "Oh please, Samuel, you are the king of avoidance."

"Likewise. May I remind you who ran out on Thanksgiving?"

"And may I remind you who bailed on us in the first place?"

His mouth snapped shut. I'd seen Samuel's face turn red on many occasions, but he'd been rendered speechless on precious few—clever man always had an answer to everything. But now, he simply flushed and remained silent.

Answers. Answers. Answers. Just fire back, Samuel. Tell me why you bailed, don't make me ask.

He wasn't going to tell me. It should *be* that easy. "Go ahead, Kaye," he murmured, "play the vengeful ex-wife, if it helps. But you should know that I'm not going to step aside and allow you to mess with me. I won't have a choice but to fight back."

"What are you going to do? Write another book about me?" His hand was warm on my arm despite the chilly air. But I still shivered and wrapped my sweater tightly around me.

"Maybe."

"Well, consider this payback for all the years you've messed with me. That ridiculous alimony check every month, all of your books. Do I even need to mention the whole New York thing? You've got it coming, Cabral."

His eyes burned an angry blue. Good. "If this is the way you want to have it out, let's have it out. Game on, *Cabral*."

"Been wearing that old letter jacket around, too? Or are you just talking high school sports trash?"

Stooping down, he swiftly kissed the top of my head. "You and Jaime look incredibly hot together—I'm so happy for you," he said loudly, his voice reverberating across the parking lot. "We'll see the two of you around." He gave my rear a swat and jogged across the parking lot to his roadster rental.

Some things never changed.

But I noticed Caroline chose to wait for him at the car, rather than hover with her hydra glares. Now that I batted for the other team, she was no longer concerned with me and was animatedly chatting to Jaime. Jaime, however, *was* shooting me a hydra glare. My former lawyer-become-accomplice was either certifiable or an evil genius. I suspected both, but leaned toward genius.

And Sam. Passionate, maddening Samuel. Yes, we were fighting—nothing new, we'd fought since we were children. But for once, there hadn't been that worn, defeatist undercurrent in his eyes or in his words. Instead, there was fire. And I hadn't seen true fire there in a really long time. Not since...not since high school.

Now, I felt the burgeoning of my own spark. A spark that wasn't due to rafting, or skiing, or mountain climbing. It was exhilarating and ominous, all tangled into one little accelerant.

I'd forgotten I could feel like that.

Much better than that insurmountable whitewater hydraulic.

Chapter 9
ALLUVIAL

Sand, clay, and silt carried away in downstream currents and layered along river banks.

Hydraulic Level Five [working title]
Draft 2.09
© Samuel Caulfield Cabral
Bat Versus Bat

Eleven-year-old boys aren't supposed to cry. Maria tells him as much when she hears his quiet tears, passing his room on her way to the bathroom. She thinks she's helpful. Patting his back, she offers to read from *Treasure Island.* His aunt reads to them every night, usually a chapter from a classic book, and *Treasure Island* was his pick.

Before that, they'd ventured through *The Secret Garden.* It was Maria's choice, but he enjoyed it (though he'd never tell Maria). She scoffs at the rudeness of Mary Lennox and Colin Craven. They are bossy and mean, sure, but he understands them a little better than Maria. Mary Lennox was all by herself in India, with a mother who didn't like her, and Colin was the same – locked away in his manor, alone, scared he'd become a hunchback like his father. And his father didn't want him because he had strange, gray eyes like his mother's.

He thinks of his own mother...she hadn't read to him at night, before bed, the way his aunt does. She'd lie down on his fire engine bed and cry with him, clutching his father's shirts and telling him to turn over because she couldn't stand his goddamned sky eyes staring at her.

But the child he likes most is Dickon Sowerby. He runs wild, like a squirrel or a fox, and he smells like grass and leaves. Aspen is like Dickon, except she picks fights with him – a lot. Well, maybe there is some Mary in her, too. When he pictures Aspen, she is outside riding her bike, wading through creeks, climbing trees (and falling out of them), her pink youth banjo slung over her back. She smells like the dirt that clings to her knees and under her nails, dirt that muddies her hazel eyes.

Caulfield swipes away the remnants of his memories from his cheeks and realizes he isn't crying. Thinking of Aspen helps. But now his throat is dry, so he flips on his bedside lamp to get a drink. His feet hit the floor.

Squeak!

He jumps back with a yell. Something writhed beneath his toes, cold and fuzzy, like an animal. His eyes shoot down to the carpet where a...thing...is sprawled, its wings spread wide.

It's a large, black bat.

"*Mamá! Papá!*" He darts for the hallway. He doesn't dare go back to the room in case the wounded thing is flopping around. He waits for his aunt and uncle to come to his rescue, but they can't hear him down the hall. But Maria does.

She stumbles into his room, sleepy-eyed, ratty hair sticking out all over her head like Aspen's Barbie doll. She straightens her yellow flannel pajamas and glares.

"Bat." He points to the other side of his bed.

Maria mumbles something incoherent and follows his finger. "Ick!" She leaps away, then takes a step closer. "Caulfield, get me your baseball bat."

"No! You're not getting guts all over my Louisville Slugger. I need it for practice tomorrow."

"Fine." She arms herself with his baseball bat anyway, before he has a chance to block her. Handle out, she pokes at the black thing on the floor. A slow smile spreads across her face.

Caulfield moans. "Oh man, I killed it when I stepped on it, didn't I? You should have heard it squeak."

Maria prods it, harder. It squeaks once more. "*Sí*, Caulfield, *tú lo mataste.*" Then she stoops down, picks it up, and flings it at him.

He screams again. But when he catches, he feels it isn't fuzzy like he initially thought. Instead, it's...rubbery. Cautiously, he smells the bat. Yup, rubber. It's fake.

His sister doubles over, giggling madly. "Wow! For a kid, she got you good."

He thoughtfully tosses it from hand to hand. A grin wins out. "Yeah, she did."

Later, after Maria goes back to her room and the lights are turned off, Caulfield places the fake bat on his pillow and stares. "Firecracker," he whispers, just to hear the sound of her name. Instead of thinking on his mother, he falls asleep plotting ways to get even with his sly, fascinating friend. Preferably, with a prank that won't earn him another chat with Aspen's father.

SC, hmm, let's break it apart. Aspen was quite the tomboy. Knowing now that she's a lesbian, how do you think that affects her characterization? Your relationship? Maybe explore that angle—childhood girlfriend grows up to be gay.
~Caro

You've certainly hit on something, Caro. That's what's missing—Kaye's thoughts. Her REAL thoughts, not the ones I'm guessing at. I think I'll ask for her help.
~SC

We'll discuss in person.
~Caro

Chirp. Chirp. Chirp.

I heard it again. That obnoxious cricket, rudely yanking me out of my much needed dream time, just when I'd drifted off to sweet oblivion with my blankets pulled over my head.

Chirp-chirp... chirp-chirp... chirp-chirp...

And the other cricket.

ChirpchirpChirpchirpchirpChirpChirpchirpChirpchirpchirpChirp-ChirpchirpChirp...

And the rest of the two dozen crickets echoing through my home. I burrowed further beneath my down comforter. This was my second fitful night's sleep since I returned from Lyons to find my apartment above the TrilbyJones mansion infiltrated by crickets. I'd had fun with them last night, pulling out my guitar and playfully strumming chords around their happy chirps like a fricking fairy-tale princess. But when three o'clock hit and I still hadn't slept, I stumbled from my bedroom to my brainstorming room downstairs and blissfully crashed on the hard office sofa. The first item of business yesterday morning was to pick up a granular bait pest control and liberally sprinkle it around the baseboards.

That should have done the trick, but the evil little Jiminies were back with a vengeance, gleefully chirping in every nook and cranny. They scooted behind my refrigerator. Hopped into my closet. I even spotted several lazing about in my claw-foot bathtub.

I pretended I was camping, tucked into my sleeping bag while the soothing sounds of a nighttime wilderness enveloped me.

CHIRP... CHIRP... CHIRP...

Nope, didn't work. I peeked at my alarm clock—four twenty in the morning. With a frustrated cry, I flung back my comforter and blindly tripped from my bed, feeling for a light switch. *Nasty bugs. Damn them!* Snatching my robe from the floor, I wrapped it around my body and grabbed *The Last Other* from my nightstand. I'd have to call an exterminator later this morning. Until then, if you can't beat 'em, join 'em.

I tucked a throw around my legs and settled into my cushy leather armchair, flipping open to where I'd left off...

> **The sirens of the Alpine lakes were slick, wicked creatures with seaweed hair and exotic faces. Neelie**

had never seen beings so ethereal, so erotic. Men and women with willow limbs twined toward them, enticing them into the water...

This had to be it. Neelie was a goner, the evil sirens would capture her and rip her to pieces. But surprise, she escaped—barely. A whoosh of breath escaped my lungs, and I dug deeper into the book. After a while, I was able to shut out the crickets, firmly planted in Neelie's world...

The town of Val d'Isère was heavy with snow and skiers, both weighing down wooden inns, blanketing folk streets. It was the ideal place to blend, recover without the Others tracking them. Neelie breathed, reveling in how a single puff of air crackled and turned to a horde of ice crystals, glinting in the fading light and street lamps. The Alps towered high, forewarning the path they had yet to travel. Their massive shadows inched over the town, pulling it into darkness.

Neelie held up her hand. It trembled, slightly. She grew weaker. Her family could never know...she'd rather die than have them believe she couldn't battle the Others, that she wasn't strong enough...

Rats. The sirens had cursed Neelie after all. So it was to be a slow death, hmm? Nothing like two hundred pages of death scene to lift the spirits. Yet I plowed ahead.

For the longest time, I'd avoided Samuel's books. I couldn't do it—allow myself to be shrouded in his thoughts. But curiosity (and, admittedly, wistfulness) eventually drove me to read *Water Sirens*. Anger over his exploitation of my personality carried me through the other books. Being angry made me feel as though I was accomplishing something, that somehow, I made him hurt just as much as he'd hurt me. Even now, I felt a stirring of annoyance at him while I followed Neelie and her crew through the Alps, from France to Geneva. But it wasn't roiling, and I couldn't call up the fierceness of years past. Perhaps time had deadened the rawness, leaving me with only a hunger to satisfy that dull ache.

Once, the iced air raised bumps along his arms. Once, they would have built a fire to stave off the chill, frozen limbs pulsing as they roared to life like the

> **hissing logs. Now, Nicodemus's feeble bones needed neither warmth nor cold. His body decayed as lake algae decayed. If he sank to black depths, mud would preserve his bones, a fossilized ammonite churning circles in the sediment layer that had been his nacken life. His body was dead – a rock memorial for an era passing away before him.**
>
> **But his mind was not dead. And his spirit certainly wasn't. Nicodemus considered his three friends as they tucked their packs into the darkness of the mountain enclave, hidden away from these things that chased them. He watched as Noel settled a weary Neelie against the wall, making her comfortable.**
>
> **His arrested heart beat for them, his family, these vibrant flickers of life. As long as they burned, he would, too...**

I folded my bookmark over the page and pressed the book closed. Nicodemus's pain hit too close to home, and it twisted my gut. I needed to pause, to think. Something in Samuel's story—the direction it had taken—was extremely troubling.

It hit me that the point-of-view had shifted to Nicodemus.

Why Nicodemus, why now? Readers were never given much from Nicodemus. Typically, the story was told through the eyes of the other three Bear Creek sirens. I'd always assumed Samuel didn't like writing Nicodemus because there was too much of himself in this particular character, things he didn't want to share outright with millions of readers. (Of course, he didn't have qualms about sharing the rest of us with millions of people.) But at this point in the story, Neelie still recovered from her near-death encounter with the sultry lake sirens in the French Alps, and was just plain loopy. Noel and Nora, freshly reunited, were too wrapped up in their love to tell the story. So the job fell to Nicodemus.

And how much of this was truly make-believe? Samuel had hammered into my head that Neelie Nixie was a fictional character, and this alone kept me from hurling the book across the room whenever I found something about Neelie I didn't like. Nicodemus, though, was undoubtedly Samuel—I could see it even more so in this book than in any of the others. And when Nicodemus spoke of death, of the need he had for his family…

Did that mean Samuel was lonely, so far away in New York? Did he regret leaving Lyons behind?

My alarm clock blared from the bedroom. Taking the book with me, I turned it off and headed to the kitchen to dish up Oatie-O's.

My vengeful side wanted to revel in Sam's misery, if he was indeed lonely. When our marriage ended, I was the lucky one who got to keep our close-knit Lyons circle. Samuel was the one in exile across the country, in a strange place with strange people. But leaving had been his choice. He'd exiled *himself*, choosing a life of "mind-altering experimentation and artistic endeavors" (as Sofia delicately called it), and goodness knows what or who else he'd dabbled with until he'd gotten busted.

Was I reading too much into this? Projecting fictional heartaches onto a flesh-and-blood man? I had to admit, I had a hard time believing he was unhappy. He'd achieved what he set out to do—he'd broken into a ruthless publishing industry in a Cinderella move that made him the Prince Charming to a world full of women. His body of work was well-respected, hadn't had a single dud. He was frequently linked to the high echelons of Manhattan artist circles, so he had to have a happy-hour acquaintance, at least.

I stuck my bowl in the dishwasher and headed to the shower.

Samuel hadn't made friends easily. He was shy, hated being the center of attention. If his closest relationship was with Caroline...

Caroline. Of course. I could kick myself. Samuel would have been writing *The Last Other* nearly two years ago, before he'd started to date Caroline, or even Indigo. Two years ago, when he'd come home for Thanksgiving...that disastrous Thanksgiving, which had dissolved into petty name-calling. Perhaps he'd worked through his loneliness since then. Perhaps Caroline helped him to do so. I cringed, remembering Molly's words to me through a merlot-induced haze: *You can't expect him to be alone forever.*

Can't I?

Early morning purple lightened to gray and gradually, the crickets' chirping ceased. I finished brushing my teeth and again opened the book, rereading the disconcerting thoughts of Nicodemus.

"As long as they burned, he would, too..."

I needed to talk to Samuel about this book, plain and simple. It wasn't just my well-being at stake anymore. I could be the bigger person, invite him back to Friday lunch, maybe even ask if he'd like to fly out for our next whitewater trip. He'd enjoy the Shoshone stretch. The idea of sharing a kayak with him, paddling with him as we conquered rapids was appealing…

But he wouldn't share a kayak with me, would he? He'd be with Caroline. Nevertheless, I could invite him. And her. Maybe. Enough time had gone by, right?

When I arrived at work, barely put together in a black dress and flats, the first thing I noticed was the crickets had migrated downstairs. The chirping had stopped once the sun came up (supernatural little beasts), but several darted across the hallway, staking their real estate claims in prime, dark closet space.

"Call an exterminator," our webmaster said to me before I even uttered a hello.

"Believe me, I'm all over it." I rubbed my tired face. Why the heck had crickets picked TrilbyJones mansion to infiltrate, of all places?

His eyes crinkled. "Sleepless night?"

"Yup."

The second thing I noticed was our graphic designer interns, fresh from college, peering at me over their cubicle walls.

"Ah…you gals have good weekends?" I glanced over my dress to see if it was tucked in my underwear. No.

Intern Number One's toothy grin broke free. "I think we should ask *you* the same thing."

"Perfect, wonderful weekend, got to catch up with friends. I haven't gotten much sleep the past couple of nights, though."

"I bet! Lots of 'catching up,' if that's what you call it." Intern Number Two winked at me, and they erupted into fits of giggles.

Odd. Gah, I needed caffeine. "Coffee's on?"

They nodded, still laughing.

I detoured to the coffee pot before I even stumbled to my office, topping off my mug with pure, strong, fragrant brew. If coffee companies really wanted to make an impact in advertising, they should show desperate, sleep-deprived people crawling on hands and knees to the desert oasis that is the office coffee machine, not rosy couples rolling out of bed on Saturday morning, embracing over steaming mugs of French Roast. I blew across the top as I flipped through the phone book for pest control services.

"Preekit's Pest Control," a gruff voice answered.

"Thank goodness! I need you, right away."

"What sort of pests are you having trouble with, ma'am?"

"Crickets. Hundreds of crickets." I described my sleepless nights, how they were all over everything, chirping, chirping, chirping. The man a-ha-ed along until I finished my tale.

"Are you sure it's crickets, ma'am?"

"Of course I'm sure. They're black with long legs and antennas. They hop. They chirp all night long. A couple even had top hats."

"I just need to make sure. See, crickets are seasonal. They typically don't enter homes until September, October, when it cools down." I frowned. What was he getting at? "So unless someone loosed a whole bucket of crickets in your house, I don't see how it's possible."

"Look, I'm telling you..." No. NO. He wouldn't. He wouldn't *dare*.

"Do you have anyone who'd want to play a joke on you, ma'am?"

Oh, of all the frickin' cricket-loving, malevolent things to do...

I set up an appointment with Preekit's Pest Control for that evening, then promptly logged onto my computer and went to my personal email account. Sure enough, there was an email from one sccabral9, short and sweet:

> Preekit's Pest Control: (978) 555-9036

Ha. Funny. It wasn't even the right number. Out of curiosity, I Googled to see where the phone number would lead me if I called (on a cold day in hell would I dial that number). I chuckled—it was one of those phony hotlines, created specifically so people could give out fake phone numbers to get bar prowlers off their backs. This particular hotline appeared to be for drunk dialing.

I hit reply and typed:

> Crickets? CRICKETS!? That's it? Watch your back, Cabral. Someone might dump a bucket of leeches or fire ants, or those flesh eating Egyptian beetles in your bed. And then Sofia would be really upset because she'd have bugs in her house. You flaming son-of-a-pebble-brained lemming, please tell whoever gave you a spare key to my apartment that I want it back. K
>
> P.S.—Thanks for the hotline. I'll use it the next time a man hits on me, maybe.

I clicked send, so proud of my handiwork, I considered forwarding it to Jaime. I perused my inbox.

The next was a mass email from best man Santiago with the details of our skydive and overnight camping trip in two weeks. Clear skies were promising.

The third email was from Jaime, explaining that, strangely, no gossip blogs were interested in the drag picture of Samuel. She was going to give it a week, then try again. In the meantime, we were moving forward with the next phase, which would require Sharpies and restraints, if necessary. I hoped it wouldn't be necessary.

The fourth was a brief message from Molly: "I want in." In? I scanned. Ah, Mickey-gate. She'd figured it out, too, no surprise. I'd give her a call tonight, ask how well could she wield a Sharpie.

There were several other emails from old college friends, probably about the wedding, but I didn't have time to bother with them.

As I dived into my business email, I tried to figure out when Samuel drove all the way to Boulder to plague my apartment with those vile crickets. It must have been Sunday afternoon, before I'd gotten home. A wicked part of me hoped curiosity had gotten the better of him and he'd snooped in my apartment, maybe even my bedroom. Was he disappointed to find that it was all mine, free of any reminders of our old life together? I shivered at the thought. My mind drifted to memories of our old studio apartment in Boulder... the squeaky wooden floors, garage sale furniture, wedding gifts still in boxes, and numerous photos from our youth.

And, like every time I mentally browsed through our studio apartment, I relived the afternoon he left me...

That ill-omened day, I'd just returned from the University of Colorado's bookstore, my bag weighed down with ridiculously expensive textbooks needed for my final year of college. My back and arms were slick with perspiration from lugging my bicycle up two flights of stairs to the stuffy studio apartment Samuel and I rented. After he graduated from CU, his father helped him land a job as a copywriter for *Latin Colorado*. Between insane hours spent hammering out concert reviews, his late-night work on his new book, and my crazy internship schedule, our paths rarely crossed. I hadn't even read a word of his manuscript, not that this was anything new—Samuel only shared completed stories with me. But he explained the new book was unlike anything he'd ever done, something about water nixies, and surreal landscapes, and allegory.

I leaned my bike against the hall and fumbled for my keys. The door was unlocked. Odd, what was he doing home so early? I dropped my bag with a thud on our wobbly kitchen table and peered around the silk screen we used as a divider between our "bedroom" and the rest of the apartment.

How many times since that sickening afternoon had I replayed this old home movie? Samuel, lying on our bed, drenched in sweat from his jog, exhausted to the point of collapse. Every single time I watched it, I willed my former self—that flickering, naïve girl—to halt at the bedroom threshold. *Don't take another step, don't ask him what's wrong. Why won't she stay behind that silk screen and simply savor Samuel, lying in their bed?* In that moment, he was still my husband, still my lover. If I'd known it was our final reel, I would have lingered, wordless, in his presence. *Don't ask...Don't ask...Don't ask.* But how could I have known? So I asked...

"Is everything okay?" My fingers rubbed his back. I felt his sigh.

"I'm moving to New York City, Kaye." His voice was hoarse.

I frowned. This was nothing new. We'd move there next year, after I graduated, so he could attend New York University. Had I missed something?

"I hate it here," he said, his face still turned from me. "My job, Boulder. I need to leave before I end up in Colorado forever. My life is practically over and I'm only twenty-three."

I winced. He was stressed. Something must have happened at work. "Just stick it out for a few more months, *mi vida*, until I finish my degree. I know it's hard, but after that we can go wherever you want."

He pushed himself up from the bed to gaze at me. His face was expressionless, and it disturbed me. I reached out to run my hand through his hair, but he evaded before my fingers reached the mess of tangled, sweat-soaked brown. He never did that, not anymore. In that single action, I realized something awful was about to come out of his mouth.

"I need to leave. I need to leave alone."

I shook my head, refusing to hear him. "Don't be ridiculous, Samuel. We can't just pack up and leave. Give me time to make arrangements—"

"Kaye."

"I can transfer to New York," I rushed on, not allowing his words to take root. "Or I could take a year or two off from school, try to sort through this. We've always managed before— "

He dug fingers into his hair. "It's no use, Kaye. I've already made up my mind. I'm sorry, so sorry. I can't be married to you anymore."

I was bewildered, struck mute. Of all the things he could have possibly said...

"Why?" I began to crumble from the inside, out. "Is...is there someone else you want to be with?"

"No." Samuel's voice broke. He stared down at his fingers, twisted his wedding ring. "We're becoming different people. It turns out I was right—we were too young to get married, before we had a chance to grow into ourselves. I'm so very sorry," he repeated. "I was wrong to have..."

I saw it in every crevice of his despondent face. He'd decided.

Why, why had I ever let my guard down around that silent, unhappy little Latino boy with odd blue eyes?

My phone buzzed, yanking me back to the present. Hector's number flashed through my blurred vision. I tossed it in a desk drawer and slammed it shut in a fit of self-disgust. Samuel's re-emergence in my life did a rigorous tap-dance on my psyche, and if I wasn't careful, I would drag others down with me.

I'd never get the marketing plan done for the Great West Caving Club in my office today. Grabbing my project binder and dry erase markers, I shut myself into the brainstorming room for the morning, away from calls, and email, and memories.

Chapter 10
CARTWHEELING

To avert a collision with a boulder, a paddler will spin a craft off and around the boulder.

It was one o'clock when I broke away from the office for lunch with Santiago at Fisher's Deli, enjoying the last days of May.

Santiago frowned, looking over his shoulder. "Is someone watching us?"

I followed his gaze across the deli's patio but saw no one. "I don't think so."

Having Santiago as a friend was particularly important to me, because he was too young to have really known Sam and me as children, which was why I broached this sensitive subject with him. I set my soup spoon down and studied Santiago, halfway through devouring a robust Reuben sandwich. "Can I ask you something?"

He paused mid-bite, then set his sandwich down. "Sure. What's up?"

"This might seem completely random…"

Santiago snickered. "Sorry. I've already hustled my way through half the female population of Lyons, and I just don't think I could go that route again—the gossip's a killer."

"I'm serious, Santiago. Although, there has been an influx of folk-singing hipster chicks, lately."

He nodded, as if he were actually considering it. "You and I could clean up at Planet Bluegrass."

"You know, you're the second person who's insinuated I should kiss men goodbye and go for the ladies."

Santiago laughed, dark cheeks dimpling. "I think I need to hear about the first person."

"Later." I waved him off, struggling on how best to word my question. "Back to random left field. I know you weren't around Samuel a lot after we graduated high school, but do you remember if he seemed happy?"

The laughter faded from Santiago's face as he considered my inquiry. "It's hard to say, Kaye. I mean, I really wasn't close to Samuel. He seemed nice, confident, people liked him, talented. The guy's a freaking prodigy."

"But did he seem happy to you?"

"I guess I'd call him quietly content. You'd know better, I s'pose."

Did I? Quietly content was not the same as happy. I knew as much.

"Cabral was crazy in love with you, though. We can tell when another guy has it bad—it's obvious. He'd follow you around a room with his eyes, relax when he heard you laugh, stuff like that." He shifted, clearly ill at ease. Santiago typically steered away from what he called "feeling talk." If a female even came close to tearing up, Santiago was out of the room before the first sniffle sounded.

My mind turned to the stretch of time between the day Samuel put an engagement ring on my finger to the day he left. The job and apartment hunting, wedding planning, college classes—the busy stuff. Then there were the tender moments like early morning runs. Cooking dinner and washing dishes, our shoulders brushing. Going to local music venues and stumbling home, reeking of bar smoke and stale beer, then making love in our little studio apartment. I couldn't remember Samuel smiling much through any of that. Life just...happened to him.

Santiago was right. Samuel had been content, but not the over-the-moon boy I'd dated in high school. "College Samuel" had reverted to the person I'd first met as a child...more sober, less playful. I'd been so wrapped up in chasing our happily-ever-after, I hadn't noticed until it knocked me flat.

The Last Other plagued my head. What else had my keyhole eyes failed to perceive about Samuel, my friends, family? There were no excuses for the part he played in the detriment of our marriage and friendship. But maybe, with fresh eyes, I could see him more clearly…and myself.

It was as if an alarm clock had just gone off and a long, long dream fell away. How could I have slept through so much of my life? Even now, I rubbed sleep from my swollen, squinting eyes.

"Hey, Molly." I knocked on her open door. "Brownies."

"Yes!" She swiveled away from her monitor and grabbed a walnut chocolate-chunk hunk of deliciousness from the box.

"How'd the meeting go?"

"Decent." She pushed her glasses up her nose and flipped open her binder. "The National Park loved the new website design. They rattled off a few changes, namely an interactive map of the park."

"Something like that might push our deadlines back, but if they're willing to renegotiate the launch date, I don't see a problem with adding the map."

"One step ahead of you. I told them we'd come back with a rough estimate of time and cost tomorrow."

"Great! Thanks, Molly, you make my job a heck of a lot easier." I started to head back to my office.

"Kaye, my sister called during the meeting," Molly blurted, "and I may need to take some time off to help her."

Worry lines crept into my friend's face. Oh no. Molly's stepsister, Holly, had given birth to her second child a month ago, and struggled with the baby blues. The little girl had trouble gaining weight and rarely slept for more than an hour stretch without crying. Specialists adjusted her formula and that seemed to help. But mother Holly wasn't eating well, and her husband and Molly were concerned. To top it off, Holly and Derek were strapped for cash, even without the doctor bills and special formula, but refused to take her stepdad's money. Every family had its drama.

"Just show me what you want covered and I'll do it. Let me know if I can help Holly in any way."

Molly leaned back in her chair, rubbing her eyes behind her glasses. "Thanks, Kaye. If I end up watching the kids for a few days, I might take you up on that, have you buy groceries or something."

"Will do." I gave her a hug and headed back to my office.

I dropped into my swivel chair and shook my computer to life. Holly's struggles with her daughter put my grievances into perspective. I wanted to do more for Molly's sister and niece. A babysitting schedule, maybe, to give Holly a breather? Perhaps a weekend getaway for Holly and Derek when the baby was a little older? Then there was that alimony stockpile…

A rattling sound coming from my desk drawer startled me. My phone. I'd forgotten that I shoved it out of sight when Hector called. In a better frame of mind, I fished it out of my drawer, expecting to see his number. Instead, unfamiliar digits flashed across the screen. 2-1-2…New York area code.

It was Samuel.

I held the unanswered phone in my hand, hunting for composure. Just as I answered, it went to voicemail. If it was important, he'd leave a message. He didn't, and I dove into my work. Then, five minutes later, the same number flashed as my phone danced a jig across my desk. I took a deep breath and tucked it under my good ear.

"This is Kaye."

"Hello, Kaye. It's Sam."

"Yeah, I know. Hey, Cliff-hucker."

He chuckled. "Do I even want to know what a cliff-hucker is?"

"I'm guessing you already Googled it. By the way, tell Danita not to pass out my phone number, please."

"I couldn't get a hold of Danita, so Angel gave me your number. And you're right, I did Google it."

I heard a woman's muffled voice in the background, something about flight times. "Where are you?"

"La Guardia. My return flight to Denver is delayed, so we're killing time at the gate. I thought it'd be easier to call you instead of emailing, less chance of misinterpretation—I don't do emoticons."

"Aren't you supposed to be a famous writer? Can't you get around the emoticons?"

"I've learned my lesson not to assume anything when it comes to you and my writing. I'd hate to have you mistake my very sincere words for sarcasm. Although sometimes, I wonder if you do it deliberately."

I chose not to bite at his subtle baiting. "What do you want, Samuel?"

"To apologize for the photo. I'm sorry you've been dragged into the media again."

"Wait, what photo?" My heart raced. Had the Halloween drag photo surfaced after all? But why would he apologize?

He groaned. "You didn't watch *The Morning Show*. I thought maybe you tuned in. You used to."

"I usually do, but I was a little preoccupied this morning with Boulder's tiniest choir—which you'll hear about, *believe* me. But what photo?"

"Someone at the café took a picture of me holding your hand. Now it's all over the Internet, along with renewed speculation about my love life, whether I cheated on Indigo, that sort of tawdry thing. Typical tabloid garbage—they cheapen everything," he snarled. "I know how you hate it when the spotlight's on you."

Breath whooshed from my lungs. The drag picture was still under wraps. But then I absorbed what he was saying. The café? Holding hands?

"Which website?" He rattled off several. I turned to my monitor, cringing as the slew of email notices that popped up from friends, family, even old college acquaintances clicked into place. *Crap crap crap, not good.* I pulled up a gossip blog, searched his name. Sure enough, there was Samuel and me in a grainy photo, his hand wrapped around mine. Caroline and Jaime were cropped out, making it appear as though we were enjoying a cozy dinner for two. The quality was poor, but it was still us, nonetheless. The headline read: "*Siren* Author and Real-Life Neelie?" Beneath the photo, a blurb:

> Bad news for Indigo Kingsley if rumors are true that author Samuel Cabral and his ex, Aspen Cabral, are back on. Does this mean that Hollywood's hot writer/actor couple is officially Splitsville? Both Cabral and Kingsley have yet to issue statements about the photograph, taken in Cabral's hometown

> of Lyons, Colorado. Rumors have long persisted that the former Mrs. Cabral is the inspiration behind beloved *Water Sirens* heroine, Neelie Nixie, though Cabral has repeatedly denied it. Kingsley scored the coveted movie role last year. *Water Sirens* is set to hit theaters in November.

Ah, so that's why Interns One and Two were making doe eyes at me this morning.

"Oh, this is bad. I'll have to stay at Molly's again." One good thing about their lack of fact-checking, though—they hadn't figured out I'd changed my name, so I still had a chance to tell Samuel myself.

"I think that's best, especially with Indigo's rabid fan following. You and I both know it was innocent, but the gossip blogs can be ruthless when my name is linked to hers. I was completely blindsided by Geneva Botsworth in the interview this morning when she pulled up the photo. Just a moment, please."

A muted voice asked for his autograph and he replied, his voice pleasant enough. Still, I could hear the subtle irritation. It was surreal, this Samuel—the jet-setter with fans, photographers, and celebrity acquaintances. He was all business, going through the motions like this happened every day. I could barely glimpse the boy who'd collected fossils and baseballs, read tirelessly, and test-ran everything for me, from tree limbs to bicycles. Grown-up Samuel was so familiar, yet I felt like I didn't know him at all.

I don't anymore, do I?

I studied the picture again, cringing at my faded sweater and frizzy hair. Samuel was as sharp and beautiful as ever. All things considered, it really wasn't that bad. It looked like two friends having dinner...kind of.

"Back," he said, breathless. "Anyway, I explained the situation to Geneva Botsworth as best as I could without going into too much detail—old friend of the family, my sister's wedding. I'm truly sorry about this, Kaye."

I sighed, wanting to muster anger that wasn't in me, not after my lunch with Santiago. "It's not your fault. You couldn't have known anyone would take our picture. It looks like whoever did it used a camera phone."

"But that's the thing. I know better." I heard the voices around him abate. He must have been walking. "Usually, I'm so careful about appearances in public. I think being in Lyons has lulled me into a false sense of security."

"Sam— "

"And now you're right back in the press where you didn't want to be. I never, never should have published *Water Sirens* without rewriting Neelie."

Ugh, here we go again. I'd almost forgotten how exasperating Samuel's tizzies could be. "You're right, you should have rewritten Neelie. But Jacques H. Cousteau, quit beating yourself up over the stupid photo. There's no reason you have to behave differently than the rest of us, in Lyons of all places." I still sensed his self-inflicted knock-out, even over the phone. I needed a red herring, fast. "Don't you have anything else you'd like to apologize for?"

"Do I?"

"I think you do. The crickets."

There was a long pause, and then a chuckle. "Are you referring to the insect or that iconic be-bopping back-up band of the fifties?"

I smiled. "Impressive alliteration. The insect."

"No. Nothing to apologize for."

"Listen, Cabral. I have a hundred noisy buggers selling waterfront time shares in my bathroom. They've even opened an all-you-can-eat buffet in my closet. I've gotten a combined total of five hours' sleep the past two nights. And, funny story—when I called an exterminator today, he scoffed at me. Want to know why?"

"Why?"

"Because cricket infestations are seasonal. Which means someone *deliberately* loosed hundreds of those little suckers on my home."

"Hundreds? A bit of an exaggeration, wouldn't you say?"

"How many, Samuel?"

"Two hundred tasty crickets from neighborhood pet stores."

"So when I said hundreds, I was correct."

"Can't you just be happy I saved them from certain death? They would have been eaten by lizards—imagine the trauma."

"They'll be dead anyway as soon as the exterminator gets here."

"Tell you what. Let me pay for the exterminator and we'll call it even."

Hmm. Tempting. I had to admit, I wasn't too keen to see what he'd come up with next. Spiders? Snakes? I shuddered. Then again, the idea of having Molly wreak her special brand of havoc on the massive Thursday night prank was also appealing. That decided it for me.

"Not a chance, Cabral. I'm going to see this one through to the bitter end."

"So you're going to keep pranking me, even if I fold?"

"Yes."

"Those aren't the rules."

"I make my own rules now, Samuel." I twisted a blond curl around my finger, letting it spring.

"I've noticed." He cleared his throat. "So did Caroline. She wants you and Jaime to double-date with us, incidentally. You've painted yourself into a corner."

I smacked my head with my palm. Son-of-a-shrew. "Um...please tell her thanks, but Jaime and I aren't ready to go public."

"Oh no, I'm not doing your dirty work. I'm very aware that if I hadn't figured out your ruse on my own, you would have let me believe a lie. I'd still be thinking I was complete crap in bed."

"Fishing for a compliment, Cabral?"

"Only confirmation, Cabral."

I picked apart a brownie, grumbling. "Fine, you were great in bed. Best sex ever. Much better than lesbian sex, not that I'd know." I could practically see his cocky grin all the way in New York. "I'll see if Jaime wants to go skydiving. That's all I'm willing to offer."

"You might want to check with Danita before you invite her."

Argh! "You think I don't know that? Look, Samuel, I'm the one who sees Danita every single weekend."

"Point taken." He paused, the silence between us curdling like soured milk. "Sometimes I forget you know my sister better than I do, now. I understand how much time has passed, but it still catches me off-guard..." He cleared his throat. "Kaye, I really am sorry about the hand-holding, if it made you uncomfortable. You looked like you were ready to bolt out of the booth when Jaime and Caro went for blood, and I had to keep you there."

Ah. He'd been trying to soothe me by holding my hand—that was it. I felt a little let down, and I couldn't fathom it. *You should be relieved, Kaye.*

"Samuel, I'm not upset. We've done that since we were children. It was just…natural, I guess."

"Yeah," he said quietly.

Memories washed over my head and trickled down my fingertips. The feel of Samuel's hand. How it grew and changed from a boy's hand, fitting mine perfectly, to the point where he could wrap his long writer's fingers completely around my fist. "Do you remember the first time we held hands? I was eight."

"Of course." A smile was in his voice. "Just before your ninth birthday, actually. It was our first Rocky Mountain Folks Festival, at the Tripping Marys concert. You told me you wanted to learn how to play a guitar. Your fingers were sticky from eating cotton candy, but I held them anyway because I didn't want to lose you in the crowd."

"Wow." *There. There's my Samuel again.* Man had a memory like a steel trap. I swallowed the lump building in my throat. "So…I'm not upset about the picture."

"I'm glad." I heard the buzz of a gate announcement, and more movement. "Kaye, my flight's boarding and I have to let you go—I'm not keen on sharing my conversation with other passengers."

"Just a sec." Crap! I hadn't even asked him about Nicodemus in *The Last Other*.

"Kaye, my flight—"

Answers, answers, answers. "Samuel, I need to talk to you about something important. Several things, really, but I can't right now," I said in rush. "Can we meet tomorrow? We could do dinner in Boulder, or I could drive to Lyons."

"Kaye, slow down, please." I had a hard time hearing him above the boarding calls. "Can you repeat that?" I did, more clearly. He met my request with silence, then, wariness. "Tomorrow won't work."

"Oh." I tried not to be disappointed.

"Hold on." I heard him speak to somebody, followed by Caroline's distinct shrillness. After that, Samuel must have put his hand over the phone because there was only rustling. "Change of plans, tomorrow is fine. Can we meet at the art gallery in Boulder, say four o'clock?"

"Four o'clock works." Ha. *Eat it, Caroline.*

"Great. I'll make arrangements for a conference room there. I've got to run, Kaye, or I'll miss my plane."

"Okay. Have a safe flight."

"Enjoy your afternoon with the exterminator. Your digression with the crickets was well-played, by the way," he said, and I laughed. Never could fool that man. "I appreciate your distracting me, but sometimes...just let me take the punch when I need it."

"Go board your plane, Samuel."

"Goodbye, Kaye. See you soon."

It was with immense reluctance that I hung up the phone. I exhaled, feeling the weight on my chest lift as I turned back to my work. Maybe Molly could dig up Geneva Botsworth's *The Morning Show* interview with Samuel. If that prying host with helmet hair and pastel suits had him this flustered, I really needed to see it.

Then there was the next step in Jaime's master prank plan, assuming my *Answers Answers Answers* chat with Samuel didn't completely implode in my face. After Jaime all but slapped Samuel with his drug record, I didn't trust her not to cross the line. But Molly knew when to say when.

It was time to loop in my cheerleader-of-a-best-friend.

"So, Cabral really wasn't behind the café photo? I don't know if I buy that."

A flare of static crackled through my phone. Hector was up in the Rockies clocking climb time. "He's truly not as manipulative as you want to believe, Hector. I wouldn't put it past his publicist, though—she's brutal. Although, I can't figure out how she'd benefit from it."

"Hmmm. You know what they say: All publicity is good publicity."

"Maybe. And Caroline does think that...oh man, I don't know if I should tell you what Jaime Guzman did."

"Spill, Trilby."

So I ran through the entire lesbian story, from the moment Samuel and Caroline caught us on our "date" to Jaime going for Caroline's throat, pausing only to let Hector catch his breath between guffaws.

The evening was balmy. I sat outside on my balcony, swinging my legs between the rails. My Boulder neighborhood was idyllic in late spring. The rustling of hundred-year-old trees. The occasional chirp of a cricket—most likely from my apartment. Charcoal and wood smoke hung in the air, from a family grilling burgers a few houses down. A man and woman pushed a stroller along the sidewalk while two boys on bikes weaved along behind them…

There were the two photographers parked on the street—Tweedle-Dee and Tweedle-Dum—presumably waiting for Samuel to swing by and "fertilize my flower bed," as Molly had put it. *Nope, sorry boys. Just an exterminator tonight.* I gave them an acerbic, friendly little wave. They smirked and waved back. I had a feeling they'd been snapping pictures of Santiago and me at Fisher's Deli, and I wondered how long they planned to stay here. Maybe they thought Indigo Kingsley would swoop in with her posse of starlets and beat the everlovin' tar out of me. Something like that would buy their bread for a year.

"Do you think I need to keep on my tux coat for the reception?" Hector asked. "Tuxes in the summer are damned uncomfortable, and I already sweat like a hooker in church."

I didn't even know how to respond to that.

"Don't worry about it. Just support your brother, don't abuse the open bar, and show your friend with the pathetic love life a wonderful time, as only friends can. I'll be the one in the aubergine bridesmaid dress, stumbling around in peep toe heels."

"Kaye, I have no clue what aubergine is, let alone peep toe heels."

"Eggplant. Purplish, almost brown."

"Sounds tasty, rawr."

The corners of my mouth curled. Hector was such a guy.

When Dani chose her wedding dress, she saw it on the rack, pointed to it, and declared, without even trying it on, "I want that one." The boutique owner didn't know whether to ring her up or hunt for a hidden camera crew. The dress was tailored to be svelte, with a sash to keep it sweet. It was exquisite and it was very Danita.

My own wedding dress flitted through my mind in a sweep of lace. I'd wanted to have our ceremony on my mother's front porch. Alonso's Roman Catholic mother, in Ciudad Victoria, nearly had an apoplectic fit when she heard there wouldn't be a mass, even though Alonso and Sofia left the Catholic Church not long after his brother's death. So we'd compromised—ceremony in the old community church, reception on my mom's farm. Farm meant tea length. My mother and I'd found a lovely tea-length dress with a delicate, daisy-embroidered overlay in a Boulder boutique. It was clean and simple, and suited me tremendously. It had suited Samuel, too. Before wedding pictures, he'd helped me out of Dad's car near the cluster of quaking aspens. His hand gripped mine, too tightly. So much had been in his boyish face, it was hard to piece apart emotion from emotion. He'd settled on awe.

He'd asked if he could touch me. I'd told him he could. Two trembling hands slowly swept down either side of my dress, fingering the lace, circled my waist. He pulled me to him. *Thank you, Firecracker,* he'd breathed into my skin. *I love you, so much.*

My own hands had smoothed over the lapels of his crisp, black tuxedo, strong column of his neck. They'd settled into his half-tamed hair. I'd pulled him down to my mouth so I could speak to him, and only him. *I love you, Samuel. Always have...*

So warm, so secure. So close. I shivered, realizing the air had grown cold on the shadowed balcony.

"Kaye? Are you still there?"

My heart twisted. "Yeah. I'm sorry. I've been a space cadet, lately."

"*Mamacita*, we'll show Cabral you know how to have a good time without him, whether you're on a skydive or a date."

"Thank you. We'll have a blast, I promise."

"I'm counting on it. Hey! Got a new one: How do you hide money from Hippie Tom? You put it under a bar of soap."

"Horrible." But I laughed, in spite of myself. Just then, Molly's car pulled into my driveway. "Gotta run, Hector."

Molly had insisted she stay with me, excited to see real life paparazzi. "That cliff-hucker and his tramp Aussie actress are *not* running you out of your own home," she'd declared earlier, when I called.

Pushing past the cameras in my face, I jogged across the street to meet Molly. She pulled me into a tight hug. Several cameras flashed behind us.

"Don't say anything at all until we get into the house." I picked up her overnight bag. "These guys will twist your words around like nobody's business."

"Hey, Kaye, is that Samuel's sister?" asked one of the photogs.

"No, I'm Molly Jones!" she replied cheerily, all but skipping past them. "That's M-O-L-L-Y, not I-E. I'm Kaye's hip, indie-stylin' best friend and life consultant. Be sure to print it just like that."

"Cripes, Molly, you just had to."

"Should I goose you for good measure?" Her arm rested on my waist as we made our way back to the house.

I gave her a playful swat on the rear. "That should keep them busy for a while, until the exterminator arrives. I hope you don't mind crickets."

"Nope! I have to admit, the crickets were good, almost as good as Mickey-gate. Sam was asked about Mickey and PETA on *The Morning Show*. Oh! I found the Geneva Botsworth interview on YouTube, and I've got two bottles of champagne in my bag—no merlot this time—to toast the comeback of the Trilby. Such a fashionable little hat."

"Ha ha ha. Did you bring your Sharpies?" I tried to sound ominous.

Molly scoffed. "Oh please. Any generic olive oil takes permanent marker out of skin in seconds. Did you and Jaime even play pranks in college? Now, I've compiled an entire list of pranks specifically designed to irritate the hell out of Sam…"

And so we settled in for another evening of fancy toasting and YouTube, cataloging everything we'd need for Molly's prank night to end all prank nights—potting soil, tomato plants, milk powder, icy hot. The exterminator stayed for dinner, terrified to leave and face a barrage of paparazzi questions about whether he was dating me, if he really was a pest control guy, and if Samuel Caulfield Cabral would be furious at him. The poor man didn't even know who Samuel Caulfield Cabral was.

At some point between the macabre cessation of chirping crickets and making fun of Samuel's deer-in-the-headlights expression when Botsworth flashed the hand-holding on the big screen, I thought about showing Molly the top-secret dossier. Jaime had copied all of Samuel's records for me: the poor NYU grades, a public intox charge, the arrest for possession of illegal substances and paraphernalia. (I hadn't even known about the first two until Jaime showed me the folder, though I wasn't surprised.) Keeping the file a secret was like a boulder on my back. But I left it in my bedroom, safely tucked in my underwear drawer.

When we crawled into bed at eleven o'clock, a bottle of champagne and an entire block of cheddar cheese later, my courage was armed and fortified for my serious talk with Samuel. I wanted *my* Samuel again, the one with fire pulsing beneath his quiet demeanor… not this cool, aloof Samuel. I knew exactly what I wanted to ask him.

Now it was just a matter of forcing the words from my mouth.

Chapter 11
UNDERCUT

Paddlers should be aware of the dangers in current flowing beneath ledges, branches, and rocky overhangs and evade them.

Samuel was the picture of contentment behind the wheel of Cassady's classic 1973 VW Campervan, a sky blue behemoth named "Betty."

Okay, not quite contentment. He was a bundle of nerves as he drove the beast west into the mountains, fighting the blinding afternoon sun. His fingers drummed the steering wheel when they weren't white-knuckling it. He tried to pass it off as jamming to the Elvis playlist I ran through my iPod. Watching my clean-shaven, Italian sunglasses-wearing ex maneuver this epitome of hippiedom around the hairpin curves of steep mountain roads was...well...frigging hilarious.

Betty rarely made it out of the car port of Cassady's rental bungalow. He biked everywhere because it was A) healthier, B) greener, and C) cheaper. We planned to take the Campervan on our skydiving trip next weekend, and Samuel was entrusted with "stretching her tires" today after a long winter's hibernation. It was a perfect solution—the paparazzi knew Samuel drove a roadster rental, so Angel arranged for him to take Betty for a spin. (Angel also thought the idea of uptight Samuel behind the wheel of Betty was better than a mini-skirted bowling league.) Betty was decked out in pure seventies wood paneling, burnt orange upholstery, kitchenette, a custom stereo system, and sleepers Cassady kept in immaculate condition. She was his pride and joy, and I was staggered he'd let a stranger drive her. Of course, the Samuel we'd all known was nothing but obsessively responsible, and I'm sure Angel had told Cassady as much.

"You're certain you don't mind forgoing the art gallery?" he asked for the third time.

"Like I said, I've been there a lot. They're one of our clients."

"Right. That's right." One of his hands ruffled his thick hair, an all too familiar nervous tic. "The gallery seemed too whitewashed, quiet. I wanted to get outside, see a few of the old haunts."

"Yeah, it's a nice afternoon."

We climbed up Ute Highway, heading to Button Rock Reservoir. It'd been years since Samuel had seen that tucked-away bit of grandeur, and he wanted to pay it a visit before he returned to New York.

"There's soda in the cooler if you want one," he offered. "Diet Coke, a ginger ale. A lemonade, too. You still like lemonade?"

"Thanks, but I'm okay. Really."

A fraught silence settled between us. He'd been all anxious energy since he waved me over to the van parked in the gallery's lot, and I wouldn't have recognized him if it weren't for the old frayed Lyons baseball cap, now tossed in the back seat. I began to regret requesting this face-to-face conversation. Yesterday, our phone call had come so easily, my confidence was boosted tenfold, but actually seeing the soft mouth that formed his words was the difference between Pikes Peak and a paperweight.

Maybe we were trying too hard to be ourselves...or the selves of eight years ago. I gazed at my trembling fingers and tucked them beneath me. It was time to loosen up.

"So...you really need a tie-dyed tee and vintage Levi's. This whole dark and depressing New Yorker thing you have going is an insult to Betty."

He smiled, not once diverting his eyes from the road. "I like to think I'm channeling Steve McQueen—you know, the King of Cool?"

My gaze swept over his gray tee and jeans that just hinted at lithe muscles beneath. I ignored the twinge that ran the span of my body.

"Doesn't every man? Besides, the King of Cool drove a motorcycle, not a VW Campervan. You are not Steve McQueen cool. More like…"

"Smokey and the Bandit cool?"

"I was thinking Scooby Doo Mystery Machine cool." I tapped into my inner ditz. "Jeepers, Fred! This ride has GPS and everything!"

"Let's split up, gang," he said in his best golden boy voice. "You go after that ghost while I take Daphne for a ride!"

Samuel had never really liked cartoons when we were kids, and preferred to read or play outside. He said the endings were too easy to figure out, but he'd put up with them for my sake. My eyes darted to him—he was perfectly at ease. I relaxed, mission accomplished. By the time we bumped along the back road to the reservoir, we'd found our comfortable rapport.

Slopes steeped in green prickled conifers and clay the color of sunset rose high above our windshields as the mountain lake came into view. The van crawled to a stop, and I hopped down, thin, pine sap air hitting my nostrils. Somewhere overhead, birds squawked at our intrusion. I slipped out of my sandals to exchange them for my Tevas and felt Samuel behind me, hovering.

"Hey, what happened to your foot?"

"What do you mean?" I wiggled my bare feet. He crouched next to me.

"Is that a scar?"

Ah. "No, it's a white-ink tattoo. A little trilby hat. One of our TrilbyJones clients did it for me."

Samuel whistled. "Nice. May I?" He glanced at me over his shoulder. It was a boon that I couldn't see those ice eyes behind his sunglasses.

I swallowed. "Um, sure."

He lifted my foot to get a closer look at the delicate etching above my toe. A long finger traced the edge of the hat's brim, brushing my skin. He studied the tiny, translucent detail, and his mouth stretched into that lazy smile.

"This is fascinating. I've never seen a white-ink tattoo before." My breath caught in my throat. Sweet mother, what was he trying to do to me? "You always surprise me, Kaye," he said quietly. "It's very unique—I like it. Did it hurt?"

"Yeah. The top of your foot is a really sensitive spot...lots of nerve endings. It doesn't...doesn't really go numb when they ink it." Lord, he needed to set my foot down or I'd soon yank it free.

Sensing my unease, Samuel patted my heel and released me to my sneaks. I jerked them on and laced up with shaking fingers while he dug through the van for his messenger bag, cramming it with sodas and sandwiches.

"So, why the tattoo?"

I mustered my courage for our talk. There would never be a more natural segue than this. "I got the tattoo because of my last name—Trilby."

"I picked up on that." I zipped my fleece, and he closed up the van. Swinging his bag over his shoulder, he motioned for me to lead the way. "I meant, what made you want to get a tattoo?"

"I guess it was on impulse. I thought they were pretty. That, and the idea of having a tattoo made me feel like a bit of a rebel." I wasn't a rebel, I was a coward. *Kaye, Kaye, just tell him about your name change—such a simple thing.* "I worked on a project several years ago for the TatnGo Tattoo Parlor, helping to reinvent them as upscale artisans. The first thing to go was the business name."

"'TatnGo not classy enough?" Samuel teased.

I shook my head, wrapping my pullover around my waist and grabbed the lantern. *Great, Kaye, you stupid lamppost. Way to step up. How can you possibly get answers if you can't even do something as easy as tell Samuel about your name change?*

This late in the afternoon, the reservoir was nearly devoid of people, the last of them trickling home for supper. Samuel and I used to come here occasionally on clear evenings, because the low sun peeking between the mountain range cast the entire lake in orange. Rock and scatters of bleached timber stretched beyond us as we made our way along the coastline.

"Oh! I'm reading *The Last Other* page-by-page this time. No skimming." I hopped over a toppled tree, careful not to bang my shin.

"Really?" Samuel's eyebrows lifted. "What do you think so far? How much have you read?"

"I'm about three-fourths through. It's...it's brilliant, Samuel, but you already know that. The metaphors frustrate me like nobody's business and it takes forever to read, but all personal stuff aside, it's even better than the others."

He grinned and wrapped an arm around my shoulders. "See? I knew you couldn't resist the dark side."

"Well, you did all but dare me to read the thing. But I wouldn't get too excited. Neelie's still alive, but barely. I might crash another book signing once I finish."

Samuel climbed onto a boulder and offered me a hand up. "That bothers you, doesn't it—Neelie's eventual demise?"

"It weirds me out a little, reading and waiting for the final ousting of Fiction-Me." I let go of his hand.

"It was never my intention to 'weird you out.' I guess I thought putting Neelie to rest would help both of us. She's always bothered you, and I'm sorry for it. You have to admit, though, that she's not a bad gal."

"Honestly, Samuel, lately I'm more troubled by Nicodemus."

"Oh? How so?"

"He's...I dunno. He just seems so sad to me."

I watched our feet as we walked, navigating the slick, natural cobblestones and sand along the lake coast. Samuel bent over and picked up one of the smooth, weathered stones, deep in thought. Finally, he answered, his eyes fixed on the stone.

"He was sad, but that was years ago. He's a lot better now." He gave me a reassuring half-smile. "I'd tell you more, but I don't want to ruin the ending for you." Chucking the rock in a pool of water, he watched it land with a plop and walked again.

My heart thudded sickeningly. Thanksgiving, I was right. I should have at least heard him out, then.

We sauntered along while I shared what I enjoyed about *The Last Other*. I asked if he'd really been back to the Alps. He had, and it was as beautiful as ever. I repressed the jealousy bug gnawing in my gut as he described the places he'd visited all over the world, the people he'd met. Samuel had always been an amazing storyteller, and his words allowed me to see the places he'd seen. He loosely committed to sending me some photos.

The sun began to set as we trekked further, me swinging a lantern and Samuel scouting out a place to sit down and eat. He finally found the perfect spot in the recess of two bleached logs. The breeze turned chilly. I pulled my hood over my head and dropped onto the dirt. Samuel took his time, spreading his jacket over the ground.

"You can sit on this with me, if you like."

I opened my mouth to say no thanks. But the shadowed ground was freezing, so I caved and scooted next to him. The long line of his body was warm, and soon the cold tingling in my arms vanished.

He dug through his messenger bag, passed me a turkey swiss sandwich and the only lemonade.

"We can share this. It's your favorite, too." I offered him the lemonade.

"That's okay. You can have it." He twisted open a cola.

We watched a couple make their way down the trail, holding hands, fishing rods swinging from backpacks. I thought I recognized them from Planet Bluegrass. Samuel ducked his head until they were gone, intent on his sandwich.

"What's the matter?"

"You know, this looks really inappropriate for me to have you out here, alone, after the café photo. I'm sorry. If someone snapped a picture..."

I smiled at him sadly. Button Rock preserve was serene, isolated. "Samuel, those photogs have done a number on you, haven't they? It hasn't always been this way, since the book was published?"

He shook his head. "My name started to show up outside the context of my books when I dated a musician a few years ago. It wasn't serious, but it put me in the limelight—walking the red carpet with so-and-so at the Grammys, attending benefit concerts, and the like. Authors rarely struggle with paparazzi. I guess I got caught in the crossfire between photogs and the people they stalked."

"But what about now? I mean, late night talk show appearances aren't run-of-the-mill. And you were on a *People* magazine list, for crying out loud."

He tugged the hair above the knob of his neck. "Yes, the *People* list was strange for me. It's like I don't even know that person in the gossip rags, on TV, in pictures. Fortunately, Caroline keeps most of it corralled so I don't have to deal with it, save for an irritating photographer...or five."

"But that picture of us got through."

"That's my fault, I wasn't careful. Caro's using her Midas touch to turn this in our favor. She's been shellacking paparazzi left and right, tracking down who released the photo. I told her not to stress, but with the press sniffing around my break-up with Indigo…" He paused. "You probably don't want to hear any of that, though."

I took a shaky breath. "Samuel, it's okay, I'm a big girl. Caroline seems very loyal. I'm glad you have somebody who cares about you." I could barely choke out the words.

"Loyal?" He chuckled. "Yes, I suppose she's very loyal. Caroline reminds me of Danita, in a way. You have to know how to handle her. She can be self-centered and affected, but she knows what needs to be done and goes for it. She's pulled me through some really awful times, and deserves my loyalty, too. I'd hate to keep repeating my mistakes, over and over." He looked at me from the corner of his eyes. I couldn't miss the implication.

"That's…admirable. She's very driven." It was the best I could do.

Samuel sighed. "She'll also cut down anyone she sees as a threat. Look, Kaye, I'm not a fool when it comes to Caroline. I know she most likely did something to rile you up—enough for you to loose Jaime Guzman on her. Whatever she did, I'm truly very sorry for it. That's why I've let the whole lesbian hoax go on as long as it has. Just…please don't goad her. I've asked the same of her."

I very nearly retorted that Caro was the one who started it, but there was no sense in sounding like an eight-year-old. "I'll try, but I can't promise anything. If she hounds me, I'm coming after you, of course."

"Of course. I look forward to your knock-out punch, as long as you don't do anything that interferes with Danita's wedding." Hmm, that was familiar. I wondered if Danita had gotten to him, too.

Honestly, who was I to be upset at him for learning from our painful mistakes? I just really, really hated that Caroline was the one who benefited. She'd been there after our split, helping him with his book, making that life he desired happen when I'd wanted to do that. Heck, I'd been entitled to it after supporting his fairy tales for seventeen years. Grudgingly, I understood why Samuel found a forceful woman attractive. Perhaps Samuel really did know who Caroline was, and liked her anyway. He had to know her better than I did, at least.

Samuel gave me a nudge. "You look like you're ready to bolt. What are you thinking?"

"Sorry."

I'd heard him say the same words to me a thousand times. Now I had an extra seven years of maturity to my name. So did he. Yet I danced around his head like a gossamer wing butterfly.

"Kaye, you're doing it again." He laughed, taking a bite of his sandwich. *Mother cliff-hucker, he's right.*

"Sorry, just thinking." I pulled myself up by my boot straps and took a swig of lemonade. "I was wondering. This new life of yours—celebrity, acclaim, travel—is it worth it?"

"Ah. Worth what?"

"I mean, is the success worth the life you left behind, here in Colorado?"

He didn't answer right away. Instead he wrapped tawny arms around his knees and squinted at the fading sun.

"Are you happy?" he asked.

I stuttered, not expecting that. How to answer? I'm content? I'm not happy, but I want to be? I settled for ambiguous. "Sure. As happy as the next person, I suppose." What did my happiness have to do with his leaving? "I don't know what you're getting at, Samuel."

"Two years ago, you told me I'd left you like a spoiled little boy." He scrubbed his chin, the gears of his mind cranking. Finally, he turned to me with intense eyes. "You and I always had this weird sort of symbiosis. Ever notice that?"

I shook my head, not sure what he meant.

"We fed off of each other's emotions, even as children. More often than not, you were the one with those overpowering moods—so much life, so happy. I couldn't help but bask in it. But I remember some days I'd think about things, sad things, and I'd look at you and see it all reflected back at me—same furrowed brow, same pained eyes."

"Okay, so we felt each other's sorrows and joys. Isn't that one of the points of marriage? Heck, of friendship?"

"Yes. But I think we influenced each other a lot more than most people. I didn't realize it until I went to college, saw how other couples behaved."

"Screw other couples. They weren't us." His cryptic language irritated the crap out of me. "So you're saying we were too dependent on each other?"

"Kind of. Toward the end, I think our symbiotic relationship leaned toward the selfish, parasitic end of the spectrum, rather than mutualism. I wasn't strong like you, Kaye. I needed you to stay above water, but instead I dragged you down."

That was just so...*Samuel.* "You and your science analogies. Basically, you're saying you would have eventually drowned me?"

"Something like that."

"Great. It always comes back to water sirens with you."

"Kaye, please be serious." He packed our empty bottles and wrappers in his messenger bag, ready to hike back to the van. I hopped up from the ground and tossed my empty lemonade bottle with the other garbage.

"I'm sorry, Samuel, but it's hard to take your 'symbiosis' theory seriously. Symbiosis happens to fish and coral reefs, dirt and plants, algae, bacteria, stuff like that. Not people."

"It was just a metaphor."

"So answer this: if we were so symbiotic, why was I happy when you were unhappy? In theory, shouldn't both of us have been happy or unhappy?"

His pale blue eyes sought my hazel. "Are you sure you were happy? I remember it a bit differently. The last time we...you cried in the shower. I heard you."

A memory gripped me...Doubled over beneath a stream of lukewarm water, sobbing after we'd had sex...he hadn't been able to meet my eyes. I squeezed my eyelids shut and banished the images from my head.

"Of course. I think I'd know if I'd been unhappy, Sam." My chin jutted out in defiance.

He nodded, not saying anything.

"Look, it boils down to this: I never felt burdened by you, emotionally drained, or damaged in any way. Not once. That is, until you left."

He sighed, pressed the heels of his hands to his eyes. This scene was rapidly becoming too much like my movie reel from many years ago. "I needed to leave, Kaye. I needed to leave alone."

"But *why?* I mean, why did I make you unhappy? Was I too demanding, too hard to live with? Too busy? Did I talk you into a marriage you didn't want?"

His head shot up. "No. Never. Please understand, I had issues—things I never told you—that would have ruined us if I'd stayed. I just...I couldn't be married to you anymore." Even he winced at that horrible cliché.

"What issues?"

He lifted a shoulder, eyes downcast, fingers tracing the lines of his palm. Still Samuel, still as closed off as ever.

"That's complete bull. Obviously I factored into your decision to leave somehow. I was the one asking for the real life fairy tale, and you played along. Maybe you got tired of the game."

He held up his hands in futility. "Marriage wasn't a game to me, Kaye. We weren't kids anymore."

Ugh. I couldn't believe we were going down this exact same path. "Please, Samuel, you gotta give me something concrete here or I'll go nuts. I refuse to end up alone because of you."

He strode several steps ahead, his long legs widening the distance between us. I watched his aggravated hands run through his hair, then slip down to his face. I was weary of his clear-as-mud explanations. My arms folded over my chest, either holding my anger in or keeping it at bay. Why couldn't he give me a straight answer, just once in his life? Let down that barrier he'd built around his mind when all I asked for was honesty. But he wouldn't, would he? Still the same old, frustratingly careful Samuel.

The sun finally sank beneath the mountains, leaving the moon and the light from the lantern to illuminate the ground as we weaved our way back to the Campervan. Old pines towered over the edge of the lake, casting colossal, swaying shadows over us. Despite my anger, I instinctively moved closer to Samuel as the night swept chills through my limbs.

He was quiet the rest of the walk, loading up the VW, even pulling away from Button Rock Reservoir. His brow furrowed as he guided the van around the dark, curving highway. I flipped on my iPod, skimming The Twiggies, Tripping Marys, New Greeleys, until I found my stash of good ol' southern rock. But even some Free Bird couldn't lighten the mood.

"Kaye," he blurted out, breaking the silence. "Are we ever going to talk about what happened in New York? I thought...I guessed... that's what you wanted to do today."

Bile burned my throat, a classic reaction whenever I thought about what I'd seen. New York was the last place I wanted to go.

"No."

"I really think we should discuss this before I leave. If you want answers, *real* answers, it needs to happen." He anxiously twisted the steering wheel beneath his hands.

"Did you know Audrey is going to propose to Dad?"

"Listen, that night— "

My voice broke. "But Dad doesn't know, yet, so please don't mention it to anyone. I'm really afraid he's going to say no, break her heart. Just like Mom."

His mouth clamped shut. I saw his jaw tighten, grind. "I'm sorry," he choked out.

"You've been saying sorry a lot the past week."

"There's a lot to apologize for."

Almost too much, was my grim thought.

His hands froze on the steering wheel, almost as if he had heard my unspoken words in the stifling quiet of the van. The veil of distress was more tangible, now that the outside world was invisible inside the confines of the retro van, save for the stretch of road beneath the yellow beams. Samuel glared straight ahead. Headlights from the opposite lane bounced off the glass and swept over his face, briefly bathing him in cold blue light. But it was enough to show me that his eyes glistened. I felt a stirring in my chest, in spite of myself.

"Samuel…"

He shook his head. "No, Kaye. I deserve this. Let me feel it, please."

"Hey. I'm sorry, too. I should have seen how sad you were back in college."

"To your apartment, then? You don't want me to take you to the farm?" So we were back to this again, our coils of barbed wire unfurled.

"Boulder, please. Molly is staying with me, and I shouldn't bail on her." I glanced at the time—nearly nine o'clock. If he took me to Boulder, he wouldn't get back to Lyons until almost eleven. "Samuel, you're welcome to crash on my couch. Heck, you've got the Campervan, you could just park it in the TrilbyJones lot. I'd hate for you to be on the roads with this thing."

He stared into the windshield, thinking over my offer. "Kaye, that's kind of you. But if any one of those photogs happened to see me coming or going from your place, it wouldn't be pretty."

"I forgot about them. Probably a good idea. I'll see you this weekend, though."

"I won't be at Friday lunch. I'm flying to LA for a couple of interviews. But Sunday, maybe?"

"Maybe." The fight in me fizzled to flat acceptance. He was leaving soon. He had Caroline. He was happy now. And he'd given me my answer—there weren't any concrete answers. Answers he was willing to share, anyway.

Before long, the lights of Boulder skimmed the hilltops. As the glowing globe grew, it reminded me that I still had one more item to check off my list. What the heck? It couldn't get any worse.

"Look, Sam, I need to come clean about something before we get back to Boulder."

"Oh?"

"Yeah. Um, how to put this?" I took a deep, shaky breath and forced out the words. "I changed my last name. It really is Trilby, not Cabral. I should have changed it sooner, but..." I studied my fingernails, grimy from our walk. "Sorry I didn't tell you." I waited for him to wince, or exhale, or even run his hand through his hair. Nothing.

"Kaye, it's all right. I already know."

"Wait. What do you mean?"

"The name change—I already know about it. I've known for a while."

My narrowed eyes studied him, so calm and collected.

"How long have you known?"

He shrugged. "Just after the book signing in Boulder. You didn't think my sister would keep it from me, did you? Really, it's no big deal."

"But you've been calling me 'Cabral' since you've been home. Why on earth didn't you say anything? To laugh at me?"

"Kaye, come on." His eyes darted to my nail-bitten fingers. "What was I supposed to do, congratulate you?"

"No, but you could have at least clued me in..." I hesitated over my words, horribly hypocritical once I said them aloud. Neither one of us had been forthright.

"Besides, it was kind of fun to watch you jump out of your skin every time your name came up."

I smirked. "Jerk."

We rolled up to TrilbyJones mansion around ten. Samuel jogged around to my door and helped me down from the van. He wavered, then sighed and pulled me into a hug.

"Goodnight, Kaye Trilby," he murmured. I gave him a half-hearted hug back.

"Night."

He pecked the top of my head and let me go, watching until I unlocked my door.

When I slumped up the stairs and into my home, I found Molly perched on the edge of my couch, intently watching the Lifetime Network. Ha. Even *I* could have a sense of humor.

"How'd it go?" She peeled her eyes from the television.

"Eh. I learned that Samuel's a lot better at moving on than I am. Of course, I already knew that, it's what started this whole thing. I learned he calls our childhood friendship a 'weird symbiosis.' Oh, and apparently I shelter him, hide stuff from him, and I'm the dirt to his emotive-drowning nacken plant."

"That good, huh?"

I sprawled on the couch next to her. "I'm sure once I have time to process it all, I'll feel better. But right now, I'm just…done. No more pranks, no more messing with Caroline, no more answers."

Her horrified face was a study in German Expressionism. "No! You can't bail, Kaye, or I swear I'll drag you there by your hair. We have to do prank night, please? I…I have everything bought!"

"No, Molly."

"And I even talked Danita into slipping a Benadryl in Samuel's tea tomorrow night. I tried for a Lunesta, but she flat-out refused. But she said he takes Benadryl to sleep, sometimes, so she'll swipe one of those. He'll be out for sure." Molly gave me a weepy, pleading look.

I frowned. "You brought Danita into this?"

"Well, how else were we going to accomplish any of this stuff and not wake him up? Kaye, don't be rash. Let's just do this and then you can be done with Samuel. You *need* this, trust me."

"No. That's final. Leave him be. Leave *me* be." I stood and headed to my room for my nighttime rituals: wash up, PJs, alarm clock, lamp off.

I'd call Jaime in the morning and break up with her. Give her the old "it's not you, it's me."

The Dream visited that night…Not the one in our Boulder studio apartment as he left me. This dream was different. It hadn't made a nighttime appearance in years, not since the aftermath of my divorce. I'd channeled my pain into other avenues, and it went away…

A dingy, sparsely-furnished New York City apartment that flickered orange.

A thin blanket of frost, or snow, or something stuck to the walls and floors.

In the corner, a rickety metal bed, twisted sheets heaped in the middle of the mattress.

Samuel hunched over, his naked back glistening with sweat in the dim light.

And beneath him…a cascade of brunette hair, spilling over his pillow.

I clung to the doorframe, that well-known despair already clenching in my gut.

I couldn't close my eyes. Why didn't I just close my eyes?

But, for the first time, the brunette wasn't brunette.

Her hair was straight and sleek, almost black…

"Shhhh. Is she asleep?"

"Yes, I think so. Do you want to wake her up?"

"No way."

"Okay, you hold her legs, I'll get her arms."

"Lemme open the front door, hold on."

What the heck? Was I dreaming?

"On three. One…"

I groaned, rubbing a hand over my face. Where was I? My bedroom. It was still Wednesday night, I thought.

"Two…"

My eyes fluttered open. Two shadowed shapes hovered over me.

"Three!"

I sat straight up in bed, my hands flying out to protect myself from the shapes. "Argh! What the frick?"

Four strong, female hands grasped my ankles and wrists and dragged me from my bed. I kicked out, but they held me firm.

"Sorry, *hermanita*, but you need this," came a commanding, oh so recognizable voice.

"Danita, let me down, right now!"

"No. This ridiculousness has gone on long enough. You're going to prank *mi hermano cabrón* tonight, damn it. Give him what he deserves!"

"Last time I checked, Danita, you get livid when I call your brother '*un carbón*.'" I landed a pretty good kick to her stomach. She *oofed*, then dug her nails into my shin. I hissed.

"Things change." She got a better grip on my legs. "Which we'll have a nice chat about on the way to Lyons for prank night. You have some 'splainin to do."

"But…it's not even prank night yet!" I squinted through the dark at the person gripping my arms.

"Change of plans." Molly, the traitor. "We've bumped up the schedule. I warned you this was going to happen, Kaye, if you wussed out on us."

"Jaime's meeting us at my parents' house in an hour. If we don't hurry, she'll string up Samuel by his testicles, which might not be a bad idea, actually. Anyway, I've already drugged him and I don't know if I can pull it off two nights in a row."

"Fresh air and sedatives make for sleepy boys!"

"I'm serious, Danita, Molly. Let us deal with our baggage our own way." *Just let me go back to sleep. That's all I want.*

"But you don't deal with it," Molly argued.

"And this is dealing with it?" I tried once more to wrench my feet free.

Danita gritted her teeth as she and Molly dragged me toward the door. "Quit being difficult, Kaye. I don't want to have to use the bungee cords, but so help me if you don't stop squirming, I'll put you in the trunk."

Bungee cords? Would they really tie me up with bungee cords? Yes, they would. I had ghastly visions of being tossed in a trunk by my two friends, bound and gagged as we bounced along the road to Lyons. Crazy, crazy people. My body slumped to the floor in a massive exhale, the fight leaving me.

"Fine. At least let me throw on a fleece over my camisole. Let's go prank the unholy cliff-hucker, woo-hoo. Then will you let me go back to bed?"

Danita flipped on the light switch. Light flooded my room, blinding me. "Yes." She flipped her long plait over her shoulder like she was friggin' Nora Nixie.

"I've already got your overnight bag, briefcase, and laptop packed and ready to go!" chirped Molly.

Tonight would be rough. I missed those crickets.

Chapter 12
T-RESCUE

When a kayak capsizes, a second kayak maneuvers perpendicular to the first.

Hydraulic Level Five {working title}
Draft 1.12
© Samuel Caulfield Cabral
The Weeping Lady

Their empty heads are filled with his sister. All the gangly, pubescent thirteen-year-old boys in Bear Creek who wake to a sticky mess in their pajamas dream of Maria. They talk about her now, his baseball team, as they tromp along the gravel road toward the cemetery.

Caulfield wants to vomit.

It is May twenty-third, his birthday. His aunt wakes him with "Las Mañanitas." She invites his entire team to spend the night after their game. They eat arroz con leche and Mexican birthday cake that looks like a baseball wearing a sombrero, open presents, and break a piñata. They put on a movie no one watches, bashing each other with giant beanbags in the basement instead. Now it's nearing midnight and his parents have long since gone to bed. These are the days before Caulfield's family moves out-of-town to the foothills, and there is an entire nighttime world of parked cars, lawn gnomes, and rolls of TP at their disposal.

But all his friends yap about as they weave around dew-coated graves in Bear Creek Cemetery is Maria. "Shut your face." He shoves at the ball players, their flashlights bobbing across time-weathered tombstones. "She's my sister!"

"Oye! You can score her panties for us!" exclaims a pig-eyed pudge who habitually gave Caulfield swirlies a couple years ago. But Caulfield is now a head taller than most of them, a welcome development in recent months. He can stare them down like a Rottweiler if he chooses, save for Esteban. It is Esteban who beats Caulfield to the tackle. He sends the pudge flailing across the ground, freshly-mown grass clinging to legs and arms.

Caulfield trudges through the dark, leaving behind the skirmishing boys. If he is honest, he also aches and strains for a girl – a friend of Maria's from school. She is a frilly redhead with barely-there hips and breasts, and her lips are perpetually glossed with cherry ChapStick. He's never physically hurt for someone like this before. He follows her around the house when she visits, shyly averting his eyes if she catches him watching while she and Maria do homework or paint their nails. Aspen notices his crush after he stands her up. She angrily bikes over to his house, pink banjo slung over her scrawny shoulders, demanding to know why he keeps bailing on their music sessions. Maria's friend smirks down at Aspen through thick eyelashes, asking Caulfield who the kid is.

"This is Aspen, the girl who lives down the street."

After an argument in which Aspen calls Caulfield a barnacle-brained wombat and Caulfield laughs (which incenses her even more), he convinces her he can have crushes and still be her friend. She watches him through coarse eyes, arms twined to her childish frame.

"Just don't kiss her. That's gross."

Caulfield wrinkles his nose. "I'm not going to promise that."

"Well, at least promise me you'll wait a long, long time."

"Whatever. I'll wait."

She smiles a victor's smile, and Bear Creek is a brighter place.

He never did kiss Maria's friend with the cherry ChapStick lips. But, three years later, on Halloween night, he did kiss Aspen.

The boys still toss each other around several yards away, behind a cracked marble obelisk. Esteban cusses at the pudge, forcing him to take back what he said about Maria's panties. Good. He wants a chance to see the stone woman before the others do.

They are supposed to be hunting for the Weeping Lady – a life-sized statue of a woman draped in robes, near one of the more prominent crypts. Like every small town, Bear Creek has its ghosts. Legend is, she weeps for lost love, stolen from her before life had barely begun.

Even in the dark, across the cemetery, he sees two worn streaks where thousands of tears drip from her eyes and slip down granite cheeks. Hers is the expression of a tender mother – the way mothers should look at their children. He obsesses over her expression.

In daylight, Caulfield examines her cold, beautiful face countless times, silently probes her dead eyes with the fingertips of a blind boy. He logically determines that she cries because rain and dew collect in the hollow gouges of her eyes and spill over. It is just science, nothing more.

He and Aspen test his theory. He hands Aspen his water bottle, wraps gangly arms around her legs and gives her a boost, bringing her eye-level with the Weeping Lady. She streams water over the stone woman's head, and sure enough, tears gather and spill over her cheeks, just like he expects. Aspen's own face falls.

"It's just...I didn't want to know. I like that she cries because it makes her real. Now she's just...cold. Made of stone."

Caulfield frowns, hard-pressed to figure out why she feels that way. "Aren't you happy she's not suffering all the time? I mean, being around forever and crying is kind of miserable. I hate to think of her like that."

"No. If she's crying, at least it means she feels something. Now I could kick her or hug her, and it's sad because she won't feel a thing."

Caulfield works a lump back in his throat, biting his lip, finding a pain that is sharper, more immediate than the cracks spreading through his chest. He can't comprehend why the Weeping Lady affects her the way it does. The Weeping Lady is just a statue.

But Aspen has a soft, sensitive heart. He is a complete ass. A selfish bastard for ruining her fairy tale. Would it kill him to let her believe, a little longer, the Weeping Woman cries tears for the loss of an idyllic love, an idyllic life? He gave her cold, ruthless reality, and now he can never take it back.

Gathering her up in his arms, he embraces her tightly, willing her to be happy. "Firecracker, I believe she's real. I think she can feel, and see, and hear everything we say and do. And I bet she enjoys our visits."

Her face is pure sunshine for him, warming his chest, searing the web of cracks closed. He will give her fairy tales, pages and pages of fairy tales, in exchange for her sunshine.

He should have just lied in the first place.

Samuel, don't you DARE start this self-loathing metaphorical prose garbage on me again. Are we going to have to hash this out like we did with The Last Other? Because if I wanted to feel pointless pain, I'd just smash my fingers between copies of War and Peace. First of all, thirteen-year-olds don't call themselves "selfish bastards" (which is cliché, by the way). Second, why are you sending this to me at four thirty in the morning? The LAST thing you want to do is start with the late nights again, in the middle of a BOOK TOUR AND MOVIE PROMOTION, of all times. You are driving me INSANE.
~Caro.

Caro, I'm sorry about the tour and promotion. I know this means more work for you. But I've got to mend some fences first, and the rest will have to come second. Please be patient.
~SC

SC, fine. It usually does come second. It usually does mean more work. And yes, you are an ass (but a damned gorgeous one, and there's my weakness).

In the back of Molly's lime green Subaru, cruising roads after midnight on the way to Lyons, I finally spilled my guts about my trip to New York. Danita fanned the fire, cornering me from the front seat with the fury of a windstorm.

"All right, Kaye. I haven't done this yet because you and Samuel actually seemed to be getting along, though I don't know why stupid pranks work so well for you two. But you better start talking about your top-secret New York excursion, right now."

"No."

"Why?"

"Because…I can't."

"Because he was screwing a woman and snorting coke in New York?"

"Danita!" Molly barked.

My eyes went wide. "How…how do you know about that?"

Molly gawked at me in her rearview mirror. "It's *true?* No, you've got to be kidding! *Sam?* I don't believe it."

"That's what I said," Dani grumbled.

"Wait, when did you go to New York?" Molly's face was rife with bewilderment.

My heavy skull fell back against the headrest. I'd have to spill. There was no getting around it, now. "This does not leave the car, understood?"

They both agreed.

"Remember that this happened almost seven years ago. And it was all really fast, so some of it's jumbled." I sighed. *Here goes nothing.*

"After Samuel packed a bag and left, I wasn't doing very well. Sofia called every night, checking on me, making sure I went to classes, prying information from me about what went down between the two of us. She and Alonso hadn't heard a thing from him—did you know that, Danita?"

"They asked me if he'd been in touch. Keep going."

"I was really frightened. So was Sofia. And my head…I wasn't sure what I thought, then, my mind was scattered marbles. When he left, I was convinced it was just a big misunderstanding, that he was mired down in stress. His job, new marriage, finances, things every post-honeymoon couple has to work through. But when he didn't call, and no one else heard from him…

"Then, finally, Samuel phoned Sofia. He told her not to worry and gave her his address because he wanted some of his belongings shipped. The minute I had that address, I flew into action. I printed a Google map, threw some things in a backpack, yanked our savings and bought a plane ticket to New York."

"Where was he living?" Danita asked.

"He had some writer acquaintances from his Colorado University days who attended NYU, and they shared a brownstone in the East Village. I'd only met them once or twice. They really weren't friends of ours—kind of spoiled rich kids."

"Yeah, I remember a few," Danita muttered. "Togsy was a piece of work. Used to saunter around campus with a joint between his fingers, like he was daring security to do something about it. Artist asshats."

A nail crept into my mouth, and I yanked it away. "Anyway, I got into JFK late at night. The subway was…interesting. I'd never even been to New York City before, let alone on the subway. It was dark, grimy, smelly. A scattering of bizarre, ragged people stared at me. I should have just gotten a cab, but I couldn't afford it after dropping so much money on the plane ticket. It was scary, but I kept telling myself once I got to Samuel, it would be okay. I needed to keep plowing forward, keep moving. I got off at the wrong stop, doubled back, hopped a different line—I ended up at NYU, then walked until I found the brownstone in the East Village." My voice crept higher. I took a deep, calming breath.

"People were going in and out of the house, so I followed them in. It was so crowded…people everywhere, students maybe, I don't know. Shabby furniture, stacks of garbage. Pot hung heavy in the air, broken glass and stale booze. I stalled in the foyer because I knew I couldn't be at the right place. I felt like a stupid, lost little girl. But then I saw one of the guys from CU. He was startled to see me, but he took me up to Samuel's room anyway. 'You Cabral's wife? Damn, this should be cracked,' he laughed."

I pressed my palms against my eyes, not wanting to relive any of this. My stomach churned violently at the memory.

"Kaye? You can't just leave us hanging!" Molly cried. "What happened?"

"There were more men and women in the upstairs room, straddling laps, shirts hanging open, groping each other…I'm not sure how many, I didn't look closely. There were a few candles on the floor, and the rest of the room was dark. There weren't curtains on the window, so the moon cast odd shadows from all the limbs…of all the details to recall, huh? I started to panic, scared the CU guy had lied just to get me upstairs. I asked where Samuel was, and he pointed to this old metal bed in the corner, the only furniture in the room except for a desk. I stared at the corner, not seeing him. There was just a half-naked man hunched over, all sweaty. And a brunette woman, nearly naked, too. His nose ran up her torso, and I thought he was smelling her at first. But then I saw white powder blowing across her skin and sticking to his fingers, rimming his nostrils, and I realized it was a coke line."

"Oh no, not Samuel," Molly murmured. Danita was stone-silent.

"But the way he was touching her…so greedy and demanding, his hands tugging her skin, her lace bra…it wasn't him." My voice cracked. "'I don't see him,' I told the CU guy. He rolled his eyes and pointed directly at the corner. It took me a full minute to understand the man in the corner wasn't some random, horny coke head."

"What did you do?" Molly asked.

I fought to keep my voice detached so I could finish my story. "I said his name, several times. The other people in the room stared at me. I felt my knees go weak, so I hung on to the doorframe for support. Finally, his head shot up. His eyes found mine. They were so…wild. Brittle. That's what frightened me the most, I think—seeing the warmth missing from the blue. I know it was because he was so high, but still…" I shuddered. "He told me to get the hell out of his room, said I wasn't supposed to follow him. 'Go home to Colorado, and don't you ever come back here again, Aspen Kaye. I fucking mean it. You think this is a joke?' His voice was snarling, harsh, just like his eyes. I didn't know what to do. My knees finally gave way." I pressed my fingertips to my temples, as if they could shove the memories from my brain.

"It gets really vague from there. A couple of the people in the room helped me off the floor. A woman took me across the hall, to a bedroom. She settled me onto a bed—a wicker bed—then pulled out my cell phone and saw all the missed calls…"

My phone call to Alonso played through my mind. Relief was in his voice when he'd answered…

"Kaye! *¡No hubo heridos graves, gracias a Dios!* Sofia has called you all day and you weren't picking up. She's on her way to Boulder to check on you—"

"Alonso, something's wrong with Samuel."

He paused. "What do you mean?"

"I'm in New York. I think he's high. He's with this woman—" It didn't even sound like my voice. This voice was edged in hysteria. "You need to fly out here, now. Something's wrong."

I heard shuffling and doors slam through the phone, as Alonso tore through the house. "Tell me in detail what you saw, even the little things. Did you call a doctor?"

"No, I called you..." Fingers of exhaustion crawled through my mind.

"Kaye?" Alonso commanded. "Focus please, *mija*. Describe what you saw."

I told him there was a woman. I told him Samuel had wild, angry eyes. "Do I need to call a doctor?"

"I will send somebody—an old friend from my Boston days. Can you sit with Samuel until he gets there?"

"I'll try..."

I did try. I banged on his door, crying and pleading for him to let me in. My face dripped with tears and snot, streaked across the sleeves of my hoodie where I'd wiped them across my nose. I remembered being trapped in the tree house so long ago, scared and soaked through, how Samuel left me there with his Keep Out sign. He wouldn't open the door. Alonso's doctor friend came, felt my heartbeat pulsing in my neck and peered into my eyes.

"Get her to bed, she's as white as a sheet." He spoke to the woman next to me, I hadn't noticed sitting there until now. "He'll be fine, Mrs. Cabral. I'll take good care of him until his father arrives."

I tried the door, one last time. "Please, Samuel. Let me in." Locked.

So I burrowed into the strange wicker bed in the strange, pitch-black room.

Time passed...

Ages later, a thin, firm hand shook me awake. Samuel. I peered into the dimly-lit room and saw not Samuel, but Alonso. He helped me sit, then wrapped two strong, fatherly arms around me. I think I hugged him back.

"Oh, Kaye," he lulled, smoothing my hair down as silent tears slid from my eyes. Heaviness lifted from my mind, leaving only panic in its absence. I clung to his neck.

"How is he? What's wrong? I want to see him!"

He pulled away, troubled brown eyes meeting mine. "He's fine now, Kaye. My son was high on cocaine, probably a few other things. I've had a talk with him, and I'm going to stay out here for a while."

I nodded. "Do you want me to look into hotels online?" I peered at my surroundings, searching for a computer. Mauve walls, flowered curtains fluttering over the window, the wicker furniture, a shelf packed with books and tiaras and knickknacks. Such a pretty room, so incongruous compared to the rest of the house. But no computer.

Alonso had the look of a man who'd just stepped off a New York red-eye. "No, that's fine. Kaye…I'm fairly certain the drugs have been going on for some time."

I shook my head. "That's not possible. I would have known."

"We'll discuss it later. For now, I think you should go home. You have school on Monday."

"No! I want to see him."

Alonso rose from the bed and turned to the window, dragging a hand through his glossy hair, so wrong in the grime of this city. "He asked me to put you on a plane back to Colorado. I think that's the best thing." His voice begged me to understand.

I was too weak, too young to fight back.

I didn't get to see Samuel. We never discussed the cocaine. I barely remembered saying goodbye to Alonso at JFK, or being in Sofia's arms at Denver International.

Three days. Three long, wretched days, and nothing. At last, I emptied my backpack, knowing I wouldn't be summoned back to New York. A letter fell out, carefully tucked away in my hoodie. I tore open the envelope. I wasn't sure what to expect, but I knew what I was hungry for. I wanted the sweet lie: I'm sorry. Come back. It wasn't real. It wasn't me. I want you. I love you.

But I got the bitter truth…his final "Keep Out" sign on the tree house, scrawled in his signature elegant handwriting…more frantic than normal, but still, his.

Kaye,

Go home to Colorado. I don't want to see you again
The roots between us are dead, we are dead…

The car was as suffocating as the grave when my voice fell away.

Dani flipped on the radio, then glanced at me in the back seat with careful eyes. "Is that all?"

"You've heard the rest. I did what he wanted: filed for divorce. Your parents moved to New York to help rein in his drug habit. I called Sofia once a week to check in, see how it was going. She gave me the same ambiguous 'fine, fine, we are all well' line. You know how your mom tends to gloss over unsavory details."

"And that's all you know?"

Almost everything...I remembered Samuel's arrest records carefully tucked away in my underwear drawer, but it would be wrong of me to share that. If Samuel wanted Danita and Molly to know, he'd have to tell them himself. My role in his life ended when I had my first meeting with my divorce lawyer.

"I would have kicked him in the balls a long time ago, if I'd known," Molly muttered, squeezing the life out of the steering wheel.

"That's just it, Molly—it's been almost seven years. I'm afraid the window for balls-kicking has passed. I'm not really angry anymore, just...done."

"Kaye, you're right. We shouldn't do the pranks. I'm so, so sorry I pushed you into this." A tear dripped from Molly's chin.

"Like hell she's getting out of it," Dani retorted. Our faces whipped to hers. "Yes, what happened was shitty, for everyone. But it was so long ago and it's time for you and Samuel to get past this."

"Danita, I don't think—"

"Shut it, Molly." Molly indignantly settled into the driver's seat.

"Why on earth do you still want me to prank him?" I asked.

"Because this prank war is the first time I've seen you take any real initiative to deal with this. You're not the only one who's stuck. You've told me, Molly, everyone else that you're angry and hurt, but have you told Sam? No. Sure, you've whined to him about the books and the alimony. But when it comes to the serious stuff, you bite your tongue and run, or divert, or make jokes. There's something about my brother that makes you bury your head in the sand, like you're terrified to takes risks with him."

"Well gosh, I wonder why?" My voice dripped with sarcasm.

"No. You both have been this way, long before you even started dating. Why can't you just be blunt?"

"Because I'm not *you*, Dani."

She slapped the dash with her manicured palm, causing Molly to flinch. "You may be done, Kaye, but the rest of us are just now catching up. For all I knew, you divorced him because of the drugs. For all I knew, you didn't even try. My brother was *beside himself* when I told him about your name change, and I didn't really understand why, because *neither one* of you bothered to clue us in. I was shocked when he told me you'd followed him to New York. Why didn't you talk to me? To Molly? You've had years to tell me!"

I rounded on Danita. "What was I supposed to say—'Oh Dani, your brother's a cheating, coke-head *cabrón*'?"

"Yeah, at least you would have been talking to me."

"Look, if your own family didn't clue you in, I wasn't going to."

"You're family too!"

"Not anymore."

Molly bit her lip, waiting for the explosion.

Danita took a deep, calming breath, but her fingernails dug into her hands. "Believe me, they've heard about it. But, Kaye, you're my closest friend. Why did you hide this?"

My voice broke. "Because it hurt too bad, okay? Because I was humiliated. How would you feel if Angel did that to you? I bet you wouldn't want to tell anyone about it, either. You'd just want to forget it happened. You have no idea…it made me question *everything*, Dani, from our childhood, to our life in Boulder, to my own sex appeal. It was too painful, too embarrassing, too frightening, and I didn't want to share it."

I ran my hands through my hair, tugging strands loose from my ponytail. I knew, *knew*, it had been wrong not to tell Danita. But for the life of me, I would not admit it.

Danita ground her jaw, struggling to rein herself in. "Kaye?"

"Yeah?"

"I told you I spoke with Samuel three weeks ago." Her voice grew somber. "Did you know he can't even remember what happened in New York? Between the brunette's story and a few serial speedballers who were in his room, he's cobbled together all sorts of ridiculous scenarios. You're the only one who knows, Kaye. You need to talk to my brother. Please. If you care about me, *please*."

I rested my head on the window, unable to comprehend what she said. How was it possible he didn't remember? He had to remember what he did—he was on the other side of that locked door. I couldn't be the only one living with this wretched memory, could I? Somehow, I felt even more sick.

Silence filled the car as I collected myself. But just as my blood began to cool, Danita pursed her pink lips—a dead giveaway more bluntness was coming my way. I braced myself.

"For the record, I don't believe Samuel ever slept with anyone else while you were married."

Oh, that was a good one. "That makes me feel so much better. He's such a saint. I'm sure he and Miss Brunette were just warming up for a friendly game of Twister."

"I'm not defending him. I only meant that they never actually—"

"What? That he was *high* when he was pawing up another woman, snorting coke off her stomach? That we were already separated? It doesn't matter. We were still married. I still loved him."

"And you don't still love him?"

"No. Yes. I didn't say..."

"Straight answer, Kaye."

I stared out the window, watching as rain began to pelt the glass. The closer the Rockies, the closer the rain. Rain was gentle, soothing. I listened to the buzz of the radio, the quiet thumps of cold drops against the car, everything but my own heartbeat, pulsing through my veins. *Just one word, that's all you need to say. Why is it so hard?*

"Yes. I still love him. Pathetic isn't it?"

Danita sighed, her head falling back, weary. "No. It's not pathetic. It's life."

"Hey, Trilby, what's Cabral's password?" Jaime whispered across Samuel's bedroom.

Calvino.

"I don't know anymore. Jaime, I wish you'd leave his laptop alone, that's his business." I kept my voice low to avoid waking him. Not that I probably would—the man was out cold, tangled up in his bed sheets despite the chill, woodsy air sweeping through his open window. He hadn't groaned, hadn't moved a single inch since we'd—no, Molly, Danita, and Jaime—began to ransack his room with the precision of a Picasso. The Benadryl did the trick, and the only sign he was still alive was the steady rise and fall of his smooth chest.

"Try 'TedWilliams,'" Danita piped up from the floor. Good guess... if the password wasn't an author, it was a Boston Red Sox player. I watched as she helped Molly fill his empty Samsonite carry-on with potting soil. I still couldn't believe they were ruining eight-hundred dollars' worth of luggage. Then again, Samuel wouldn't have any trouble replacing it.

Jaime's fingers clicked over keys, and paused. "Nope, that's not it."

"Add 'nine' to the end, his old baseball number."

It's Calvino. A hundred bucks says it's Calvino. I picked up the graduation picture, now sitting on an end table next to the futon. The silver frame was smudged. I polished it with my shirttail, studied our smiling teenage faces, and put it back.

Something nagged me, had since our roller-coaster ride along Ute Highway. Then it struck me. "Dani, was Samuel really beside himself about my name change?"

"It was the oddest thing. He got really upset. And then he was just...glad, I guess."

Glad? Yes, I could see that. But upset? No.

Molly smoothed gloved hands around another tomato plant and gently patted dirt over the roots, as if she actually thought the doomed thing would grow and thrive in Samuel's suitcase. "Hmmm. Try 'Neelie, nine.'"

"Nope," said Jaime.

She wiped her forehead, streaking it with potting soil. "You know, Kaye, you could at least help a little. There are six tomato plants for that big suitcase over there, and there's still the Sharpies and powdered milk, though I'm not sure how we'll manage that one." She scowled at Danita. "You were supposed to sprinkle it on his mattress *before* he went to bed. It has to be under him for his pores to absorb it, otherwise his skin won't stink."

"That's disgusting." Jaime's nose crinkled. "Wish I'd known about powdered milk when I was messing with Juan. His little mistress would have kicked him out of the house—she can't stand nasty odors."

"Most people can't." Danita slathered the underside of a doorknob with mechanic's grease, then knelt to check her handiwork. "The stench will wear off before we go camping, right?"

Molly nodded, extracting another plant from its container and shaking the roots loose. "It only lasts a couple of days." She glared at me over her shoulder. "Oh for the love of all that's holy, Kaye—do something. You owe me, big time. Years of owing me!" Molly's face scrunched up in what I thought was anger…I wasn't quite sure, because I rarely saw Molly truly angry.

"I'm fine where I am. You three have everything under control."

Danita jerked me up by my elbow. "Look, can you please just screw with my brother tonight? That's all I ask."

Molly sniggered in spite of herself.

Danita blushed a beautiful bright red. "Ew."

"See?" Jaime hissed, twisting around in the desk chair to point at Dani. "I'm not the only one who's done that. So why don't you tell her to clean out her mouth?"

"Screwed with Samuel?" Molly giggled.

"Yes! No! Never mind."

I pointed accusing fingers at all of them. "Every single one of you filthy women had better watch your backs. I know people."

Jaime lifted an eyebrow. "I *am* your people, Trilby. So if you're planning to put shaving cream in our hands and tickle our noses with feathers, you're—" she leered at me "—screwed."

I jumped up from my unproductive slouch on Samuel's old futon and scooted across the room. "Son-of-a-frickin' fruit bat, give me the powdered milk." Molly handed it to me, then watched as I marched over to Samuel's bed, assessing the situation.

"Got it. I used to do this when Sam sprawled over my side of the bed and I wanted him to move." I traced my index finger, ever so lightly, beneath his rib cage. "He's ticklish here." Sure enough, Samuel mumbled something incoherent, brushed my finger away, and rolled to his side like a trained puppy.

"No way." Danita came up behind me. "He's never been ticklish."

"Yeah, he is. He's just very good at controlling it. It got *you* to stop attacking him when we were kids, didn't it?"

"Huh. So how did you figure that one out?"

I opened the powdered milk and liberally sprinkled it across the bed. "He wasn't in control of himself quite so much, one time. That, and there wasn't a lot of space on the top bunk of my dorm room." Molly coughed delicately, patting the final tomato plant into place. I ignored her. "After ten minutes or so, he'll probably flop over again. Then the powdered milk should work its magic. Sofia is going to kill us, by the way."

Jaime peered at me from over the laptop screen, then at Samuel's half-naked form, then back to me. "Wow, Trilby. Sounds like somebody knows Cabral's kinks pretty well. Are you sure you don't want to tap that for old times' sake?"

A jolt shot straight through my body at the idea, but I quickly recovered. "Jaime, I think we need to have a serious talk about our relationship. I mean, aren't you supposed to discourage me from 'tapping' the male species?"

"That sounds like an inside joke I need to hear," said Dani. "Please go skydiving with us, Jaime? Or at least camping?"

"Camping, no. I'd smother all of you with your Eddie Bauer air mattresses before the night was over. Skydiving, hell no. You suicidal adrenaline junkies go ahead and jump from a plane without me, and I'll scream obscenities at you from the ground." She swiveled back to the laptop and tried another password.

Molly brushed stray dirt from her clothes, then leaned back to observe her work with a small smile. "Kaye, hand me that note card and pen in the bag, please?" I dug through the plastic bag, grabbed the note card, and tossed it to her. She scrawled what seemed like a book and propped it next to her little suitcase garden.

"There!"

I scanned her work—she'd made a care card for the plants. Typical sweet, interfering Molly. If only it were that easy.

> Emotivus Drownicus Nixius: Nixius plants deplete the soil of nutrients fairly quickly. But with a bit of knowledge and perseverance, you can eventually have some wonderful blooms. Nixius plants require five hours of direct sunlight and daily watering. Soil care is key: roots need air in the soil just as much as they need water and nutrients. Turn soil frequently, digging deeply to break up dirt clumps and keep roots healthy. Good luck with your Nixius plant!

"That's cute, Molly. But the whole symbiosis thing…I mean, seriously. You don't buy that, do you?"

She scowled at me. "Do you want me to make you a copy of the card?"

Before I could answer, Danita snapped her fingers and pointed at the laptop. "The password's 'Calvino.' I used it for emailing several weeks ago."

Crap crap crap. I braced myself behind Jaime, ready to shove her out of the swivel chair if it worked.

I was right. It was "Calvino." Windows whirred to life, giving us entry to Samuel's most private files if we so chose. For a fleeting moment, I considered searching for an electronic copy of the Planet Bluegrass draft I'd stumbled upon. But there was no way I was going to let Jaime browse through the laptop. I dug my shoulder into her side, trying to unseat her, but she held on tightly while the computer loaded and locked her hands and ankles around the desk.

"Holy shit!" she exclaimed, staring as the screen flickered to life.

"Shhhh!" the three of us hissed. My eyes flew to Samuel. He groaned and turned over, onto the scattered milk powder. We paused, waiting with bated breath for him to open his eyes, stretch, catch us red-handed. He didn't stir. I exhaled and turned back to the laptop.

And then I froze, seeing what Jaime saw. I gasped.

Two children's faces glowed above a handful of birthday candles, a little blurry because the camera kept focusing on the flickering light. Someone had tried to tame the boy's hair, but it still ran wild, sticking out beneath the blue party hat perched upon his head. His shoulders were hunched beneath his too-big T-shirt, almost as if he were embarrassed to be the center of attention. But his smile…his bright, lazy grin dominated everything about the picture. Everything, save for the girl with tangled blond hair. She chastely kissed his cheek beneath a yellow smiley-face sticker she'd placed there, minutes before Sofia brought out the sombrero cake.

"Oh wow," Molly breathed behind me. Danita silently swept a hand over her eyes.

Every day. He looked at this picture every day while he wrote, emailed, researched. Tears pricked my eyes. My hands flew to my mouth to stifle a sob.

I felt overwhelmed. I felt elated. I felt angry. I felt…

I just felt.

But something was off...I looked at the date in the corner of the image. May twenty-third...No. Oh no. May twenty-third. Samuel's *birthday*. Last week, right smack in the middle of Mickey-gate.

I'd forgotten.

Why hadn't he said anything? Why hadn't Danita or Sofia? Had the entire family eaten Mexican birthday cake and snapped pictures while I...what was I doing? Plotting with Jaime.

Now I felt like a shrew. Samuel had never once forgotten my birthday, even if it was just a simple "Happy Birthday" card tucked in the envelope with his alimony check.

I snapped the laptop closed before we saw anything more, then studied Samuel, his arm now flung across his chest. Asleep, he more closely resembled the boy in the laptop picture...the child I'd befriended and loved so long ago. Same slightly-rounded nose. Same angular face beneath a shadow of grown-up stubble. Same soft lips. His hair was still a frustrated mess from our evening at Button Rock Reservoir. I'd missed this—watching him sleep, searching out the boy in his peaceful features.

"Molly, give me a Sharpie." Confused, she dug through her bag of toys on the futon and tossed me a red one. I cautiously rested a knee on Samuel's bed, shifting my weight. When he didn't stir, I uncapped the Sharpie and leaned over him, slowly marking his forehead. I waited...no movement. Sweeping his hair away, I scribbled the other letters then eased back, gazing at my handiwork:

I'M A NAUGHTY NACKEN

I smiled, satisfied.

Molly laughed quietly. "You do realize he's supposed to be a guest on *The After Hours Show* Friday, right? Caroline's going to strangle you."

"It's a good thing olive oil takes out permanent marker, then."

"Only if somebody tells him," said Jaime.

Danita yawned, stretching. "Okay, *chicas*, off to bed. There are a couple of couches in the basement and the guest bedroom downstairs. Caroline's in the one up the hall— "

"I'm going home. I need to feed the Labs in a couple of hours," said Jaime.

"Dibs on the bedroom," Molly called.

"The couch for me, I guess."

"Mind the grease on the doorknob," Danita reminded us as we filed out to our respective beds.

I sneaked one last, greedy look at Samuel, then ducked past Dani before she could accuse me of "eye-screwing" her brother.

Just before I drifted to sleep early that morning, close to four, I feared The Dream would make another appearance.

It did not.

Instead, I dreamed of lazy May nights. Catching rare Colorado fireflies in jars as we chased their haunting glow trails across wooded backyards and marshes. Slices of Mexican birthday cake alight with sparklers. And a little boy with warm, ice eyes.

When I woke, gray morning light stretched from casement windows through the creams and beiges of Sofia's cozy family room, hitting my face.

The warm ice eyes were still there, watching me from the armchair.

The stench of curdled milk in my nose was overwhelming.

Crap.

Chapter 13
OFFSET WAVES

*A wild stretch of waves that curl and collide
into each other from all angles.*

Miles of golden clay and rocks slid past Betty the VW Campervan's windows on the road out of Boulder. Danita and Molly chatted quietly in the front, Molly at the wheel. Santiago followed behind us in his car. Angel and Cassady were passed out in the back, Cassady's body slumped over Angel's knees (Danita had already snapped several photos) after a long night of Coronas, cigars and poker.

Samuel and Caroline were settled in the bench across from me, his arm resting along the seat behind her, her creamy coffee face nestled in his shoulder. His iPod lay in his lap as his head lolled back. I was sorely tempted to crank up the volume on that thing and scare him with the force of the apocalypse. His legs stretched out in front of him, his calf occasionally bumping mine.

At least most everyone was getting in a few hours' rest before the dive.

I leaned against Hector—who was also asleep—and tucked up my knees.

"Oh, Sweet Kaye, shoes off the upholstery," Molly sang in her best "Cassady" voice, eyeing me in the mirror. "Hippie has issues with dirt in his Campervan."

"Then he's not a real hippie." But I shot her an apologetic smile and slipped off my sneaks.

Since Samuel would leave the day after the wedding, I tried to read the final quarter of *The Last Other* in the narrow windows of time I had to spare. That included now, on our way to the Rocketeers' Skydiving hangar. Rather than suffer the embarrassment of reading the book in front of Samuel, I'd snagged the dust jacket from my special edition *Hitchhiker's Guide to the Galaxy* trilogy (a present from Angel) to camouflage it.

I chewed my thumbnail, reading on…

> **She would not die. He would not let her die. Nicodemus seized Neelie's hands, her wrists, her body, dragging her away from the scores of Others spilling through the tunnels, crawling over slimy, mildewed walls like poisonous spiders. For hours and hours they hid below, in the ground. He buried his face in her hair, waiting for the Others to scatter above them. And when the creatures finally retreated, still they hid, clutching bodies. Neelie...his friend. Neelie...**
>
> **Nicodemus pulled her to him with hungry hands...**

Oh no. No! I was going to murder him. I flushed, pressing the book shut until my blood cooled. Minutes later I returned to the story, rushing through Nicodemus's musings on Neelie's scent, the feel of her skin, her mouth, all the while my mind hammered *fiction, fiction, fiction!* I breathed a sigh of relief as the narrator tactfully drew a veil between audience and the newly-aware couple. If there'd been any more references to heart-shaped freckles, I would have strangled him with his iPod cord. I skimmed over the passage again. Second time through, it really wasn't that bad. Kind of hot, actually. He'd live to see another day.

I should have finished *The Last Other* before now. The final week before Danita and Angel's vow swappin' would be frantic, whipping together the last of the decorations and entertaining the extended *familia*, traveling from as far as Ciudad Victoria in Tamaulipas.

This past week hadn't been much calmer, but for entirely different reasons…

After the ultimate prank night, I woke in Sofia's basement to find Samuel watching me, his fingers tented over his mouth. I thought

I was a goner. And he'd gotten me back, oh yes. Once fuzzy sleep lifted from my brain, the first thing I noticed was that the horrible smell of soured milk was too strong to be coming from Samuel alone.

"Ewwww." I sniffed my arms, pushing myself up from the powdered milk-coated blanket. My nose crinkled in disgust. "Did you do this?"

Samuel raised an eyebrow. "I told you I wasn't going to let you mess with me and not fight back. You really shouldn't fall asleep in someone's basement after pranking them. Poorly executed, Ms. Trilby."

"How'd you get all of this...stuff...under me?"

"Are you going to explain the same thing to me?"

"Heck no."

"Then I'm not telling, either."

"Well, one good thing about this. No one will want to be within twenty feet of me, so at least I'll be able to finish your book."

He grinned. "I hadn't even thought of that. Maybe if I keep it up, you'll re-read *all* of my books."

"Once was enough, thanks."

Rubbing my eyes, I took him in for the first time. Well-worn pajamas and T-shirt, damp hair, freshly shaven...red marker still very prominent on his forehead. After Dani's revelation last night, I saw him with new eyes. He didn't remember what happened in New York...he'd been so messed up on drugs, he only knew what others had told him.

"You're not very intimidating with 'I'm a Naughty Nacken' written on your face."

His lips curled. He crossed the room and held out a hand mirror. "Likewise."

I grabbed the mirror from him, examining my forehead:

I'M NAUGHTY, TOO

Ugh. Well, Kaye, what did you expect?

"Nice, Mr. Famous Author. Couldn't come up with anything better?"

"Well, I considered writing 'Neelie Nixie is completely and entirely fictional—kind of,' but I thought it would tick you off."

I smiled in spite of myself. Between the horrible smell and the marker, I'd probably start work late this morning. I fumbled for my phone...nine thirty. I groaned.

"I thought you could use the sleep."

"How long have you been down here?"

He shrugged, glancing at the wall clock. "Not long."

I remembered I didn't even have my car. I fired off a quick message to the office, letting them know I'd work from Lyons today.

"Caroline and I are flying out of Denver tomorrow. We can take you to Boulder for your car, if you like."

"That's okay. Wouldn't want to give your paparazzi photogs any ideas about a threesome." Horror flooded his face, and I laughed. "Kidding, Samuel. We're going to Boulder to pick up our dresses, so I can collect my car then."

He gently tugged at my elbow. "Come on, let's get you fed. Mamá cooked up a storm this morning—chorizo, huevos rancheros, *pan de yema con chocolate*—then ordered me to eat outside. Apparently she doesn't like the way I smell." His eyes flicked over a strip of pale stomach as I stretched, then darted away. Self-conscious, I tugged down my cami and grabbed my fleece from the floor. He busied himself cleaning up the powdered milk mess on the blankets.

"I bet she was incensed this morning." I gave him a hand.

"Let's just say we'll all be paying to have her furniture cleaned. Danita barely made it out of the house alive."

I winced. Together, we rolled up the offending blankets, dragged them into the laundry room, and stuffed them in the washing machine. "I'll chip in to pay for that." There was no way I was ending up on Sofia's bad side. Over the years she had perfected the art form of inflicting sweet and subtle guilt on the deserved.

"If you want."

I tromped up the stairs, scanning the house for any signs of Caroline. A radio quietly buzzed in the kitchen, pulsing with Sofia's up-and-at-em classical playlist, which usually just lulled me to sleep again. Right now, it was something familiar. Samuel would know.

"Composer?"

"Vaughan Williams. Too early for him?"

"No, no, it's fine. Relaxing." Alonso and Sofia both believed classical music stimulated the brain, which was why they'd insisted Samuel study Spanish guitar along with acoustic. My dad, however, believed rolled joints and The Grateful Dead did the trick.

The dishwasher rattled, but other than that, it was peaceful. Too peaceful. I looked at Samuel.

"Mom's at the florists. Molly is still asleep. Caro went for a run to cool her head—she was a little agitated this morning, heads up. She hasn't even seen my luggage yet." He gestured for me to sit down at one of the bar stools while he dished up a plate of leftovers warming in the oven. The fragrance of spicy sausage and chocolate flooded the room, momentarily driving away the sour milk smell and making my stomach rumble. Then he placed a mug of luscious, black coffee under my nose. I sighed. God bless Sofia Cabral and her gourmet beans.

"Thanks. And I'm sorry. I didn't mean to cause a rift between you and Caroline."

Samuel gave me a dubious look as he set the plate before me, along with the fruit bowl. I immediately went to work on my huevos rancheros.

"You didn't, really. Caro will get over it. The pranks are good for her, although, she's going to skin me alive for not correcting her about your…sexual orientation. She'll be livid, actually." He grimaced.

"Maybe Jaime and I can stage a break-up scene, then we'll both be off the hook. Not that it's any of Caro's business who I tango with."

He offered me a little smile, though it didn't quite reach his eyes. "When it comes to business, she takes herself very seriously. Unfortunately, I am Caroline's business. She works very hard, has since she first read my writing. Every social event, every dinner date, she makes connections, promotes…well, me. If it weren't for her, I would have lost my focus a long time ago. And if it were any other author, I don't know if she'd work so hard. She genuinely cares about me, and I'd be a fool not to appreciate that." Grave lines settled around his eyes and mouth, as if he wore that expression enough to make those lines permanent. I didn't like that expression. My fingers itched to reach up, smooth the worry lines away. I held them back.

"I know Caroline has helped you to become wildly successful. But does she care about your happiness, too?" I asked softly. "That's pretty key when you're dating somebody." My cheeks burned, and my plate of food became extremely interesting as I stabbed at a sausage.

Samuel wasn't going to let me play ostrich. He leaned across the counter, his intense eyes seeking mine, drawing them up from my plate. He held them captive, not letting me go until he spoke.

"I did a lot of thinking on the drive back from Boulder last night, Kaye." Blood pounded through my veins. *Uh oh, never good.* I braced myself. "You told me some things that startled me, quite frankly. The biggest is that you refuse to be alone because of me. That you need concrete answers."

"Why does this surprise you?"

"Because I've never thought of you as being alone. You're very successful, strong…beautiful." His soft lips quirked. "You have TrilbyJones. Close friends and family. You've taken up daring hobbies, like whitewater rafting, skydiving. I just assumed you had moved on, that you were happy." I started to shake my head, and he rushed on. "I was a weak man who let everyone coddle him when I needed to be stronger for you, and you should have been glad to be rid of me. I believed I'd given you more than enough reason to put me behind you…especially after New York." Confusion and doubt crept into his features, something I wasn't used to seeing in Samuel Cabral's normally self-assured face.

"What's your point?"

"My point is that I have an answer for you—a concrete one."

"I'm listening."

"I never was a true friend to you."

I scoffed. "Don't be ridiculous."

"No, Kaye, listen—this is important. Real friends don't hide vital things from each other. Real friends are truthful, even if it means making themselves susceptible to hurt, or causing the other person pain. And I wasn't truthful. I've hidden so much from you…since the day I first met you, I think. Do you remember?"

My mind skipped back to that afternoon. I could barely recall it, because I'd only been four. The Cabrals had hosted a Halloween party for Samuel to meet the neighborhood kids and parents. He'd spent the entire time in the corner, fiddling with his white sheet and plastic chains, watching other children as they played a bean bag toss game. I'd gone as a ghost, too. (Much to my mother's chagrin—she'd wanted me to be a butterfly.) I told him my mother was taking me trick-or-treating. He said his mother was taking him, too. "She's not here yet. She's in Boston, but she'll be here tonight." I scowled, asking if she was going to live with the Cabrals, too—I already had to share them with this new boy. But all of this happened before I discovered his mother was dead…

"Usually it worked and I made you happy. But this time, Kaye… I don't know. After last night, everything's mixed up in my head. I just…I need to *fix* it. I don't want to be weak or coddled anymore."

Who was this Samuel? Chasing his quick-moving mind had always been like chasing a river current. But drumming the counter, biting his lip…this nervousness was new. He was usually so decisive, so self-controlled in the slightest pinky-lift.

He said he'd hidden a lot. What? I didn't think it was just the drugs. I grabbed at what I could.

"Samuel, look. If you miss our friends and family, you don't need to stay away on my account. Don't feel things between us need to be fluffy kittens for you to come home. I think we can get along well enough."

"Kaye." My name was an exasperated sigh. He warily reached for my hand, his expressive eyes asking permission. I didn't tell him no. His fingers linked with mine. "What if I want to be *your* friend? What if I want to help you find your answers? I know it will take a lot of work and honesty, but I think we could do it."

"But what about your book tour? Let's be realistic, Sam. You're leaving in two weeks."

"I don't give a flying…*cliff-huck* about my book tour, Kaye. I want to make things right between us."

My breath grew quick, shallow. "I don't know if it's still possible. I don't know if I can…" I wasn't sure how to finish that.

"If you can what?"

"If I can trust you," I sputtered. "I want answers to tie up loose ends, not create new ones."

His face fell like a toppled sandcastle. "I thought with the pranks, maybe…" He squeezed my hand and released it. "Fair enough. Just think about it first, please, before you decide. I'll do what I can to help you find your answers, regardless." He smiled, but his brow furrowed. I brushed an index finger over it, smoothing away the creases.

Had I really just called our friendship a loose end? How jaded. I'd sent him mixed messages and I knew it, but what other message could I send when I was so mixed up myself? It struck me—the hypocrisy of it all. Here I was, telling Samuel I couldn't trust him. Yet I had a file hidden in my bedroom with information that could utterly ruin him if I wanted it to. Just hours ago we broke into his laptop. And if he considered "hiding" to be untruthfulness, then, according to Dani, I was as guilty as he. But what he'd done—leaving our marriage, the drugs, the woman—was much, much worse than my alleged hiding. Wasn't it?

He had been right about one thing. I had some thinking to do before I could decide whether or not to be his friend. In the meantime, a peace offering wouldn't hurt.

"Olive oil." My thumb rubbed the red streaks on his forehead. "Molly said it takes out permanent marker."

He'd released a shaky breath. "I'll try that…"

Muffled snoring from Hector broke into my reflections. I gave his shin a nudge and he started, his head thumping Betty's window.

"Sorry."

"S'okay," he mumbled, and went back to sleep.

Samuel's head lolled against burnt orange shag carpeting as we climbed a hill, Betty's weight and girth chugging against the incline. I studied the elegant, masculine lines of his face, noting an increased resemblance to Alonso as he aged. Samuel's father and Alonso had looked very similar, though I'd only seen a single picture of the man in Alonso's home office, taken near Boston Harbor when they were college students. Samuel's strong jaw and high hairline must belong to the English Caulfield side, as well as his blue eyes. I'd never seen a photograph of his biological mother, though Sofia had once told me she was insanely beautiful and came from a prominent Boston family. I wondered what other characteristics Samuel had inherited from her. My eyes traced the faded pink letters still scrawled across his forehead…

When I'd tuned in to *The After Hours Show* last Friday night, "I'M A NAUGHTY NACKEN" was still boldly written across his forehead.

I'd been at the farmhouse that evening, helping my mother label honey jars. We'd settled into the familiar routine, too caught up to even notice I reeked of sour milk. When ten thirty hit, we turned on the ancient television on the counter, adjusting the antenna to get a signal. We watched the program in comfortable silence, chuckling every now and then.

"So I've got to ask, this forehead art—'I'm a naughty nacken.' Is it a hint for a future book?"

The audience had laughed. So had Samuel, charming as ever. I'd noticed the host discreetly covered his nose with his hand.

"I think the Siren series has run its course. No, a friend wrote it as a joke. She believes I have an obsession with metaphorical water creatures. I suppose I've written about them for the past decade, so she may be onto something."

"I don't know, just a hunch she has?" (More audience laughter). "Your new book is *The Last Other*, being snatched up in bookstores across the country..."

They had talked about the typical topics: the book, the movie, and now the hand-holding picture and Mickey-gate. Samuel, of course, had a practiced, polished answer for everything—no, Neelie Nixie is not real. Yes, Indigo Kingsley is a wonderful woman and that's all he'd say about his personal life. No, a PETA advertisement wasn't on the horizon.

My mother had rubbed the back of her neck, leathered by the sun, and stared me down beneath unplucked eyebrows. "Did you write on your ex-husband's head?"

"I told him how to clean it off." I'd been a defensive ten-year-old again, conjuring ways to remain free from being grounded.

"He better keep his hands to himself."

"Mom!" Red had poured into my cheeks.

"I know, I know, you're an adult, you make your own calls." Her nose had twitched. "The forehead thing...is that why you smell like old sweaty socks now?"

"Sour milk. And yeah."

"You can't get rid of it?"

"I tried soaking in vinegar. It did a little good. But Samuel smells worse than me."

"Mm-hmm. Just be careful, Aspen Kaye."

"I will, Mom."

The next week passed swiftly. My photog stalkers drifted away. I even missed them—or at least having someone to greet me every time I left my house and returned. If they wanted to take a picture of me looking hot in my pencil skirts and fitted blouses (better than the tattered sweater they'd caught me in at the café), who was I to argue?

Molly was out most of the week, helping her sister with the new baby. I went over to Holly's several times to let them both get out of the house and run errands. Babies made me uncomfortable, but once Molly showed me how to change a diaper and bounce the little girl while maddening nursery rhyme songs looped, I managed well enough. After the third visit, I knew the difference between her "I've got poo in my diaper and I want it out now" wail and her "you better feed me or so help me I'll break your eardrums" wail.

Though he'd returned from LA, I didn't hear from Samuel at all, save for group emails making final plans for our skydiving and camping trip. Yet our pranks continued, becoming less sophisticated and more obnoxiously juvenile. He crammed a package of Life Savers into my showerhead, coating me in a sticky film. Of course, the only solution to this problem was to take a shower. I exacted revenge by covering the toilet seat in his bathroom with Icy-Hot. Danita said she heard the screams all the way from Jeff's Welding and Machine. He retaliated by changing all of my computer prompts, desktop scheme, and fonts to black-on-black. I panicked, thinking my hard drive had crashed until our webmaster, doubled over in laughter, showed me how to fix it. At least I didn't have a picture of us set as my wallpaper for Samuel to discover. I'd have to start securing my computer when I left for lunch.

Pranks aside, I knew Samuel played it low key while I considered his "friend's" proposal. I was pitching now and he waited for a signal.

Friends. The picture on his laptop hadn't been our wedding photo, or prom, or anything of a romantic vein. And honestly, if he'd asked for more, I wouldn't have handled it well. But friendship…more than anything I missed simply being in Samuel's presence without complications. Having him home for holidays, swapping emails or funny greeting cards, maybe even hitting Planet Bluegrass together. It was tempting, and if we could figure out how to do that again… But could we really?

Being his friend would also mean playing witness to his romances and eventual marriage, whether the woman was Caroline or someone entirely different. It would mean being there for his wedding, the birth of his children, and any other happiness that came calling. Was I strong enough for that? Was I *masochistic* enough for that?

But if I got my answers from him and moved past this…stuckness, I might have those things, too. Marriage. Children. Companionship. Love? And as my friend, he'd also play witness to *my* happiness.

It came down to this: was sharing each other's lives, and taking the joys that came with it, worth the heartache?

Could I risk it with Samuel Cabral?

I gave the opposite bench a once-over. Samuel yawned and stretched, then folded his arms across his chest and turned his back to Caroline. I wondered if he had even slept last night. I ignored him and dug into the pages of my book…

> **Neelie was gone. Gone over the cliff, dead in the void after battling the Other. Her body had grown frail under the siren's curse, but she'd fought fearlessly, driving back evil in the miserable night while her family struggled against the Others. Nora and Noel mourned for a time, and traveled on. But Nicodemus...Nicodemus snarled and tore into the Others. He would shred them, conquer them, demand vengeance with a fury for his lost love until they begged to be hurled over the same cliff that had taken Neelie. And once the Others were defeated, he knew what was left to him...he would fossilize, through and through...**

So Neelie was dead, then.

Tears trickled down my cheeks as I read. Odd, how I couldn't connect with Neelie at all, but Nicodemus moved me. I thought her death would have been incredibly disturbing to read, but I didn't see myself in her anymore. This Neelie had grown from the girl who couldn't drink a ladybug under the table to a daring, vicious, self-sacrificing young woman who'd defied Nicodemus, faced down the Others, and saved the people she loved. Nicodemus could love a woman like Neelie. He could die for her, and most likely would if his destructive mindset carried through to the end of the book.

"For the life of me, I can't figure out what scene in *Hitchhiker's Guide to the Galaxy* would have you in tears."

My eyes snapped up from my book and found Samuel's concerned face close to mine. I slammed it shut. Crap, if only I'd read *Hitchhiker's* after Angel gave it to me for Christmas. "You know… that sad part. Where he's in the galaxy…hitchhiking." I adjusted the dust jacket, making certain he couldn't see what was behind it.

Samuel's eyebrows arched in mock shock. "Are you reading something naughty, Kaye Trilby?"

"Of course not! I'm just...the book is really good, that's all."

His eyes softened. He pressed my knee and returned to his bench, leaving me alone. I was pretty sure he'd figured out what I was reading. I tucked the book away in my bag, too mortified to open it again.

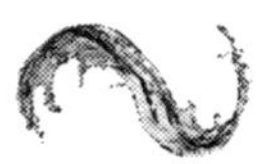

Angel's buddy's plane was a twin-engine, jet-propelled aircraft with the name "Surrealistic Pillow" painted across its body. Samuel and I grinned at each other, both catching the Jefferson Airplane reference. The plane accommodated our entire group. We were jumping at fourteen-thousand feet above ground, which would give us roughly one minute of free fall, then another five minutes of hang time.

The wedding party huddled together in the tight metal space, taking turns peering out of the circular windows as the plane leisurely circled, knees bouncing, running through dive instructions again for the newbies. All except Caroline, who was tucked in a corner beside Samuel, awkwardly crossing her heeled ankles and avoiding dirt smudges on her D&G purse—so incongruous to the warm-ups the rest of us wore. Her face was pure fury.

"Are you sure you don't want to dive, Caroline?" I shouted over the roar of the engines. "You still could if you lose the heels."

Her lips pressed tightly. "Why would I risk my life so carelessly?" She shot a glare at Samuel.

Samuel fiddled with an expensive-looking steel watch on his wrist, ignoring her. I scooted over, settling next to him.

"That's nice." I tapped the watch face. "Better take it off before the dive, though."

"Oh, yeah. Birthday present from Caro." She'd given him a frickin' Rolex for his birthday. Ugh, I felt horrible. He unstrapped it and handed it to her with a smile. She snatched it from him, tucking it into her purse for safe-keeping.

"I can't believe I forgot your birthday."

He leaned in close, his voice all but muffled by the plane. "And here I thought the donation to the guinea pig charity was your gift to me."

"I'm so, so sorry."

Samuel laughed, the sound warm on my good ear. He settled against the metal wall. "Kaye, really, don't worry. We've barely spoken for years. I don't expect anything from you for my birthday."

I felt like such a cad, if women could be cads. Feeling guilty took the fun out of pranking.

"Maybe I can buy you a belated birthday drink at Oskar Blues. I'm of-age, now." I grinned. The last time Samuel and I had been to a bar, he had to buy my drink for me.

Caroline stared down her prim nose. Samuel ruffled his hair, hesitating. "I'd take you up on it, but I don't drink anymore."

"Really? Since when?"

"Since…a while."

I remembered the public intox charge. Geez, I felt like even more of an idiot. "Oh."

"Yeah," Angel piped up, "we tried to get ol' Sammy plowed last night, but he was having none of it. Ended up cleaning the apartment when the rest of us passed out on the floor."

Danita planted a swift elbow in Angel's ribs. "At least one of you had the sense not to show up for our camping trip hung over. If you like the boys' company that much, then me and my girls are taking the Campervan tonight. You *pendejos* can crash outside."

A chorus of male groans and glares were directed at Angel for opening his big mouth, even though it was painfully obvious they hadn't followed Dani's "get some sleep" suggestion (which was really more of a threat, minus an "or else").

"Okay, skygods. We'll be over the drop zone in ten minutes," the pilot called back to us. "Certified divers, you're good to go. Non-certs, buckle up with the certs for a tandem dive."

"I call Cassady," Molly said quickly.

"Angel, strap me up good," Dani grinned. Angel began to cough, his eyes bugging out of his head. He jumped up from the floor in record time.

Samuel searched the remaining certified divers, probably trying to decide with whom would be the least uncomfortable to get up-close-and-personal. His gaze fell to me, then down to his hands.

Oh, what the heck. It's just skydiving. I offered him a hand up. "Come on, Cabral. Let's jump out of a plane together." I slipped goggles over my eyes then tossed him a pair, showing him how to tighten them. He stared at me, dumbstruck, as I secured our parachute on my back.

"Seriously?"

"Yeah, unless you want to snuggle up with Hector."

Hector waggled his eyebrows at Samuel as he zipped up his windbreaker.

Samuel chuckled. "I'll take my chances with you, Trilby. Just show me what I need to do." Leaning over Caroline, he whispered something in her ear. She scowled up at him, jerking her shoulder away from his hand. His face clouded, but he said nothing.

Now I was in my element. I walked him through the dive steps, explaining that I would do the steering and deploy the canopy. The only thing he had to worry about was paying attention to me and kicking his feet up when we neared the ground so I could keep us from crash-landing. He listened intently, nodding along as I adjusted the tandem system, harnessing us together. All the while, I felt Caroline's hydra glare on my back. She'd probably had me pegged as a spineless sea sponge.

Samuel strapped on his helmet, then looked pointedly at my bare head.

"Don't worry, my helmet is right there. I'm not that big of a risk-taker."

"Ah." But he barely relaxed, even as I tucked my thick curls under a helmet. I pushed on his shoulders.

"Crouch down a little, you're a foot taller than me. I don't want to hang from your back like a rag doll."

"Yes, ma'am." His lips twisted into a wry grin as he forgot Caroline's fury.

Hector opened the plane hatch, and one after the other, our friends tumbled into the roaring wind with wild cries.

We made our way to the hatch. "I can't believe you're so nonchalant about free-falling at one-hundred-miles per hour from a plane!" Samuel's face was inches from mine, our clothing whipping both of us mercilessly.

My eyes met his in challenge. "You aren't scared, are you? We don't *have* to do this."

"Never."

"On three, then. One!"

He braced his arms against the frame, trying not to peer down.

"Two!"

I waved goodbye to Caroline.

"Three!"

I wrapped my arms around his waist, tightly pulling him to me, praying I'd secured everything properly. He covered my arms with his. And then a wall of cold wind hit us, and blinding light. We spiraled out of the plane into nothing but sky. My stomach flew to my throat, and then settled back down as my body adjusted. I flung my arms out, squealing with exhilaration while we coasted across a canvas of endless blue. Sam whooped and hollered with me, our limbs tangling, cutting through air. I turned and steered us closer to the others.

"Tuck into a ball!" He did, and we somersaulted once…twice… tumbling in circles as if gravity were nothing more than a silly myth someone invented to keep us close to the ground. Pure laughter poured from our mouths. Our clothes snapped as wind streamed over and around us, stinging our faces, enveloping our bodies.

Danita and Angel joined us. She kicked up, and I grabbed her feet, laughing. Santiago swept below us and linked onto Sam's feet, causing him to jolt in surprise.

Farther down, I saw Hector's parachute fly open in a balloon of red and white. Molly and Cassady's chute opened, yanking them up from their free fall.

Angel checked his digital altimeter and gave us the thumbs up—it was time. Waving goodbye to Dani and Angel, I steered us away and found the cord.

"Ready?" I shouted into Samuel's ear.

He nodded.

"Brace yourself!" I pulled the cord.

Our parachute flew behind us in a cascade of blue and white and opened, halting our wild tumble with a jarring tug.

Our bodies dangled like wind chimes as we drifted down…down… through the sky. Golden platte and basin spanned to the east, and jagged gray mountain to the west, vanishing in a panorama of bright haze. We hovered above frothy strands of clouds, the earth arching over the horizon in a crazy-quilt of nature and culture.

Sam reached back and pulled my arms around him. He laced his fingers with mine. I rested my chin on his shoulder, reveling in the adrenaline coursing through my veins. My entire body trembled, head to toe. His hands shook, too.

Diving tandem with Samuel…sharing a piece of my new life…there were no words. We would reach the ground all too soon. Even now, roads snaked below us, growing bigger and bigger, until we saw the color of the cars traveling up and down highways. Evergreen forests were no longer dark blobs, but thousands of trees. Rooftops grew details—chimneys, slats, eaves. But in the bit of time we still had left, I enjoyed him. Breathed him in. Felt his body expand, back rumble as he laughed against me, flush with every single gust of wind, ping of light, twinge of muscle we experienced together.

Hector coasted to the landing strip.

Then Molly and Cassady.

Santiago.

Danita and Angel.

"Legs up." I reluctantly untwined my hands from his and wrapped them around the parachute cords, steering us to earth. Then my toes brushed along grass, dragging us to a halt. Samuel swung his long legs down and grabbed me beneath my knees to keep us from toppling backward. Our parachute fluttered to the ground behind us and I unhooked the chute, yelping as he plowed toward the others with me on his back, replete with joy. I flung my arms around his neck.

"Amazing! Kaye, that was just…"

"Amazing?"

"Smile!" Molly snapped a picture.

My hands quaked so badly, I was barely able to unbuckle my diving harnesses and hop down from his back. We joined the rest of the group, high-fiving each other, chattering like a colony of flying squirrels and shedding our gear as we waited for the plane to land.

Hector pushed past Samuel and threw a tattooed arm around my shoulders. Samuel hurled daggers at my friend.

"Kaye, did you try the somersaulting this time?"

"Yup!" I said proudly, nodding to Samuel. "Cabral here's already an old pro after one dive. Didn't bawl or scream at all!"

An oh-so-familiar embarrassed grin spread across Samuel's face and he ducked his head like a thirteen-year-old kid.

At last, the plane swooped in and crawled to a stop.

The minute the hatch opened, my diving buzz fell flat. Caroline elegantly climbed out as if she stepped onto a red carpet rather than an oil-spattered tarmac. She strode purposefully toward us, her eyes fixed upon her prize.

"Welcome back." She gazed up at him through lashes so long, they *had* to tickle her eyebrows. Reaching into her purse, she pulled out his watch and returned it. He slipped it into his pocket. Then she stood on tip-toes and pressed her freshly-glossed lips to his.

I hated her. Hated her with the fiery passion of a thousand molten Rolex watches. My stomach lurched back to my throat the minute his lips touched hers. The way she was with Samuel…it was as if she owned him, rather than loved him. I turned away, relinquishing him to her, planning to catch up with Hector and the others. Caroline's throaty laugh followed on my heels. Somewhere behind me, they crossed paths with my pride as it tucked tail and flew in the opposite direction.

Perhaps I was still riding the high from our dive after all. Maybe there was no way I could be Samuel's friend again, watching from the side as that hound sank her teeth into him. Or maybe Jaime Guzman was rubbing off on me. I imagined her in my corner of the boxing ring, loosening my shoulders and mopping my forehead with a towel, screaming at me to "get back in the match and hook that bitch like you have balls, you pantywaist." And dang it, I wasn't down for the count, yet.

I turned around and waited for them to catch up, then looped my arm through Samuel's when they did. He started, too stunned to notice my miniscule glance in Caroline's direction. Caro, however, didn't miss it.

Her lips thinned and her eyes blazed as if she tried to conjure lightning bolts to zap me down. I felt Samuel's body go rigid, ready to hold either one of us at bay if we started swiping at each other. He picked up his pace, steering us toward the Campervan.

Later, when Samuel and the guys returned our equipment and the gals ran for the restroom, she rounded on me.

"I noticed your girlfriend didn't make an appearance today."

I dug through my backpack for my water bottle.

She pressed on. "But Angel's brother—the one with the tattoos—he seems awfully fond of you. I wonder how he feels about Samuel being back in town."

I took a swig of water and wiped my lips with my sleeve. "What's your point?"

"My point is, you are a devious little flirt, and it's going to hurt a lot of people. Do you have a decent bone in your body?"

Play it cool, Kaye. "Look, Samuel and I go way back—we're talking training wheels back. So if our shared history bothers you, then maybe you're with the wrong man."

Something tender, raw, flitted across her exquisite Latina features. Then her face hardened and she was all Caroline Ortega, publicist extraordinaire. She pointed a polished nail at me. "You're the one behind that ridiculous guinea pig charity, aren't you? And that drag photo I had to squelch. Oh, and the hand-holding stunt at the café."

"Nope, the hand-holding was all Samuel." I thought it might come to blows, but she never touched me.

Her white teeth gleamed as she leaned forward. "It's okay. I can tolerate these little stunts for another week. Because when it comes down to it, the Aspen Kaye Trilby he really cares about is a thirteen-year-old kid with a backwoods name in his yearbook."

Yeah, that did it. "Nose-jobs and pretention don't fly here in the backwoods, princess. If you think for *one minute* I'm going to stand back and watch my friend with—"

Before I could finish the sentiment Samuel slid the door open, and I witnessed her face shift from angry harpy to beatific angel in a split second. I shuddered. He warily eyed both of us, probably relieved to see we hadn't dragged each other out of the Campervan by the hair. *Give it time...give it time.*

As we rattled along to Rocky Mountain National Park, I wondered if he knew just how manipulative Caroline Ortega was.

I also wondered if there wasn't the tiniest bit of truth to what she'd said.

Chapter 14
AGGRESSIVE SWIMMING

When river conditions are treacherous, paddlers should concentrate all energy on getting to safety.

"Friend Behind the Forehead?"

The tabloid headline flashed neon arrows at me from the magazine rack, innocently nestled among a rainbow of candy bars and packs of gum. On the front page was a picture from Samuel's *After Hours Show* appearance. "I'm a Naughty Nacken" was Sharpied across his forehead, and he grinned like a fool on the red guest couch.

Glancing over my shoulder to make sure Samuel and Caroline weren't nearby, I pulled the magazine from the rack and flipped it open. Nerves rippled through me as I expected to see my name printed in bold, black letters. I scanned the article:

> ...Whether Cabral's stunt was harmless payback or a declaration of something more, one thing is for certain—long-time friend and agent Caroline Ortega is the wielder of the marker.
>
> "Oh, it was definitely Caro," an unnamed source close to the duo asserted. "She and Samuel have that kind of relationship. They're very good together."

Unnamed source my lily-white tail. That statement came from Caroline, I'd bet my life on it. I read on, fingers crushing the magazine edges:

> ...Since rumors about the Kingsley-Cabral split first began to circulate, Ortega's name has repeatedly surfaced as a possible romantic interest to Cabral. "Samuel and Caro go way back."

"Are you going to pay for that?" The clerk glared at me from beneath a ball cap with a cartoon chicken on the front.

I added the crumpled magazine to my iced tea and bag of preservative-packed popcorn that would make my mother cringe, swiped my card, and stuffed it under my arm before anyone saw. When I passed the trash can in the parking lot, I disposed of the disgusting piece of print. The vile thing belonged in the landfill.

"Problems with the magazine?" Hector flung an arm over my shoulders as we headed back to the Campervan.

"Nothing that hasn't been right under my nose for a few years now. But I'm beginning to realize just how skewed the truth can become when someone is intentionally skewing it."

Hector chuckled, shaking me. "You've secretly read the tabloids for ages, haven't you, Kaye? I bet you have one of those creepy hidden rooms covered in magazine clippings. Any day now, the FBI's going to bust you." He flicked a pair of shades up from his eyes and winked at me.

"Shut up."

Hector ruffled my hair, earning a yelp from me. "Go get 'em, tiger."

I held my head high and climbed into the vehicle that would carry me to an impending night of hell on earth. On the bright side, there'd be marshmallows for the fire and brimstone.

Our campsite was a grassy clearing on the upper-east side of the Rocky Mountain National Park, surrounded by lush forest, hiking trails, and a creek so clear, an array of rocks and shells was visible along its bed. We were isolated. Our nearest neighbor was a half-mile up the road at a larger campground boasting a bath house. Our grounds had a parking spot for the camper, a rustic rock pit for a fire, and nothing more. Danita had, yet again, reminded me to pack toilet paper.

It was already four thirty when we arrived. Setting up camp was easy with nine pairs of hands. Cassady had Betty's canopy unfurled in no time, and we went to work pitching tents, unfolding lawn chairs, and finding dry wood for our campfire. The minute we finished, the boys grabbed a sports equipment bag like they'd just been released to grade school recess to "hit some balls outta the park."

Danita hopped into the game. Caroline dragged a blanket over to their impromptu ball field, along with a thick manuscript that was probably work-related. Molly and I opted to keep the fire stoked and babysit the foil pockets of potatoes, mushrooms, peppers, onions, chicken, and loads of butter we'd thrown together for dinner.

I leaned back in my lawn chair, enjoying the last bit of sunshine before it would disappear over the trees.

Molly fanned herself. "My oh my, we have a fine-looking set of friends, ya know?"

I followed her gaze to the field, seeing what she saw. Santiago peeled off his T-shirt. Even from far away, I could tell he was giving us a show—flexing his biceps, stretching his torso. He wasn't the only one. Hector pulled his T-shirt up and wiped his face, revealing a nice set of abs. Hmm, I'd never noticed those before. Angel hadn't even bothered with a shirt. He swept Danita into a sweaty embrace, guffawing as she dug her hands into his chest and pushed him away with a grimace. Even Cassady had an arm lazily resting against his abs, shorts hanging low on his hips.

"Yeah, I guess they're pretty hot. It's weird to look at them that way, though—kind of like checking out your brothers."

"Oh please, Kaye, you'd have to be a freaking blind bat not to notice those men are gorgeous! And my gosh, how is Hector still single?"

I laughed, even though I'd just wondered the same thing. "Fine, yes, they are gorgeous. I feel like 'Boys of Summer' should be blaring somewhere over our heads."

I refused to look for Samuel. I was scared stiff I'd find him flirting with his Manhattan hussy, beaming at her from under his ball cap the way he used to with me when I attended his ball games, from little league to varsity. Each game, I'd sit above the third base line near the home team dugout so he could easily find me, even from left field. When the team trotted in from the diamond to bat, he'd give me a quick wave, or a wink, or even just a smile, no matter how crappy the inning had been.

Cassady bent over, slowly picking something up from the ground, flashing his tail feathers like a strip-teasing peacock. I laughed, but it became too much for Molly.

"You can manage without me, can't you?" she twittered, jogging toward Cassady without waiting for an answer.

Sure, I could manage. What was there to watching food cook? Piece of cake…

I checked the packets of chicken and veggies.

Kept myself from glancing at Samuel's trim torso as it twisted when he swung at the ball.

Tossed another log on the fire.

Never once checked out Samuel's muscled legs from years of running as he stood on the sidelines, hands on hips, waiting for his next up-to-bat.

Dug a lemonade out of the cooler and pressed it to my forehead. Even in a tank top and shorts, it was awfully hot outside.

Didn't even ogle the tell-tale front of his black mesh shorts as he took his turn…pitching. *Crap, he caught me that time!* I turned away before my face flamed red as a firecracker.

Danita snorted behind me. I hadn't even noticed she'd left the game and returned to the campfire, I'd been so busy *not* paying attention.

"Kaye, honey, quit sexing up my brother with your eyeballs from a distance and join the fun. I swear, every time you turn your back he's gaping at you, anyway."

I snorted rather unattractively. "Actually, everyone's gaping at me. It's suppertime, they are hungry men, and this is where the food's cooking. Need I say more?"

"I *wish* you'd meant that as a euphemism," she sighed. "You are a hopeless, hopeless girl. Apparently I either have to kidnap you or get you tipsy in order for you to take any initiative at all."

"Please don't. The food is ready, anyway. Should I go get the others?"

"Allow me." Dani put her fingers to her lips and loosed the most ear-shattering, shrill whistle I'd ever heard. The game stopped. She waved the crew over to the campfire, taking charge. "Go hang out with your boy, Kaye. Cut loose, have fun. Relax." She leaned in, pecked my cheek and whispered, "Kick that cliff-hucking floozy back to the Atlantic Seaboard."

I grinned and saluted. Grabbing two paper plates, I made my way to Samuel's side—the one not occupied by Caroline.

"Good game, Cabral." I tossed him a plate.

"Sorry you missed it, Trilby. First time ever, I think."

"Hey, I watched from the back of the bleachers." I nudged his body, then wiped my arm, grimacing. "I forgot you sweat like a cold beer on a hot day."

"You never minded before." Wrapping his arm around me, he pulled me to his side and plunked his damp, smelly ball cap on my head. I screeched, but left it where it was.

Caroline mumbled something about regressing to junior high. *That's right, woman. I was there every...single...game.*

I dished up my plate.

"Hand sanitizer." Molly traded my plate for a bottle as we went through the line. I pumped sanitizer into my hand and turned around to offer it to Samuel, only to find Hector behind me.

"Hey, Kaye, I've got two lawn chairs all set up with our names on them. Whaddya want to drink?"

I peered over Hector's shoulder, looking for Samuel. He and Caroline spread a blanket across the ground and dropped their things. Jealousy churned as he handed her one of the drinks he'd pulled from the cooler. Pushing the ball cap off of my head, I tossed the dirty, stinky thing in the grass next to the tent.

"Kaye? Drink?" Poor Hector grinned at me, pulling my focus back to him.

"Ah...a lemonade. Thanks, Hector."

Hector retrieved it as I claimed one of his lawn chairs. He brushed the cold lemonade across my arm, making me jump.

"Did I scare you, *mamacita?*" Hector playfully winked.

"Kaye doesn't like it when sweaty beverages touch her arm," Samuel retorted from the blanket, not even glancing up as he pushed his food around with his plastic fork.

I ignored his jibe and took the drink from Hector with a smile.

The baseball talk continued for a good half hour as we settled under Betty's canopy, devouring our food. Angel and Samuel swapped glory days stories about the state championship team. We laughed when Angel did his free-wheeling impression of my dad.

"Hey, Cabral, do you remember when Coach had you run endurance sprints for three practices straight because you had Kaye out after curfew? It was the only time anyone ever missed post-practice chakra cleansing."

"Yes." Samuel glanced at me from the blanket where he reclined, long legs crossed, elbows propping him up. "I thought my legs were going to fall off. Never had her out past curfew again."

I frowned thoughtfully. "I don't remember that."

"I never told you about it."

"Why not?"

A sheepish grin spread over his face. "Because you'd have gotten angry with Tom and ended up grounded for three weeks instead of two." Dad's version of grounding was forced meditation in lieu of date nights.

Angel chortled. "And Cabral was a pissy *perrita* whenever you were grounded. It's like he was grounded, too. He was a helluva hitter, though, when he was pissy. Do you remember that grand slam he hit out of the ball park at the state championship game? Man!"

Samuel stiffened, his jaw grinding. His eyes darted to mine. No one except Danita knew that the state championship was when he promised to marry me.

"I didn't know you were a star hitter." Caro peered up at Samuel with shining eyes. I looked away as she snuggled closer to him on the blanket, leaning against his torso.

"Do I ever remember that hit!" Molly chimed in. "I still have the hearing loss as a souvenir, after Kaye shrieked in my ear."

I tapped my left ear and winked. "So we match."

"That was one of the best days of my life, pummeling Florence." Angel ground his fist into his palm. "And then the stands rushed the field after we won? It's a good thing the season was over, Cabral, or Kaye would have put you on the DL when she tackled you."

Samuel shifted Caroline and stood up, stretching his legs. My arms wrapped around my knees as I too grew uncomfortable. Danita's sharp gaze swept over me, then Samuel.

"Hey, Angel," she interrupted, "do you remember when we were fifteen and borrowed your mom's minivan? You were so freaked out to be driving without a license. I bet she never found out about that…"

As the conversation turned from baseball to other memories (and thirty-year-old Angel begged Danita not to tell his mom about the minivan), Samuel visibly relaxed. I breathed out, not even realizing I'd held air in. After that, the night was an easy, laid back jaunt through Angel and Danita's years together. When the sun set, we stirred the campfire to life and situated logs and blankets around the fresh pile of lumber, enjoying the orange glow and flickering shadows.

A web of stars grew stark and bright against the black sky. They were so clear, up in the mountains, in the crisp air. Pine leaves rustled. Crickets began their nightly chorus. I kind of missed the little guys at home.

Hector skewered several marshmallows and sat down next to me, holding them over the flames. I rested my head on his shoulder. I could enjoy this for years to come—having all of my loved ones together, basking in each other's presence. For a while, I was even able to forget Caroline was next to Samuel, pressed against him, stealing his warmth in the cool air.

Once the fire fully crackled, Angel and Danita slipped away for a bit of alone time. When they returned, I was surprised to see them holding Samuel's old Gibson guitars—the Spanish and acoustic. Nerves fluttered in my stomach. Dani's mouth twisted in mischief.

"Now, Kaye, I know you're going to argue, but just remember that this is *my* bachelorette party. And since you didn't get me a stripper, you owe me." Dani pouted and handed me a guitar. Angel did the same (minus the pouting), handing a wary Samuel the other Gibson.

"You…you want us to play?"

Danita rolled her eyes. "No, Kaye, I want you to strip with a guitar. I've got a stack of dollar bills with your name on them."

Samuel lifted a questioning eyebrow at me.

I shrugged and began to strum the guitar, twisting the pegs until it was in tune. Leaving the blanket to Caroline, Samuel crossed the campfire circle and stood in front of Hector, waiting for him to move. But Hector just stared at him, not even twitching a knee cap. Finally, Samuel dropped onto the ground next to my feet and tuned his guitar.

What the heck was that?

I knew Samuel's animosity toward Hector started a long time ago, when I'd spent Saturday afternoons skiing with Hector and our dads instead of lazing about with him. Hector had actually been my first date ever, not Samuel, which upped their animosity. And of course, Hector still wanted to pulverize Samuel for leaving me to move to New York.

"Any requests?"

Molly clapped her hands. "*Ruby Tuesday*. I know you guys remember that one."

"Mine first." Danita smugly tucked herself under Angel's massive arm, pleased at how easily we'd folded. "I happen to have a very special request." *Of course you do, sneaky Danita.* "You know what I want to hear, Kaye-bear, Sam."

I'm pretty sure my face went white as blood drained from my freckled cheeks. "No. Oh no, Dani. My Spanish is really rusty."

"Your Spanish is better than mine. Come on, you know it's my favorite. This is for Angel and me. We're getting married."

You have got to be kidding me. First the baseball championship, now the guitars? If I didn't know better, I'd have thought my friends were conspiring to send me off the deep end. I looked to Samuel for help.

He merely shrugged. "It's just a song, Kaye. You know, for fun?"

"Now I really want to hear whatever it is you don't want to sing." Hector grinned.

"Shut it, Hector." I tried a new tactic. "Let's do our acoustic version of *Matador*. That's a good one."

Molly groaned. "You guys just sing the song, already! It was the last song of Soda Stereo's farewell concert—if they could do it, so can you."

Cassady whispered something in Molly's ear, and she whispered back. He nodded. "Just think of it like this, Kaye. *De Música Ligera* was a defining recording of Latin Rock. It's not just a song, it's a piece of history."

"And we're all about defining moments in history," Angel added.

Samuel offered me a speculative smile. "It's pure musical poetry, Kaye. The pain of farewell, the shackles of *amor*."

"You people are pushier than a turnstile, you know that?" I was beat. My forehead fell over my guitar with a thump. "Fine. Danita, Angel—this is for you, so you both better sing loud and clear. Play it again, Sam."

His beautiful smile grew bigger as he started us off. The first stanza was awkward, like I'd expected. Jamming with Samuel again, especially to a song which encapsulated an innocent era for both of us, was difficult. But then my gaze drifted to Danita. Her eyes were bright as she watched Angel. Her face was rife with love as she swayed with him to the flourishes of Samuel's Spanish guitar. He laughed down at her, tucked a strand of black hair behind her ear. I put all of my anxieties and heartaches aside and simply focused on both of them, sharing their happiness. I was glad—no, ecstatic—they got their fairy tale.

Samuel nudged my calf with his elbow, reminding me about our added key change. I nudged him back with my foot; of course I remembered the key change. He chuckled his way into the next stanza.

Once the song ended and everyone belted "*Gracias totales*," we dove into Molly's request. Then we strummed through everything our fingers could handle. We even played around with a couple of The Twiggies' songs, something we'd never tackled together.

Guitar sing-alongs on our camping trips underscored the melding ethoses in our circle of friends. Holidays, mealtimes, weddings, and funerals carried the more obvious differences. The Mexican-Americans peppered their words with colorful Spanish interjections learned from their parents and neighborhood children. Then there were the songs we grew up singing in car rides and before bedtime. It was only logical that the vast amounts of time we spent in each other's company gave rise to the oddest, mish-mashed cultural stew—music playlists included.

All the while, Caroline's eyes burned holes into my guitar neck. It didn't unnerve me. I was comfortable here, with a guitar in my hands, next to Samuel, surrounded by our friends, and there was nothing she could do or say to take me out of my element.

"Oh! Did I mention that Samuel's taking me to Rocky Mountain Folks this year?"

And...there goes my confidence. I strummed a chord, its somber, disjointed tone hanging in the air as everyone fell silent along with it.

"Nothing's set in stone, Caro," Samuel said quietly. I knew that voice. He was pissed. He shuffled his guitar, standing up. "And August is a long way off."

"It's only two months, actually." Poor Santiago was a little behind. "When you think about it, that's not really a long time."

Don't cry...don't cry... Every muscle in my face tightened to keep those tears from welling, and I was grateful for the cloak of night. Molly slapped her knees and hopped up to diffuse the tension.

"Okay, girlies! I think it's bachelorette time! Kiss the boys goodnight, brush those teeth, and be in the VW in ten minutes!"

"'Night, Hector." I stood on tip-toes to peck his cheek. "Lay off the poker and cigars."

"You too. You can't bluff to save your life." He pulled me into a bear hug, whispered. "Don't let Cabral and his woman trip you up, 'kay *mamacita?* Just enjoy the night." He left to help Cassady smother what was left of the campfire.

"Kaye." Samuel touched my arm.

I stepped away from him, stuffing the Gibson back in its case and shoving my arms through my fleece.

"Please talk to me."

I gave him a wide berth as I picked up the leftover marshmallows and angrily grabbed my blanket.

"Oh, so now you're giving me the silent treatment?" he snapped, irritation evident.

I shot him a fierce warning glare. "It's none of my business where you take your girlfriend, Samuel. In fact, I think I'm the one who suggested you show her Planet Bluegrass, in the first place. Just go to bed."

"Fine. Goodnight, Kaye." He backed off, running aggravated hands through his hair. Stalking over to the tent, he grabbed a towel from his duffel bag and made his way into the woods, toward the creek. I watched with jealous eyes as Caroline followed.

Danita tugged on my arm, pulling me away before I could run after them. "Come on, Samuel's a big boy. He can handle himself."

"I know." I peered at Danita's concerned expression and guilt crept in. *Geez, Kaye, could you be a worse maid of honor?* I sucked it up and slathered on the biggest grin my face would allow. "Anyway, this night isn't about them. It's about you, my knock-out hot friend who is getting married to the sexiest pilot this side of the Rockies." I climbed into the Campervan, Danita following behind. "And right now, we are going to give you the best, and only, semi-bachelorette party of your life."

"Come on, Kaye! Just do one more."

"Molly, no. I've had two already and so help me, I am staying as sober as possible."

She pouted and poured another round of raspberry liqueur and Bailey's. Sweet heaven, those things were tasty, but I held my ground.

With Samuel just yards away on the other side of the campground, I was not going to risk another drunken email-type incident on a much grander, in-person scale.

"Hit me, baby." Danita held out her glass. She, on the other hand, imbibed as much as possible. We'd already opened naughty lingerie, played a couple of obligatory penis games, and moved on to spilling our guts (or getting Danita to spill, anyway) about our love lives. She adjusted the red lace bra she wore on the outside of her pajamas.

I patted her cheek. "You are going to be such a sexy, beautiful bride."

"Damn straight!" Molly raised her shot glass. "Here's to scoring the second hottest man to ever come from Lyons."

Danita frowned. "Wait, who's number one?"

"Sorry, Danita. Your brother's Mr. January on the Lyons Hotties calendar."

Dang. I'd nearly stopped dwelling on the fact that Caroline was still outside, in the dark, with Samuel.

An hour later, Caroline clattered through the door, her face stony. The rest of us exchanged cagey looks. Muttering a hello, she grabbed her bag and headed to the back of the van to get ready for bed. I ignored her and passed the snack mix bowl to Danita. Eventually, the Afghan hound emerged, sleek in green satin pajamas, and tentatively curled onto the bench next to Molly. Molly gave her a friendly little smile and handed her a shot. She declined, her cool mask firmly in place.

I wondered if Samuel had asked her to get to know his sister better, and was certain she'd put a damper on the night. But before long, even Caro quietly laughed as each of us took turns swapping stories about Danita and Angel's long, tumultuous, entertaining romance. The many years Angel spent firmly entrenched in Dani's friend corner. The high school boyfriend Dani had who perpetually smelled like peanut butter. And finally, Angel taking electric hedge clippers to his car, just so he could ask Dani to weld it. She'd invited him to Sunday dinner after that.

A couple of times during the night, Angel's or Hector's face popped up in the window, followed by faint scuffling. Then, five minutes later, scratching sounds moved along the outside of the VW, as if a pack of raccoons scaled its retro trim. Santiago's pasty cheeks (the other cheeks) even made a one-night-only appearance, but the act was cut short when Cassady bellowed, "You gunnars better get offa Betty and make as scarce as rocking horse shit!"

After that, it was quiet.

Once the boys retreated, the energy was zapped from the small camper. We toppled over, one by one. Danita was the first out, still in the red bra. Then Caroline crawled into the back of the Campervan and drew the beaded curtain, leaving just Molly and me. After another fifteen minutes of soft chatting, we curled into our sleeping bags, her head resting on my feet.

I closed my eyes, but did not sleep. Rather, I lay awake, hands behind my head. I listened to the distant bubbling of the creek. Cicadas and crickets. And the quiet, pensive strumming of a Spanish guitar.

It was eight in the morning when I stumbled out of Betty with bleary eyes and aching joints, my hair a blond haystack. Samuel and Caroline were the only two awake, the others dead to the world and probably would be for another hour. Grabbing my toothbrush, washcloth, and water bottle, I snuck around the back of the Campervan and cleaned as best as I could. Smoothing my hair into a haphazard bun, I unfolded a lawn chair across from the pair.

My anger had abated after a good night's sleep, and I couldn't help but think that both of us had been overly sensitive because of the late hour. I sought Samuel's gaze, shooting him an apologetic look.

He smiled back and mouthed, "I'm sorry."

I nodded, settled into my lawn chair and let the cool morning air wake me. Rubbing sleep from my eyes, I studied both Samuel and Caroline more closely. He had gone for his early morning run, despite our late night. She, however, had forgone careful makeup and posh clothing for an oversized, slate-gray warm-up, glowing skin and knit cap. Caro was one of those "I'm pretty and I don't even have to try" people. I struggled to figure out why she owned such ill-sized clothing when it hit me. It wasn't hers.

It was Samuel's.

Breakfast didn't seem appetizing, now.

Caroline handed me a mug of coffee. For a moment I warred with myself, very aware of Samuel's eyes on me. And I needed coffee, desperately. I took the mug from her manicured hands, muttering a thank you.

She nodded. I closed my eyes, focusing on the strong, woodsy fragrance and not on the couple across from me.

"So, Kaye, you and Samuel have played guitar for a long time, I understand." Her voice was much too shrill for morning conversation.

"Yes, that's right." Keep the answers short, polite.

"You've been playing since you were what—eight?"

I sighed, setting my mug of coffee down. Woman couldn't just let me enjoy my coffee in peace. "No, I believe I was nine."

"I'm pretty sure you were eight, because you decided you wanted to play guitars when you went to your first Rocky Mountain Folks, correct? And you learned on a pink guitar? You were eight and Samuel was eleven."

"No, I believe I was *nine*."

Samuel put a hand over Caroline's, probably a silent warning that I was about to rip out her throat. She ignored him and gave me a patronizing smile.

"You were eight, and you decided to play after seeing the Tripping Maggies."

"I was *nine*. The band was the Tripping *Marys*. And my *banjo* was pink, not my guitar." I narrowed my eyes at Samuel. Why had he told Caro all this personal stuff about me?

He rose from his chair, trying to diffuse the bomb. "Caro, let's walk over to the crick?"

She shook her head, beaming in triumph. I braced myself for her kill. "I can't wait for Planet Bluegrass."

The tears I'd repressed last night with Herculean strength tromped back to my eyes and refused to budge. My temper warred with immense gloom. I set my coffee mug on the grass, pressed fingers to my eyes, and took a deep breath. *Relax, Kaye, relax. If you fling the coffee in her face, that's assault. You don't need a criminal record.*

"No, I was *nine* when I started playing the guitar. What Samuel has probably failed to mention to you in his detailed account of my life is that my birthday is in September—just weeks after Rocky Mountain Folks. So the next time you decide to flaunt your in-depth knowledge of my childhood, be sure you have your facts straight."

I stared at my toes, unable to watch their reaction to my outburst. Jerking on my sneakers, I sought refuge on the wooded trail to clear my head.

How *dare* he betray me like that? But betrayal was nothing new for Samuel, was it? My tender memories had been exposed, violated by this wretched woman. How much did she actually know about me? How much had Samuel told her?

I shoved my way through the trees and wandered off the path, not caring the low-lying bushes and bramble scraped and snagged my clothing and ankles.

He was taking her to Planet Bluegrass, this unworthy, manipulative person who'd insinuated herself not only into his present life, but our past. Our Planet Bluegrass. I swiped angry tears from my eyes before they tumbled over. I knew I'd suggested he take her to Planet Bluegrass when she attended Danita's shower, but I didn't think he'd actually do it.

Somewhere behind me, trees and bushes rustled loudly as a second set of feet trampled through them, and I heard Samuel call my name. Crap, he'd followed me. I veered to the right in a last ditch effort to lose him, but he already had me.

"Kaye, will you slow down instead of running away from me?" He caught my elbow. I yanked it away.

"I'm not the one who ran, Samuel." I whisked away tears with grimy hands.

"You're running now. For once in your life will you just yell at me, or hit me, or show me how infuriated you are instead of hiding it?"

I rounded on him, jabbing my finger in his chest. "Fine! You want to be friends, Samuel? Well let's get one thing straight, right here, right now, you self-righteous *cabrón*. Don't you ever tell that woman anything about me again, do you understand?"

"Kaye, she's my editor, my publicist…It's not like she hasn't been hearing about you for years."

"I don't care if she's the fricking CIA. Starting now, not a word to her about me, or we're done. I'll not have her flinging personal details in my face like the pink banjo or Planet Bluegrass, even if you consider them trivial."

He shook his head. "They aren't trivial at all."

"Not a word to her."

"Kaye, I'm a writer—"

I turned to leave.

He caught my elbow again. "Wait! What if I had your permission first? Let's say you read what I write and sign off on it before I send it to Caroline for editing. Anything you don't want her to read, I won't give to her. How would you feel about that?"

I started to scoff at the idea, but paused. This would certainly give me some power over the floozy. And Samuel had never offered to let me read his drafts *before* he completed them, preferring to present a perfected, error-free copy. Would he really let me read his work-in-progress stories?

Then his words struck me like a boxing glove. Wait. Wait a second. Is he writing about me again?

"Samuel," I said through clenched teeth, "what exactly have you been writing about? Isn't *Water Sirens* finished?"

Streaks of red crept up his neck as he realized his mistake. He *was* writing about me! Mother cliff-hucker! And if his stories included my pink banjo, it was the *real* me, not some stupid mythological nixie heroine.

I spun around and stalked back to the campsite, angry fists pumping at my sides. Samuel was immediately next to me.

"Kaye, please. Yes, I'm writing about us—a memoir of sorts. Our story, when we were kids. But I'm not publishing it," he explained breathlessly. "And I planned to let you read it once it was cleaned up and edited, I swear."

"Then why are you writing it if you don't intend to publish it?"

He went quiet. The only sound was our quick breath and the rustle of tall grass as we pushed our way through the forest.

"Because I don't want to forget," he finally answered.

"Forget what?" I broke through the trees and scurried onto the trail. He followed on my heels.

"Forget *us*. Every day, more details disappear. Little things, like the color of the dress you wore on your fourteenth birthday, or the first song we learned on our guitars. Every day, you slip farther and farther away from me."

"You made the choice to leave, Samuel. At Button Rock I asked you, point blank, if it was worth it. And you couldn't even give me a straight answer!" I frantically scrambled over a dead tree, trying to lose him. Still, he kept pace.

"*Por Dios,* Kaye, will you stop *running?* Yes, I chose to leave. And no, it wasn't worth it, because I don't think that either one of us is happy, are we?"

I pushed a low-hanging branch out of the way. It swung back and thwacked Samuel in the face.

"Ow!" He doubled over, hands flying to his nose. "Shit, shit, *shit!*" he cried painfully, his eyes watering. Blood began to seep between his fingers.

Horror at what I'd done swept over me and I flew to his side, easing him to his knees as I crouched next to him. "Oh, Samuel, I'm so, so sorry. Is it bleeding badly?"

"I dunno," he said nasally. "Sorry for the swearing."

Only Samuel would apologize for cussing when he was in pain. Prying his fingers away, I gingerly touched the deep cut on the bridge of his nose. No breaks, thank goodness, but he'd need a couple of butterfly stitches from the first aid kit. I pressed my cuff over his injury to clot the blood, wiping away the stream of red trickling down the inside of his cheek.

After several minutes he exhaled. "Isn't that your favorite sweater—the one your grandma made?" His voice was muffled by my ruined sleeve.

"Yeah," I admitted.

Grasping my hands in his, he rolled my blood-soaked cuff back until it wasn't visible. Then he leaned his forehead against mine, his sad, perceptive eyes so close, they blurred and doubled in my vision.

"Kaye, this is why I'm writing." His voice was weary, resigned, as if he'd just lost a long, brutal battle. "I'm scared—no, terrified—to forget this. *Us.* I need to get it down on paper before it's too late, and those little details are completely gone from my mind. I don't want to lose them. Tell me it isn't the same for you, and I'll leave you alone."

Tears gathered in my eyes. I knew what he was feeling. I was terrified to forget, too. I had my photo albums, my memories, my family and friends to remind me. And still, I'd forgotten May twenty-third—his birthday.

The photo of us as children on his laptop. The graduation picture. The Friday lunches. The draft about Planet Bluegrass. Even Caroline's callous, cruel remarks about how Samuel cared only for my thirteen-year-old self told me he was being truthful—he was writing to remember. Well, maybe he did care more about our childhood than our present. So be it. But dang it, that thirteen-year-old girl was still inside this twenty-seven-year-old woman's body, somewhere. And if he cared about that little girl, then he *had* to care about the woman she'd grown in to.

My forehead dropped to his shoulder, and I leaned into him. He was my fury and my comfort. Familiar arms, circling me. This heartbeat thudding against my skin when I'd rest my cheek on his chest, now pulsing rapidly beneath his sternum. I knew, *I knew*, I couldn't live without it.

"My dress was cream with sprigs of burgundy flowers. The first song we learned was—and I can't believe you don't remember this, it's deliciously ironic—'Paperback Writer.' It was very watered down and only had three chords, and we really sucked." I exhaled, breathing mint into his neck.

"Kaye?" His voice was a whisper, as if he were afraid to destroy the frail threads being spun between us, stitching us back together.

I understood what my decision had to be. I'd already made it long ago, when I was four years old. Yes, there was the pile of lies we both had to sift through. There was a world of hurt to be dealt with, namely the betrayals of New York. But we could work through that together as friends, couldn't we?

"I'll try to be your friend, Samuel." I pulled away from him, meeting his cloudless eyes. "And I'll screen your drafts before they go to Caroline, only because I don't want to forget, either. We can start after Danita and Angel's wedding. But, so help me, if you ever try to publish it I will— "

He didn't give me a chance to finish my threat. Rather, he pulled me into a tight embrace that forced the air out of my lungs. His fingers burrowed into my hair, his chin came to rest on the top of my head. He pressed his lips there, warm and soft.

"I'll do everything I can to ensure you don't regret this," he breathed into my hair. "I promise."

"I know you will."

I felt the corners of his mouth turn up. "So, are you up for Rocky Mountain Folks this year? Just you and me?"

"Yeah. You and me." I sighed against him, knowing I'd just placed my heart back on the chopping block.

Chapter 15
ROOSTERTAIL

When the current hits an underwater rock,
sprays of water explode into the air and resemble
a rooster's tail feathers.

Hydraulic Level Five [working title]
Draft 1.15
© Samuel Caulfield Cabral
Baseball Posters

Thirty-seven days and six hours. That is the amount of time Aspen has been in Durango visiting her grandmother.

Twenty-two days and eighteen hours. That is the amount of time until Aspen returns to Bear Creek.

His mother comments over chile rellenos how lovely Aspen has become, with her cascade of blond curls and skin as smooth as silver bark. Caulfield stares down at his plate to hide what must be plain in every sixteen-year-old line of his face – he wants Aspen.

Aspen will be a freshman this year. That makes him a little less of a pervert, if they both attend the same high school. Because only perverts eyeball eighth-grade kids. And Aspen is a kid. A talented, savvy kid he's proud of in a big brother sort of way. She is consistently first in her class, has already tackled algebra, and works from the same classics reading list as he. She can pluck most songs from the radio and cobble them out on her guitar like no thirteen-year-old has any business doing. But she is just a young girl who still has bony knees and elbows, cornhusk hair, and hazel eyes that make her owlish.

Except her legs aren't quite so gangly. And when his gaze follows them all the way up, he feels twinges all the way up his own body. Her hair isn't stringy, but thick and shiny, and curls over her white shoulders. And her eyes, heaven help him. They are still Aspen's eyes. Yet when she stares at him through her eyelashes, he goes embarrassingly hard. And she is clumsy, tripping over her unfamiliar feet, but somehow even that is a turn on because he is there to catch her.

It is confirmed. Caulfield is a sixteen-year-old pervert. A pervert who, for nearly seven months, has ogled someone who might as well be his little sister.

Except she isn't.

It's Maria's fault. She stuck Aspen in her junior varsity cheerleader uniform over Christmas break, complete with pom poms and face paint. The costume wasn't an exact fit, but Maria folded and pinned until it was passable. When Maria told him what they were going to do, he laughed. He expected his friend to bounce down the stairs swimming in the bright blue uniform, a young thing playing dress-up in adult clothing.

She didn't. Rather, she flipped that short skirt, flirty as hell, and winked at him. Aspen winked.

Horrible Maria. She put his innocent friend up to it just to mess with his head. After recovering from his shock, Caulfield staggered to the family room, every inch of him tingling as if a cardiac defibrillator had sent a thousand volts jolting through his body. He barely met Aspen's eyes the rest of Christmas break.

Twenty-two days and seventeen hours.

It is a summer of firsts. Caulfield scores his first job, selling tennis shoes. He acquires his license. His family leaves the home he's lived in for nearly ten years for a luxury cabin in the foothills, near the Hispanic neighborhood. His father wants him to find a deeper appreciation for his Mexican heritage, and perhaps it will give him aspirations beyond baseball and storytelling. Caulfield is lost when it comes to labels. He isn't quite Mexican, but he isn't quite Caucasian. Not quite a jock, but not quite a hipster. He's just Caulfield, who is Aspen's friend – and that's a label he can live with.

A fierce scowl graces Aspen's face when she helps him take down his baseball posters and pack his books in boxes. She thinks his family is abandoning her. He assures her he'll see her every day once school begins. And he has his license now, so he can drive into Bear Creek whenever he wants.

This summer is also the first time he conscientiously decides to think of his aunt as his actual mother. He makes the tactless mistake of referring to her as his aunt in a conversation with a woman at the DMV when he applies for his license. She doesn't correct him, but he sees her raw hurt. When they return home, freshly-minted piece of legal plastic in his wallet, he goes up to his room and puts away the last of the things he brought with him from Boston, so long ago.

Now that baseball season is over, Caulfield works Saturdays. If Aspen starts dating Esteban's cocky little brother, he might keep the job into the school year. Her mom agreed to let her group date when she turns fourteen...and she'll be fourteen in two months. What else will Caulfield do while she holds hands in shadowy movie theaters and shares popcorn with someone else? He can find a girlfriend, he supposes.

Only Esteban knows he hasn't so much as kissed a girl – he'll get mercilessly pummeled by the team if they find out. He's had his chances. When he and Esteban made the varsity baseball team their freshman year, the girls at Bear Creek High School doubled their efforts to snag him. Some were even senior girls. He's lying if he claims he hasn't thought about pulling them under the bleachers to grab their hips and kiss their soft lips. But he isn't on the market for a girlfriend, and he has no desire to inflame the small town gossip that comes with groping a girl then ignoring her as he passes her locker. If something like that reaches Aspen's ears...

Twenty-two days and sixteen hours.

He can see her up in the bleachers, her skinny, sunburned arms holding high a homemade poster with his jersey number scribbled in blue marker. She never misses a home game, refusing to go to Durango until the season is over. She even attends half of his away games with his family, chatting with his mother or cheering with Maria and his father. Sometimes she brings the cheesy #1 foam hand he gave her, emblazoned with the Boston Red Sox.

Caulfield will to take her to Boston someday for a Red Sox game. He's never been to Fenway Park, even though he has every last beam embossed on his brain. They don't get much Red Sox baseball in Colorado unless they play the Rockies, but he religiously follows them in sports magazines, newspaper box scores, and now on the World Wide Web.

He drove past Fenway Park countless times with his real mother, but never once entered the historic ballpark. His real father was a Red Sox fan. His mother's bedtime stories were of brilliant sunsets over the "Green Monster," and how they used to be season ticket holders until he was born. Caulfield asked her to take him to a Red Sox game, just once. She slapped him hard across the face – the first time ever – screaming at him to never ask again, that it would be a fucking disgrace to have him set foot on hallowed ground like Fenway. Not an hour later, she clutched at him and kissed his five-year-old cheeks slathered with tears and snot, murmuring *I'm so sorry, Sky-Eyes, so fucking sorry.* His mother bought the foam finger and a Wade Boggs poster to make him feel better.

Caulfield finally takes the poster off his wall. It is rolled up, in a case, in his closet.

Twenty-two days and fifteen hours. That is the amount of time until Aspen returns to Bear Creek and closes the growing crater in his chest.

Whether it makes him a pervert or not, when she returns to Bear Creek, he will kiss her beautiful mouth.

"She knows you're not a lesbian." Jaime flipped through the tabloid mag—the same issue proclaiming Caroline's Sharpie-wielding prowess I'd tossed outside the convenience store—thoughtfully tapping the article.

"But I haven't given her a reason to believe otherwise. At least I don't think I have."

"She tried to eat Samuel's face in front of you, right?"

"Yes."

"Uh-huh. She can tell you're still hung up on your ex boy-toy. Actually, anybody with half a brain can, which is why Cabral is clueless, ha ha ha." She tossed me the magazine and picked up a rubber ducky. The one-year-old Labrador she worked with, Tango, made a grab for it. She held it away until Tango stood up on his hind legs. I watched, awed and slightly disturbed, as the dog gnawed on the adorable yellow ducky.

The minute the VW Campervan pulled into the Cabrals' driveway earlier this afternoon, I said quick goodbyes, slid into my Jeep, and barreled down the hill toward the Hispanic neighborhood. Jaime Guzman had a handsome two-story log cabin on the very edge, down a gravel drive lined with arching pines.

Tonight, Samuel planned to discuss his new book arrangement with Caroline. He likened it to pulling a grenade pin inside an armored tank. The weekend with the floozy had been truly enlightening. My guess was she'd pull out the big guns once Samuel hit her with the news, and I needed to be prepared. And being prepared meant consulting Jaime.

"The more I see of her, the more I wonder if she bought into the lesbian thing to begin with. Maybe she played along for Cabral, thinking she could use it to padlock his balls to her chain. But once she realized Cabral knew you weren't chasin' skirt, she's back to keeping you close. *Qué chinga*." Amazing, how I didn't even cringe at Jaime's bluntness anymore. "Man, I wish I could nail down this Botox-frozen yuppie slag's M.O." Jaime tossed a liver treat to Tango and scratched his ears. I scratched Tango's ears too, working through the dilemma.

"Okay. She knows a lot about my history. Samuel obviously has feelings for her if he brought her home. He also trusts her opinion as an editor, and apparently she's earned it."

Jaime lifted a suggestive eyebrow. I gagged.

"I said as an *editor*, Jaime! Please, I can't even speculate about that."

"Just don't rule it out. You know how with men, one head tends to override the other. Right, Tango? Got to keep you away from the girl doggies for now, don't we? Dat's a good boy." She scratched the sire dog's neck while he stupidly panted with glee.

I pointedly ignored her. "I don't think Samuel expected Caroline to go after me with the info she'd gleaned from his writing. He seemed really upset about it."

"And that's where you have power over her—Samuel's onto her jealousy. You and Samuel have a past, and it's got to be eating away at her. She cracked under pressure. And if she goes after you again, I'm willing to bet he'll side with you."

"Yeah, but now she's on her guard. And she hates my guts."

Jaime put Tango in his kennel and brought out two puppies, handing one to me while she trimmed the toenails of the second. I held the squirming, yipping thing in my lap as he batted my face with his tail. "I agree. If your little buddy time with Cabral interferes with whatever plans she has for him, she'll try to take you down, I guarantee it."

"I think she'd steamroll him in a minute as well, if it came down to him or her. Ugh!" I held the puppy away from me as he drooled down my neck. "I need leverage, more than just Samuel's friendship—I don't want to risk that. I just have to understand her better, the way she seems to understand me. Being runner-up Miss North Carolina tells me nothing, except that she's gorgeous, knows how to fake smile, and probably stabbed several women with her stilettos on her climb up the ladder."

Jaime traded puppies with me, instantly calming the little squirmer with a surprisingly gentle brush of her hand.

"Oh, Jaime—" I smiled, stroking the puppy like an evil mastermind "—any chance you might do some extra digging into Caroline Ortega's PR tactics? I imagine a few of her strategies are fairly shady."

"For crying out loud, Trilby, don't you own a PR agency? I mean, this should be second nature to you."

I glowered. "My clients are Mom-and-Pop B&Bs, national parks, and art galleries. We don't exactly have a high demand for celebrity image management in Boulder. I like to keep my hands clean. But the one thing I know about celeb PR is that the media will put you on a pedestal and then knock you off just as quickly if it sells papers."

She frowned, but nodded. "Okay, so let's figure this out. We know Caroline's able to either shut down or spin most negative press. Case in point: the drag photo never saw the light of day."

"And neither has Samuel's arrest record. My guess is her firm has made some heavy deals to keep it quiet."

Jaime began to pace the kennel, her Labs following her with watery eyes. "The question is, what sort of deals? Because as a lawyer, I better have something really juicy to hand over if I'm going to get the deal I want."

"It could be leaked book info, movie details, or advance notice on his schedule so the paps can snap their pictures."

"Romantic entanglements with other celebrities?"

"Yeah, that too. Caroline obviously has insider information about Samuel's personal life, and an 'inside source' is currency when it comes to media bargaining. I hate the idea of this woman bargaining with Samuel's secrets."

"So now I'm your henchman. What do you want me to do, Prank Princess—put Nair in her shampoo?"

"Tempting." I racked my brain. "I'll do some digging and find out who a few of her media contacts are. Once I get them, I want you to research what's been published about Samuel and her other authors, see if you can find patterns. Then we'll have a better grasp on Caro's M.O."

"Whoa, Trilby. You're turning me on by going all PR business bitch on me. Why don't you have this kind of buoyancy when it comes to your personal life?"

I handed her the puppy. "Jaime, come on. I need your help."

"It'll cost you. You better be prepared to pony up for all the work I've put into this sad little variety show."

"What do you want?"

"It's for my brother, actually." Jaime's normally gruff voice lost a bit of its edge. "He's training to mountain climb, but doesn't have anyone to go with. I dunno, he's stupid."

Ah. I knew what she was getting at. Except for Hector Valdez, the Mexican community cold-shouldered Jaime Guzman. Unfortunately, her twin brother, Luca, suffered because of her past mischief. She never would say it, but I knew she hated she'd put him in that position.

"I'll talk to Hector about Luca. We're doing a Longs Peak climb this winter, and if he passes muster in Hector's opinion, count him in."

Placing both of the puppies in the dog run, she held out her hand for me to shake. "The sordid business strategies of Caroline Ortega, coming up."

Odd, how I felt like one of her trained Labs as she shook my paw.

I should have worn running shoes on my final day of work before the long wedding weekend. From the minute my heels clicked into the TrilbyJones conference room, it was one of those days. My eight o'clock with the Boulder Community Theatre was delayed because the director had to go to the city jail and collect "Daddy Warbucks" in the upcoming production of *Annie*. The actor's friends were supposed to shave his head the previous night, and much alcohol was involved to bolster courage. Too much. After that, my entire schedule for the day was pushed back by half an hour, and I skipped lunch to finish the natural history museum slogan samples for their new exhibit: a complete dinosaur skeleton. The tagline? *"Remains to be seen."* I was pretty proud of that one.

Molly was also taking time off to help Holly. Her stepsister still struggled to care for her infant, and Molly and Derek feared she would need psychiatric help.

I staggered up my outdoor staircase, heels wobbling, only to see the back of a familiar floppy fishing hat, its owner reclining in one of my patio chairs.

"Cassady?"

"Nope." Samuel swiveled around, tipping the hat with a dopey grin.

I stifled a laugh. Yikes. Cassady could pull off the hat. Angel could even pull off that hat. But on Samuel, even with faded jeans and an old Vail ski T-shirt, it looked ridiculous. I grabbed the stairwell as my feet wobbled again. His eyes shot down my legs, to my feet.

"Since when do you wear heels?"

"Since Danita said I'm not allowed to go into my client meetings wearing shoes that make me look like a little girl. And hello to you, too."

"You like the hat? The lone paparazzo who's still tailing me knows my ball cap."

"Um…it's a different look for you. Isn't that Hippie's?"

"Yes. After you took me out with the tree branch and 'ruined my mug for wedding photos,' as my loving sister put it, she told Cassady it's his job to keep me safe until Saturday."

I stepped closer and studied the bruised, scabbed bridge of his nose, chagrinned. The cut wasn't long, but it was ugly. Danita would probably sic Molly on him with foundation and face powder.

"Sorry about that." I unlocked my door and motioned him inside. "So I've been demoted, huh? Not living up to my maid of honor title?"

"Dani couldn't have a better friend than you." Samuel eyed my apartment, hands jammed into his pockets. "Can I interest you in a stroll to Pearl Street? We can grab dinner on the way, if you're hungry."

I kicked off my cursed heels and smoothed down my pencil skirt, debating whether I just wanted to put up my feet and veg. But it was a nice evening and a walk wouldn't kill me.

"Um, sure. Give me a minute to change and we can take off. Make yourself at home, grab a drink, whatever." I darted into my bedroom and my hand flew to my chest. Samuel was in my living room, seeing where I now lived. Yes, he'd already been here for his grand cricket prank, but this time, it seemed more real. Fricking monkey rump, now I'd have that image of him standing there, in that stupid floppy hat, burned into my mind.

"Where's Caroline?" I called from my closet. I paused halfway through pulling a maroon sundress over my head, listening for his answer.

"Denver Airport. I dropped her off an hour ago."

Yes! "Oh? Where's she going?"

A pause, and a muffled answer. Stupid ear. I shrugged into a pair of sandals and pulled my hair into a ponytail, then changed my mind and let it tumble over my shoulders. Oh yeah. Hair was good today. "What was that?"

"Raleigh. Caro said she needed to take a few days to sort out some personal issues there before the wedding."

"I take it she's not happy with our book arrangement?"

"She'll be fine. She's just used to the two of us working on a book, that's all. I don't think she anticipated involving you, screening what she reads." Yes. Oh freaking yes. I'd make sure that Caroline never again read a single thing about me. "That, and she's concerned the longer this personal project takes, the longer it will be until I begin a publishable book."

"Why do you even need her help if you aren't publishing?" I touched up my light makeup and slicked ChapStick over my lips. What the heck. I pulled out a tube of dusty pink lipstick.

"Just because I've been successful doesn't mean I should stop pushing my work to the next level. Caroline has a knack for asking tough questions and improving my writing. She usually sees angles I never considered."

Leave it to Samuel to perfect a book that would never see the light of day. Still, he wouldn't be Samuel if he didn't. At least I could enjoy a few days without operating under Caroline's hydra stares. Pouting my mouth in the mirror, I frowned and wiped off the pink lipstick. Lipstick was for dates and meetings, and this was a night with a friend. I grabbed my purse and waltzed into the living room, *hound is gone, hound is gone* dancing through my head.

Samuel studied one of my black and white framed photos on the wall. "This is gorgeous. Longs Peak?"

"It's Molly's. She gave it to me for Christmas several years ago. Ready to go?"

He stared at my beaded Elvis purse and chuckled. "Some things never change, do they?"

"Hey, if we're going to do the buddies thing, we are going to do it right. Oh, and lose the hat. I refuse to be seen in public with you while you're wearing it."

He tossed the hat on my table, then messed his hair. "Aren't you worried about having your photo taken with me?"

"We're friends, right? Unless your plan is to make out in the middle of Pearl Street—then you might need the hat."

Samuel's eyes gleamed. "Behave, Trilby, or I won't buy you any Cherry Garcia after dinner." Yum. He had me. Darn that fat, bearded Deadhead and his tasty ice cream.

We sauntered through the neighborhood, enjoying the summer evening as we made our way to Pearl Street. Kids flew down sidewalks on bikes or threw footballs across yards. Two little girls in swimsuits blew up floaties as their father tested the water temperature in their wading pool. The pool toys deflated as quickly as he could blow air into them.

"I have a plan," Samuel said as we turned onto the busier strip. He guided me toward a panini shop.

"Big surprise there," I teased. "What is it?"

"Okay. I think we both agree our chat at Button Rock didn't go well for either of us. You have struggles of which I wasn't even aware. And I was prepared to discuss something entirely different, so you caught me off guard. Do you agree?"

"Yes. You called me dirt."

Samuel ordered a sub crammed with mozzarella, spinach, and red peppers. I chose the same.

His lips quirked. "And you're deliberately misinterpreting my symbiosis theory, Miss Trilby. But that's beside the point. So, you know I have a tendency to hem and haw over decisions. Save the sarcasm." I kept my mouth shut, swallowing the retort while he paid for our sandwiches. "And you have a tendency to make snap decisions. You do, don't deny it."

"Your point is?"

"We need to meet somewhere in the middle."

"You mean compromise? What a foreign concept." I tried to take a bite of my sub without the contents tumbling down my cotton dress as we wove through the crowded sidewalk, past shabby boutiques and restaurant patios draped with twinkling white lights.

"What was that I said about sarcasm?" Samuel nudged me. I nudged him back, just as he took a bite of his sandwich, dotting his chin with marinara. He wiped it off and gave me a patronizing glower. "Anyway, we both agree there are discussions that have to happen — 'answers,' as you've put it. Here's the thing, though. If we just dump our baggage on each other all at once, we'll end up more confused, overwhelmed, and angrier than before."

"You mean if we rashly fire questions at each other, we won't have time to process?"

"Yes."

"And if we overanalyze everything, we'll never get a straight answer."

"Right. So here's my proposal. Each week, we both ask the other one question. You ask your question on one day, and I'll ask mine the next day."

"Just one question?"

"As a discussion prompt, yes. For as long as it takes, until we are both on the same page."

"Have you spent time in therapy? This all sounds very shrink-like." I squinted up at him, the setting sun casting his profile in silhouette.

"Is that your one question?"

"No. You think I'd waste it on a 'Yes or No' answer?"

"Of course not." He wadded up his sandwich wrapper and tossed it in a trash can. Ahead, charming shop signs and striped canopies flanked either side of the road until it disappeared into the open blue of the sky.

"So, the questions...are you willing to give this a try?"

"Why just once a week? Is this a stall tactic?"

"Because, Kaye, we'll need that week to ensure we really understand the implications of what we reveal to each other."

"You must have some whopper secrets." I only partly kidded. Spotting the ice cream parlor, I threw the rest of my sandwich away and grabbed Samuel's hand, pulling him toward dessert. He chuckled.

"I see where your priorities are."

"Can it, Cabral. You promised me Cherry Garcia and so help me, you better deliver. You can't tease a girl like that."

Once we purchased ice cream—mine in a waffle cone and Samuel's in a neat little cup—we found a green space near the sculpture of a lovely girl on a front porch swing, her bronze tones warmed by an array of brightly hued tulips. We settled onto a park bench and ate our ice cream. An occasional pedestrian stopped to ask if Samuel was that *Sirens* author. He explained this was fairly typical, unless he was in New York. People tended to mind their own business in the city. They either didn't know you, or didn't care.

"So, do you have any more non-discussion questions?" Samuel asked after he'd politely autographed the back of someone's receipt and smiled into their camera phone.

"Yes. How is any of this going to work? In one week, you'll board a plane to wherever you're going for the book tour. You'll be crazy busy. I get the whole email concept, believe me. Email convo will work just fine when I read your memoir, but..."

Samuel's blue eyes gently read me as I broke off a piece of my waffle cone. "I promised you I'd do whatever it takes to mend this friendship and I intend to keep that promise. You have my cell phone number. I have yours. If you need to call me, you can, whatever the time. If you want me to fly back for a visit, I will."

"And you'll be back in two months for Rocky Mountain Folks?"

"Yes, pink banjo in tow."

I smiled and offered him a chunk of waffle cone. He took it, even though I was certain he still didn't like them.

"Do you want to ask first, or should I?"

"You mean we're starting with the questions right now?" I asked.

"Sure, if you want. No time like the present."

Shoot. I had to give this some thought. What could I possibly ask him first? Samuel, were you really that unhappy with me? Were you doing drugs in Boulder? Why did you leave? Why didn't you come back? Did you love me as a friend or as a lover?

"Geez, there are so many questions—this is like having to choose from a dessert tray. Well, a really crappy, ingestion-inducing dessert tray. Why don't you go instead? I'll give you time to come up with one."

"I already know what I want to ask."

"Oh! Fire away, then." I nervously crumbled the rest of my waffle cone, bracing myself for the New York question. I sorted out all of the ways I could tell him what happened that night without crying in public. But he didn't ask.

"Other than the fact that you've been wonderfully successful and enjoy taking ridiculous risks—" he smiled when I bristled, teasing me "—I know very little about what you've been up to for almost seven years. And I want to know, very badly. So my first question is, why extreme sports?"

I blinked. "Seriously? That's it?" Hmmm, that was easy. "Okay… what do you want to know about them?"

"Anything. Everything. Why don't you start by telling me how you became a certified skydiver?"

Skydiving. That was a safe place to begin. I explained how the Paddler boys wanted to become certified as part of their adventure guide careers, and I tagged along. I talked about whitewater rafting, expounding on the difference between a hydraulic and a wave. We talked about TrilbyJones and some of my crazier client requests like the ski shop who wanted to unload merchandise and simultaneously promote the Green movement—buy a thousand dollars' worth of ski equipment, get a free goat to replace your lawn mower. He listened while I spilled my story, my hands waving enthusiastically over things like ice rappelling or backcountry skiing in Vail. He cringed as I flung my dangerous stunts in his face, but he wisely didn't comment until I finished.

"Why do you do the ice rappelling, the backcountry skiing, the rafting, all of these risky things?"

"Didn't I just answer that?"

"No, you told me what you like about them. Not *why* you do them. There's a difference."

"Oh. Well, I live in Colorado, so they're in my backyard."

"What else?"

"I guess I do them because they're thrilling. I'm addicted to the adrenaline rush."

"And?"

I shrugged. "What other reason would there be?"

"So you like risking your life simply because you get a temporary adrenaline rush."

"Look, you asked and I answered. If you believe there's more to it, then why don't you come right out and tell me what it is?"

"That's not the way this works, Kaye. I can't ask a question and then answer it for you."

"Well obviously you know the answer better than I do. But that's nothing new, is it?"

Samuel ground his jaw, and I thought for a moment he would argue with me and demand that I tell him what I really meant by that. He didn't. Instead, he offered me a contrite smile.

"I'm sorry. You know your own mind and I shouldn't argue otherwise."

The playful charm of the evening had all but deflated. The sun sank below the row of brick storefronts and would soon be gone, leaving us in a world of violet. Throwing away our trash from the ice cream, we left the green space and wandered up Pearl Street, gazes bouncing over the mountains that shadowed the city.

Soon, Boulder would be decorated in its red, white, and blue regalia for its Independence Day celebration. Our group of friends usually made an evening of it, listened to live music and hung around until ten o'clock for fireworks. Colored fire would fill the sky and drift down as Sousa marches pounded from loud speakers. For a fleeting moment, I thought about inviting Sam—he'd enjoy the music and the company.

"I miss this in New York—how everything catches on fire before sunset. The mountains, particularly." He gestured over his shoulder to the starless mounds blackened by the extinguished sun.

I studied the faint circles under his eyes. "You look tired, Samuel."

"It's been a long weekend."

We watched a thin, haggard man shuffle past us, his hair gray and skin weathered and rough like canyon crags. A black garbage bag was slung over his shoulder and clanked with bottles and cans. I leaned my head against Samuel's warm shoulder. His arm came around me.

"Sometimes it's strange to me, seeing homeless people wandering around Boulder, not like it is in Denver. And I bet it's an everyday occurrence for you in New York."

Samuel shifted so he could see my face. "It depends on the part of the city. But yes, most people get used to it. I don't, though."

"I wonder what happens in a person's life to drive them to the streets? How does someone go from having a family and a home, and a school, to picking up cans for a living and sleeping in a doorway?"

"I suppose a number of different factors. Addictions. Mental illness. Physical disabilities. Criminal record. Natural disasters. Maybe all of the above. Most of the time, only a single twist of events separates their lives from ours, you know? Seeing them reminds me that if it weren't for certain people, I could have been one of them."

His arm tightened around my shoulders as he became lost in thought. I let him have his silence while my mind drifted to his troubles in New York. I'd have to ask him about it, soon, but it would be on my terms. Already, a million questions formed. By the time Samuel's grip on my shoulder loosened and he pulled me from the bench, I'd decided what I would ask him next time we talked.

At last, the sun was gone. Stretching our limbs, we made our way back to TrilbyJones, past the colorfully-lit boutique displays packed with sporting gear and artwork. We moved quickly this time, stopping occasionally to peer at something in the windows.

"So, I've been curious but never wanted to ask. Why aren't you Angel's best man? At first I thought it was because you never see each other, but rumor has it you still keep in touch. He's closer to you than he is to Santiago or Hector."

"Angel and I talk to each other once a month. Don't worry, we never discuss you," he rushed on. "Usually Danita hands the phone over to him after she chews me out for not coming home more often."

"You deserve it, after the coercing Sofia has to do to get you to come back to Lyons, even for holidays. But you didn't answer my question."

"Angel did ask me to be his best man. I declined."

I halted. "Why on earth did you do that?"

Samuel rubbed the back of his neck. "In retrospect, I probably shouldn't have. But when he asked me, I wasn't sure I'd be able to manage the requirements."

"You mean planning the bachelor party and renting a tux? Wow, those are *hard*."

Samuel began walking again. "You know what I mean, Kaye."

I sighed. "Yeah, I know. Jaunting down the aisle together in the church where we got married. Talk about déjà vu. I have to admit, I stressed about it, too. But, Samuel, I think you should have told him yes. It would have meant a lot to him, and you'd have managed just fine. Me, however…you know what a nostalgic sap I can be."

Samuel kindly pulled me around to face him. "Having a sensitive heart does not make you a sap, Kaye. Please don't degrade it. You have such a bent for caring about people and you don't even realize it."

"Oh yes. Downtrodden guinea pigs are singing my praises across all of Los Angeles. Kaye Trilby: friend of furry rodents."

"Well, undeserving as I am, I'm grateful to call you my friend again." He lightly touched a finger to my cheek.

"Me too."

Samuel walked me to my front door. He leaned against the frame, his arms crossed over his chest.

"Can I see you tomorrow, Trilby? Don't forget—you have to ask me a question."

"Ugh, tomorrow's crazy." I flew through everything I had to do to get ready for the wedding. "And I have to help my dad's girlfriend and Molly put together eighty welcome baskets for out-of-town wedding guests at The Garden Market, then distribute them to hotels. You may not have a lot of extended family, but the Valdez's—flippin' stapler, that family is huge!"

"Most of 'em are Roman Catholic." Samuel grinned. "I have a feeling the Valdez family's descent upon Lyons will be the biggest party the town's ever seen. Anyway, I can help with the bags. Let me drive you around—we can talk, then."

"How can I possibly refuse extra help?"

He pulled me in for his customary hug and head kiss. "Goodnight, Kaye."

"Don't forget Cassady's floppy hat."

That night, I couldn't sleep. I considered finishing the last few chapters of *The Last Other*, but that would probably cause my brain to floor the gas pedal and peel out. Instead, I made myself a mug of hot chocolate, put on The Twiggies, and relaxed in my comfy leather chair. The music smoothed the rough edges from my thoughts until I could fall into the pile and not be cut.

Something bothered me, but I couldn't put my finger on it. I flipped on the television, losing myself in an old black and white movie in which an heiress, Claudette Colbert, ran away with secret reporter Clark Gable after escaping her father's yacht to find her rich flyboy. In the end, of course, she fell for the scoundrel reporter and ditched her flyboy. I had to smile at the innocence of it—splitting a room with a curtain to avoid impropriety. It was probably considered risqué in the day. After another mug of hot chocolate while the credits rolled, I pinned what nagged me. Samuel had intimated I hadn't answered his question about extreme sports. Why *had* I chosen extreme sports? I'd never pondered it before.

I'd told Samuel it was the adrenaline rush. And I had to admit, I could see a few parallels between the high he got from his drugs and the high I got from jumping out of a plane. Our habits were kind of alike, although *mine* was a lot less likely to royally screw up my life and my family. And it was legal.

I wrestled with the question for a good hour until I had my answer.

I called Samuel. When he didn't answer, I nearly hung up.

"*Hey, this is Sam. Leave a message…*"

I kept up my courage through his voicemail.

"Hey, Samuel. I thought about your question—why extreme sports? And you were right, there is more to it." *Come on, Kaye, you can do this.* "Yes, I love the adrenaline rush. But I started doing the dangerous stuff because it was the only way I could feel sure of myself. When you left me behind, you also left me numbed, my confidence shattered, and I wanted to *feel* again, prove I was still breathing, still strong. The extreme sports helped."

I exhaled, feeling the pressure on my chest lift.

"Also, I suppose it was a passive aggressive way to get even with you. I thought maybe Angel or Danita would rat me out, and you'd be irked because I'd found something you were so wholly uninvolved in. Even if you'd never found out, I believed I was spiting you, somehow. But the adventure trips are more than that now, and I'm not going to quit just because you think they're dangerous.

"That's all I wanted to say. Talking to your voicemail's actually therapeutic. Maybe we should do all of our weekly discussions like this." I cringed, feeling stupid. "That was a joke. Um…sleep well. Goodnight."

I hung up before I could say anything else completely embarrassing.

Chapter 16
HIGH WATER

The higher the river flow, the faster the current.

Petulant mouth. Sad, sagging eyebrows. Avoidant eyes. Yup, guilt. Whether thirteen or thirty, that expression hadn't changed. If he was ninety, I'd still know guilt in his beautiful face.

Summer heat hit Lyons full force two days before Danita and Angel's wedding. Rainless days and high winds only notched up the heat and baked the east Rockies beneath a gigantic hair dryer.

Samuel glanced at me again, and this time I caught him. Three hours and still no mention of the phone message I'd left. Granted, we were in the presence of my dad's girlfriend and Molly—not the best time to bring it up. But I knew, without a doubt, he'd received it. I poked him beneath his ribs to lighten his funk. He gave me a little smile, the guilt only deepening in the creases around his eyes.

Three hundred bud vases were washed and ready for pink gerbera daisies. Stacks of programs were folded, sealed with wax, and boxed. And eighty gussied-up baskets packed with apples, trail mix, bottled water, and Spanish-language greeting cards covered every spare inch of space in the back room of Audrey Wexler's organic grocery store. We were tackling the last of the gift baskets and stacking them in crates to carry out to my Jeep. Our fingers stalled over the ribbons, reluctant to abandon the air-conditioned room for the parched air outside.

I paused over my basket and watched Samuel smooth another pink ribbon between his fingertips.

"Unbelievable." I pushed up the strap of my brown tank top for the umpteenth time. Of course he could tie a perfect bow. His nimble, elegant guitar fingers had no trouble weaving two ribbon ends together into perfect loops. I'd seen those hands fly across strings and pluck out the fiery rhythms of Albeniz, or sweep pristine sentences across letterhead. Samuel was also the only man I'd ever known who could tie an immaculately straight necktie.

I, however, could not tie a pretty little bow to save my life.

"Oh for the love of—Samuel Caulfield Cabral! It doesn't have to be even. Just whip the ribbon around the handle and knot it."

"Admit it, Kaye. You are envious of my bow-tying dexterity."

"No. I just don't want to be stuck in here the rest of the afternoon." I rolled my neck, worked out the kinks. "Let's get these crates loaded, delivered, and crash in front of a TV for a ghost hunting marathon and cold drinks. You can put those magic fingers of yours to good use, Cabral."

Samuel's lips twitched. Molly snorted into her hand.

I bent over the basket to hide my chagrin. "*Neck rubs*, you creepers. What is wrong with you people? I can understand Samuel having a dirty mind—he's a writer. But seriously, Molly."

"I grew up around my stepsister. I knew what French kissing was by the age of seven, thanks to her and her boyfriend. And once Samuel started cramming his tongue down your throat, you weren't much better."

"Molly!"

She waved a dismissive hand. "Back rubs and ghost hunting, huh? I'm in..." She glanced between Samuel and me. "Unless the two of you just wanted to hang out alone. Because that's fine. In fact, I think Cassady mentioned something about biking tonight, so I'm busy anyway, and that ghost hunting show is kind of lame. Really."

Samuel discreetly hefted a crate and carried it out of the room, escaping Molly. I sighed. My perky friend was bound and determined to solve the world's problems, starting with her immediate circle, and there wasn't much I could say to keep her interference to a minimum.

Audrey returned with a crate of plump red apples, her brown curls bouncing around the paisley scarf tied over her head. She pointedly avoided Samuel, had been since he'd arrived at The Garden Market just after lunch. Whenever he addressed her, Audrey offered him a biting little smile, which clearly said, "you poor boy, you really screwed up, didn't you?" I'd been on the receiving end of that look a million times.

"You've done a remarkable job with the store, Ms. Wexler," Samuel said as he returned from the Jeep. "It seems to be doing very well." Son of a shrew, could he be any more Eddie Haskell?

She lifted her shoulder. Oh yes, she was in the playing-it-cool mode she'd perfected over the years—the classic shrug I'd witnessed a thousand times with my dad. "The Market draws quite a few loyal customers. Did you know your mother shops here regularly?"

"She's told me you have the best produce in the area, and you know how choosy she is."

Audrey flushed at the compliment. I rolled my eyes and Molly silently laughed. Samuel was certainly laying it on thick, even pulling out that killer white smile he used when he really wanted to charm someone.

Dad, however, seemed more than willing to forgive and forget with his golden boy.

"Hey there. How's Lyons' star ballplayer?" He emerged from the storeroom with an armful of bulk trail mix containers, strutting like a perpetual sixteen-year-old and beaming like one, too. He set down the containers and slapped Samuel on the back with a tanned arm. "I heard you were in town and wondered if I'd see you around at some point."

"Nice to see you again, Mr. Trilby." Samuel pulled his hand from Dad's strong grip.

"Call me Tom."

Dad and Samuel had gotten along, for the most part. There was the time Samuel nearly punched him when I'd found out he was sleeping with Audrey, mom's friend. After catching them *in flagrante delicto* on our Formica countertop, I'd wailed into Samuel's T-shirt like the emotional fifteen-year-old I was, about how Dad was ruining my life and how, for once, I wanted him to think of my feelings first. After taking me home, Samuel hauled it over to Dad's and nearly got himself benched for the next three games. The whole thing was convoluted and seedy, and I'd never loved Samuel more for throwing himself into the middle of it for my sake.

Audrey turned her cool look on Dad. His jaw set in stubborn defiance. Ah, they'd argued about my ex-husband.

"Hey, Samuel, when are you going to dish on your celebrity pals?" Molly asked, breaking the uneasy silence.

I stacked another ten baskets in a crate, fluffed the white tulle in each, trying my darndest not to appear interested. Audrey tried, too, but her greatest vice was celebrity gossip.

"I'm not going to dish, Molly. There's nothing to tell—just a bunch of people who move in circles which happen to be splashed across tabloids." Samuel eased past my dad and Audrey, lifting the crate from my arms.

"So you have no issues 'dishing' about Kaye, but celebrities are off limits? At least tell me if Indigo Kingsley's had work done. Molly says nose and boobs, but I'm pretty sure those puppies are real. What do you think?"

"Audrey!" I hissed.

Streaks of red crept up Samuel's neck as the three of them stared him down, waiting for an answer. He cleared his throat. "I wouldn't know. I was never in a position to find out what sort of work Indigo may have had done."

I was torn between complete embarrassment and amusement. Fortunately, Dad stepped in.

"So, Samuel, have you been down to Lyons High's ball field lately? We put in new dugouts last year..."

We loaded crates as quickly as possible and hit the road before Audrey pounced again.

"Kaye," Samuel asked as he stretched his long legs in my Jeep's passenger seat, "how much have you told your dad about what happened between us?"

I fiddled with the air controls. "Not a lot. You know how he is. If I remember correctly, our split happened during his *Zen and the Art of Motorcycle Maintenance* phase. He was already trying to talk me into a 'Chatauqua' visit to discuss truth in the modern world, said it would 'cleanse my spirit.' If I'd told him everything, he would have strapped me to the back of a motorcycle for a three-week quest to achieve inner peace of mind."

"And so the Paddler Outdoor Adventures crew strapped you into a kayak, instead."

Ugh, he had me there. "Okay. I probably should've talked to my family, but honestly, if they knew the entire truth, you wouldn't have lasted five minutes in that store."

Samuel tensed. "The entire truth?"

"The drugs. On second thought, Dad might have offered to toke it up with you at a Buffett concert."

He nodded, but his fingers still clutched at the seatbelt across his lap. Once more, guilt infused every inch of his face. Reaching over, I pressed his hand.

"Hey, relax. The whole question and answer thing isn't so scary. I survived, didn't I? Albeit, I *did* have to resort to a voicemail."

Samuel threaded his fingers through mine, his hands and wrists clammy. "I'm sorry for what I did to you, Kaye." He grimaced. "That apology sounds pathetic, doesn't it?"

I pulled my hand away and wrapped it around the steering wheel. "I didn't tell you those things to make you feel guilty or to fish for an apology. I told you because you asked for honesty, so there you have it."

"Do you want to talk about your voicemail?"

I shook my head. "I told you everything I wanted to say. Now it's time for *my* question for *you*. Brace yourself, Cabral. I have about seven years' worth of questions stored up, ready and aimed at the big ol' target on your forehead."

"Whenever you're ready, fire away."

But only silence drifted between us as I stirred up my courage. I fiddled with the radio, settling on a mellow alternative station. In between navigating the empty road to Boulder and ignoring Samuel's hints that I drove too fast, I glanced at him, gauging his mood. Tired. It was most noticeable when I caught him unaware—the way his entire body sagged into the seat, purplish, puffy eyelids, limp lips. Something ground him down, and he was doing his best to hide it from me.

"You still look exhausted. Worse than yesterday."

He rolled his head, gave me a half-hearted smile. "I haven't slept well the past couple of nights."

"From the looks of you, I'd say you haven't slept all month. The trip home is really doing a number on you, huh?"

"You know what they say about vacation: you need a vacation to recover from it. Normally I have a very strict daily routine. Wake up at six. Go for a run. Breakfast. Work. Lunch. Work some more. Dinner. Then entertainment, public appearances, or more work, depending on what Caro's booked. In bed by eleven. My body's thrown off, that's all."

"Wow. That's…glamorous. I would have expected your days to be a bit more exciting."

He shrugged. "I know, lifestyles of the rich and famous."

"Why the stringent routine? You were anal-retentive, but never *that* anal-retentive." I treaded carefully, instinctively knowing I was prying open a sensitive topic.

"Is that your one question?"

I grinned sheepishly. "No. This is just a warm-up question."

"Breaking the rules already? Cheeky." He tugged my ear, eyes crinkling thoughtfully. "Why my strict routine? It's necessary to keep me focused. And I suppose it's a way to cope."

"With what? Stress?"

"Yes."

I chewed my lip. "In the short time we were married, I knew you were stressed out. We both were. When you left, I tried to blame it on your stress, but I think I knew, deep down, it wasn't just stress." My mind raced, sorting itself out as I spoke. I kept my eyes riveted to the windshield because if I dared look at him, he'd see my weakness for him. "You were restless. Dissatisfied. For so many years, I believed you were dissatisfied with *me*, and that's why you left. But now I wonder if it was more than just me…"

"Kaye, I told you it wasn't you."

"I know, but you never gave me another explanation."

"Well, for what it's worth, I handled it poorly."

I pulled into the first hotel's parking lot but didn't kill the engine. Unbuckling my seatbelt, I turned to him. "I've thought a lot about this lately…Nicodemus really got me stewing. Ever since you were six, there was this unfathomable sadness in you. I couldn't do anything about it, so I pretended it wasn't there. And finally, it disappeared. But it never really went away, did it?"

Samuel's ice eyes searched my face. "It would come and go. Usually, I could push it back and simply enjoy being with you. But each time it returned, it was a little bit more intense. It began to linger, even when I was with you. Sometimes, especially in college, it grew so strong that the only way to keep my head above water was to steel myself against it. I reminded myself how much I would disappoint you, my parents, our friends if I ever let it swallow me. And when that didn't work…"

"The drugs."

He nodded.

"I wish you'd told me." I folded my arms around my ribs, suddenly scared for him. I didn't want to ask what he meant by it swallowing him, and I was extremely glad we'd never found out the hard way.

"When Alonso told me in New York you'd been doing cocaine for a while, I was sure he was wrong. I never believed I could be so incredibly blind as to not know my own husband was doing coke. But then, I never saw how sad you were until it was too late. I guess I *was* blind, huh?" Tears pricked my eyes, and I flipped my sunglasses down to hide them from Samuel.

Samuel leaned closer to me, his voice also quiet. "I intentionally hid it from you, Kaye. The more practiced I became, the easier it was to hide the sadness and the drugs. And I justified lying because the truth would only hurt you." Samuel glanced at my hands, and I thought he was going to pry them away from my body. But he stayed where he was, giving me my space. He closed his eyes, his head falling against the seat.

"The cocaine stimulated my mind, zapped me out of my funk to the point where I could come home from work with a smile. I added an extra mile to my morning run to hide my weight loss and cope with the restlessness. I worked on my book late at night to hide the insomnia. And the increased sex drive…well, we were newlyweds. Lots of sex was never our problem."

I felt my cheeks burn. Correction: sex was never a problem for us in the heat of the act. The problem was post-coital guilt, even after he'd put a diamond engagement ring on my finger. Before, to my twitterpated, teenaged self, our decision to wait sucked about an hour before curfew on Saturday nights, but was a relief Sunday morning in the church pew.

It was this very values system that made everything he revealed so hard to swallow. This was *Samuel.* Straight-laced Sam Cabral. Even now, it was difficult to picture him snorting white powder or simply *carrying* the paraphernalia with which he'd been busted.

He continued. "I also led you to believe my job with *Latin Colorado* kept me busier than it actually did. I wrote about *music*, Kaye. There wasn't a whole lot of research I needed to do because you and I lived and breathed the local music scene."

"So where were you if you weren't at your job in the evenings?" My voice cracked, and I knew I wouldn't be able to hold back the tears much longer. I bit the inside of my mouth and tasted metal on my tongue.

"Lots of places. Parks, mainly. Lakes. Empty car lots. Anywhere I could go to do a line and crank out several pages of surreal nonsense on my laptop. When the high wore off, I'd work with the gibberish and shape it into something coherent."

I remembered how bizarre and brilliant some of *Water Sirens* was. "How often did you use?"

"It started out sporadically, in college. I'd do a bit of pot with the other writers during poetry slams. Then I graduated to a coke line or two after evening workshops. But once you come off of a high, you crash hard, so I used it more and more to compensate for the crashes. Obviously I wasn't thinking clearly. Around the time I went to New York, I'd moved from a few lines every two to three days, to craving a binge. And if I started binging, I knew I wouldn't have been able to hide it from you. I even kept a separate bank account with my parents' money to cover the extra expense."

My jaw dropped. "You spent Alonso and Sofia's money on drugs?"

"No. My other parents."

I blinked in surprise. He very rarely mentioned his birth parents, unless he couldn't avoid it. "Oh. I forgot about the trust fund."

He smiled bitterly. "I wouldn't touch it for anything else. Wasting my mother's money on my own self-destruction seemed fitting." Samuel's eyes iced over, chilling me with their strangeness. One, then two tears spilled over my cheeks and I wiped them away beneath my sunglasses. Samuel dug around in my glove compartment and handed me a paper napkin.

"So you left," I sniffed, angrily rubbing at my eyes with the scratchy napkin. "You chose *it* over me."

The frost left Samuel's pleading eyes. "I didn't see it that way—my head was all screwed up. Right before I left, I tried to stop, so many times. And each time I tried, I failed. You have to understand how my mind worked. The very thought of dragging you into my hell was repulsive."

"But you just left. You didn't even give me a choice—you took that away from me."

"How would you have chosen?" he asked quietly.

"I would have stayed and fought, of course. We would have got you better, together."

"No. You would have sacrificed yourself for me, and you would have lost."

"I guess we'll never know, will we?"

"*I* know. You were twenty, Kaye. I would have destroyed you, along with myself. You just don't *do* that to someone you love."

"So you left to keep me from being a casualty to your destructive behavior, only you destroyed me, anyway. Being two years younger didn't make me naïve or weak." Anger pressed against my chest. I straightened my back. "Samuel, you have to get it into your head that when you shield people—me, Danita—from the big bad world, you cause more harm than good. I'm not even going to start stewing over the implications of this, because all I want to do is dig out your old baseball bat and beat you with it."

He fell silent, allowing me some peace. After a while, he exited the Jeep and carried the crates of welcome baskets into the hotel to give me space.

He said he left because he didn't want to drag me down with him. But he didn't let me *choose*. What in Tom's name had he been thinking?

Sure, Colorado had its pot-heavy air. Heck, my dad used to light up when he thought I was napping. But I had to admit, I knew next to nothing about hard drugs. The only knowledge I'd gleaned was from articles I'd read online months after my trip to New York as I tried to make sense of Samuel's behavior. They had explained the physical implications but not the cognitive. Why was he so sad, and why had he hidden that sadness? Had he believed I was so fragile, he couldn't rely upon me?

I could only understand if I asked. When he finally returned to the Jeep twenty minutes later, I pounced before I chickened out. "Samuel, I'm ready to ask my one question."

"Go ahead." His blue eyes warily skimmed my face.

"Did you really want to leave me?"

Please say no, please say no…I squeezed my eyes shut, braced for his answer. So I felt, rather than saw, his fingertips brush my damp hairline, slowly coming to rest under my chin. His warm breath hit my cheek, then my mouth. For a frightening, fleeting moment, I thought he was going to kiss me. I held my breath, my fingernails digging into my thighs.

"No." His voice was soft on my ear.

My eyes popped open. He was right there, bright blues inches from mine. My heart pounded wildly, echoed in my ears, and I couldn't think with him so close. I backed away and asked him to repeat it.

He must have sensed my distress because he also leaned back, his hand falling from my chin to his lap. I suddenly felt like an idiot for panicking.

"Of course I didn't want to leave you, Kaye," he sighed. "How could you possibly think I'd *ever* want to leave you after I spent years doing everything I could to keep you next to me?"

I frowned. "Um…because you told me you didn't want to be married to me anymore? Was there any other way to interpret that?"

"No, I said I *couldn't* be married to you anymore. Never once did I tell you I didn't *want* you." His frown mirrored mine.

"The whole 'leaving' thing kind of implied the 'want' aspect, don't you think?"

Samuel held up a calming hand. "Let's not argue semantics. Truly, the only thing I understood that summer afternoon was I had to get as far from you as possible."

I shook my head, unable to wrap my brain around what he told me. "Once you got clean, why didn't you explain any of this to me?"

"It's a rather convoluted story," he said, trying miserably to lighten the mood. "It's also a third question, which I'll answer next week if you ask. That furrow between your eyebrows tells me I've given you more than enough to ponder."

"You're wicked."

"So you've written." He grinned that stellar grin and tapped his forehead. Charmer. I conceded, knowing he was right about needing time. His story was a field of prairie dog holes to stumble through.

As we delivered the rest of the baskets, I struggled to reconcile the Sam I thought I'd known with the Samuel he'd just introduced.

He had loved me, but *how* had he loved me? He obviously valued our friendship, very much, and wrote to remember because he felt its loss so keenly. He told me he wanted it back. But there was a difference between romantic love and friendship love…more and more, I wondered if Samuel had confused the two. Perhaps the drugs simply quickened the destruction of a marriage already doomed to fail. Perhaps that was why, once he got clean, he never came back.

Samuel sat silent beside me, arms folded over his chest. The late afternoon sun bounced off of his dark head as he watched the hazy outskirts of Lyons through the window. The hairs on his olive arms shone. I used to smooth my hands over them, tug them when he teased me. I used to clutch his bicep and lean against his solid shoulder while we watched movies, his other hand weaving into my hair, pulling me to him. A dull ache flared within me, a longing particularly painful on quiet nights alone in my apartment. Despite my anger, right now I wanted nothing more than to feel the warm lines of his long, lean body tucked against me on my sofa, complications be damned.

"Do you have plans tonight? The extended family descends tomorrow, so you might like a quiet evening before then. The ghost hunting show is still on the table, and I can whip up a taco salad."

His smile was all apology. "I'd really love to, but Caroline's flying in tonight and I need to pick her up in Denver. She decided to return a day early."

Oh, right. His girlfriend. "Why didn't you say anything? We could have gone on to Denver and saved you the backtrack."

"I'd rather pick her up by myself, Kaye. We have some issues to sort through as well, and it would be easier with just the two of us. I'm sorry."

My face fell, his rejection stinging. Of course Samuel didn't want a third wheel. He reminded me he'd fly back to Lyons any time I wanted—even if it was just to watch TV and eat taco salad—and that appeased me, slightly. But my stomach still twisted at the thought of Samuel and Caroline working through their issues…kissing each other, whispering apologies, holding each other tightly. Jaime had better be digging up dirt on her. I needed a distraction from the revelations swirling through my head.

He hadn't wanted to leave me, but in that warped, protective way of his, he'd thought leaving was for the best…

Every inch of me felt lighter…and heavier. How much of our marriage's disintegration could be blamed on the sadness and drugs, and how much on plain dysfunction? This bothered me as much as the idea that he didn't want me because, in the end, it still meant we had failed each other.

It was eleven o'clock when I crawled into my father's basement guest room in Lyons. A bizarre idea flitted around, blocking me from sleep…as much as Sam rationalized and reasoned, did he organize his thoughts or make lists of the lies he'd told, the things he kept hidden? The idea was funny in a horrible sort of way, but it was so Samuel. I could see him feverishly typing away on his laptop, creating a spreadsheet.

I wondered what such a list would look like…

He'd hidden the drug use, first and foremost.

Also, Samuel had hidden his unhappiness under the guise of stress, at least until he left.

Ice raced up my spine at the thought of him deliberately lying to me. I wondered what other lies he'd told. And then, with shame, it occurred to me that he wasn't the only one. I should be keeping my own list.

That wasn't such a bad idea.

Opening my laptop, I took a page from Samuel's anal-retentive book and began to type out a list:

My Lies (forthright and by omission)

1. LIE: I'm a lesbian.

   TRUTH: Lie told in rash decision to stick it to floozy and ex-husband.

   STATUS: Continued because of strong dislike for floozy and success in her retreat. However, Jaime thinks floozy knows truth. Agree.

2. LIE: I had nothing to do with Mickey-gate.

   TRUTH: Prank conducted to embarrass ex-hubby and throw wrench in floozy's publicity plan.

   STATUS: While PETA still causes problems, fervor has died down and both floozy and ex are aware of lie.

3. LIE: I had nothing to do with drag picture.

   TRUTH: Obtained picture from Danita.

   STATUS: While ex (presumably) does not know of picture, floozy claims to have squelched media exposure.

While I was being honest, I might as well acknowledge I did each of those pranks because I enjoyed getting a rise out of Samuel.

4. LIE: I hate Samuel's books.

Hmm, gray territory. This lie hadn't been told so much to Samuel, friends, and family, but to myself.

   TRUTH: Not hatred, per se. The Last Other is actually really good. And while I'm confessing, I've had time to finish Samuel's book, I just don't want to—not sure why.

Along those lines…

5. LIE: I didn't have time to change my name back to Trilby.

   TRUTH: I had nearly seven years, enough said. Why didn't I? Was it the finality? Giving up a claim to the Cabral family? May require further introspection.

6. LIE: I didn't think Samuel was perfect.

   TRUTH: Uncertain about this. However, Mom and Samuel claim I thought he was. Also may require further introspection.

7. LIE: I'm glad Samuel has moved on.

Wow. Could I truly be happy if he was with another woman, given the woman was a good match for him?

   TRUTH: I might be glad if the woman he moved on with wasn't such a harpy.

8. LIE: I'm not angry anymore.

   TRUTH: I like to believe I've moved on, but every time I think of New York, I want to claw out Samuel's eyes. If that's not anger…

Ah, and then there was the New York "lie by omission." Amazing, how the list grew.

9. LIE: I never traveled to New York to see Samuel.
   TRUTH: Told Dani and Molly I hid it because I was embarrassed and hurt—truth? I think so.

And the last one. I almost couldn't write it, because making it more than a hurriedly-answered question under Danita's pressure meant I'd have to face it, eventually. And facing it meant facing Samuel. Yet it flowed from my fingers:

10. LIE: I don't love Samuel anymore.
    TRUTH: Is it possible to stop?

There it was: my list of confessions. Now what to do with it?

The bottom few made me heart-heavy. A part of me almost hoped Danita or Molly would tell him the truth so I wouldn't have to. Another part wanted to fall out of love with Samuel and move on before I ever had to face it.

A little past midnight, I locked my laptop and snuggled under my blankets in the black, windowless room, glad to have exorcised so much on "paper." I was on fire. Unstoppable, solving the world's problems as puzzle pieces fell into place. I began to believe that maybe Samuel was wrong—that we really could just sit down and hash out all of our issues in one go, rather than this plodding one-question-at-a-time method. So when Jaime called at nearly one a.m., I stumbled for my phone and answered with passion, ready to uproot the Manhattan yuppie once and for all.

"What have you got for me on Caroline?"

Silence.

"Jaime?"

"Wow, Trilby, if I didn't know better, I'd say you're coming down from some mind-blowing sex. What the hell have you been doing... Cabral? You both need to get laid so badly, it's painful to watch."

I choked, reining in my exhilaration. "Just sorting stuff I'd stuck on the backburner. What did you find on Caroline?"

"Do you have your dossier handy? I ran across something in there tonight that I'm kicking myself for missing. It's your fault, you know. If you hadn't gone after me at the café like I was plotting to rip off your teddy bear's head, I would have noticed it earlier."

The dossier? Not what I expected. "It's in my apartment in Boulder."

"Hold on, I'll send you a picture of my copy. Call me back once you look it over."

My phone blipped. I opened the file to see the top of Samuel's drug arrest record glowing in my screen. I scanned it several times, but nothing jumped out. I called Jaime back.

"Okay, I give up. Tell me."

"Well, I puzzled over this one for a while—how Samuel managed to stay out of prison for this drug arrest—the one right after your divorce went through? New York State has extremely tough drug laws, which almost always carry mandatory prison time as part of sentencing. And yet unconnected ol' Cabral gets away with a slap on the wrist and community service. So I perused the file again. Lo and behold, what did I find?" Jaime paused dramatically.

"Just spit it out, Jaime."

"Fine, *caray*. Samuel wasn't arrested in New York. He was arrested in *North Carolina*. Which means that, after he signed the divorce papers, he barely returned to NYC before scooting down to Raleigh—if he even returned at all. I can't believe I missed this!"

I sucked in my breath, only to find I had never exhaled. I patted behind me. When I couldn't find my bed, I sank to the ground, stared at my wall in disbelief. No. *No.* Please not *her*. It *had* to be a coincidence.

"And you know who's from North Carolina?"

"Caroline?" I rasped.

"Caroline."

Chapter 17
HORIZON LINE

When looking ahead for potential waterfalls,
paddlers will notice a line where the river falls away.
The harder it is to see the bottom of the drop,
the steeper the drop will be.

There are key events in our lives which mark imminent change. Accepting a diploma. Attending the funeral of a loved one. Witnessing a friend walk down the aisle. Suffering through a divorce. It's expected. But there are little, everyday events that whittle away at who we are, steadily shaping us into someone different, for better or for worse. Things that cause our perceptions to shift.

I thought it might be one of those days when, for the first time, I downed strong, black coffee without the fixings…and didn't flinch.

When I pulled into the Cabrals' driveway bright and early Friday morning, workmen already swarmed around the extensive lawn like bees, manicuring and pruning hedges, scrubbing siding, making way for tomorrow's onslaught of reception vendors and guests. I wove around them, careful not to stumble over my already awkward, sleep-deprived feet. Danita would kill me for being half-dead during bridesmaid spa time, a.k.a., Connie's Nail Salon on Lyons' Main Street. I'd have to sneak in a nap before Hector picked me up for the wedding rehearsal.

But now I needed to see Samuel before the bridal buzz engulfed the day.

Samuel left me just before fall semester of college began. I went to New York in September, then filed for divorce. According to Jaime's dossier, his NYU grades slipped all of that semester, even with Alonso and Sofia there. Given his drug history, the poor grades were understandable.

At some point during the semester, he met Caroline Ortega—an associate editor with Berkshire House Publishing. Or had he known her before he moved to New York? Did she help him get an eleventh hour NYU admission?

He ignored Jaime's repeated phone calls, letters, and emails to discuss divorce proceedings. Finally, he contacted her after New Year's and said he wanted to sign the papers in person.

We divorced late January. Samuel was arrested in North Carolina for drug possession in mid-February. Why was he in North Carolina when spring semester should have been in full swing? Was it because his associate editor was from Raleigh?

Next logical question: Why ditch classes just to visit your associate editor, and right after a nasty divorce? But if said associate editor was more than an associate editor…

I kicked a rock that had escaped a flowerbed, sending it skipping across the driveway. Attacking a rock was better than attacking husband-seducing debutante tripe. In the light of day, I told myself that Samuel needed friends, too. But why did it have to be her? Had he been attracted to her from the moment he met her, and ran to her when he was free to pursue a relationship? I couldn't see him doing that, but I also hadn't believed Samuel was amped up on coke lines.

I spotted Queen Bee Sofia up to her elbows in dirt. White columbine and delicate blue flax encompassed Mamá Cabral as she pushed back her floppy straw hat and waved to me with a gloved hand and spade. Her wavy black hair was loosely braided over her shoulder, her curvy frame swam in denim overalls.

"You're up and about early, Kaye. I thought you and the girls weren't going to Connie's until ten."

"Good morning, Sofia. Sorry to bother you on such a busy day, but I need to speak with your son." I shoved my hands into my pockets to hide their trembling. I needed answers now—forget the one-question rule.

Sofia's face fell as she studied my demeanor. "He and Caroline are on their morning jog. After that, I have them scooting to Denver to meet family at the airport. But you can come inside, have a cup of coffee and a bagel."

Jogging together? Samuel and Caroline must have worked out their "issues." Cringing, I followed her up the back stairs, knowing I wouldn't be able to eat anything. She shucked her gardening gear and washed her hands in the sun room. I slipped off my flip-flops.

Alonso sat at the kitchen island in his flannel PJ bottoms, slippers, and robe, the back of his bed hair standing up in a cowlick. A newspaper was in his hands, his eyes scanning headlines. When he saw me, he jumped up from his paper.

"Kaye, what a nice surprise." He dished up a bagel and mug of steaming coffee, then gestured for me to sit. So polite, just like his son. "Are you here for Danita?"

"Can't I just visit my second-favorite mom and dad?" I glanced around the kitchen bathed in soft gray light, gauzy curtains fluttering over an open window. Gershwin quietly tinkled from Sofia's morning playlist. I loved this kitchen. It had brought me such peace, especially when I'd spent nights with Danita after fighting with my mother. Sofia was always there with hot chocolate and hugs, encouraging me to give it another go with my mom. Samuel was there, too. And Danita, once she stumbled out of bed, her black hair pulled into a skewed ponytail on top of her head. Even Alonso joined us on the mornings he wasn't swamped with deadlines for *Latin Colorado* magazine. My ideal family.

But this morning the kitchen didn't bring me peace. It felt off, knowing what I did about Samuel's arrest in North Carolina. Because I understood, now, that Sofia had misled me.

"Sofia, I didn't come here just to speak with Samuel. Do you mind if we chat?" My eyes shifted to Alonso, indicating I wanted to keep this private. She caught my drift. Nodding to the hallway, we left the kitchen for the library.

The first thing I noticed when I entered the hallway was the Rivera *Girl with Lilies* print above the mahogany hall table was gone. In its place were two newly-hung portraits: one of Danita and Angel, and one of Samuel. Each was an exquisitely-done, antiqued sketch. I wasn't an artist, but the unfinished appearance reminded me of DaVinci's intricate, feathery etchings. Around the cream-colored matting of each picture was a quote done in flawless calligraphy. I tilted my head, reading the Spanish around Danita's and Angel's:

"The first symptom of love in a young man is shyness; the first symptom in a woman? It's boldness."

Victor Hugo—I knew it before I'd even finished the quote. Tomorrow's date followed the quote, commemorating their wedding. I smiled.

I studied the portrait of Samuel next. The artist had captured him perfectly. Not just the strong angles of his face, but subtle nuances like the barely-there scar above his eyebrow and the sensitivity of his mouth. Around the matting was one of his favorite quotes—he used to scroll it across his laptop screensaver years ago.

"A writer is not a great mind, he's not a great thinker, he's not a great philosopher. He's a storyteller."

Erskine Caldwell, that was it. A modestly successful Southern writer, in his time. Certainly controversial.

Sofia came up next to me, her fingers skimming over the gilded frame. "It's beautiful work, isn't it? She's captured them all so well." She sighed. "It's too much, really, for a thank you gift."

I frowned. "Who?"

"Caroline. She gave them to us in appreciation for welcoming her into our home the past month. I had no idea..."

"Wait. Caroline commissioned these?"

"No, Kaye. Caroline *is* the artist." Sofia tapped the corner of one of the portraits, indicating the signature. "I can't begin to imagine having this kind of talent. But I've always said the same thing about you and Samuel, too."

I studied the initials closely...CRO. So Caroline was a brilliant artist, as well as a successful agent, editor, publicist, journalist, equestrian, cheerleader, socialite, jogger, and frickin' beauty queen. Jealousy burned deep. I grudgingly admitted I should appreciate the tremendous talent that lay behind the portraits, but I didn't stand a chance in hell.

Sofia continued on to the library and I followed, escaping to the safe-haven walls of beautifully bound books. She gestured to one of the overstuffed chairs by the fireplace and settled into the other, opposite me.

"What is on your mind, *mi corazón?*"

I took a deep breath to calm my jealous stirrings. "Do you remember when you were in New York, how we called each other weekly to catch up? We'd talk about how I was coping, the good things that happened, the books you'd read...all of that?"

She nodded.

"Okay, so you probably remember the night I called just a couple of weeks after the divorce. You were upset because Samuel had been arrested for drug possession."

Sofia shifted uncomfortably, but again nodded.

"Here's the thing." I drummed my fingers on my armrest, trying to phrase my thoughts without sounding accusatory. "I told you I was going to fly out to New York to be with you and Alonso. That I could leave Denver in two hours and be at JFK by midnight."

"I remember."

"Why didn't you correct me, Sofia?"

Honest confusion blanketed her features. "What do you mean?"

"Samuel was arrested in *North Carolina*, not New York. I know it seems like a minor thing, but...what was he doing in North Carolina to begin with? I think you know and you didn't tell me for a reason."

Understanding dawned. "How do you know about that?" It was my turn to squirm. I couldn't exactly tell Samuel's mother I had a dirt file on him. "You've been speaking with Samuel. I know, he's told me. He's explained his reasons for leaving Colorado?"

"Yes."

Sofia studied my face and saw my fears, plain as day. She leaned forward and placed her brown hand on my knee. "Kaye, Samuel wasn't involved with Caroline in the way you're thinking. She was a friend of a friend who eventually became his editor. That was it."

"Please explain, Sofia."

Her expression became pained, far-away. "You have to understand—he'd made progress in New York before the divorce. He had his little setbacks, but he was able to fight through them. So brave. My son wanted to get himself together so he could repair the damage he'd done with you. He was racing against time, avoiding Jaime Guzman's requests until he could see you and sort through the mess. But then he had a major setback and it 'changed the game' for him, so to speak. All of his hard work...he threw it away, just like that."

Poor Samuel. A lump formed in my throat for the umpteenth time this tumultuous week. "What happened?"

She shrugged, giving me an apologetic half-smile.

"Fine," I conceded, "I'll ask Samuel. Please continue."

"He agreed to the divorce, believing he could never overcome his problems. When he returned from Colorado after signing the divorce papers, he planned to journey across Mexico and write, no phone, little money."

"You mean he was just going to disappear?"

Sofia's eyes welled with unshed tears. "*Sí,* more or less. *'Donde hay amor, hay dolor,'* and there was so much hurt in my son, Kaye. Please don't think it was all because of the divorce. His burdens were too heavy, and he believed if he extricated himself from his current life, it would make those troubles go away. Alonso and I couldn't tell him otherwise. But Caroline—she didn't coddle him. She said his book was nowhere near the shape it should be in for publication, and threatened him with a lawsuit if he reneged on his contract. He was too tired to fight back. So they agreed to a compromise. She took him to Raleigh. They could work on his book and he could get the change of scenery he desperately needed."

"But he still kept up the drug use."

"Like I said, he'd thrown in the towel. The police picked him up for public intoxication and noticed his erratic behavior, so they searched his messenger bag…"

"And found his stash of goodies."

"Cocaine powder as well as diluted cocaine in vials, another step further into his…experimentations. But the arrest was a blessing in disguise. I don't know if you are aware, but Caroline comes from money—old money, from the vineyards of Spanish California. She contacted one of her father's golf friends, who happened to be the best defense lawyer in North Carolina. They bailed him out of jail, gave Samuel a good shake, and managed to avoid jail time. On the condition, of course, he'd go to full rehab—not just the therapy sessions in New York."

So now I could add "savior" to Caroline's list of accomplishments. No wonder Samuel was so loyal to her. Crud, I didn't want to like her.

"What about NYU?"

"He dropped out, then later returned once he was able to focus on his studies again. It was a tough road, but he finished that degree."

"Sofia…he could have died." A shudder ran up my back as I spoke the unreal words, the reality of them hitting me. Gone. Samuel could have died somewhere in Mexico in an overdose, or a car crash, or, heaven forbid, a kidnapping, and I hadn't even comprehended the possibility was there, lurking. At twenty-one, who really believes they will lose the one they love until reality comes knocking? A tremor of the same fear I'd felt in New York gripped me again, and I wanted nothing more than to put my arms around Samuel and assure myself that he was alive.

"I'm so sorry, Kaye."

I bit my lip, feeling awful for having missed so much. My irritation turned to Sofia. "Why didn't you or Alonso tell me about this? Didn't you think I deserved to know? Was I not good enough, not trustworthy?"

"Kaye, you and Samuel were divorced," she said gently. "You had your own life to live. You were in bad shape too, dear heart, even if you put on a brave face. We knew how it would look to you—Samuel running off to Raleigh with some woman, right after your divorce. It would have crushed your already fragile self-esteem, even if we'd explained."

"But what if…what if the divorce was a mistake to begin with? Didn't that cross your mind?"

"I wonder every day, *mi corazón*. But then, forcing two young people to listen to their mother is like forcing the tide to turn. It must happen naturally, on their own terms."

I pressed my fingertips to my temples, knowing deep down that she was right. I hadn't been in good shape, then, hadn't listened. But something still gnawed at me. It had to do with the fact that my warm, perfect Cabrals had hidden things from me. They claimed it was for my own good, but how could keeping secrets like these possibly help? Unless—and I couldn't even think it—Alonso and Sofia wanted to put distance between me and their family. Because of the divorce? Because I wasn't Hispanic? Perhaps that was why Danita was so blunt—she overcompensated for her family's secretive tendencies.

Another thought hit me: if Dani was my friend, why hadn't *she* told me about Samuel's North Carolina arrest?

"Sofia, did Danita know what was going on?"

"At the time she didn't, no."

"But she knows now?"

"Our family has discussed it recently. Despite my daughter's often brusque attitude, she really loves you, Kaye, and is very devoted to you. But sometimes she strong-arms you into doing her bidding, so to speak. And she has her own way of clearing the air, which often brings about more trouble than solutions."

"So you thought Danita would use me to try to fix Samuel's drug problems, if she knew."

"It was wrong of us to keep her—both of you—in the dark for so long. But we learn as we go. Parents make mistakes too, Kaye, so many. No one is truly an expert, but our hearts are usually in the right place." Guilt crept into her face. Even if they weren't blood-related, Samuel had certainly adopted many of Sofia's expressions. Sometimes it hurt to see him in her—and this was one of those times. My compassionate side urged me to go to Sofia and hug her. But I refrained, not able to forgive so easily. Samuel was more than just an ex-husband to me, and she knew it. And Danita…she must have been incredibly hurt.

In true kismet timing, there was a rap at the door and Samuel poked his head around. His hair and limbs were damp with sweat, as was the dark blue T-shirt clinging to his torso. He looked more rested today—bright-eyed and energetic, though the circles beneath his eyes were still there.

"I thought that was your Jeep in the driveway. There are so many people here and it's only seven thirty." His eyes darted to his mother, then back to me. "Ay, *lo siento*—I'm interrupting." He began to close the door, but I hopped up from my chair to stop him.

"Samuel." Despite his stinky, sweaty state, I threw my arms around his neck and pulled him to me tightly, terrified to let him go. Samuel jerked as if he'd touched a live wire, but wrapped his arms around me, lifting me from the ground. He pulled back to search my face.

"Firecracker, what's wrong?"

"I'm just glad you're okay," I mumbled into his neck.

His brow knit as he gazed over my shoulder at his mother. "Why wouldn't I be okay?"

I shook my head, suddenly feeling foolish. "It's nothing. I'm just all over the place emotionally, with Danita getting married."

"Are you sure?" He ran fingers up and down my spine, comforting me as if I were ready to crack.

I nodded and awkwardly pulled away from his arms. I didn't miss the hopeful gleam in the eyes of my former mother-in-law as she watched her son and me.

"Well then, I have a favor to ask of you." Samuel linked his index finger with mine and swung our arms back and forth, studying me more closely. "Actually, never mind. You look like you're ready to drop from exhaustion. Trouble sleeping?"

I shrugged off his concern. "Just tell me what you want, please, Samuel."

"Aunt Lucia and Uncle Carlos fly in this afternoon. Would you like to pick them up at the Denver airport with me? I'm sure Aunt Lucia would love to see you again."

Lucia was Sofia's older sister from Southern California, and I'd always liked her. "With you and Caroline?"

"Caroline would prefer to stay here. But I'd enjoy your company—as much as you'll allow before I have to return to New York." He leaned in, whispering, "You'd probably be able to sneak in a nap on the drive, too."

It was my turn to refuse Samuel in payback for ditching on the ghost hunting show. But payback didn't seem so important, and I was sad to tell him no.

"Sorry, Mr. Cabral, unless you want to take my place with the other bridesmaids for manis and pedis later this morning. I've seen guys there before. Really."

Samuel playfully grimaced. "That's okay. You'll see the family tonight." He started to lean in for a hug, but changed his mind. He quickly kissed my temple and released my finger. "Be good, and no crazy hair changes before wedding pictures. I don't want to scrape you off the bottom of Danita's shoes." Kissing his mother's cheek, he ducked out of the room.

It was time for me to be off, too, if I was going to shower and put out a few TrilbyJones fires before ten. But Sofia grabbed my elbow as I tried to leave.

"Kaye?" Her voice wavered. "That cookie-cutter dream…ideal spouse, beautiful kids, successful business, SUV packed with baseball gear, fireworks on the Fourth of July…Don't let it trip up the two of you, *sí?* As parents, our dream is to leave a legacy for our children that is even greater than the legacy left to us. But sometimes we forget, there are lots of different kinds of happiness. The dream that works for some doesn't work for others."

"Sofia, I can barely keep myself together right now, let alone a car packed with little leaguers. I know what makes me happy, don't worry."

"Does Samuel know what makes you happy?" she asked softly. "Or for that matter, do you know what makes him happy?"

Warning bells sounded in my head. "What does this have to do with anything?"

"It's *everything*. And if you were honest with yourself, you'd know that."

Are you happy? Three little words, written by Samuel in the cover of a book. Oh, but what a book they'd opened. I backed out of the room, unwilling to have this discussion with Samuel's mother.

"I appreciate your candidness, more than you know. But I should say hello to Danita before I head out." Never mind. I'd see her in two hours at Connie's Nail Salon.

Sofia sighed. "Wedding rehearsal, six o'clock, *mi corazón*."

Dun...dun dun Dun...dun dun Dun...dun dun Dun...

I started awake, the sharp scent of nail polish remover and patchouli tingling my nostrils. Arena rock wailed from my purse and echoed through the salon. Crap, my cell phone. I looked helplessly at my purse as the fresh polish on my fingers and toes dried under the salon's blue-light.

Molly, still waiting for her turn along with Angel's little sister, dove for my purse and dug out my phone.

"Hello? Hi, Hector!...Um, she's got wet fingernails right now. Hold on." She held the phone next to my ear and lifted an eyebrow.

"Hey, Hector, what's up?"

"*Hola*, just want to double-check on the gig tonight. Pick you up at five thirty at the Cabrals' house, casual dress?"

"Yes. Don't forget, the rehearsal dinner is on your folks' property near the crick, where we used to play? So when I say casual dress, I really mean casual dress." Because of the high number of out-of-town guests, there was no place in Lyons to accommodate the rehearsal dinner. Instead, the Valdez family opted for backyard *zacahuiles*—huge tamales cooked underground in a clay pot. Mariachi and local brews would flow aplenty, tonight. The Valdez clan knew how to throw a party.

Of course, to get to the rehearsal dinner, I had to make it through the rehearsal. If I kept my eyes away from Sam, maybe I would survive unscathed. Already, my stomach was a mess of nerves. So was Danita's, though she did her best to keep up that tough-girl exterior. I toyed with the idea of asking Molly's stepmother for a Xanax, something Dani and I could split.

"Kaye?" Hector asked. "Look, it's going to be okay. Remember why you asked me to be your date?"

"Yeah." I smiled in spite of my nerves, recalling my sobbing phone call to Hector. "You said we'd show 'dickhead' what he was missing. Give your dear friend Kaye, with the pathetic love life, a wonderful time and all that." Danita glanced up from her magazine and scowled at me. I stared at the black-and-white striped wall just beyond her head.

His tone grew sober. "*Mamacita*, you know your love life doesn't have to be nonexistent, right? I'm single and fairly decent to look at…"

"I know, Hector." Molly's hand squeezed my shoulder. My eyes darted up, seeing if she'd heard. Yup, she'd heard.

"Just think about it, okay? No pressure."

"I'll think about it. That's all I can promise."

"That's all I'm asking for. And, Kaye?"

"Yeah, Hector?"

"Saint Peter stood at the gate when Hippie Tom walked up…"

When I finished my call with Hector, I felt three sets of eyes on me. Danita fumed. Molly worried. And the poor junior bridesmaid was confused.

"Okay, I think it's time for some discussion, ladies." Molly checked my nearly-dry nails, then dragged me from my seat and across the slick wood floor. I plopped into the pedicure chair next to Danita, where she soaked her feet. Angel's little sister scooted up a chair and leaned in, sensing good gossip.

Danita gave her pre-teen sister-in-law a piercing look. "Not a word or so help me, I tell your mother about that text you accidentally forwarded to me." The girl blanched and nodded.

"Dani, tell Kaye about Sunday night," Molly whispered. A knowing look passed between my two friends.

"Wait, after the camping trip?" I asked. "What happened?"

Dani leaned forward, her eyes shining. "Okay, but keep this on the down-low. I wasn't supposed to hear it, and the only reason Molly knows is because there was something about you being a lesbian that totally confused me, so I had to ask her if she had any clue what they were talking about."

"Dani! Who was talking? I'm dying here."

"Sunday night I was in the living room digging through old photo albums for the slide show tomorrow. There's this vent in the corner, right? So when people are in the basement, you can hear their conversations. Well, Samuel and Caroline just happened to be in the basement, having a pretty heated argument."

"You were eavesdropping."

Danita puffed. "Yes, but that's not the point. Caroline was really working Samuel over with drivel about you not being a lesbian, I don't know. That part lost me. But here's the good part. Caroline accused him of bringing you in on some book project because he just wants to—" she covered the junior bridesmaid's ears "—get into your pants—exact words. *Jesús, María y José,* did that make Samuel angry. He fired back, saying—get this—his sex life *isn't any of her concern.*"

Dani smugly sat back in her pedicure chair, hands perched on the armrests like she sat on a throne. Molly beamed at me, waiting for my reaction. I blinked, trying to make sense of it. If Samuel told Caroline to stay out of his sex life, then that would mean…

Yes! Eat it, harpy. A toothy grin spread across my face as I pumped the air with my fists. It meant Samuel and Caroline weren't together, or at least they weren't Sunday night. Even if they'd sorted out their issues—which now seemed to pertain to Caroline's accusations—it meant their romance was definitely on shaky ground.

"There's more," Dani rapidly continued. "So Caroline fires back that instead of spending his time writing something worthwhile, he pours all of his energy into a foolish book about dismal little kids with guitars and mommy complexes. After she said that, it got really quiet. I could just see that furious look spread over Samuel's face—the one where he purses his lips together like he's just sucked a lemon? And then he told her, really low, to quit cheapening relationships. 'I know I've hurt you, Caro,' he said, 'but let me be clear. If you go after her again I will drop your agency so fast, you won't have time for damage control. And with the movie publicity on the horizon, that would be extremely unfortunate for your firm.'"

Molly gasped, her hands flying to her mouth. "No way! You didn't mention that!"

Danita shrugged. "Caroline flounced off to Raleigh to see Togsy, supposedly to give them both time to cool down. But I think she just threw the guy out there to make Samuel jealous."

"Who's Togsy?" Molly and I asked at the same time.

"Caroline's ex-boyfriend."

I frowned, something clicking with Sofia's words, earlier…friend of a friend. "Surely not writer Togsy? From Colorado University?"

"Maybe. I don't know, I didn't ask. But apparently they were together for years. Of course, now she's back and on best behavior," she groaned. "Two more days and then she leaves for New York, thank God."

Still leaving with Samuel, though, I silently added. The others might be tolling the victory bell over Samuel and Caro's falling out, but I was hesitant to start kissing people in the streets. After all, Caroline had since unveiled those exquisite portraits. If that wasn't a big "I'm sorry," I didn't know what was.

Molly snapped her fingers. "You know that Friday lunch several weeks ago, when Kaye implied she had a date?" I rolled my eyes while Dani eagerly wagged her head. "Well, apparently Samuel called Santiago that night to ask if he'd seen you around town."

I struggled to remember. "That was the night he and Caroline showed up at the Lyons Café, when I was there with Jaime. They were arguing…"

Molly squealed. "Don't you get it, Kaye? Samuel was trying to *track you down* on your 'date.' That man is still head-over-heels in love with you, I'd bet my life on it. Tell her, Dani."

"Molly, he's my brother. I just can't—"

"It was kind of apparent Saturday night at the campfire," Molly continued. "The way he looked at you when you were playing guitars?"

"Wait, wait, wait, hold on just a minute." I jumped up from the pedi-chair, waving my hands to ward off my friends. "Let's not jump to conclusions, girls. I know you're trying to be helpful, but this isn't. I can't…I can't hope like this, not with our history and everything that's gone down between us."

I pointed a shell-pink nail at them.

"Molly, the only thing Dani's eavesdropping tells me is that Samuel is willing to stand up to Caroline for a friend. Which is very honorable, but it doesn't mean he's in love with me anymore. Let's not bring up that he brought a girlfriend home to meet his family, in the first place."

"But things can change, Kaye."

"And earlier on the same camping trip, you hinted I should go for Hector. So whatever you guys see in Samuel, I'm guessing you're skewing it out of proportion because of this bit of gossip. Bottom line: if Samuel was still in love with me, I'd see it better than any of you, plain and simple."

Molly shook her head. "Not necessarily. What if *you're* the one with skewed vision?"

I pressed a hand to my chest, trying to squelch the ache. "Molly. I've *made love* to this man countless times. I know what it looks like when he wants me." The junior bridesmaid's eyes widened, and I reined myself in. "I don't see it there, anymore. Heck, he doesn't even know me anymore. So please, just…stop."

"He still knows you," Dani said firmly, "even if he doesn't know everything *about* you."

A wave of exhaustion washed over me. I sank into the pedicure chair and rested my head in my hands, waiting for the dizziness to pass. I needed sleep, badly. I gazed up at Danita, feeling guilty for letting my personal grievances intrude on her wedding.

"Dani…" She cut me off with a surprisingly understanding smile.

"Go get some rest, *manita*. You've been there for me since you were a toddler, and you're allowed to take five every now and then. Just do one thing?"

I nodded, gathering up my purse and sandals. I should have waited to hear what she wanted before agreeing.

"Tell Samuel what happened when you found him in New York City. That can be your wedding present to me—along with the crystal stemware set you and Molly knocked off the registry." She winked, drawing a little laugh from the last bit of humor in the air. Of course Dani diligently watched her registries online.

"I'll do it," I sighed.

"That means tonight, Kaye, if it's going to be a wedding present. Maybe then you can *both* get some sleep."

My mother was on the back acre weeding her young squash plants, so the farmhouse was quiet when I staggered through the door. The rooms were stuffy. I adjusted the thermostat, closed the blinds, and sank into the old vine-print couch. But, once again, sleep wouldn't come. Dread pulsed through my veins as I sorted through what I'd tell Sam about New York. Finally, I hopped up from the couch and pulled out a spiral notebook. Carpe diem, and all that.

For a full hour, I jotted down everything I could recall about that time, from finding his address to finding his note in my backpack, the smells, and feelings, and fears. That way, when I almost certainly began to unravel, I would have something to simply hand him.

I folded the notebook paper and slid it into an envelope, feeling better now that I'd gotten it out of the way. Curling into my mother's couch, I crashed.

Two hours of blissful, uninterrupted sleep. And then I tossed fitfully, starting awake as brown, then black hair spilled over Samuel's pillow. Other times, there were flashes of Samuel dead on a lush, Tamaulipasian roadside. The Dream just had to make an appearance right after I'd committed to telling Samuel about my excursion into his East Village Den of Sin.

But this time I wasn't the girl at the door. I was the woman beneath him, feeding his addiction…

> *Me…moving hands to his sticky, muscled back, dragging along his spine, tangling in his thick hair and taking what was someone else's. Me, pulling his face closer, breathing in the rim of white powder above his lip.*
>
> *The girl in the doorway…a slight, mousy thing, no more than twenty. Jeans, sweatshirt, no makeup. Backpack resting next to her feet where she'd dropped it. A Post-it note fluttering from her fingers to the ground. Too thin, too sickly.*
>
> *Me…smacking his shoulder, getting his attention, pointing at her…"Who's that?"*
>
> *Him…his entire body going rigid above me, caging me between him and the twisted sheets as if he could hide me, cold eyes riveted to the girl at the door…so much anger for this out-of-place, pale-faced person standing in his room.*
>
> *A black-haired woman helping the girl up.*
>
> *Why were his eyes so cold? Something was wrong with him…so wrong…*

An annoying buzzing vibrated against my cheek. I batted at it, then realized it was my phone. I answered.

"Sam?" I groaned, still asleep.

A laugh. "No, *hermosa*, it's Hector. Hey, where are you? Everyone's waiting at the Cabrals' place."

I sat up, running my free hand through my snarled hair. "Crap! What time is it?"

"Five forty-five. Were you asleep or something?"

I shook the remnants of the disturbing dream from my system. "Argh!" Stumbling out of bed, I tore into my closet, peeling clothes from my clammy body. "Yeah. Geez! Tell Danita I'm so, so sorry. I must have silenced my phone."

"Hold on, Kaye." I heard muffled speaking in the background, then Hector's voice. "Yeah, she's fine. You were right, *princesa*. Tell Cabral to get the hell out of his roadster and a grip on his pansy-ass… sorry Sr. Cabral."

I grabbed my body mist and sprayed myself down with apple-scented stuff. Hector was moving—I heard a door slam.

"*Mamacita*, I'll be there in ten minutes. Can you be ready?"

"Hector, I can be ready in five." I pulled my orchid-colored sundress over my head, adjusting it until it draped correctly—snug high waist, flowing skirt. I dragged a comb through my hair and spritzed it, then brushed my teeth, touched up my makeup, and put on my pearl stud earrings. Ack! Where was the bouquet I'd made from the bridal shower ribbons?

Just as Hector rang the doorbell, I yanked on my sandals and at the last minute, grabbed a light sweater in case the creek got cold. Crap, the letter. I stuffed it into my purse and took a deep breath. Five fifty-four—yes.

I opened the door to my date.

"Sleeping Beauty, hot as always." Hector kissed my cheek. He looked cool and easy in khakis and an untucked, white button-up. "Let's go show Cabral what real fun looks like."

"Sounds like a plan, Prince Charming." I grinned. After my week, I was ready to unwind.

Chapter 18
WATERFALL

A sudden, vertical drop, often over six feet high, that culminates in turbulent and treacherous water below.

Hydraulic Level Five [working title]
Draft 3.18
© Samuel Caulfield Cabral
The Farmer's Front Porch

Heavy black clouds obscure the sliver of a Halloween moon as neighborhood children make their way from lighted door to lighted door, crunching over dry leaves. Soon, Bear Creek is awash in witches, mice, superheroes. Caulfield muses how the streets resemble a nostalgic Norman Rockwell painting, glazed in the muted grays of his mountain home. And in the forefront of his Americana portrait is his "girl next door." Caulfield tucks away her image for his collection, another moment of happiness encapsulated by amber.

Aspen sits on the crumbling front steps of her mother's farmhouse on the edge of town, a large plastic witch's cauldron filled with fun-sized candy resting in her lap. They just finished decorating her porch with carved orange pumpkins and spider webs draped between railings. Aspen even procured a pair of old jeans and a work shirt from Mrs. Trilby, stuffing them with hay to make a headless scarecrow. Caulfield hits play on the scary sound effects tape and takes his post next to his friend, "accidentally" brushing his thigh against hers. But the autumn wind is brisk tonight, and Aspen doesn't seem to mind the extra warmth.

This year, he and Aspen go with pun costumes. She is resplendent in flower leis, grass skirt, and coconut bra (worn over a long-sleeved T-shirt and jeans), and he has borrowed Esteban's boxing gloves.

"A hula girl and a boxer?" A little cowboy scoffs as he holds out his candy bucket.

"No, we're Hawaiian Punch," Aspen says matter-of-factly, as if their attempt at humor is the most obvious thing in the world.

The kid sneers. "That's stupid."

Aspen digs deep into the bottom of her chocolate pile and tosses a half-crushed packet of Smarties in the kid's candy stash. She winks at him as he stomps down the stairs, calling out, "you forgot to say trick-or-treat!" to his retreating back. Scaring the piss out of neighborhood children is one of her most beloved Halloween pastimes.

Por Dios, Caulfield wants to kiss her.

She peels a wrapper from a chocolate bar, splits it, and offers half to Caulfield. He absently pops it in his mouth, watching Aspen's warm lips close around the chocolate between her fingers, melting it as she drags it into her mouth.

Earlier that afternoon, Caulfield took Aspen on their first date. Only he was too much of a coward to actually inform her it was a date.

"Do you want to grab a bite to eat before the kids make the rounds?" he eagerly asks after school is out for the day. He plans to buy her an early dinner at the Hungry Bear Café because it is always done up like a haunted house to mark the holiday. Her mother won't see it as a date, will she? *Mierda*, he should have just asked her out the minute she turned fourteen, and they could have doubled with Esteban and Maria to a movie. But taking her on a date date means kissing her goodnight. What if he sucks at it? What if he kisses her and she hates it? What if she just wants to be his friend?

An after-school date, though...

"Um, sure." She digs into her coin purse for a quarter. "Lemme call my mom and let her know I'm just out with you. She'll freak out if I don't."

Just out with you. As in, just hanging out with my old friend, Caulfield.

He ogles her hips swaying toward the pay phone in the school lobby, ignoring students as they jostle by him in the hallway or high-five him on their way out the door.

She doesn't know it is a date. He'll have to be blunt. Now he has to kiss her afterward. He'll never sleep another night until he does, for all the visions of that soft mouth tearing through his dreams, making him ache with his need to put his lips on hers.

Aspen's first official date hadn't been with him, and Caulfield feels like a chicken-shit for letting her first anything not be with him. Yes, it is selfish. The minute Aspen turned fourteen, Esteban's little brother swooped in like a vulture and whisked her away to a bonfire with his friends. The kid and Aspen shared a blanket at the bonfire. They held hands. She let him buy her ice cream afterward. She never let him buy ice cream for her.

Caulfield has been on dates before, too. Nothing special, a parade of poodle girls with permed hair stiffened by hairspray, hell-bent on scoring quality backseat time. A couple of girls try. One misses and hits her forehead on his car window. He even took Maria's friend – cherry ChapStick girl – to the Homecoming dance just two weekends ago, but only because Aspen flat-out refused to go with him.

"The upper-classmen make me nervous, especially the Hispanic girls," she admits. "They call me an ugly gringa."

"They are ugly for saying that."

"They don't like how you hang out with me. Besides, you're the big man, friends with everyone. You wouldn't want to spend the evening entertaining a freshman."

"But I want to spend it with you," he retorts. "This is your first Homecoming, Firecracker. We don't have to talk to anybody. We can sit at a table and watch everyone try to dance."

She rolls her eyes at him and whips her hair into a ponytail, the down of her neck taunting his itchy fingers with its softness.

"I'll go to the football game, but please don't make me go to the dance..."

So now Caulfield sits next to hula-girl Aspen on her front steps, agonizing over the best approach when moving in for a kiss. Should he just lean in? Lift her chin? And does he tilt his head to the left or to the right? She pops another chocolate in her warm mouth and catches him staring.

"Do you want a piece?" Aspen asks innocently.

He groans and drops his head into his boxing gloves.

"Caulfield, did I do something wrong? You've glared at me half the afternoon. If you didn't want to do the whole Halloween thing with me this year, you could have just told me no. I had a nice flower-power dress and go-go boots I snagged from my mom."

He peers at her feet, watching as she tugs slippers around her bony ankles. His own feet bounce with nerves.

"Firecracker, can I ask you a left-field question?" Caulfield props his chin on his gloved hand, eyes searching hers. Rich hazel, with fleck of brown at the center...like the chocolate melting between her fingers. Funny, he always thought they were the color of pond algae – not so rich. He licks his lips.

She frowns. "You can ask, but I'm not sure I'll answer."

Caulfield sucks in his breath and blurts it out. "If I kissed you, would you kiss me back?"

Hazel eyes blink once, twice. Her mouth falls open, and Caulfield is fairly certain she is going to slap him. She reaches up and grabs his shirt collar. He grinds his gloved fists into the porch slats, bracing for the sting. But she tugs him closer. So close, her nose touches his.

"Yes," she breathes, her eyes bright with excitement. Her lips curl, so soft...

He rests a boxing glove on either side of her face, and leans...

It is Halloween night, on the farmer's front porch, when Caulfield kisses Aspen for the first time.

And the second time.

And the third.

Jaime—who is Caro's ex, Togsy? See what you can find.
Check CU creative writing alums.

I finished texting Jaime Guzman and stuffed my phone in my purse.

Christ the King was an old brick church with stained-glass windows and a creaky balcony. The interior had lately been painted bright white, but the rosy, glass-filtered light and Lyons' gray day still made the interior seem dingy. Danita had covered the place in tulle and vivid red roses. A stack of programs was placed next to a guest book in the musty church narthex. I picked up one, scanning for my name.

Maid of Honor: Aspen Kaye Trilby, Friend of the Bride.

No question mark.

A sad little smile played on my mouth. I caught Samuel's eyes on me and he smiled back, putting me at ease.

As it turned out, I didn't need a Xanax to get me through the wedding rehearsal (though Molly's stepmother was more than willing to oblige). Our friends kept it light, helping us to forget another wedding which took place in this tiny community church eight years ago. Santiago crossed his eyes at me across the sanctuary. We hummed "The Bridal March" because the organist had another engagement this evening. Molly gifted Danita and Angel with matching bride and groom T-shirts that said, "Game Over." Angel thought they were hilarious, and immediately stripped off his button-up dress shirt to pull on his tee. Danita shrugged it over her red strapless dress after vowing to burn it later in the fire pit.

I looked over Sam's shoulder at the small gathering of family and dates (and Caroline) in the audience, tuning out the minister's droning as he explained the ceremony to Angel and Danita. I had my duties down: hold the bouquet, fluff Danita's train, give a wedding toast. No stress here, thank you very much.

Once the rehearsal was over, though, my nerves did the conga back into my stomach. I was jittery the minute I slid into Hector's truck, my knees bobbing against the dash until my friend placed a calming hand on them.

"Ay, Kaye. The last thing this poor truck needs is another dent."

I pushed his hand from my knees. "Quit trying to grope me, Hector."

"*Mamacita,* you don't know the meaning of the word 'grope.'"

I choked on the Tic Tac I'd been sucking. Hector smirked and I relaxed.

The heady scent of roasting pork and chiles hit my nose before I even left Hector's truck. Long pine tree shadows stretched across the driveway as we made our way around the Valdez family home to the extensive backyard. Green and yellow Chinese lanterns were strung between canopies and tiki torches. The giant *zacahuil* tamale had just been removed from the clay pit, and six feet of *papatla* steamed and sizzled on a table. Two of Angel's cousins rolled in kegs from a local brewery while Mr. Valdez rigged up a stereo system to pump out mariachi.

Other guests were just arriving, many I recognized from the Hispanic neighborhood. Angel helped his *abuela* down the hill and settled her into a lawn chair. There were Sofia's sister Lucia and her husband, Carlos — two quiet people overshadowed by the roisterous Valdez family. A few out-of-town Cabrals milled about, too. Samuel's great aunt, who'd retired to Baja, California, once Alonso's mother passed away, and another great aunt and uncle from Ciudad Victoria were there. But the vast majority of guests were Angel's large extended family. The Valdez clan had established roots long before white settlers came in their wagons, and had farmed west of Lyons well over a hundred years. If locals weren't related to the Valdez family, they at least went to school with a Valdez. They were a rowdy pack of mainly agricultural workers who told crude jokes and tried to toss each other into St. Vrain Creek. I thought they were fantastic.

"Hungry, Hector?" I shouted over the thumping stereo speakers as my date tugged me toward stacks of fried plantains and pickled things.

"If I'm going to show you a good time tonight, Kaye, I need some fuel." He winked at me and popped a cheese cube in his mouth. Just beyond him, a brown-haired man stiffened. Ah, Samuel and Caroline beat us to the party.

Caroline was slumming it, couture-wise. She'd finally ditched the heels for more sensible sandals, capris, and a pale green top that showed off her coffee-cream skin. I grimaced as I glanced at my own white forearm, tinged a blotchy pink by the sun.

Hector's roaming hands were little better at the fiesta than they'd been in the car, and it began to tick me off. At first it was funny, but now I wondered if he was using his status as my "date" to get in a lifetime's worth of digs at Samuel. Kissing my cheek whenever Samuel watched. Snaking an arm around my shoulders. He even grabbed my tush, which earned him a death glare from both Samuel and me. Enough was enough.

"I thought I told you to quit groping me," I demanded as we set up our lawn chairs near the gurgling creek. I chucked my sandals at him.

He placed a hand over his heart in mock hurt. "I thought this was what you wanted, Kaye. To piss off Cabral?"

"No! You are supposed to show me a good time, not play the revenge game."

"Isn't that what he's doing with the yuppie chick? Playing the revenge game?"

I stared over at Caroline and Samuel, where Samuel dug a soda out of an ice-filled cooler for her. "I don't think so. Samuel doesn't play head games like that."

"Why else would he bring her? Come on, Kaye, it's obvious the guy's not into her. The way he looks at you..." Hector bit his tongue, his eyes growing angry.

"What do you mean?"

"He looks at you like he wants to nail you seven ways till Sunday, and I don't like it." I had to laugh at his dirty twist on that old expression. His ire only grew. "I just don't want you to break your heart over this guy, *mamacita*."

I stopped laughing. Hector was truly worried about me. Sighing, I pressed my face into his shoulder. "It was broken a long time ago, Hector. If anything, I'm trying to mend it. Thanks for your help with that all these years—the kayaking, the ski trips, the jokes. I'm not sure I ever told you how much it means. You're a great friend to me."

"Friend," Hector grumbled, messing my hair with his big hand. "You are gonna kill me, Trilby. But I can be a friend..." A sly smirk spread across his face as he stood and stretched. "If you let me try to pick up Samuel's hot date."

I snickered, imagining the horror on Caroline's face when my bald and goateed, tattoo-sleeved, pickup-driving friend hit on her. I smacked his butt in payback.

"Go get 'er, tiger."

"Sam, did you put baby powder in the air vents?" I caught Molly's words as I joined my friends crouching like thugs behind Angel's hatchback that evening. The sky had fully darkened, and it was prank time.

"Remind me why I'm the only person who can pull that one off?"

"Because Danita can't kill her own brother when a twelve-foot high cloud of powder whooshes in her face. Besides, you'll be long gone to New York by the time she'll have a chance to exact revenge." Molly tossed me a box of condoms and told me to get to work.

The bridesmaids and groomsmen were blowing up condoms like balloons and stuffing them in the hatch-back's interior. If we tried anything after the wedding reception tomorrow, Danita would "string us up by our ta-tas and hoo-hoos," as Cassady so elegantly groused.

"And she can't exact revenge from a distance? You know she will." He looked at me with an unfathomable expression.

"Oh, go write about it in your padlocked diary," Molly mumbled.

Somewhere below, Hector put the moves on Caroline to keep her out of my hair for a bit, bless him. Not quite what he had in mind for the evening, but having Samuel's dour-faced, disapproving date hovering would suck the joy right out of our mischief.

"Did you stick a potato up the exhaust pipe yet?" I buttoned up my sweater. Santiago giggled like a girl, already trashed. I ignored him.

"Done." Molly held up an empty Ziploc bag. Flaming stapler, she'd even labeled it.

"You know, having you for friends is enough to convince me to never tie the knot," Cassady commented. "Almost feel sorry for Angel and Danita."

"Don't. Hey, Sam, tell Cassady what they did to you at our wedding."

Samuel thought, and then a slow smile lit his face. "You see those four little teenagers over there?" He pointed to the fire pit. "Well, they're Angel's cousins. They were probably seven or eight when we got married. Anyway, they attended our wedding as Danita's and Angel's 'plus-ones'—counting each cousin as a 'half.' Angel paid them to go around to Kaye's out-of-town relatives, point at me, and say, 'That's my daddy...don't you think he's pretty?' I kept getting cold-shouldered by my new in-laws and I couldn't figure out what I'd done. So this?" Samuel gestured to our latex handiwork. "This is tame."

Molly knotted off a condom balloon and tapped it through the window. It floated down and settled next to the brake pedal. "Don't forget about him." She pointed an accusing finger at Santiago. "He told Kaye's college friends Samuel was the biggest prick at Lyons High."

Santiago had the class to blush. "Yeah, I was a real jerk back then."

She flung a condom at his face. "You were just jealous of Samuel."

"Well, who wouldn't be? He could have had half the girls in Lyons in the backseat of his Subaru if he'd wanted, with that pretty face."

Molly landed an elbow in Santiago's ribs. "If he'd wanted to. But he didn't. You still are a jerk, aren't you?"

Samuel became incredibly interested in unrolling a condom and blowing it up. I jumped in to finish the "man-pretty" story, saving him.

"Anyway, my great aunts and uncles and cousins kept coming up to me, asking if Samuel had been married before. I was so confused, replying, 'Nooo, he's only twenty-one.' Then I caught Angel and Danita busting their guts by the greenhouse and put two and two together."

Samuel cracked a smile.

Later, after a near case of latex poisoning, I munched on a plate of shrimp mole and churros when Samuel made his way over and plopped into Hector's vacated chair. That odd expression was back—mouth and eyes tight. He wasn't happy; I could tell as much. I glanced down the beach where Hector replenished his beer.

"So I hear you've been skirting our one-question rule."

Crap. Sofia'd talked. "What makes you think that?"

"Kaye, come on. You could have talked to me about my arrest in North Carolina. You didn't need to pry it from my mother."

"Your mother was more than willing to talk." I waved a fork in Sofia's direction. "And for the record, I would have talked to you, but you were busy breaking in your running shoes with your new best friend."

A smile twitched at the corners of his mouth. "If I didn't know better, Neelie Nixie, I'd think Caroline's behavior on the camping trip isn't the only problem you have with her."

Ooh, he *knew* I hated that nickname. "You think? Let's see…she knows far too much personal info about me and isn't afraid to throw it in my face, she struts around with this elitist attitude that is, frankly, off-putting. Oh! And don't forget how she ditched my PR agency for some West Coast media machine who doesn't know a thing about the Boulder area." I grabbed a churro and snapped it in two, imagining it was one of Caroline's spindly arms. A waft of shrimp mole hit my nose, and I grimaced, dropping the food. Dammit, my appetite was gone. I dumped the plate in a trash bin and stalked off toward the rocks stacked along the creek, away from the crowd.

Samuel followed. "Kaye, don't get upset. All I'm saying is that you can come to me if you have questions."

"I didn't know it was taboo to talk to your family now." I scooped a rock from the water, smudged away wet clay, and saw it was ribboned in pale pink like the Rose of Sharon shrubs that bloomed along my mother's property line.

"Talking to my family isn't taboo. But digging up an old arrest record is rather shady, don't you think?" He gave me a pointed look.

My hand froze over the stone. "How did you know about that?"

"I didn't. It was a hunch, but I guess I'm right." He frowned, scratching his neck. "What could you possibly want with my arrest record?" The deductive wheels churned in his mind as he fitted puzzle pieces together.

My phone buzzed. Saved! I glanced at the screen—it was Jaime. Oh thank you, thank you, bitter divorce attorney. I place the pretty rock in Samuel's hand with a promise to chat later and walked farther down the creek.

"This is Kaye."

"Well, hello to you too, sugar-booger. How's your straight date?"

"He's competing in another pissing contest with Samuel. You know, the lesbian thing is sounding better and better. I should have invited you as my wedding date."

"Hector Valdez is a walking penis, and there you have it. Someone needs to teach him how to take down opponents with his brain instead of caveman grunting."

I stepped into the slimy creek bed, letting currents break over my feet. "What did you find out?"

"Okay, Trilby, brace yourself, here's what I dug up on this Togsy person. Lyle Togsender, age thirty-one. Originally from Raleigh, but moved to Boulder for his undergrad at CU. Get this—he was also in NYU's Creative Writing grad program, where he shared an East Village house with several other writers. Namely, one Samuel Caulfield Cabral."

Shared a house…"Crap! The guy who answered the door at Samuel's brownstone—that was Togsy! I *knew* he looked familiar. So Samuel met Caroline when she was visiting her boyfriend at the East Village house."

"Ahhh, no." Jaime cleared her throat. "Now don't go all soap opera on me, Trilby, because this really isn't that big of a deal if you think about it. But Caroline wasn't visiting. She *lived* in the brownstone. Actually, her daddy owned the home. Pretty swanky place."

"I don't remember her living there." I retraced my steps through a house littered with trash, staggering party-goers, Samuel's nearly-bare room…

No way. Tiaras. Stacks of books. Classic wicker furniture. I'd been in *Caroline's* room. Who else's could it have been? And if she'd lived there, she'd witnessed Samuel unceremoniously tell me to "fuck off." Embarrassed fury flooded my skin. Of all the people I would *never* want to see the lowest, most heartbreaking moment of my life, Caroline was at the top of that list.

"There's more. I found a change of address for Lyle Togsender from six and a half years ago. After that, I couldn't dig up anything romantically linking Caroline and Togsy. My guess is they split around the same time you and your man-meat divorced."

So Samuel and Caroline both became single in January, almost seven years ago. How long *had* Samuel known Caroline? If he'd been invited to live in her brownstone, he would have met her when we were in Boulder, especially if she'd ever visited Togsy there. Brown hair…black hair. It had been dark, only candlelight. Was it possible the woman I'd seen beneath Samuel had been Caroline? Horrible scenarios played themselves out in my mind, despite Sofia's assurances that Samuel and Caroline weren't together then. Black hair could have easily appeared brown in candlelight…What if they'd orchestrated their respective break-ups so they could be free to date each other? The possibility made me sick.

Caroline's laughter echoed through the trees, and the cord of jealousy wound tightly in my gut snapped.

"Gotta go, Jaime." I hung up on her protests and stormed back to where I'd left Samuel, only to find he had once again settled into Hector's lawn chair. Seated next to him, in my chair, was none other than the black-haired, brownstone-owning Afghan hound, her sleek legs curled beneath her.

Heck no. She may have stolen Samuel, the book tour gig, and the Cabrals, but I'd be damned if she was going to take my purple lawn chair.

"You're in my seat."

"Do you mind if I sit here a bit? Just until I finish my conversation?"

Argh! Floozy was dead. "Get out of my chair."

"Kaye," Samuel cut in, "what's the big deal? It's only a chair."

"There's no need for rudeness," the hound added.

That was it. Screeching, I wound back, ready to do some serious damage to the Manhattan yuppie even though I'd never thrown a punch in my life. Samuel leaped up and grabbed my elbows to keep me from tackling her, but not before Caroline rolled out of my chair onto the ground, pure panic on her face.

"Kaye, what's gotten into you?" he hissed.

I yanked my arms back and rounded on him. "Was the woman Caroline?"

"What do you mean?"

"The woman you were a coke line and two pairs of underwear away from screwing in New York. Was it her?"

Caroline's mouth dropped open, and she spilled a small, disbelieving laugh. Several people on the edge of the fire pit turned their heads at my loud words.

"*¡Válgame Dios!* Keep your voice down, my family is here." Samuel placed a hand firmly on the small of my back and steered me away from the party. I stumbled along next to him, bare toes digging into the grass to keep up. He led me up to his roadster and dropped his arm, staring down at me with flaring nostrils.

"Talk," he said.

Fricking monkey rump, I'd nearly attacked somebody. I had never been in a real physical fight before. "Caroline lived there in the brownstone," I sputtered. "Togsy—the guy from CU—answered the door. Oh cripes, I'll just ask. Were you sleeping with her?"

"No!" Samuel threw his hands in the air. "Yes, she was with Togsy. No, I wasn't sleeping with her. Kaye, please be rational!"

How was I not being rational? My temper flared again. "Rational like you? Leaving our marriage because it was the logical thing to do? Rational, like locking me out in New York, asking your father to put me on a plane home without so much as a goodbye from you? You couldn't even be kind in your note—just cold."

"What note?" Confusion suffused his features, which only fueled years' worth of hurt.

"The note you wrote to me, Samuel! You didn't have the courage to give it to me in person, so you stuck it in my backpack while I was asleep."

"I don't— "

"Remember? Oh, that's right." I wiped my cheek with the back of my hand, only then realizing I was crying. "You can't even remember sending your wife packing because you were getting high off of some skank. And you would have slept with her if I hadn't shown up. Right?"

"Kaye..." His hands hovered around my shoulders, not sure what to do.

"Was she Caroline?" I demanded again. "That woman?"

"No!"

"But you said you can't remember."

He groaned, running his fingers through his hair. "I can't, but others can. Yes, Caroline lived with us in the brownstone, but she wasn't the woman you saw me with. She told me so, herself."

I took a deep, hitching breath, forcing myself to calm down. Samuel reached for my hand and tried to lead me over to his roadster to sit. I jerked it back. He sighed.

"Kaye, I want to answer your questions, but I need to know what you saw in New York. So far, the only information I have about it is from people who were also half out of their minds and my father's vague second-hand story from you. Frankly, we should probably wait until you're not so upset, but..."

"Are you sure the woman you were with wasn't Caroline?"

He met my eyes, all earnestness. "Positive."

I exhaled and reached into my purse. Samuel watched me warily, as if I might pull out an eight millimeter. Instead, I handed him the letter I'd written.

"This is everything I can recall about that night, down to the last details. I wouldn't give this to you now, but Danita wanted me to, as a wedding present, of all things."

"She knows what's in this letter?"

"Most of it. Molly, too. I shared a few additional things with you—only you. Mainly about some dreams I've been having."

"Do you want me to read this now or later?"

"Whenever. We can talk about it next week in our one-question convo. You can call me from New York," I said, my voice tinged with bitterness.

Samuel tucked it into his jacket pocket, cagey eyes not leaving mine. When his hand re-emerged, the rose marbled rock was clutched between his fingers like a stress ball. "Kaye...that woman. She wasn't anything to me."

"You know, that doesn't make it better—messing around with someone you don't even care about."

"How could I care about her that way? She wasn't *you*. No one has ever been you. Not Caroline, not Indigo, or any of the others Page Six likes to flash around."

"You're right about that one. Beauty queens, actresses, musicians. You certainly found the good fishing spots in the pond." It was meant to be a passing jibe, but he didn't let it go.

"What do you mean?"

"Oh please. I'm not elegant or refined. I'm a hick." I gestured to my wrinkled cotton dress and bare feet. "I'm scrawny, a year behind in fashion, and I've hardly been out of the state, let alone vacationed in Cannes. I have a modestly-successful business, but wouldn't stand a chance in a New York agency. And if you stuck me in a room full of your Manhattan friends, I'd vanish into their designer wall."

Samuel was honestly puzzled. "Why would you even compare yourself to them, Kaye?"

"I'm just saying I understand, even if it pisses me off. I'm a trout, not a bluefin tuna." I bit my tongue before I said too much.

But it was too late. Confusion melted away, and his thumb restlessly rubbed over the rose rock. He loosed a quick, sardonic bark. "I don't know whether to laugh at the absurdity of your fish analogy or shake you for even thinking something so preposterous. Is this really how you see yourself? Inferior to those shallow people?"

"Look, Samuel. You outgrew me, I get it, but I don't need patronization from you. You harbored this little crush for your best friend when we were young and you never had a chance to see what else was out there."

"Little crush?" he sputtered, eyes widening. "That's not it at *all*. Starting a romantic relationship with you wasn't something I did on a whim, Kaye."

"Really? So we didn't just fall together?" I stared at him dubiously. "You consciously made a decision to kiss your best friend, considering all of the ramifications?"

"Yes, mostly. Obviously there were some things I could never have foreseen at sixteen."

I shook my head. "You know, you plot way too much. I'm starting to wonder if the drugs were an excuse."

His thumb furiously traced the rock ribbon. "For what?"

"To get out of a marriage you didn't want to be in anymore... didn't want in the first place, but went along with because you wanted to give me my fairy tale." I already knew I'd probably made a mistake in voicing the thought. But resentment still coursed through my blood, and I was ready for the bell to ring on round two. "You told yourself you left to give me a better life. But maybe you just didn't want to face the fact you'd mistook friendship for something else. That you really didn't love me like you thought you did."

Furious red streaked up his neck. His fists dug into his hips as he paced in front of me, rose rock still firmly in his grasp. "That is the most ridiculous thing I've ever heard, Aspen Kaye. Don't you think I know the difference between loving someone and being in love? You may have forgotten, but *I* wasn't the one who filed for divorce. Perhaps *I* should be the one asking if there was someone else."

Was he referring to Hector? Oh, that put me over the edge. "And I had good reason to file, given what happened! You actually did me a favor, Samuel. New York sealed the deal. Before, I hadn't accepted it was over. In spite of *everything*—you leaving me, not getting in touch just to tell me where you were—I still held out hope that maybe you wanted me, that it was just a horrible misunderstanding." I crossed my arms over my chest like body armor as the scene played through my mind...the cold eyes...the drugs...the brunette. "But I got doused with ice water and it woke me up. You may have left to 'spare' me, but I know you didn't *want* me. Because you don't screw around on someone you're in love with. I don't care if you were high or not."

Up to this point, he'd remained relatively in control throughout our exchange. But I knew, once the words left my mouth, I'd found his breaking point. Heavy silence descended, a gambit of emotions dancing across his features. Anger won out above the others. His face twisted dark, fierce. A fist flew into the side of his rental roadster, the Rose of Sharon stone I gave him still clutched by ragged knuckles. I yelped, stepping back a few feet in case he took another swing at the vehicle. But then he leaned into the car, his arm hiding his face.

It had been too soon to have the New York conversation, for both of us. I should have told Danita no. Samuel stayed still for so long, I began to worry.

"Samuel?" I gingerly touched his shoulder. He whipped around, eyes clouded with self-loathing.

"I'm sorry I filled your head with lies." He pushed off the roadster and took a step toward me, fingers twisting around the stone. "I'm sorry you don't know how lovely you are." Another step. "And I'm sorry I've made you feel undesirable. It's shameful."

Gone was the golden boy he played so well. In his place was just a troubled man. So stunning it hurt, but still, so flawed. And strangely, I didn't feel disappointment…only sadness for him.

Face set in determination, he clutched at my arms, kneaded them, and the rock dug into my bicep. The knuckles on his right hand bled, where he'd pummeled them into his car.

"It's shameful, because I have never desired *anybody* the way I desire you." His voice grew hoarse. "And I should have told you a long time ago. I should have told you *every single day*."

I knew what was coming. Before I could tell him no, I felt his warm hands slide to my face…felt the heat of his mouth when it covered mine.

Shock jolted through my veins as Samuel's strong lips pushed against me, working over my mouth like a half-starved man. Every alarm system in my body flashed and wailed, their warnings beating through my brain. I grasped at his shoulders and warred with myself. Pull away? Let go? Samuel was kissing me. Oh lord, *Samuel's kissing me*. I couldn't think.

Sam's hands left my face and circled my waist, the rose-ribboned rock falling to his feet. "Firecracker," he breathed against my ear, "please, just kiss me back."

Those words. Oh…

Warm blue eyes addled my eyes, and I *knew*. I recognized it… No, remembered it. Samuel *wanted* me. It was there, plainly written in the lines of his body. How could I have forgotten what it meant when he watched me like this? Meeting my challenge in the café parking lot. Tracing my foot at Button Rock. Sitting in silence as I slept in his basement. Kissing the top of my head. So many times in the past weeks, I *saw* it…and I'd been blind to it.

So I kissed him back. How could I not? With every last muscle weeping to stretch up and meet him, I *had* to close the space between us. My fingers ran along the ridges of his shoulders and threaded into his windblown hair, tugging him to me. I tasted a hint of spearmint on my tongue, so comforting.

"Kaye." His grip on my waist tightened. His mouth skimmed down my neck and up again, drawing a wet line which caused me to shiver when cool night air flitted over my skin. Samuel felt the tremor run through my body and smiled against my jaw. His lips gentled. Reverent. Persistent. Soft lips…tugging at my lips…talking to me like they used to. So much heat, flushing my face. So much aching, twisting my heart.

My twisting heart…

Sudden panic forced its way into my brain as reality caught me in a choke-hold. *What the hell are you doing, Kaye?*

Samuel dipped his mouth to mine once more. With the last bit of resistance I could muster, I turned my face.

"Stop."

The word hung between us, ringing as Samuel froze. Then his arms slackened.

I don't know how I left his arms. I didn't think I was strong enough to tell Samuel no. But something in this—giving in, forgetting our promises of friendship—wasn't right. I took one step back, then two.

"Why?" His voice cracked.

"I didn't see it coming, you wanting me. We shouldn't go down this road again, Sam."

Already, I witnessed the reality of my rejection hit its mark, driving out hope. His shoulders slumped, resigned. He was that six-year-old boy in a ghost costume, sitting alone in a corner. Hurt radiated off of him, crushing him like he'd crushed me.

"It *is* too late, isn't it? For us."

"It's not good for us," I choked, skirting his question. Because I knew—we *both* knew at this point—I'd wanted his kiss. "And I care about you too much to pretend otherwise. I'm sorry."

"Kaye—"

"Your hand is still bleeding."

He gazed down at his bruised, bloody knuckles as if it was someone else's hand. My sweater sleeve was streaked with blood where he'd grasped it. Shrugging out of it, I bunched it up and pressed it over his scrapes. He winced. My ratty sweater for his nose, now my dress sweater for his hand. What else could I possibly lose to his injuries?

"You can have this." I bit my swollen lip, gesturing to the ruined gray sweater. "Just keep it pressed to your knuckles—it'll stop the bleeding." Turning away, I hurried back to the fire before he saw his pain reflected in my face.

I avoided Molly, Alonso, and Sofia, all of my friends as I tromped down the hill, seeking Hector. Caroline was there, smirking at me like a triumphant harpy. She thought she'd won. Maybe she had. I ignored her, too.

Hector chatted with Angel and a burly Valdez cousin, cheap cigars hanging from their mouths. When he spotted me, he quickly tossed the stub in the fire and grinned with a guilty expression. But the grin faded.

"Kaye?" Hector asked, taking my elbow. "*Mamacita*, you look like hell. You wanna go home?"

I nodded, not trusting my voice. Plastering a smile to my face, I kissed Dani goodbye, telling her I'd see her bright and early at the salon—no oversleeping. I refused to drag down her big day.

"Don't turn on the air in Angel's car," I whispered as I hugged her goodnight.

Her brown arms squeezed me back. "Thanks for the warning."

We passed Samuel on our way to the parking lot. Both hands were jammed into his pockets, despite the blood. My sweater was neatly folded and tucked under his arm. His eyes were downcast, feet dragging across the sand as we crossed paths. It was dark and I couldn't see his face. But the moon was bright, and under its glow his cheeks glistened with tell-tale wetness.

Samuel called me four times that night. I let them go to voicemail, too frightened to speak with him. Any chance we still had at resuscitating our flat-lining friendship depended upon how we resolved this, and I was petrified to start.

The first time he called, he apologized for kissing me.

The second, he asked me to pick up the phone.

Third, he said he would try to reach me at Hector's home phone number if I didn't answer.

Two glasses of wine and a mild buzz later, I curled up on my bed, clutching my pillow like a teenager, my cell phone in hand. I watched the display glow each time he called.

Samuel Cabral. 212-555-0368.

Samuel Cabral wanted me. This beautiful, brilliant, damaged man—he told me he still desired me, had never stopped desiring me. No matter how many times I replayed our kiss in my mind, I couldn't hammer it into my psyche. The thought was so foreign after so long. A warm light burned in my gut, searing through stone limbs all the way to my toes. Despite my fear, it felt good to be wanted.

The fourth time he called, he spoke with my voicemail. "I'm such an idiot." He sounded like he'd scalded his throat with hot sauce. "I really screwed this one up, didn't I? So much for taking our friendship slowly, easing into it again. Here I was, lecturing you on rash behavior and then, like a horny sixteen-year-old kid, I turn around and beg you to kiss me. Firecracker...I'm sorry. Please call."

I called him back after I listened to his message.

"Kaye?" he answered. "Where are you?"

"I'm at home, Samuel. Where else would I be?"

Relief infused his voice. "I'm sorry, so sorry. *Por Dios*, I wish I'd handled that differently."

"Samuel, let's just get through the wedding tomorrow, okay? It's taking an emotional toll on both of us, more than we realize. Besides, you can't take all the blame for this—I kissed you back."

"I don't regret it, Kaye. Maybe I shouldn't have kissed you. But this idea you have in your head about not measuring up? It's got to stop, and I'd do anything to dispel it."

"Like tell me you want me?"

"It was the *truth*." He sounded affronted.

And I had asked for truth. But the truth left me reeling, as if the rug I'd walked on for nearly seven years had been yanked out from under me and I'd hit the ground, hard. Now I got a good, close look at the bare floor for the first time.

"I don't know if I can trust you. And I don't see how dredging up old feelings is going to help either one of us. We have a helluva lot of baggage."

"Would you rather have me lie? Let you believe for a while longer those casual dates were somehow better than you? That I wanted them with a modicum of the way I want you?"

"No."

"Kaye," he sighed, "I'm not perfect and I'm going to screw up. I know you don't trust me, and that's a consequence I'll have to live with. But I promised you on the camping trip I would do whatever it took to make sure you didn't regret giving our friendship another go, and I meant it. I just…I need to know if you're with me in this. Because as long as you still want this friendship, I want to fight for it."

"I want it, Samuel. I just need to sort through a few delusions." Like the fact that my friends could read Samuel better than me. Molly would have a field day with this. "You threw me for a loop and I'm not sure I've caught up."

"Next week—can I count on you to ask your question? I'll read the letter you gave me, and don't forget about our book."

The book had completely slipped my mind. Dang, the man was persistent. And pushy.

"I'm still in, but so help me, Samuel, I don't know if I can handle another week of turmoil. Please promise me your book doesn't have anything about a long-lost brother in it."

I heard him exhale. "No. It's all us, Firecracker."

"Thank you." A whoosh of air escaped my lungs as well. I ran a hand through my hair, shaking my head at the unbelievable turn in our relationship. Oh, if the tabloids only knew. I quietly laughed at how they'd spin it: *Siren Author Drowns Ex-Wife in Kisses, Drives Her Over Edge.*

"What?"

"I was just musing about the tabs. The other evening in Boulder, when I teased you about your plan to smooch your ex-wife in the middle of Pearl Street? I didn't know you were serious."

"Hmm. It *is* rather daytime talk show-ish, isn't it? Now all I need is for some fan to charge the stage and claim I'm her baby's daddy."

I cringed at the phone. Ugh, was that even a possibility? I didn't want to think about him picking up women at his book signings. What if it was a signing TrilbyJones had scheduled? Frickin' craptastic.

"Kaye? That was a joke. A pretty bad one, evidently."

I breathed out. "Too soon, Cabral. Too soon."

"Kaye?"

"Yeah, Sam?"

There was a pause, and I heard a smile in his voice. "I still want you."

"Shut up." I bit my bottom lip, holding back a smile of my own.

"Kaye?"

"Yes, Sam?"

"You're lovely."

"I'm going to bed now. Goodnight."

"Kaye?"

I groaned. "What, Samuel?"

"Sleep well." Ha. Fat chance.

"I hope the ghosts of all those crickets I killed come back to haunt you." But I smiled regardless of what my brain told me. "Sam?"

"Yes, Kaye?"

"You sleep well, too."

Chapter 19

BELAY

To keep a raft from slipping down river, one person will wrap a rope around tree or rock, allowing them to hold fast under the tremendous pull of the current.

Danita Cabral had forced me to play "wedding" with her when we were children. She'd been the bride and I'd been relegated to various roles, such as *madrina*, cake-maker, or groom (one time she even scribbled a goatee on my face with a black marker). Sofia purchased old *quinceñeara* dresses at a consignment store for us to play with, and one was a fluffy, white number with poufy sleeves and lace trim. Danita snatched it as her "wedding dress." With several clothespins and a rhinestone belt, she tailored the frilly frock to her eight-year-old frame. If Angel and Samuel made the mistake of showing their faces during dress-up time, they were stuffed into Alonso's old suit coats and obliged to join the wedding party.

As much as Dani had loved to play wedding, when it came to the reality of marriage, like her brother, she was stone-serious. Many in Lyons thought it odd that Angel Valdez and Danita Cabral were just now tying the knot after a decade of dancing around the other like mating birds. I wasn't surprised. Dani and Angel always did things in their own time, never bowing to pressure—even as our classmates settled into married life, two by two. I think Angel always knew he'd marry Danita, so he waited her out, biding his time in the Air Force. And given the disastrous outcome of Samuel's and my short-lived marriage, they were determined not to marry until both were ready to walk down the aisle.

Today, they were ready.

My friend was a portrait of regal beauty as her mother finished with the row of tiny buttons along the back of her wedding dress. Only Danita could carry off the gown she'd chosen. It was not-quite white, but more of an antiqued, silvery white Dani called "candlelight." With hair piled high on her head, like a blackened wick gracing the top of her long neck, she really did remind me of an elegant candelabrum. She turned in front of the full-length mirror in her bedroom, showing off every ruched curve.

"Well?" she asked, taking a deep breath.

Molly's eyes glowed, her aubergine skirts rustling as she bobbed up and down. Tears gathered in my own eyes. I swiped at them, already forgetting Molly's earlier threat not to smear my mascara.

"Danita, Angel's going to faint dead away. You are, by far, the most beautiful woman I've ever seen. Supermodels got nothin' on you."

She nervously smiled at me in her mirror, tucking one final bobby pin with a trembling hand. "I know this is right. But *Ave María Purísima,* I can't stop shaking!"

Sofia wrapped warm arms around her daughter and whispered encouraging words into her ear. Molly and I exchanged quick looks. But Danita closed her eyes and nodded, breathed in, and grabbed her beaded purse and shoes.

"Kaye," she said as settled onto her vanity bench, tightening the ankle straps of her shoes, "about Samuel."

My smile fell. "I'm working on it, Danita."

"No, no, I'm not hounding you. I just…" She glanced between me and the other three women in the room, biting her lip. "Can you give Kaye and me a minute?"

"We'll be in the living room, baby," Sofia said. "Don't be too long." They picked up their things and left.

Danita turned to me and grasped my hands. "This is difficult for me to do. I need to apologize for pushing so hard with my brother. It's hard on you, I know, but I've wanted the whole family together for so long, united for my wedding day, one way or the other. I thought changing your name would help you move on, once I discovered

Caroline was in the picture. That maybe Samuel would feel like he could come home more often if he had evidence the divorce was water under the bridge," she admitted. "And then that backfired, so I pounced on New York."

"Danita, come on. You're getting married in a couple of hours. Don't do this now."

"I just want to get this off my chest—go in with a clean slate, you know?"

"You're getting married, not walking the aisle to the electric chair."

She half snorted, half sniffed. "I just want my family together again."

I sighed. "Dani, you have nothing to apologize for. We *are* together, aren't we? We're all here for you and Angel. We love you. And if you want Samuel to come home more, just ask him."

Danita nodded, her grip on my hands tightening. A tear dripped from her eyelashes and splashed onto our fingers.

"I'm just so scared, Kaye. And if you tell anyone, Samuel included, I'll—"

"String me up by my ta-tas, yes, I know." I met her eyes. "Why are you scared?"

"Don't get me wrong, I want to marry Angel more than anything. But what if we completely suck when it comes to marriage? We've managed so well up to now...what if we screw it up? He'll be deployed again..."

I hugged her neck. "Dani, being terrified just means you aren't cavalier about exchanging vows. But you can't be self-defensive in a marriage. Go into it balls out. Just love hard." Her pink lips twitched and I realized what I'd just said. "Okay, so I'm obviously speaking from past mistakes. You want some real advice? Don't eff it up like your stupid sibling and BFF did."

"That was really inappropriate." Danita was fraught to hold her laughter.

"Hmmm, more advice from my past mistakes...Oh! The first time he says, 'That's not the way my mom makes it,' smack him. You can't let that crap go."

Dani rolled her eyes. "Yeah, I've already heard that one."

"And never, ever tell him he reminds you of one of those *Family Circus* kids, even if he does. Samuel fumed for a full week over that one."

Danita couldn't contain her laughter anymore. Soon, we both heaved and clutched our ribs, our faces red and tear-streaked.

"Oh man, he does!" Danita wailed. "I can just remember Samuel when he was a kid, tugging on Mamá's pants and asking her how to spell 'spell.'"

"Or when he used to shove all of his hair forward and he'd have that cowlick sticking up in back? All he needed was a closet full of purple T-shirts and black pants!"

Molly pounded on the door.

"So help me, Danita Cabral, if you or Kaye ruin those fabulous up-dos again, I'll shove your bouquets so far down your throats, your asses will sprout flowers!"

We pulled ourselves together, touched up our hair to save the flowers, and hit the road.

"All right, floozies," Danita exclaimed with fierce determination, "let's go take Angel Valdez out of the game."

I tried not to follow him from the corner of my eyes. When he mingled in the foyer while Angel and Danita posed for altar photographs, I only saw a blur of crisp, black tuxedo and lightly bronzed skin. When he clasped Caroline's hands and kissed her cheek as she arrived, I kept my face firmly riveted on the wall. Fascinating wall. Lovely old bricks.

This man wanted me. This man kissed me, and what a kiss it was... Pink heated my cheeks and spread across my skin...not good in a strapless dress. Even with Caroline drifting around him, willowy perfection in a jacquard dress, Samuel wanted me. And because he wanted me, I had the power. Control. The Afghan hound could have been sniffing up his leg and rubbing her scent all over him, but I no longer felt threatened.

"Holy crap, you're friends with Taralie Rocheford!?" Angel's little sister exclaimed, grabbing Caroline's elbow. "Wow, I always read about her in the New York social diaries, especially now that she's involved with Prince Henrik von What's-his-face..."

Okay, maybe I felt a teensy weensy bit threatened.

Hector sidled up to me, also looking dapper in a tux and new cuff links he'd purchased just for the wedding, sweet man. I linked my arm with his as Samuel and Caroline joined our chattering circle of friends. As Cassady and Santiago went on about a nasty thunderstorm during a biking trip, I peered at Samuel, getting an eyeful of his lithe, tuxedo-clad frame. Starched white shirt, skinny tie and black vest, freshly-shaven jaw. Heat scorched through my body. My throat went dry, leaving me with cotton-mouth, ugh. I left Hector's side and wandered down the stairs into the fellowship hall, alone, in search of water.

Samuel didn't follow me. I tried not to feel thwarted.

So far, so good, as long as I didn't eyeball him. *Right, Kaye, because you can go an entire evening without a single glance at him.*

But the past reared up and kicked us both in the teeth as we stood at the altar and witnessed Danita Cabral and Angel Valdez vow to love one another in sickness and in health, joy and sorrow, good times and bad. We fought valiantly to focus on our friends… the light in Danita's eyes…the comforting curl of Angel's lips as he held her shaking hands. But every now and then, my gaze drifted past Angel's and Santiago's shoulders.

"I, Danita Maria Cabral, take you, Angel Esteban Valdez, to be my husband, secure in the knowledge that you will be my constant friend, my faithful partner in life, and my one true love…"

I studied the intricate little buttons on the back of Danita's shimmery dress, my vision focusing and unfocusing while she recited her vows. Samuel and I had both royally screwed up. When we exchanged them, I thought our vows would be easy to keep. We'd been childhood sweethearts, after all. Piece of cake. But now, seeing the solemn set of my two friends' faces, it hit me that we hadn't kept a single one of them.

"I promise to comfort you in times of distress, encourage you to achieve all of your goals, laugh with you and cry with you…"

He met my eyes, and I saw it again—that warmth, that urgency. That want. But overshadowing it all was profound guilt. Once again, his shoulders slumped. Once again, his mouth sagged sadly. Eyes rimmed in red. Tired. World-weary. I'd seen him like this too many times the past couple of months…warm, cold, warm, cold.

"I, Angel Esteban Valdez, take you, Danita Maria Cabral, to be my wife…"

Each time I sought him, his troubled blue eyes found mine. The reminder of our broken vows was killing us, even though we managed to plaster smiles on our faces. If we didn't find a way to relieve our guilt, and soon, it would crush us.

"I promise to love you without reservation, honor and respect you, provide for your needs as best I can, protect you from harm, always be open and honest with you..."

Vows.

That's what we needed. I perked up, growing animated in my idea. We could write new vows. Friendship vows. We'd both decided that, more than anything, the very foundation of our relationship needed to be re-laid. What better foundation was there than spoken vows? Friendship was a lifelong commitment, too, and having that contract would go a long way to re-solder our trust.

Samuel looked at me strangely as my demeanor shifted. I grinned at him. He returned my grin, and some of the misery fogging his features burned away.

"This ring I give you, as a sign of our constant faith and abiding love..."

Yes, friendship vows would serve us well.

Unluckily for Samuel, celebrity trailed him to Lyons—even to his sister's wedding. One would think his hometown offered a breather from fan-girls. After all, these people had known Samuel when he was a gangly kid with braces. But that history also carried a sense of entitlement, because they *had* known him for a long time. And with so many new "best friends" vying for his attention, it was tricky for anyone—including me—to garner his attention for more than five minutes.

I watched with emulous eyes as Samuel's first crush, frickin' Jennifer Ballister with her red tresses, tight pink dress, and cherry ChapStick, rested a hand on his bicep and tittered at something he said. Several tables over, Caroline shot daggers at her, too, ready to clobber her like a minute steak. Several other old Lyons High gals were jonesing for time with Samuel Caulfield Cabral: World-Famous Author, Renowned Hottie. And now that Indigo Kingsley was allegedly out of the picture, they tacked "Eligible Bachelor" onto his title. If Jennifer wasn't careful, she'd be torn limb from limb.

Women weren't the only ones with Samuel in their scope. Alan Murphy had a blatant man-crush on his beloved author and spent half the night hovering, stalking, bringing him drinks, and firing questions as he clutched a precious, plastic-wrapped first edition of *The Last Other* to his chest. It was peculiar watching Samuel work the crowd. Before, he would have been too reticent to venture far beyond his assigned seat. He still didn't enjoy playing the part of socialite author, but he was all politeness, subtly ditching cocktails on random tables. Just another script to follow.

Pushing my envy aside, I absorbed the magic of the Cabrals' garden, transformed to a world of tea lights and hydrangea. Sheets of filmy white tulle and ivy were draped from tents. Crisp linens covered dozens of round tables, each set with glistening porcelain and silverware. Beyond the dining area, a dance floor and stage had been assembled, where the mariachis crooned sultry bolero. And the lights…thousands of little white lights twined around trees and dangled from canopies, bathing the entire banquet area in luminance against a dusky sky.

Hector rested a hand on the back of my tulle-covered chair, chortling with the rest of our table as we watched Samuel towed between classmates, classmates' moms, and classmates' younger sisters, sending "help me" glances my way. Frick, I even used to babysit a few of them.

Santiago chuckled. "I think Mr. June wants you to rescue him, sweet pea."

I felt a little wicked. "I'm his ex-wife, sugar tush. People expect me to let him suffer."

"If you won't chase off those girls, then I will," Molly huffed. "Get ready for your toasts, honey muffins. It's that time."

Santiago cleared his throat, becoming very stiff and very anxious. I gave him an incredulous look.

"You did write a toast, didn't you?"

He ran a finger under his collar. "Well yeah, but it wasn't very good. Too saccharine, not personal enough. Samuel helped me revise it. You?"

"Danita sat on me and jabbed my ribs until I promised to leave out the embarrassing stories, so that didn't give me much to work with."

The wedding party slid into their respective seats, Samuel diving for his as if he'd just bounded through a pit of pedicured crocodiles. Caroline gracefully settled next to Samuel and leaned over, flashing a hint of cleavage for the entire table. Tart.

Molly flipped on a mic, cringed when it squealed, and handed it to Santiago.

Showtime.

Despite his obvious nerves, Santiago did a fantastic job toasting the new couple. "It's been said that marriage is an adventure, like river rafting…" That was all Santiago. Then came a couple of embarrassing stories about Danita and Angel: "I'm not going to tell you about the night they spent in jail after mooning the town sheriff. Second date, right, Angel?" (I was shocked this particular story cleared Samuel's screening. Judging from his quaking shoulders as he hid his face in his hands, I gathered it was an ad lib).

Santiago grew serious. "Remember to listen to the *un*spoken words as well as the spoken. Wake up each morning, loving to give and giving to love." He lifted his glass. "Angel, Danita—may you fall in love every evening, only with each other."

I pressed a hand to my throat, feeling a lump swell. That. Now that was vintage Samuel. I gulped my ice water, loosening my voice so I could speak.

When I stood, I thought my kneecaps would pop out, they wobbled so badly. I closed my eyes and imagined I was prepping for a TrilbyJones presentation (the whole "audience in their underwear" method didn't work for me), and plunged in.

"Phyllis Diller said 'Never go to bed mad…stay up and fight.'" *Laughter, not stunned silence—good.* "And for all of us who have been blessed to watch Danita and Angel's love for each other deepen, we have seen them perfect 'the fight,' infusing it with passion, love, and humor…"

I kept my gaze schooled on the newlyweds, not hazarding a look at Samuel. I shared a bit about growing up with the couple. How she braided my hair and forced me into my first pair of heels. How he taught me to ride a bicycle. Angel brushed away a tear as I thanked both of them for putting up with me, for tormenting me, for becoming siblings to idolize.

"Thank you, Angel, for being *so* wonderful, Danita relentlessly gushes to me about her perfect boyfriend." *More laughter.* "And thank you, Danita, for making this mountain man grin and drool every day of his life. When I see the two of you together, I know what home looks like. So each day you come home, revel in each other. Never take that home you've found for granted." Dani grabbed my hand, and I raised my glass. "Congratulations, Danita and Angel Valdez."

Setting my glass down with a clink, I fell into my chair and tucked my shaking hands under my thighs. Angel hugged me, followed by Danita squeezing the breath out of my lungs. I downed the rest of my champagne, glad to have survived the toast without stuttering, flubbing, or tripping.

Something small, like a pebble, beaned me in the forehead. I rubbed the spot and scanning the table for the object.

Another hit me. And a third. This time, it bounced across my half-eaten lime chicken and settled next to my dessert plate. I leaned closer…a piece of wadded-up wedding program.

A fourth hit me just below my collarbone and my eyes flew up, catching Samuel mid-toss. *Busted.* I picked up a wad of paper and chucked it back. He deflected and it bounced off his hand, onto another table. Hector snorted. Caroline hid her face in embarrassment.

"What are you, five?" I quipped.

A lazy smile stretched across Samuel's face. "Will you dance with me tonight, Firecracker?"

"Nope. I'm dancing with Santiago."

"After Santiago, then."

"Hector's called dibs on that one."

Hector gave Samuel two thumbs up. Samuel groaned. "The third dance, then."

I relented, deciding not to tease him too terribly. "Fine, but only if it's a slow song. I don't do fast."

"Deal. Great toast, by the way."

"Ditto." I shamelessly winked at him. Caroline turned her back to Samuel and started a conversation with Cassady. I knew it was wrong to flirt with Samuel in front of his wedding date. But then, I'd already crossed the Rubicon when I kissed him back. She was a big girl and she'd get over it, I hoped.

The newlyweds cut their cake—a magnificent, four-tiered *tres leche* with clusters of roses and vibrant strawberries. They managed to feed each other without face-smashing or any other naughtiness that would earn Angel a night at the plane hangar. They danced their first dance to a mariachi version of "Ain't That a Kick in the Head?" Angel was surprisingly nimble. Dani was, of course, all class. The mother-son dance followed, then the father-daughter (dang, Alonso was still gorgeous), then the wedding party. Santiago was a fabulous partner who didn't complain when I stepped on his feet (thank Jiminy for tea-length hems). He only stepped on my feet twice. Maybe we could invest in dance lessons.

Then the floor opened and Hector swept me into his rebellious arms.

"You look hot tonight, Kaye. Your hair's really curly, kind of like Shirley Temple, but all twisted up and stuff."

"That's borderline pedo, Hector."

"Eh. I get the whole eggplant dress thing now. Yum."

"You clean up really nice."

His white teeth gleamed brighter than the starched linen surrounding us. "With you all sexy in this pretty dress, I couldn't look like a bum."

I laughed and let him swing me across the floor.

When the next song began, my eyes skimmed through ebullient dancing limbs for Samuel. He was across the floor, circling with Caroline, her arm snaking around his neck. Grinding my teeth, I grabbed Hector for another dance. Then Santiago. And then my father. Finally, my nonsensical jealousy subsided and I decided to hunt down Samuel for a dance. But when I turned around, a light blinded me. My hands flew to my eyes, blocking the camera flash.

"Murphy! What the heck?"

"Sorry, Kaye, I need a picture to post on my *WS* blog. Hey, you wanna dance?" Before I could object, Alan grabbed my hand and pulled me back onto the dance floor.

I'd finally found someone who was worse than Santiago and me. Alan mercilessly stomped my toes in a junior-high swaying sort of way as he rambled about how awesome it was to dance with Neelie Nixie (despite my insistence she was fictional—I began to sound like Samuel). More than once, he whipped out his phone and snapped a picture, even kissed my cheek. Before the night was out, they'd probably be posted on some Neelie Nixie fan site.

"Hey, Kaye, before you leave can you sign my book?"

"Um…okay."

I followed Murphy back to his table, where several of his friends mooned up at me over *tres leche*. Grabbing Alan's pen, I hurriedly scrawled my name in the front cover and flipped it shut. Thankfully, my father spotted me and waved me over. Returning Alan's pen, I excused myself and shuffled through the crowd, grateful to be away from the scrutiny of twenty-eight-year-old horndogs.

"Hey, flower."

Dad had finagled an outdated tie and sport coat for the wedding, and was decidedly awkward in it. I hugged his neck and straightened the tie.

"You look really handsome, Coach Trilby. Where's Audrey?"

He hugged my shoulders. "At the bar. You're real pretty too, Kaye. Nice toast, by the way. Almost made me want to get hitched, myself."

I noticed Samuel beyond my father, making his way through the crowd in our direction. His great aunt from Ciudad Victoria (Bonita? Belinda?) swooped in and patted his cheeks with gnarled fingers. He politely nodded, sipping a cola as they conversed in Spanish. At eighty-something, she was slightly deaf and had a tendency to speak loudly. I had to step closer to my father to hear him, but I couldn't turn off my internal translator.

"What was that, Dad?"

"…and so handsome."

"I said not to break a leg in those heels. Say, how's Hector?"

"He's as happy as a clam after all the free food and beer the past couple of nights. See him out on the dance floor? That's two G and Ts at work, right there." My dad watched my date, scratched his ponytailed hair.

"All of the Cabrals are so proud of you, Samuel…"

"Quite a dancer, isn't he? Just don't let him drive you home, now…"

"…so difficult, especially after your father died…"

I started at the mention of Samuel's father. Holding up a hand, I halted our conversation and brazenly listened. My father frowned at my eavesdropping.

"Well, yes," Samuel answered.

"You are so much like her, you know—your American mother. She had that same lovely brow, and such a beautiful voice. And the way you smile just takes me back…"

I chanced a look at Samuel. His face blanched, paleness ringing pressed lips. His hands balled into fists so tight, his knuckles turned bone white. His aunt didn't notice.

"Definitely your mother's boy, even your eyes. What did your father call them? Blue skies? Sky something?"

Samuel rasped an answer, too quiet to hear.

Aunt Bonita or Belinda clapped her hands. "Sky-Eyes! That's right. Well, you'd have made them really proud, Samuel—"

Samuel cut her off with a muttered apology and darted into the darkness, away from the white lights and canopies.

"Dad, I'll chat with you later, okay?" I pecked his cheek and chased Samuel into the night before my father could stop me.

I wasn't the only one who'd noticed Samuel's bizarre reaction to his aunt's words. Alonso was also hot on my heels. Samuel tripped up the stairs of the house and stumbled down the hallway, toward the bathroom. I halted, unsure of whether I should enter. Alonso brushed past me and pushed through the door. I caught a glimpse of pale blue tile and Samuel collapsing to his knees, and then the door swung shut in my face.

"Samuel?" I mouthed to the closed door.

What just happened? I'd never, not once, seen anything affect Samuel so swiftly, so violently. On the surface, his aunt's comments were harmless. So he looked like his birth mother—wasn't that to be expected? I'd learned a long time ago that conversation about Antonio Cabral and Rachel Caulfield Cabral upset him, but that was years ago. Why on earth would a thirty-year-old man still react so negatively?

Enough was enough. I'd be damned if I'd let Alonso handle this one without me. Mustering my courage, I pushed through the bathroom door, not even bothering to knock. It creaked shut behind me.

Retching sounds echoed from the corner of the room, beyond the washstand. Samuel hunched over a toilet, his fingers clinging to the rim as he heaved. His father crouched behind him, rubbed his shoulders. Neither one of them saw I'd entered.

"Another migraine?"

Samuel shook his head, his entire body trembling from exertion. "I'm fine, Dad. Just didn't sleep well last night."

Worried brown eyes swept over his son, taking in his worn appearance. He opened his mouth to say something, but Samuel gave a little shake of his head, staring up at me with blood-shot eyes.

Alonso frowned. "You need to sleep."

"I'm *fine*, Dad," he repeated, his eyes not leaving mine.

"Are you still— "

"Yes."

Alonso followed Samuel's gaze, seeing me for the first time.

An uneasy feeling settled into the pit of my stomach over the exchange. This was more than just passing concern. And even though Samuel played it down, fear still lingered in his father's face. Alonso all but confirmed my worry: revisiting our troubled past wasn't just taking an emotional toll on Samuel. It was affecting his physical well-being.

But just as fear crept through me, it cleared from Alonso's face and he smiled, giving his son's shoulders a brief pat.

"Sorry, Samuel. Once a father, always a father." It happened so quickly, I wondered if I'd even seen the fear at all. But I wasn't so easily appeased.

"You aren't *fine*, Samuel." My voice quaked. "Don't pretend you are."

Alonso took a step toward me and gestured to the door. "*Mija*, you probably need to step out for a while. Give Samuel some air."

"No. I'm not leaving until someone tells me what's wrong."

"Kaye," he stated, more firmly, "you need to go."

I turned to my former father-in-law, stubbornly planting my feet. "I'm. Not. Leaving."

He sighed and reached for my arm. For a moment, I thought he would bodily drag me from the room, but he just ran frustrated hands through his gray-streaked hair, at a loss.

"Kaye..."

"Dad, I want her to stay."

Samuel pulled himself up and took my hand, tugging me to him. I wrapped my fingers around his, a united front, despite the knowledge those fingers had clutched a toilet bowl seconds earlier.

Alonso studied Samuel, then me, some unreadable emotion passing through his face. He relented.

"If you think it's best, son. I should return to the reception, anyway." He stepped around me, giving my shoulder an affectionate squeeze. "Don't hole up in here forever, okay, kids?"

The door swung shut behind him, leaving us in silence. I dug through the medicine cabinet and found a bottle of mouthwash. When he was done rinsing, I sank down across from him, a clownish task in heels and fluffy skirt.

"Kaye, your dress."

"Tell me what's wrong."

Samuel pulled up his knees, resigned. I wrapped my arms around them and rested my cheek on his kneecaps. For two full minutes, we stared. In the silence, conversations and well-wishes floated through the house as guests and vendors entered and exited, the screen door ceaselessly thudding. I kneaded circles against Samuel's legs with my thumbs, waiting. Finally, he spoke.

"You shouldn't want to be around me, Kaye."

"That's a different tune than the one you sang yesterday. What's changed?"

"I read your letter last night." He pulled the piece of paper from his inside pocket and held it up, absently crushing it in his fist.

"I figured as much."

"I didn't know. I never believed I could hurt you the way I did." Samuel reached out and rubbed away a lipstick smudge from the corner of my mouth. Then he dropped his hand, as if he were ashamed to even touch me.

"I see someone attacked you with foundation," I murmured, brushing his healing nose, the week-old injury barely visible.

Samuel caught my pointing finger and drew my entire hand into his. "Kaye, remember what I said about letting me take the knock-out when I need it? Well, I really, really need to feel this one."

I shook my head. "No, Samuel."

"I need to feel that same pain I caused you in New York." He began to choke up. "The things I did and said to you…"

"You're getting worked up again, and it's not helping." I pulled my hand back.

He looked at me incredulously. "I violated every single marriage vow within a handful of minutes. I wasn't loving or faithful, I didn't honor you—"

"Samuel, please stop."

"—or even protect you. The shock you were in…What if you'd left the brownstone? What if those drunk guys—"

I tightened my grip on his knees. "*Samuel.* You need to breathe." His face twisted as he grappled for control. He took a deep breath. "Take another. And then you need to calmly tell me what this was that I just saw. A panic attack?"

He offered me a half smile, the fakeness of it marring his otherwise handsome face. Today had been tough on him—on both of us. Samuel gently pried my fingers from his knees, wincing as my manicured nails relinquished their grip. His eyes on mine, he brought both hands to his lips and kissed them, running his thumbs over the tendons trailing from each knuckle. I sighed and returned them to his knees, resting my chin there.

"Tell me what happened to your parents," I whispered.

His head fell against the wall tiles, eyes closing. "I can't. Not yet."

"Why not?"

"Because…there are other things. Things I need to explain. And this all just takes time."

"Samuel, the mere mention of your parents made you vomit into a toilet. This is really serious."

"Most days I can handle it better, believe me. Today is more stressful." His eyes cracked open and bright slits of blue greeted me, pleading for understanding. "Please, Firecracker, let me tell you when I'm ready. I swear I will tell you."

I nearly acquiesced to his pleading, gave in to that damaged, haunted boy, circling in that endless hole of forward and retreat. All the old fears surfaced—that if I didn't back off, I'd lose him forever, that I had to protect this fragile thing floating between us. But love is not meant to be fragile, and regret is a hard thing to live with. I remembered: *Perhaps I should have pushed.* And if I didn't push now, then I'd lose him forever.

I shook my head. "No."

"What?"

"I said no. No, I won't wait. For years I waited for the tiniest crumbs of information from you, telling myself that this was painful, that you'd open up some day because you trusted me and loved me. But you never did. So no more waiting."

His back stiffened in cageyness. "That sounds a lot like an ultimatum, Kaye."

"I suppose it is."

"And if I don't tell you? What?"

"You want to earn my trust? Well, you've got to trust me back. When there's no trust…nothing. We shake hands and maybe see each other in a few years."

He shot up from his slouch. "Bullshit! I'm *trying*, Kaye. Do you have any concept of how much I want to make this right? But maybe I'm a little reluctant to drag you down a path that would be extraordinarily unfair to you. Maybe I don't want to hurt you, to watch you throw your life away trying to fix someone that can't be fixed!"

I ripped my hand from his sweaty grip, wiped the dampness on my dress. "Now I call bullshit. This has nothing to do with self-sacrifice. It's plain old self-preservation! You're not protecting me, Samuel, your protecting *yourself*. It's always about protecting yourself. That's the *real* reason you ran away to New York."

"What a heaping load of insanity. That's…" His mouth slid open in shock and his eyes unfocused as he stared past me. He blinked once, twice. "Dammit. That's what my therapist said, too."

My eyes sought his. "Do you see? We can't rebuild on air. We've both got to be truthful and…and honest. Otherwise we might as well say goodbye and walk right out that door."

He rolled the hem of my dress between his fingers. "I don't want you to go."

"Then don't make me beg for honesty."

Long minutes passed. More silence, save for the faint pounding of dance floor speakers…*thud thud thud*. Panic that we were well and truly finished burned in my chest. Then he spoke, so softly.

"My mother…she…she was ill. Very ill. And there was no one there to help her, no one to…"

My breath whooshed out. "To help you?"

"No one to stop her." The implications of his words hung heavily between us. "When I was a child, I loved my mother beyond reason. When I was older, I hated her. She was my world for so long…and she didn't even know it."

"And now?"

"Now…both. Neither." He exhaled slowly, a mess of nerves and trembles. "I try not to resent her because I know she wasn't well. I like to tell myself that if she'd had help, she would have been a good mother. But I just don't know...I'll *never* know. And there are some things that are hard to forgive."

"Did she hit you?"

"A few times."

"Did she do other things?"

"Not in the way you mean. Most days she forgot me. I was a ghost to her. Some days I longed for her to hit me, because it meant she knew I was there and that she felt something—anything—toward me. But then she would, and I'd wish to be forgotten again. I'd bring snacks home from kindergarten and hide them under my bed, just in case she forgot to feed me..."

My eyes fluttered shut. He'd only been a baby.

He continued, voice a detached whisper. "I remember her crying every night when she was home, the waterbed sloshing each time she turned. Sometimes she came into my room when she thought I was asleep and lay down with me. I learned quickly to pretend I wasn't awake, or she'd get angry and yell. It was the strange little things which set her off—things that seemed like nothing, but were significant to her. Like my asking to visit Fenway Park to see the Red Sox."

"How did she die?"

"I think you know."

"Did your mother take her own life?" I asked carefully.

"Both of my parents did."

Both? I hadn't seen that one coming. I gaped like a fish, trying to form words.

"I don't remember my father—he died when I was a baby. My mother died just before I came to Lyons."

"I met you at the Halloween party. You told me your mother was taking you trick-or-treating."

His face was all raw reminiscence. "She packed me into her car and we drove to a hotel near Fenway Park. Before we left, she tucked a letter for Alonso in my backpack, asking him to keep me instead of her parents. She checked us in, requested a top floor balcony, and jumped."

I bolted upright. My eyes flew to Samuel's, though he wouldn't meet them. "She jumped from the balcony?" I asked incredulously. "With her six-year-old son in the room?" Oh dear God, the things he must have seen. The aftermath…I covered my mouth to hide my gagging.

"For years, I convinced myself she'd accidentally fallen over the wall. But as I grew older and realized such a thing as suicide existed, I understood."

My fingers weaved through my loosely pinned hair, tugging bobby pins free. "Oh my God, Samuel. I can't believe…" I stumbled around for a way to finish my sentence, but there was nothing. A foggy memory from long ago clarified in my head, and I gasped.

"When we were little," I said, "I remember your greatest fear was falling from high places. Alonso and Sofia took us to the national park to climb up a five-story look-out tower and see the tops of the trees. You screamed bloody murder the whole way up the stairs, and finally Sofia had to carry you back down." I drew in a deep breath, my arms wrapping around my middle. "I get it now."

He touched my knee. "I grew out of it, Kaye. Do you think I'd go skydiving if I hadn't?" He offered me a faint smile. "Figuring out my mother's death wasn't an accident helped, in some respects. I didn't walk around terrified of open windows, anyway." He paused, his voice trailing lower, quieter. "It also taught me to cherish and protect the people I love, though I know I've done a disgraceful job at it."

He'd been such a brave, sad little boy in that ghost costume. So quiet, so well-behaved.

And, I now understood, so traumatized.

I gazed at him, tenderly placed my palm against his face. I noticed it was slightly less clammy. "Why did she do it? Why did they both do it?"

"No one knows, though Dad and I have speculated. Neither was ever diagnosed with anything. But in retrospect, it's apparent they were sick. I think, maybe, that's why they fell in love to begin with. They must have recognized themselves in each other…fed off each other." His trembling hand rested on top of mine.

"Symbiosis."

"Symbiosis."

My fingers curled around his, willing him to hear me. "Samuel, we are *not* your mother and father. I'm not, and neither are you."

"Am I not?"

"No, you're not." I said adamantly.

"If you say so."

"I say so."

He closed his eyes and sighed, threading his fingers through mine. "Kaye, please, no more tonight. My sister just got married. Let's just be happy for her and Angel."

I relaxed my grip on his hand, willing to let the rest go…for now. Relief flooded his eyes as he realized I wouldn't force the issue further tonight.

"When are you flying back to New York?" I asked after several minutes.

"Tomorrow morning."

I grimaced, dreading that goodbye. We didn't have much time. "Can you meet me tonight, after the reception? I know you need sleep, but you can sleep tomorrow away after you board the plane, can't you? Oh shoot!" I slapped my forehead. "You have to drive to Denver, don't you? Never mind, get some sleep."

"It'll be fine, Caroline's driving. What do you have in mind?"

I hesitated, but he insisted. "Bring the letter." I pointed to the crumpled piece of paper he'd dropped in his lap. "We're going to talk about it. And then we're going to get rid of it, once and for all. It's killing us, Samuel. We need to let this rest in the past."

"Okay." His voice was tentative.

I drummed my fingers on his knees, trying to lighten the atmosphere. "I also had an epiphany while Angel and Danita exchanged vows today."

"I noticed." He smiled a bit, for real this time.

"I'll share my idea later. I think it will help us."

We sat for long minutes, perhaps even an hour, simply absorbing each other's pain, driving it away. We shared the small things we'd learned in the time we'd been separated: I'd tried sushi for the first time and actually liked it. Samuel had given *Legends of the Fall* another go and still hated it. We discussed philosophy—I now thought that truth really wasn't as relative as postmodern society believed. Samuel agreed, saying we had to have some sort of basis for reality. I admitted his big brain sometimes made me feel less smart. He admitted he envied my risk-taking, even if it made him worry.

Something momentous was shifting…Rather than guarding our Achilles' heels, we exposed them to each other, so very slowly, while shielding each other's weaknesses.

A set of feet tromped down the hall and jiggled the handle. The door opened a crack as a hand clutching a champagne bottle sluggishly pushed it open. Cassady popped in his shaggy head inside. His jacket was long gone, and his tie hung loosely around an unbuttoned collar and rolled-up sleeves. One of Danita's lacy garters circled his bicep. He cursed as he sloshed champagne on the floor and immediately shut the door.

"Sssorry, gunnars," he called to the closed door. "We'll jus' go upstairs. Sssorry."

I snickered. "It looks like Cassady won the garter toss. I suppose that means I missed the bouquet toss, too."

Samuel checked his watch and whistled. "Nine forty. We've been in here way too long."

I groaned as I shook the numbness out of my feet and tailbone. Pushing myself up from his knees, I held out a hand and helped him to his feet. We brushed our backsides and took deep breaths.

"Are you ready to return to reality?" I asked.

"Only if you are." He tried out a full smile. "The quiet is nice. I felt like I was leaping from circus ring to circus ring out there."

I reached for the door, but Samuel's arm came out, halting me. He wrapped his long fingers around my wrist, pulling me to him. One arm secure around my waist, he peered down at me.

"I don't need your pity," he said gently, firmly.

"I know." I smoothed my hand over his finger-raked hair.

"I'm a grown man, Kaye—not that little boy anymore."

"But it doesn't mean I can't feel pain for that little boy. Or that I love him any less," I quietly added.

He shook his head and kissed a drop from the corner of my mouth. I hadn't even realized I was crying. "I wish…"

He didn't finish his thought. There were so many ways to finish it, and he probably couldn't decide on one. His palm cupped the back of my head and he pressed me to him, kissing my hair once, twice. "I guess I wasn't quite ready to let you go," he said sheepishly and released me.

We walked up the hallway, the ruckus of the caterers in the kitchen having died down now that dinner was well behind us. As we passed the pantry, I heard a soft, feminine whimper.

I paused, tugging on Samuel's sleeve. There it was again.

My eyes widened. I tried the knob—the door didn't open. Was someone locked in?

"Hello?" I called, rapping on the heavy oak door. "Are you okay in there?"

There was a deeper moan and a giggle, followed by a flurry of rustling clothing and muffled cursing. I began to panic.

Samuel snorted.

I glared at him, baffled. Only then did I notice Cassady's champagne bottle and black tie on the rug next to the closed door. The bride's throw bouquet was propped up against the floor board, as well.

And then it hit me. Oh crap, oh crap, oh crap. There was a reason the door was locked. Stupidly, I knocked again.

"Ahh, never mind! Forget I even knocked the first time! Go back to...whatever."

A full-out laugh burst from Samuel. I poked him in the ribs, completely mortified. Dragging him behind me, we escaped the Cabral house before the pantry occupants emerged.

"You know who was in the pantry?" He lifted an eyebrow at me.

My lips twisted. "I have a hunch. Now we know who won the bouquet toss, too."

As we re-entered the party, Samuel placed a hand on the small of my back and steered me toward the dance floor. The mariachis pounded out a samba and dozens of guests shuffled and grinded to the steamy number. Even Hector was out there, his collar popped as his hips swayed to the music. I quickly scanned the crowd for Caroline, but didn't see her.

Once I realized Samuel was actually dragging me onto the dance floor, I did an about-face and retreated. But he caught my elbow, every inch of him sparking with naughtiness.

"Oh no," he laughed, lifting my waist. "You have gotten away with this 'I can't samba' garbage far too long."

I squealed and kicked as he plopped me down next to Angel and Danita. Danita shamelessly high-fived him.

"Samuel, you know I can't dance to this stuff. Slow dance, yes. Rock even. Latin, no."

"Be good or I'll carry you off to the pantry." He placed his hands on my taffeta-clad hips and moved them with his, careful to leave a bit of space between us despite his pantry threat. He wasn't going to push his luck. "You don't seem to be having a difficult time dancing, Trilby. In fact, you're pretty good at it."

"Say that when your toes are broken, Cabral." I scowled, but let myself go a little. His eyes flashed with approval.

Before long, I partied with Angel and Danita, thoroughly enjoying the beats pulsing from the stage. I turned under Samuel's hands and tipped my head back against his shoulder. White lights spun over my head, warm halos hitting the stark night sky. A cooling breeze brushed my skin and carried the faint smell of pine onto the dance floor.

"See?" he whispered into my hair. "Not so scary. It's just music, Kaye."

I laughed again, reveling in the place, the night, my friends, Samuel. I saw Cassady and Molly sneak across the lawn toward the dance floor, his arm flung around her long torso. Her hair was a sexed-up mess and she winked at me, conveying what I already knew. I hoped he wouldn't break her heart.

In my periphery, Hector and Santiago bickered, Hector vainly trying to convince his brother that his "sultry" dance moves weren't all that smooth. Even my own parents were being civil to each other, the two of them and Audrey sitting at a table, chatting over drinks as they watched us dance.

And somehow, all of it faded to the background as my best friend's arms circled my waist. I felt the muscles of his stomach beneath starched cotton. Smelled his sweat as it crept to the surface of his skin. His breath tickled the nape of my neck, and it reminded me of making love to him, so much. Too much. It reminded him, too. A familiar warmth pressed into my back, the space between us forgotten. My lips curled and I felt a bit of the seductress return to my bones.

The song ground to a close and another one started, slower. I turned in Samuel's arms as the band strummed out sweet contemporary strains.

He gently pressed his fingers into my back, urging me closer…I rested my cheek on the lapel of his tuxedo vest.

"You know what I mean when I tell you I want you, right?" he murmured.

He took my hand in his and held it against his chest…I let my other hand creep up his neck, into his hair.

"It's kind of hard to miss," I teased, leaning into his body.

He chuckled and trailed a hand up my spine, all the way to my neck…I allowed him to play with the ringlets on my head.

For years and years, we'd spoken those three little words to each other. An innocent "I love you, I'm sorry" after playing too rough as children. A quick "love ya" as we flew past lockers on our way to class. A sad "love you so much" as he left for college, leaving me in Lyons. So many meanings, that saying "I love you" became common—like hello and goodbye.

I'd never doubted our friendship love. But Samuel telling me he wanted me…I hadn't heard it much from him, in the past. We'd shown it, we just didn't say it. And when our marriage ended, it left me wondering whether I'd been the only one who'd truly felt it.

But he had. He still did.

"You are glowing tonight. Lovely."

I brought my eyes to his and returned the smile. "So are you."

Samuel moved me around the dance floor. I knew people watched, talking about the exes. I didn't care. My face burrowed into his neck, breasts brushing lightly against his chest. A wave of nostalgia washed over me as I inhaled his faint cologne. Spicy cardamom, juniper, and cedar. He still wore the same scent, even so many years later. Despite the changes in him—clothing preferences, grown-up confidence, the ability to work a room—the recognizable little things reminded me that he was still Samuel.

Had he known I'd wanted him too, back then? How often had I told Samuel I desired him? I needed him? I bit my lip, searching my memories for one occasion when I'd shared those words, confessed how good he made me feel.

I couldn't think of a one. For all he knew, *I'd* only loved *him* as a friend. I had begged for his last name, but never explained why. Not telling him was a costly mistake on my part, and I would have given anything to go back to the years we were together and tell him, every single day, that I wanted him too. But mulling over "woulda coulda shouldas" didn't fix a thing. The past was just upstream driftwood, out of reach. The present, though, still sloshed against my trailing fingers.

"Welcome home." I kissed his neck—a promise—and wiped away the trace of lipstick I'd left there.

His entire body sighed.

With a final flourish, the song ended.

As the music died away, I felt eyes on me, yanking us down from our high. Samuel held me to him a moment longer, his lips brushing my hairline so subtly, it might seem unintentional to anyone watching. And then he let me go. Disappointment surged through me as he hurriedly kissed my cheek, thanking me.

Before I could gather the courage to ask him for another dance, one of Angel's enthusiastic teenage cousins claimed him. Samuel relented, and I made my way to the back table where I'd left my wrap and hour-old champagne. The corner was partly obscured by shadows, so I didn't see anybody sitting there until it was too late.

Caroline Ortega glared up at me, onyx eyes two pinpoints of hate.

She was crying.

I nervously grabbed for my champagne flute, hoping to clear out as quickly as possible. But in true disastrous timing, my hand missed the glass and sent it clattering across the table, spilling sticky champagne down the front of Caroline's designer jacquard dress.

"Frickin' swizzle-stick." I picked up a pink linen and stopped short of dabbing Caroline's dress. She swiped the napkin from me and brushed the material, then her eyes. Once she finished, she tossed the thing on the table and rounded on me.

"You did that on purpose."

I thrust out my hands. "Look here, if I'd wanted to spill champagne all over you, I would have picked the thing up and dumped it on your head."

"No. What you are doing is worse, and you know it."

"I haven't a clue what you mean." I busied myself by mopping up the table with the pink linen.

"Samuel. You're playing with him. Instead of cutting him loose like an amicable *ex*-wife to let him live his life, you string him along."

"Bull."

"Is it? You've dangled Hector Valdez in front of him since you were kids and when he reacts to it, you berate him for it, don't you?"

"No! Hector and Samuel are my friends—nothing more." My fingers tightened around the cloth napkin.

"There's no point in lying, it's written all over your face. You can't have it both ways, you know. 'Friends with benefits' never works."

My fists dug into my hips. "Hey, let's calm down, okay? I'm sorry you're upset, but it's not my fault Samuel doesn't want to date you, Caroline. You have no right to take your bitterness out on me."

"I have every right to despise you. It drives you insane that I know him better than you do, now, doesn't it?"

"And yet, he still wants me." I chucked the champagne-dampened linen on the table. The woman just could not keep her mouth shut, could she?

"So what are you going to do when he's back in your arms? Destroy him again when you realize you don't want the real him?"

"You don't know the first thing about me, so back off." Grabbing my empty champagne flute, I stalked away from the table, weaving my way toward the bar. But Caroline jumped up and stalked after me.

"Don't I? Apparently it isn't enough that he's been hung up on you for *seven miserable years*. You want him to be miserable for the rest of his life. You just couldn't stand to see him move on with someone else, could you?"

Tears stung my eyes. I jabbed a finger at her. "I can't stand that the woman is a selfish, manipulative harpy."

"Take a look in the mirror, you podunk piece of trash."

"Enough." A calm, forceful voice sounded behind me. Sofia Cabral stepped forward, her face grieved. "There will be no more fighting."

She took the empty champagne flute from my quivering hand and set it on a nearby table. Touching a calming finger to my cheek, she turned to both of us.

"The two of you mean the world to my son. But if you must force him to choose sides, please don't do it tonight. This is my daughter's wedding."

Only then did I glance around, noticing for the first time that several guests—Mrs. Jones included—stared at us, whispering about Samuel Cabral's ex-wife and new girlfriend going toe-to-toe like a tawdry reality show. I sought Samuel's tall frame on the dance floor and was relieved he hadn't witnessed the ridiculously embarrassing girl-fight.

Caroline bit her tongue and carefully schooled her features into a deliberate nonchalance. I mumbled an apology to Sofia like a thoroughly-scolded thirteen-year-old. How was it that Sofia, with a single stern look, could bring me to my repentant knees?

"Come with me, Caroline. I can help you treat your dress in the laundry room." Sofia held out a firm hand and Caroline had no choice but to follow. But as she left, she got in one final dig.

"You are just another addiction," she hissed for my ears only. "You're going to destroy him, Kaye. And the disgusting thing is, you can't even comprehend you're doing it."

As I watched her elegant, retreating back, I chewed on her words.

I wasn't an addiction to him, was I?

No, she was wrong. If it was the last thing I ever did in this life, I would prove Caroline wrong. Samuel Cabral would never face destruction because of me.

A destructive path…

I slapped my head at my stupidity. Samuel's last *Water Sirens* book. The entire thing was about destructive paths. Now I had to finish it before we discussed New York after the reception.

Scanning the crowd, I spotted the person I was looking for—kind of scrawny, goofy-looking ruffled shirt, matted blond hair. Alan Murphy sat at a table, chatting away with several old Lyons High friends about some graphic novel.

"No way, dude, I'm telling you—if *WS* was illustrated, Neelie Nixie would totally have huge tits. She'd wear leather, too. Head-to-toe…"

His friends frantically waved to him, motioning "cut it." He gave them an odd look. "Oh come on. You can't tell me you don't think Cabral wrote 'em bigger than in real life…"

I ground my teeth, struggling not to slap Murphy upside the head.

"And…she's standing right behind me, isn't she?" Alan swiveled in his chair, his face flooding crimson. His Adam's apple bobbed in his throat.

"Kaye, hehe. Look, I totally didn't know—"

"Forget it. I need to borrow your book, please. The one I signed?"

"Yes! Um…you aren't going to throw it in the dumpster, are you?"

"Don't be ridiculous. I just want to read it. I'll return it when I'm done, I promise."

He just stared at me, protecting the book as if he shielded his kitten from a hungry hawk.

"Look, if anything happens to it, I'll see if Samuel can get you a signed galley copy. How about that?"

Alan reluctantly handed over the precious first edition copy of *The Last Other*. Muttering my thanks, I scrambled for the house, the book tucked under my arm.

It was time to finish *The Last Other*. Neelie Nixie was already dead. Now I had to know, once and for all, what happened to Nicodemus.

Chapter 20
RIVER SIGNALS

Like baseball signals, paddlers use a series of signs while on the river in order to communicate from a distance.

"Kaye, please!"

"Just a sec', Alan."

Music from the mariachis floated through the window of the Cabrals' spare bedroom—last dance type of music.

"My friends need to leave and I need my book back," he whined through the guest room door, where he'd finally tracked me down.

"Another fifteen minutes?"

"Fine." I heard him tromp down the stairs and back to the party.

I bit my thumbnail, flying over paragraph after thrilling paragraph of action. This was it. Nicodemus had picked off the rest of the Others, one by one, until he'd cornered their mastermind in a deserted Alpine village somewhere in Austria...

> **Nicodemus righted his fossil limbs and threw himself into the dream-fray, desperately striking against the furious strength of the last Other. A defeated soldier in a battlefield of blood he swung, aimless,**

heedless of the carnage beneath his feet, of the stench. Scatters of stone and smoldered flesh...remnants of a final, failed stand against the overpowering evil that had taken Neelie and left his world in miserable ruin.

He had been so very sure. When the Others began to drop, mysteriously, by a hand other than his, he'd hoped. When he'd trailed bands of demons across the mountains only to come across their dead carcasses along the road, he'd been so sure...

The last Other leered down at him with glistening black teeth, hitting him with yet another vision. Neelie, grasping at loose rock, tumbling over the edge. Neelie's body, crumpled at the bottom of a cliff. Neelie, gone, gone, gone. Nicodemus clutched his head and tried to root out the Other...

I closed my eyes, pressing the book to my chest until panic subsided. I forced my coward eyelids open and gazed out the window, down at the twinkling lights of the wedding reception. Guests had steadily left over the past hour as it crept closer to midnight.

A knock at the door yanked me out of Samuel's fantasy world. My mother, working the beads and bell sleeves, peeked around, noticeably relieved to find me alone.

"Kaye, your father's going to drive Hector home. He's a little worse for wear after that open bar."

Guilt clamped down and twisted my chest like a lug wrench. In my haste to secure time with Samuel, I'd completely forgotten about Hector. "Thanks, Mom."

"Don't you get into any trouble with that Cabral boy tonight."

I groaned. "Mom, I'm not fifteen."

"All the same, I saw you on that dance floor. Make sure he—you know. Covers up."

"Mom! Your Free Love card is being revoked."

"What? It's getting cold out." She smirked and ducked out of the room. Shaking off my utter humiliation, I locked the door, opened the book again and plowed ahead.

> He'd hoped for this. Death. The lashing, the destroying, and now the peace. Wherever Death was, she was. He'd failed to bring down the last Other – this was his fate. But now the fight faded, and he wanted nothing but to feel the stone filament creep through his veins, thicken his blood until his body was encased in the sediment lake bottom. Until his brain petrified. Dear God, he wanted this. Lost...Lost...Lost...
>
> "Get the hell off of him, you repulsive bastard," a vicious, feminine voice snarled at the creature. From the haze of fossilizing eyes, he saw a beloved face, twisted in hatred and brandishing a well-known weapon...

"Son of a—!" I read on. No way. No. Way.

"Kaye?" Alan Murphy called behind the door, having returned from the party. "What happened? Is my book torn?"

Ignoring Alan's panicked cries, my eyes flew over the page. Cripes. Cripes! It was *her*—Neelie.

> Nicodemus watched helplessly as his lover and the last Other writhed and tore at one another, her deadly blade flashing against the creature's neck. The beast flung her from his back and leaped onto her tiny body, pitilessly seeking to crush her.
>
> Now Nicodemus cursed the scum weighing him down, rendering him inadequate. With a savage cry, he fought to lift an arm – just a single arm. But it was enough to distract the thing. The Other whirled around, hissing at Nicodemus. He dragged a limp Neelie behind him as he stalked closer...closer.
>
> Nicodemus saw the slightest stirring in Neelie's hand as it brushed her discarded knife. Her steady fingers reached for the hilt and she kicked away, toppling the creature. Without mercy, she raised her hand high –

Alan pounded on the door. "Kaye, come on! Talk to me!"

–The Other loosed a last, fierce growl and grew still. Between them, they heaved the dead weight of the black, hulking thing behind the thatched hut. It was there, beneath the fractured ice of the Alps, they burned the last Other...

"If you don't open this door, I'm going to get Mr. Cabral!"

"I knew." Nicodemus framed his world, this face, between his fingers. "Neelie, I hoped. How I hoped. I was turning to stone without you, can you believe it?"

Neelie pushed away the film of her tattered sleeve, displaying soft, ivory skin. She wiggled several fingers and Nicodemus saw they weren't ivory but gray... stone gray. Warming gray. Gray fading back to flesh, like his fingers.

"I believe it..."

"That's it. I'm going for help!"

"Oh for the love of all that's holy, Murphy, this is the best part!" I leaped up from the bed, unlocked the door and swung it open, staring down a baffled Alan. "You told me Neelie died!"

"Well, she did. At least you're supposed to think she did." He twisted the leather *WS* bracelet circling his wrist. "Wait, you just now figured it out?"

"I... I hadn't read that far."

He snorted, making me feel like I missed something obvious. "If you'd paid attention to the rest of the series, you would have guessed at it. Cabral has been setting it up for the past two books, now."

"Faking her death?"

He nodded.

"But why? Why would Neelie let her friends and family believe she was dead?"

He rolled his eyes. "So she could lay a trap for the Others. See, Neelie figured out a long time ago they weren't after her, remember? They were after Nicodemus. And in the process, they planned to take out Neelie, Nora, Noel, anyone who could lead an attack against them. So she faked her death, quietly traveling the same path as Nicodemus and picking off the Others until she could strike. Get it?"

"Yeah, I g-guess," I stuttered.

He scratched his head. "Um, look. I don't mean to be a jerk, but can you finish that thing up? I really need to leave."

"Oh! Sure, just a sec." He slid down the side of the wall as I tucked into the last chapter.

It was as I'd remembered before, when I skimmed it on the way to Samuel's book signing. Nora and Noel, taking up the reins of power. The mythological creatures rebuilding their world after years of oppression at the Others' hands. No Neelie. And no Nicodemus — now I knew why. Like Arthurian legend, they'd vanished into the Alps, vowing to return when there was need of them.

So epic. So Samuel.

I turned the final page and closed the book.

"That doesn't make sense, though." I flipped pages under my thumb. "I never helped Samuel fight the Others."

"Yeah, I guess that's why it's *fiction*." Alan carefully extracted the book from my hands. "Happy endings occur more often in stories than in real life, that's for sure. Maybe Cabral just wanted to write a happy ending. I dunno."

He fled the room, precious book in hand, and I slumped against the bed and fought to make connections to Neelie.

Neelie had swollen keyhole eyes — battle wounds. Now that was definitely me, watching Samuel plow ahead in his constant need to shield, to pave the way. I could see now how I'd been blind to so many things when it came to Samuel, like his reasons for leaving and his overwhelming sadness. I shuddered as the gruesome things he'd revealed to me about his parents burrowed through my mind.

And Neelie had been touched by the curse of the wicked sirens, whatever the hell that was. If the Others were Samuel's demons, then what was the curse?

Both Neelie and Nicodemus were turning to stone without each other, their love bound them together so inextricably. Samuel's whole "symbiotic relationship" theory again, taken to the extreme. But again, it didn't make sense. Until we'd talked at Button Rock Reservoir, Samuel had believed I was happy. He'd wanted me to be happy. So why was Neelie turning to stone?

"Did you like the rest of the book?"

I jumped. Samuel stood in the doorway, sober eyes on mine as he munched a piece of wedding cake.

"I ran into Murphy downstairs, muttering about getting a galley proof because you'd wrinkled the dust jacket. There's no chance I'm giving him a galley, by the way. It would be online in a minute."

I self-consciously tugged up the strapless bust of my dress. "Sorry about that. And yes, I loved the ending. You gave Neelie and Nicodemus a happily ever after, so what's not to love?"

Samuel smiled. "I had originally intended to kill off Neelie and Nicodemus. I knew you hated them."

"I don't hate them anymore."

He offered me a bite of cake, and I refused. Discarding his plate on the dresser, he settled next to me on the comforter. "Also, it wasn't healthy for me to keep writing about us, dwelling on us."

Just like an addiction, my mind answered. I hastily repressed the thought.

"So I resolved to end them and move on. But when the time came…I just couldn't kill them. I'd left a second option open—Neelie faking her death—and I used it."

"It's refreshing, I suppose. You don't get a lot of happy endings in real life."

"No, you don't." He played with the ruffle of my skirt. "Grief is a natural part of life, like happiness. But honestly, Kaye, if I see you get your happiness, then I can find mine, too."

"I know what you mean." My voice was soft. I tapped my forehead. "Symbiosis and all."

"No, not there." He lifted my fingertips from my forehead and pressed them to the pulse-point on his wrist. "Symbiosis," he corrected. His eyes not leaving mine, he slowly moved them to the pulse at his neck. I gulped. When he slid them along his collarbone to his sternum, I felt the swift pounding of his heart. My own heart mimicked his. Suddenly, I was very conscious that I lounged on a big, beautiful bed while Samuel bent over me, and all I wanted to do was tangle my fingers in his tousled hair and yank him down to my body. I shyly pulled my fingers away.

"Are you going back to the party tonight?"

"No," he breathed, inching closer to my face.

"Okay." *Talk time, Kaye, talk time.* My stomach fluttered with nerves. I glanced at the duffel bag I'd left here this morning. "Um, I'm going to go change out of this dress," I mumbled, grabbing the bag and slipping past him, up to Danita's room.

As I pulled out the rumpled yoga pants and tee I'd worn that morning, I chided myself. *Way to go, Kaye. Only last night you tell the man you shouldn't have any sort of physical relationship, and now you want to lick frosting off of his chest. What the heck is wrong with you?* It didn't escape me that ten years ago, my seventeen-year-old self wouldn't have thought twice about stripping off my dress in front of Samuel and yanking on comfy clothes. Funny, how much had changed. Huffing, I slipped my discarded dress onto a hanger and grabbed my flip-flops, not caring that my fancy up-do was completely incongruous.

I found him in his bedroom, zipping up the last of his suitcases (now potting soil free), tux discarded for jeans and a T-shirt and still six feet of delectable, lanky limbs. I schooled the lust out of myself, silently cursing and rejoicing over his departure tomorrow morning. If this friendship thing was going to work, I had to get my sex-starved libido away from him. Yet, when he took my hand, I linked my fingers with his.

"All packed. Where do you want to go?"

"The ball diamond." I scanned his room one final time, smiling when I couldn't spot our framed graduation picture. He was taking it with him to New York.

He didn't ask why I wanted to go there—he didn't need to. Instead he grabbed his old, tattered stadium blanket and tugged me from the room, away from the reminders that tomorrow, he'd leave Lyons behind and resume his fast-paced publicity tour.

"Grab your laptop, please. Oh, and we'll need a lighter."

We hopped into Samuel's roadster and weaved through the remaining cars in the driveway. The night air had bite now that we were away from the heat of the party, and I soon realized I should have brought a jacket. Gooseflesh popped up all over my arms. I rubbed warmth into them.

"Cold?" Samuel fidgeted with the heat. "There's a sweatshirt in the backseat."

I felt around the clutter-free car until my hand hit fabric. I put the black hoodie to my nose and inhaled.

"It's clean, I swear. I haven't been jogging in it."

I pulled it over my head, embarrassed. "It smells nice, that's all."

It was even chillier when we reached the windy, wide-open baseball field, completely black save for the lone streetlight washing the loose-graveled parking lot in pale orange. We'd spent long hours here in our youth. Dani and I tagged along, taking up perches in the bleachers while Samuel and Angel practiced hitting. Then there were the times Samuel and I came here alone and spread a blanket in the middle of the field. We'd watch the sky and chat. When we were older and clichéd horny teenagers, we'd move our rendezvous under the bleachers where he pushed an eager tongue into my mouth and I wrapped jean-clad legs around his waist in youthful oblivion.

The wooden benches were as rickety as ever. We climbed up and down, chipped paint flecking our feet.

"This is a lot smaller than I remember." Samuel gazed over the old ballpark with a faintly wistful turn. "Time tends to do that, doesn't it? Change our outlook of what is big."

"Location does that, too. You're used to New York City—skyscrapers, armies of yellow cabs. Of course the park's going to look a lot smaller. Lyons probably seems incredibly dumpy to you, now."

I don't know why I was suddenly snippy. Samuel, ever-perceptive, picked up on it. He rested a hand on my shoulder, halting me.

"Hey. This isn't the end, Kaye. I'm coming back this time, I promise."

I nodded. "Rocky Mountain Folks Festival."

"Rocky Mountain Folks Festival. Sooner, if you like. I told you, whatever it takes."

I gritted my teeth, trying to be strong and not beg him to stay, if for no other reason than to prove to Caroline that she was wrong, that I wasn't stringing Samuel along. After all, a lesser woman would have jumped his bones by now.

"Let's go down to the field, okay?" I said.

He dumped his laptop bag and spread the stadium blanket across the outfield grass, on the edge of the diamond. We sprawled next to each other, my head resting on his stomach. Samuel took a deep breath, causing my head to loll.

"So, are you going to tell me what your epiphany was? It sounded foreboding."

"It's not, trust me. You know how you told me a few weeks ago you were never really a true friend to me? Which I disagree with, but that's beside the point." The bottom of his lightly-scruffed chin bobbed once.

"Okay. So…I was listening to Danita and Angel's wedding vows, thinking about how we really screwed up. Both of us."

"Kaye— " he started to protest, but I silenced him by bouncing my skull against his abs.

"*Both* of us. Anyway, what we need is a new set of vows." Samuel jerked, and I thought he was going to bolt for the roadster. I smothered a laugh. "Not marriage vows. Friendship vows."

"Friendship vows?" He propped himself up on his elbows, his face dubious.

"Cripes, Samuel, I'm not proposing we prick our fingers and swap broken-heart necklaces like a couple of little girls. Just go with me." I sat up, my hands beginning to wave with excitement as I explained. "True friendship is a lifelong commitment too, right? So why shouldn't we say vows to each other for that? I mean, people used to do that all the time hundreds of years ago—blood oaths and all. Countries vow friendship to each other, too. And don't forget about the whole 'no greater love than laying down your life for a friend.'"

Samuel cracked a smile. "Are you quoting scripture to me, Trilby?"

I patted his shin. "Just listen. Having friendship vows would give us something concrete to hold on to when our talks with each other get really rough, like they did tonight. When you want to bail on me or I want to claw out your eyes, we'll remember them." I shrugged. "What do you think?"

"I think it's a very clever idea, Kaye. Let's try it."

Pride warmed me like a radiator as I absorbed his praise.

Samuel opened his laptop and typed in "Calvino" (I'd have to tell him to change it, now that his password was pretty much public knowledge). A new desktop picture blurred to life—the two of us decked out in our skydiving gear, flush-faced and exhilarated. He flipped open a case and pulled out a pair of square, rimless reading glasses.

"What the heck, Cabral?" I balked. "When did you start wearing reading glasses?"

"Oh, these?" He peered at me over the lenses. "About three years ago. I should use them anytime I'm reading, but sometimes I forget. My eyes are tired, though, so my laptop screen is fuzzy."

"They're kind of sexy. Smart sexy." He waggled his eyebrows. I flicked the bridge of his glasses and sighed. Yet another little change I was only now discovering.

For an entire three hours we brainstormed over our vows, laughing, pushing, cobbling out and struggling to define what friendship was. We discussed things we'd learned from our parents. We combed through scripture, Aristotle and Cicero, Lewis and Tolkien. We observed traits of the greatest friendships we could recall. I heatedly debated. He calmly reasoned. We compromised. And then we added "compromise" to our list, too. When all was written and grammatically sufficient for Samuel's perfectionist urges, we'd carved our list to five vows:

1. I, [insert name], will make myself available to [insert name] when he/she is down, as well as happy. I recognize that this is a lifelong commitment.
2. I will provide emotional and physical warmth to my friend. I won't suck the life out of him/her, but will instead offer encouragement.
3. I will fight for [insert name] and his/her reputation. I will guard my friend's back, not stab it.
4. I will sharpen my friend, helping him/her to grow in character and in mind—I will always want the best for [insert name].
5. I will be honest and truthful with my friend, even when the truth is difficult. I will not judge until I have spoken with [insert name], and will compromise when necessary.

Samuel flipped his laptop to sleep mode and reclined on the dew-damp stadium blanket, the late hour and late nights catching up with him. I returned my head to his stomach, content as a cat. I'd been spoiled, having him so close, and would feel it keenly when I could no longer pluck him from his parents' home on a whim. We hadn't wasted these two months, either. The fights, the pranks, the heartache, the talks, even the kiss. I could see now, we'd regrown our roots. Broken through dirt clumps to keep our roots healthy. And the sturdier the roots—

"The stronger the Nixius."

"Huh?" I was sure he'd fallen asleep.

"You mumbled, 'the sturdier the roots,' and I was just completing the thought. Molly's care card, remember?" He patted the blanket for his wallet, opened it, and handed me the creased care card: *Emotivus Drownicus Nixius.* I skimmed Molly's loopy handwriting, wondering.

"Is it really this simple, Samuel—the key to a strong relationship? The vows, the nourishment?"

He grew thoughtful, the coiling light of his laptop screensaver bouncing off his forgotten glasses. With his hair sticking every which-way and his glasses askew on his nose, he resembled a bumbling professor. And when he spoke, he sounded like one.

"In theory, yes—it is that simple. In practice, no. It will be very difficult at times, Kaye." He didn't ask me if I was ready for this, and I was glad. But the way he rubbed my back, so comforting, told me he had faith in us.

Hector had essentially said the same thing to me years ago, and it stuck with me. It was the day after Christmas, and my father and I trekked through pelting sleet to the Hispanic neighborhood for leftovers with the Valdez family. I was seventeen, smoldering and hissing like green wood. Samuel wouldn't play Christmas songs on his guitar because he was exhausted after college finals. I argued that he'd been granted ample amounts of rest and was acting like a hermit holed up in his room. When he refused to humor me, I turned to Hector, hoping for a sympathetic ear. Hector didn't humor me, either. "Look, *mamacita*, I don't know what's up with your moody boyfriend, but ragging to me about your relationship isn't going to help. You need to talk to him, 'specially when it gets all rough and shitty..."

I restlessly shifted against Samuel, and decided I was ready to deal with New York, once and for all.

"Did you bring the letter?"

"Yes." Easing me off his torso, Samuel sat up and pulled it from his pocket. "May I ask you some things?"

"I'd planned on it."

Samuel fidgeted with the piece of paper as he rattled off question after question. What did I mean by "greedy and demanding?" How frightened had I truly been of him, of his wildness? What was the last straw—the thing that pushed me to file for divorce?

"The note," I answered simply.

"Were the people in the brownstone kind to you?" His distressed eyes were shadowed by his hand.

"Togsy was a jerk. The rest weren't unkind—just indifferent. Except for the woman who helped me off the floor."

"Caroline."

I blinked. "Wait. It was *Caroline* who got me off of the floor? Caroline put me in her room and helped me call Alonso?"

"Yes. Caro and Togsy." His brow furrowed. "I thought you knew that. That's why I was so confused last night, at the cookout..."

"Wasn't she high with the rest of you?"

"Oh no. Caro steered clear of the drugs, called us a bunch of crackheads who would never meet our creative potential. She put up with a lot of garbage for Lyle's sake. Anyway, she'd been shut up in her room, using my laptop to edit my work when she heard a commotion in my room. She found you in the doorway and got Togsy to help carry you to her bedroom."

I racked my brain to place Caroline. "Are you sure the brunette wasn't her?"

"Positive. The woman you saw me with? I only met her once more, just to ask her what happened between us. She 'recalled' a lot more than what actually happened, apparently." Samuel shifted uncomfortably. "But Caroline had very short hair, if that helps. Togsy had a thing for pixie hair."

Hmm. Togsy seemed a bit of a control freak, as well as a jerk.

"Kaye, do you still have the note I wrote to you?"

"I think so. Why?"

"I want to read it."

It was my turn to shift uncomfortably. There was no way I wanted to see that thing again. "If I still have it, it's over in Boulder. Why do you need to read it?"

"I want to see the actual writing."

"Samuel, I'm not making up the note."

"No! I know you aren't. I just...I don't understand how I could have written something so straightforward given the shape I was in. And from what others have told me, after you left the room, I was outside, jogging." Samuel picked at the strap of his flip-flop, unable to meet my eyes.

"Oh...I thought you were in your room..." Bile crept up my throat. Jogging? I suddenly felt like such a naïve idiot when it came to drug highs. I'd been so upset by the note, not *once* had I considered its origins when I'd found it stuffed in my backpack.

"Maybe you dictated it to someone."

"Maybe."

"When I find it, I'll mail it to you." At the moment I wouldn't, couldn't entertain the possibility that I'd lived under the shadow of a deception for so long. But if it wasn't from him, who wrote it? Alonso, thinking it would keep me in Colorado? No. Not possible. I shook the thought away.

"Do you have any other questions?" I asked, my voice cracking.

"No, I think I'm finished. You?"

"When did you start remembering again? Was it before or after I left the city?"

"After."

I chewed my lip. "Okay, so you don't recall telling Alonso to put me on a plane. But why didn't you ask me to come back, once you found out what had happened?"

Samuel dropped his hand. "Would you have come back?"

"I...I don't know. Maybe."

He sighed. "I wasn't in my right mind, Kaye. For weeks following, I couldn't think straight. Withdrawals, confusion...I was really messed up. When I came down from my high, I was ashamed. Guilty. Terrified to let you see me like that, but terrified to lose you. So I made up my mind to pull myself out of my black mood before I saw you again. It was wrong not to have you there, and if I could change the past, if I could just have Mom or Dad call you and ask you to come back, regardless of what you found...God, I wish I could go back. But I was so hell-bent on being the perfect man for you, I forgot I just needed to be *your* man."

Ire began to stir...not at Samuel this time, but his parents. "Why didn't Alonso or Sofia tell me what was going on?"

"Because I wanted to handle it."

"No, not good enough." Alonso had to have known Samuel wasn't able to make wise decisions at the time. Yet he'd kept me away—Samuel's own wife. And Sofia...she usually deferred to Alonso's opinion, but why hadn't she seen what they were doing was wrong? It was jarringly off, the damage my former in-laws had done. This was not the loving Cabrals I knew.

Samuel saw the anger building in my face and he lowered his eyes, the familiar clouds signaling a dither behind that flawless hairline.

"Kaye..."

I forced my anger to dissipate and cupped his beloved face. "No more regrets, Samuel. Years of guilt and grief and rage is enough. So..." I fished for the Bic lighter between the folds of the blanket and flicked it on. "What do you say we burn this piece of paper?"

He blew out the little flame. "Are you sure you're ready to forgive me?"

"Yes. If you forgive me for bailing and not standing firm as your wife. For not questioning your parents."

"There's nothing to forgive, Kaye."

I flicked the Bic again, leveling stern eyes at him over the tiny flame. "Yes, there is."

He relented. "Very well. I forgive you."

Samuel twisted the letter containing my New York memories into kindling and held the corner to the flame. When it caught fire, he rose from the blanket and carried it to the diamond dirt, dropping it there. I joined him over the orange glow, lacing my fingers with his as we watched the letter curl and crumble to ashes.

When I was eleven, I was quite the stargazer. We'd constructed constellation wheels in my science class that, at any given time of year, would display which stars were up and which were below the horizon. The first clear, spring night, after begging my mother and Sofia to let us out after dark, I dragged Samuel to the baseball diamond. Flashlights, hot chocolate, and graham crackers in tow, we wrapped ourselves in blankets and waited for the moon to push away all traces of dusk. When the stars gathered enough strength to form constellations, we picked them out, wheel-to-heavens. Perseus. Cassiopeia. Canes Venatici. Samuel forever poured knowledge into his reservoir head, particularly stories. So for each constellation we pinpointed, he shared the myth behind it. Perseus, severing the head of Medusa. Cassiopeia, perched on her throne. Canes Venatici, two hunting dogs leashed by the herdsman. This constellation was rich with galaxies, Samuel told me, many of them real showpieces. As he spoke, I imagined billions of planets spinning in solar systems, spinning in galaxies, all contained within those two hunting dogs. It blew my mind.

But when we took the paper wheel out again in September, I was disappointed to find Canes Venatici missing.

"Timing is crucial," Samuel had explained. "Not only the season, but the hour. Canes Venatici's window has passed and won't come again until April..."

Time. It ticked away so swiftly as, once more, we pointed out stars through drifts of cloud cover. Samuel folded his glasses and tucked them away. We talked. We slept a little. All too soon, the sky was a rose hue and we watched the sun rise.

"It's time for me to go." Samuel's tone was tinged in sadness. "I have to be in Denver by noon to board my flight, and I told my parents I'd go to church with them."

I groaned and shifted against him. "It's too early. The sun isn't all the way up."

"If we wait for the sun to be all the way up, it'll be noon."

"Are you afraid to miss your flight?"

"No." Samuel didn't put up much of a fight. He turned toward me, propping his head on his hand. "I'd stay here all day with you."

"Really?"

He lowered bright eyes to mine, brushed his lips against my temple. "Yes."

I realized, then, all I had to do to keep him in Lyons was ask him to stay. He was serious. And if I were selfish enough to let him quit his book tour, he'd do it for me. Here, then, was my first test of friendship—fight for Samuel's reputation. If he bailed on his commitments for me, it would cause him immense professional damage. I couldn't let him do that. Time for a compromise.

"When do you have free time again?"

"Um, let me check." He glanced at the time on his cell phone—six thirty—and dialed a number. "Caroline? Sorry to bother you so early."

Oh frick.

"I know that, but still...At the ball diamond. Look, can you please check my schedule over the next few weeks and tell me when I have a couple of days free?...Okay...Right...No, decline that...I'm positive. Block those days..."

My heart thudded, fast and hard. Samuel was going to come back before Rocky Mountain Folks. I nervously tucked a loose curl behind my ear. He pulled the curl out again, playing with it while he talked.

"Yes, I packed yesterday...Yes...No. I'll be at Mom and Dad's in a bit..." Samuel glanced up at me, frowning. "Yes, she is. Caro... *Caro*..." He tossed his phone on the blanket, falling back.

"She's angry?"

"More hurt than angry."

I folded my arms over his chest, resting my chin there so I could look at him. "That doesn't give her the right to be rude."

"I gave her my word on something that I never should have."

A current of fear lurched through me. "What did you promise her?"

"That we'd try the romance thing once the final *Water Sirens* book was published. But my heart was never in it, and it was over before it even started. It was grossly unfair to her, and I called it off the night of our camping trip. I guess—" He ran an aggravated hand through his hair. "I guess I was at a crossroads in my life and I didn't know which way to go. Neither direction seemed better than the other, so I just chose. If I'd known a third road was open to me, I would have taken it in a heartbeat."

I noticed for the first time he wasn't wearing the Rolex Caroline gave him for his birthday. I tried not to smile.

"What's the third road?"

"The one that you're on."

His soft mouth curled and man, did I want to kiss him. I smoothed the hair from his face, relaxing the furrows beneath. "There's nothing you can do about hurting her, now. Don't let this spoil our last few minutes together, okay?"

He nodded, his sleep-heavy eyes refusing to leave mine. "I have four days open in the second week of July. Can I see you then?"

"Mm-hmm." My eyes flicked to his mouth again. *Don't do it, Kaye. Don't you force that window open.*

"Yes...oh crap." Molly and I were spelunking that week with a client—the Great West Caving Club. I explained my dilemma to

Samuel, struggling to keep my eyes off his mouth. *Don't kiss him. Where is your resolve, you jellyfish?*

"Is caving something a beginner can pick up easily?"

A smile spread across my face. "Absolutely. I'll help you! If you're in, of course."

"No Hector?"

"No Hector."

"I'm in." He parted his lips and leveled warm blue eyes on me and, screw it, there went my resolve. I hovered over him, placing a chaste kiss on the corner of his mouth.

"Thank you for giving Neelie and Nicodemus a happy ending," I murmured. "Knowing they're somewhere in the Alps, alive and loved…it's the way it should be."

"You're welcome." His hands froze over my waist. "I'm happy it makes you happy."

I kissed the other corner of his mouth. "Thank you for wanting me to be happy."

He grunted in reply and started to move. I shook my head, kissing each of his eyelids.

"And thank you for wanting me, period," I whispered.

His torn eyes held mine. "Don't think I'm complaining, but you said *no* to this at the cookout. I'm not—I'm not sure what you want from me, Kaye."

Crud, I didn't know if I could answer that. "It's probably good we'll have some physical distance between us for a while, give us a chance to get to know each other again. That would be the right thing to do. But then we have Rule Number Two: provide emotional and physical warmth."

"Don't forget Rule Number Four: want what is best for each other."

I brushed a finger along the ridge of his nose. Samuel watched as it slid away.

"What do you want?" he repeated.

"What do I want?"

"Yes."

Don't tell him. Don't string him along.

But you just vowed to be honest with him, you twit.

He's leaving. You'll tell him and then he'll be gone five minutes later.

But that's just it—he's leaving for New York. He needs to know before he leaves.

I scrunched my eyes shut and called up my reserves of courage. "I want *you*. A lot. And I should have told you every single day, too—that was just as much my failure as it was yours." I opened one eye, then the other, not sure what I would find.

He sucked in a breath, his entire body rigid and intent on my next move. "Now tell me what is best for you, Firecracker. Because truthfully, I'm not sure."

Even though every tingling nerve in my body protested, I rolled off his chest and settled into the crook of his arm. "Friends for now. I think it's best, don't you?"

"How so?"

I brushed the tiny white scar between his left thumb and index finger. When he was nine, he'd accidentally put his hand through a window pane after rapping it too hard, because Danita had locked him out of the house.

"I know all of these little marks," I said wistfully. "Yet there's so much we don't know, as manic as we were about each other."

His arms tightened around me, his only response.

For me, it would never be enough to simply call him "friend," and I could now see that it wouldn't be enough for him, either. Samuel was a part of me, as much as the veins in my arms or the muscles in my legs were a part of me. We'd waited this long to suture ourselves together. We could wait a few months for each other, couldn't we? There was something sublime in the waiting, despite the dysfunction… a painful devotion to each other that spanned time and circumstance.

So, despite "friends for now," there in the quiet morning of Lyons High's baseball field, I closed the gap and pressed my lips to his. It was a gentle, careful, goodbye kiss. One that left me aching when I released his bottom lip. One that begged him to wait for me. To wait until our window returned.

As ever, he kissed me back.

Continue reading for a short preview of the upcoming sequel: *Skygods*

SKYGODS

Skydivers, arrogant in their ability to navigate the heavens, rejects their fragile state and calls themselves gods of the sky…

Chapter 1

BLUE SKY, BLACK DEATH

A skydiver's mantra or greeting: Enjoy the exhilaration of the open sky, but never forget the mortal earth below.

Hydraulic Level Five [working title]
Draft 1.22
© Samuel Caulfield Cabral and Aspen Kaye Trilby
22. *An Inheritance and State*

Three million dollars. All of it in a trust fund left behind by his dead parents which, now that he is eighteen, is at his disposal. According to the lawyer, the fortune would've been nine million if the estate hadn't been obligated to pay his mother's debts after she jumped. Not that he wants a dime of it. Caulfield scowls at the memory of the piggish man with squinty eyes and a stupid-looking bowtie that choked his fat neck. He doesn't need a stranger to remind him his mother had preferred ski slopes, sports cars, and spending sprees in Boston's Back Bay to her son.

"Caulfield, hit the on-deck circle!" Coach bellows from the opposite end of the dugout. Caulfield scoops up a bat and sprints to the circle for warm-up swings. He has to get his head in the game, his last ever with Bear Creek High. He's wanted the state title for so long, and now it's three colossal runs away – so impossible just fifteen minutes ago, yet Bear Creek managed to load the bases in a ninth inning rally.

Bright stadium lights wash the field in white, heightening the exhilaration of the night game. He pushes his hat brim down to shield his eyes from the glare.

"Straighten out that swing, you're a little wild today." Caulfield nods to the hitting coach and focuses on the next pitch, clobbering the imaginary ball. "That's better."

The odd thing is, baseball has begun to lose its sheen of magic. The University of Colorado, along with several other colleges, offered him baseball scholarships. He turned them all down. The idea of playing ball another four years seems daunting. Really, all he wants to do is plow through the next two years until Aspen graduates from high school, and he can once again see her every day.

She's up there in the stands, like she always is – screaming his name when he's up to bat, waving as he takes to the outfield. To her, he's Caulfield: attentive boyfriend, hell of a ballplayer, and best friend since five. How would she feel about Caulfield: child of a disbarred lawyer and nutcase socialite? Or Caulfield: sack-of-shit millionaire who's too scared to touch his inheritance, even to buy his girlfriend a reliable ride? Caulfield tears through another swing.

"Number Nine, you're up!" Caulfield shoulders the barrel as the hitter before him strikes out. A thrill shoots through him every time he hears "Number Nine." Ted Williams – the Splendid Splinter himself – wore the number nine for two decades in Boston. Someday he'd see that retired number flying high above Fenway Park. Maybe he'll use his mother's money to do it and hopes she burns with revulsion, wherever she is. The more he learns of her, the more he can't stomach thinking of her as "mother." He should just call her Rachel Caulfield. No, just Rachel.

Caulfield digs one foot into the batter's box, then the next. *Time to focus. Ninth inning, down two runs. Runner on third, runner on second, runner on first.* He has to hit it deep. The crowd behind him is a roaring machine. He hears Aspen's voice, and Maria's and Esteban's. Zoning them out, he studies the pitcher as he shakes his head once, twice, and wind-up. The ball's coming in high – too high. He holds his swing. *Crud, slider.*

"Strike!"

Coach roars at him to watch for breaking balls, as if he doesn't already know. He plants his feet, pure fury pulsing through his veins, his heart pounding *Ra-chel...Ra-chel.* Fuck her. Fuck her for distracting him during the biggest game of his life, for keeping him from Fenway Park, and for despising her only child. He hates her money. He swings hard.

Too early.

"Strike!"

"Fuck!" Caulfield growls, earning him a warning glare from the umpire.

"Come on, Caulfield! Get your head out of your ass and in this game!" "This isn't tee-ball, this is State!" The crowd behind him jeers, and Caulfield knows they will hang, draw and quarter him, then stick his head on the fence post if he screws this up. He narrows his vision to the pitcher, watching his wind-up, the angle of his arm, bracing himself. This one's coming in low. He holds his swing.

"Ball!"

He whooshes out. *There we go, Caulfield. Eye on the ball–first rule of baseball. Channel the rage. Carry it through in your swing. Wind-up...no break, coming in fast, just how you like them. Swing through...*

CRACK!

Yes. Caulfield tosses the bat and sprints for first as the crowd's untamed screams propel him forward. He rounds first as the other team's outfielders stumble around the fence, the ball out of the park and lost to them. A manic grin claims his face as he slows to a jog, savoring the trip around the bases. One runner crosses home plate...then two...then three. Caulfield's grand slam pushes the score to 6-4, bottom of the ninth. The game is over.

His teammates flood from the dugout and Bear Creek students and parents spill onto the field, but the only face Caulfield seeks is Aspen's. Strong arms lift him and he can see above the hundreds of heads. He spots her, wildly waving her arms and jumping with sheer joy. Gone is the inheritance. Gone is the piggish lawyer, his father and Rachel. It's only her. Always her.

Caulfield stiffens.

I love her.

Not some high school crush or infatuation with her hair, her eyes, her body. He loves *her*. Enough to forget everyone else. Enough to give her everything he can. Enough to protect her, to marry her.

He slides down from his teammates' shoulders and whips Aspen into his arms, clinging to her.

"You were...Ack! Amazing!" she cries into his ear, heedless of the sweat dripping from his forehead, his neck, his arms. "So brilliant, so perfect!"

He laughs and set her down, plopping his soaked ball cap on her lovely blond head. Framing her face with his hands, he kisses her, hard.

"Let's do the fairy tale. All of it." His voice quakes with adrenaline and emotion. She can't miss his meaning. *Don't scare her, you idiot. She's not even sixteen.* But it's not fear in her wide eyes. Nothing but joy stares back, and it fills Caulfield's own heart with trepidation.

He smooths her cheek, eases his agony. "That's a long way out, though, getting married? Far, far in the future." She nestles beneath his arm. He stoops and pecks her cheek.

"Only you, Firecracker. Don't forget it."

Kaye, well, here it is. One hundred plus pages of our story, told as truthfully as I can recall. I know it's one-sided. It's missing your thoughts, your memories. Thank you again for agreeing to share them with me.

You should know, I feel like that eighteen-year-old kid again, terrified you'll read this memoir and lose respect for me. I'm ashamed of how I resented Sofia. How I both idolized and hated my birth mother. Or the secrets I kept from you, for years. The way I longed for a thirteen-year-old girl who was little more than a child. But this is life, and we make choices and we suffer (and grow) because of them.

Read our story. Give me your honesty. Question everything, not just the passages I've marked, because this is us and I want it to be right.

~Sam

Acknowledgments

To my husband and beautiful children: you will always have first claim on my hours and my love. Thank you for your ceaseless support and encouragement.

To Mom and Dad: you raised me to believe I could achieve most anything with hard work and creativity. Thank you for your guidance.

To my editor Jennifer, to Elizabeth, and the Omnific staff: thank you for your respect, time and care in making this book "shine."

To Jenny and EBJ: You were the first to tackle these pages with the "red pen of honesty." Thank you for helping to shape this tale.

To Tricia and Amelia: You brought this story its first readership. Many, many thanks.

To Renee, Katie, Erin, Dana, and Kelly: You were the first of my friends to read my work. Thank you for believing in me as a writer.

To my DSM dinner ladies, Team WTFISGOINGON, and the online community: Thank you for your enthusiasm and endless patience these past years. You made me want to keep writing.

About the Author

Sarah Latchaw was raised in eastern Iowa and appreciates beauty in mud-splattered gravel roads, weathered farm faces, and combine harvesters powering through cornfields. She also loves to explore the world, thanks to countless family minivan trips across the States to coastal cities, kitschy attractions, and national monuments. This passion for finding stories led to college adventures to Israel and Palestine, Jordan, Slovakia, Germany, and other European countries. Each place's story rests in the back of her mind and in her childhood photo albums.

In 2002, Sarah received her BA from Wartburg College in public relations and media, and entered the workforce, ready to climb the ladder. However, when researching MBA applications evoked feelings of dread, she realized the last thing she wanted to do was spend the next years of her life in a passionless corporate marketing career. With the unfailing support of her loving husband, she chose to pursue a career in creative writing and received her MA from Iowa State University in 2009.

While writing more "serious" works for grad classes, Sarah dabbled with a fun online writing project, titled *Hydraulic Level Five*. As often happens, this particular little story evolved into something more important, more personal to her and those who read and enjoyed it. Once the story was complete, Sarah loved it enough to desire a proper place for it on bookshelves. This began her relationship with Omnific Publishing and the anticipation of *Hydraulic Level Five*'s official release in Fall 2013.

These days, Sarah wakes every morning thrilled to cuddle her toddler son, show him the world, then capture that world and shape it into stories on paper. She also enjoys her piano, volunteering in her community, and reading anything with a cohesive plot. She and her family reside in Des Moines, Iowa.

check out these titles from

OMNIFIC PUBLISHING

Contemporary Romance

Boycotts & Barflies and *Trust in Advertising* by Victoria Michaels
Passion Fish by Alison Oburia and Jessica McQuinn
Three Daves by Nicki Elson
Small Town Girl and *Corporate Affair* by Linda Cunningham
Stitches and Scars by Elizabeth A. Vincent
Take the Cake by Sandra Wright
Pieces of Us by Hannah Downing
The Way That You Play It by BJ Thornton
Poughkeepsie by Debra Anastasia
Cocktails & Dreams by Autumn Markus
Recaptured Dreams and *All-American Girl* by Justine Dell
Once Upon a Second Chance by Marian Vere
The Englishman by Nina Lewis
16 Marsden Place by Rachel Brimble
Sleepers, Awake by Eden Barber
The Runaway Year by Shani Struthers
Hydraulic Level Five by Sarah Latchaw

New Adult

Beside Your Heart by Mary Whitney
Romancing the Bookworm by Kate Evangelista
Fighting Fate by Linda Kage

Young Adult

Shades of Atlantis and *The Ember Series: Ember & Iridescent* by Carol Oates
Breaking Point by Jess Bowen
Life, Liberty, and Pursuit by Susan Kaye Quinn
The Embrace Series: Embrace & Hold Tight by Cherie Colyer
Destiny's Fire by Trisha Wolfe
Streamline by Jennifer Lane
Reaping Me Softly by Kate Evangelista

Erotic Romance

Becoming sage by Kasi Alexander
Saving sunni by Kasi & Reggie Alexander
The Winemaker's Dinner: Appetizers & *Entrée* by Dr. Ivan Rusilko & Everly Drummond
The Winemaker's Dinner: Dessert by Dr. Ivan Rusilko

Paranormal Romance

The Light Series: Seers of Light, Whisper of Light, and Circle of Light by Jennifer DeLucy
The Hanaford Park Series: Eve of Samhain & *Pleasures Untold* by Lisa Sanchez
Immortal Awakening by KC Randall
Crushed Seraphim and *Bittersweet Seraphim* by Debra Anastasia
The Guardian's Wild Child by Feather Stone
Grave Refrain by Sarah M. Glover
Divinity by Patricia Leever
Blood Vine and *Blood Entangled* by Amber Belldene
Divine Temptation by Nicki Elson

Historical Romance

Cat O' Nine Tails by Patricia Leever
Burning Embers by Hannah Fielding
Good Ground by Tracy Winegar

Romantic Suspense

Whirlwind by Robin DeJarnett
The CONduct Series: With Good Behavior & *Bad Behavior* by Jennifer Lane
Indivisible by Jessica McQuinn
Between the Lies by Alison Oburia

Anthologies

A Valentine Anthology including short stories by Alice Clayton, Jennifer DeLucy, Nicki Elson, Jessica McQuinn, Victoria Michaels, and Alison Oburia

Singles

It's Only Kinky the First Time by Kasi Alexander
Learning the Ropes by Kasi & Reggie Alexander
The Winemaker's Dinner: RSVP by Dr. Ivan Rusilko
The Winemaker's Dinner: No Reservations by Everly Drummond
Big Guns by Jessica McQuinn
Concessions by Robin DeJarnett
Starstruck by Lisa Sanchez
New Flame by BJ Thornton
Shackled by Debra Anastasia
Swim Recruit by Jennifer Lane
Sway by Nicki Elson
Full Speed Ahead by Susan Kaye Quinn
The Second Sunrise by Hannah Downing
The Summer Prince by Carol Oates
Whatever it Takes by Sarah M. Glover
Clarity by Patricia Leever
A Christmas Wish by Autumn Markus

coming soon from

OMNIFIC PUBLISHING

Fix You by Beck Anderson

Unreap My Heart by Kate Evangelista

On Best Behavior by Jennifer Lane

Client N°5 by Joy Fulcher

Forced to Change by Stephanie Caldwell

Flirting with Chaos by Kenya Wright

The Sacrificial Lamb by Laura Pintus

Love in the Time of the Dead by Tera Shanley

CPSIA information can be obtained
at www.ICGtesting.com
Printed in the USA
LVOW10s0808300917
550672LV00001B/112/P

9 781623 420222